EDEN

BURNING

EDEN BURNING

ELIZABETH LOWELL

HarperLargePrint
An Imprint of HarperCollinsPublishers

HarperCollins books may be purchased for educational, business, or sales promotional use. For information please write: Special Markets Department, HarperCollins Publishers Inc., 10 East 53rd Street, New York, NY 10022.

FIRST HARPER LARGE PRINT EDITION

Printed on acid-free paper

Library of Congress Cataloging-in-Publication Data has been applied for.

ISBN 0-06-008330-1

02 03 04 05 06   10 9 8 7 6 5 4 3 2 1

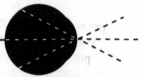

**This Large Print Book carries the
Seal of Approval of N.A.V.H.**

For everyone
who ever dreamed
of falling in love
in Paradise

EDEN
BURNING

PROLOGUE

Y ou've never seen anyone like her. That picture we sent doesn't begin to do her justice. No picture could."

Sitting in Oregon—on the bed, because the motel room chairs were piled with reports—Chase Wilcox frowned at the phone and the eager affection in his younger brother, Dane's, voice. His **married** younger brother. The younger brother who had a lovely wife and two wonderful children. The younger brother who couldn't stop talking about some glorified shimmy dancer who was giving his daughter hula lessons.

Hula, for God's sake.

Not that Chase objected to his niece, Sandi, learning the dance. From the little he had seen of hula dancing, it looked like good exercise. The problem was Sandi's daddy. He was much too enthusiastic about the instructor for Chase's comfort.

And that instructor was sexy enough to set fire to stone.

Almost reluctantly he touched the facedown photo that had come with his brother's latest letter from Hawaii. Slowly he turned it over, hoping it wasn't as bad as he had first feared.

It was worse.

Lust hit him hard and low and hot, the kind of heat even his very beautiful, very skillful, sexually manipulative ex-wife hadn't been able to generate in him.

The woman in the snapshot apparently had been caught just as she finished turning in a swift circle with Chase's little daughter in her arms. Lisa was laughing with a freedom he had been afraid would never come again after her mother's casual cruelty. He owed Dane's wife, Jan, for helping Lisa. Jan had a gentle patience and welcoming love that came to her as naturally as breathing.

Chase owed the dancer "Pele" something entirely different. She of the hip-length, flame-red hair and luminous gold cat eyes. Pele, who radiated sexuality like fire radiated heat. He couldn't see what kind of body she had beneath the seething curtain of hair, but he was certain it was showgirl caliber. Women who strutted their stuff onstage for the benefit of cheering, leering men generally had something to strut.

"Hey, bro, you there or are you trimming your mustache?" Dane asked.

"Yeah, I'm here, yawning and listening to you run over like a plugged toilet about some exotic dancer who isn't your wife."

In Hawaii, Dane laughed despite the frown that came from his brother's sour view of humanity in general and women and particular—except for Jan, his sister-in-law. For her, Chase had a well of tenderness as great as he had for his own daughter. That was what gave Dane hope that his brother was coming out of the bitterness that had followed losing custody of his daughter.

"Hey, don't worry. Jan is the first to sing Nicole's praises," Dane said. "She's good with kids and has real talent as an artist. In fact, wait until you see the drawings she does. You'll see why we wanted her to do the illustrations for . . ."

While his brother ran on and on about Pele/Nicole's skill as both an artist and a scientific illustrator, Chase drummed callused fingers silently on the desk in the generic motel room that was presently his "home." Outside the window, invisible beneath the Pacific Northwest's customary lid of clouds, the shattered cone of Mount Saint Helens steamed, brooded, and waited for the energy to blow its top again.

Chase wouldn't have to wait as long for his own personal eruption. He was fed up to the teeth with hearing his brother rave on and on about the paragon of womanhood who just happened to be a shimmy dancer. If Jan was too gentle and good to see the danger to her own marriage, Chase sure as hell wasn't. Having once been married to a gorgeous home wrecker, he had no problem recognizing one when she started swinging her hips around his little brother.

Abruptly Chase decided he couldn't wait any

longer. His life's work was studying the return of life to volcano-scarred slopes; he didn't want to have to help his brother survive devastation of the kind the dancer Pele would bring. Chase knew too much about that kind of personal agony—the numbing self-doubts, the despair, the cold blaze of hatred. He wouldn't let it happen to Dane, to his wife, or to his children.

With the ruthlessness of an older brother, Chase cut Dane off in mid-word. "I got the go-ahead to study kipukas. I'm coming out to Hawaii as soon as I wrap up a few more details here."

"Really?" Dane said instantly. "Lisa will be over the moon. She misses you."

"Not as much as I miss her."

His voice was rough. He hadn't known how deeply he loved his little daughter until he had stood in court two years ago and silently raged against the judge who had been too dazzled by Lynette's angelic beauty to see through it to the absolute selfishness beneath. Lisa—tender, shy, intelligent Lisa, a little girl who had just turned five—had been given over to the sole care of a woman who shouldn't have been trusted with custody of a gravel pit.

Chase's hand closed into a fist against the pain of being separated from his daughter. He ached to hold her, to feel her small fingers patting his "tickle fur" while she giggled with delight and he blew "furry bubbles" against her cheek. He needed to reassure her of his love and to reassure himself that the sins of her parents hadn't scarred the little girl's self-confidence beyond healing.

"You did the right thing to leave her with us after that bitch dropped her on your doorstep," Dane said quickly. "Having Lisa crawling around with you on Mount Saint Helens or your pet South American volcanoes just wasn't possible, especially with her recovering from pneumonia. And even if you had found a wonderful nurse/nanny . . . well, it's just not the same as family."

"I know." Chase's voice was tired and angry. **He** was tired and angry.

It seemed like he had spent a lot of time that way since the final custody hearing. He certainly had spent the past few weeks living with too much work and anger. He had put in eighteen-hour days in order to turn over enough of his old projects so that he could take a week or so in Hawaii, set up the new project, and sort out his blissfully stupid younger brother's life. Then, finally, Chase would be able to settle with Lisa on the Big Island for at least a decade of studying Hawaii's fascinating balance of destruction, creation, and the stubborn ability of life to survive no matter what the odds.

"After Lynette, Lisa needed the security of a loving family, of a woman like Jan," Chase said, trying to keep the old bitterness out of his voice. "Lisa needed to love and be loved by a mother. From the smile on her face in the pictures you sent, I owe you and Jan more than I can ever repay."

"Our pleasure. And don't forget Nicole. She's really good with kids. She and Lisa—"

"Oh, I won't forget Nicole," Chase interrupted. "That's a promise. Give Jan a big hug for me." **And give yourself a big kick in the butt for being so gullible,** he added silently.

He hung up and stared down at the photos of Lisa and Dane, Lisa and her cousins, Lisa and Jan, Lisa dwarfed by one of Hilo's giant tree ferns, Lisa smiling shyly up at a dark-haired, tanned Hawaiian boy whose facial bones gave promise of future strength and beauty. Like Lisa's face; even at seven she had a loveliness that made people stare.

Like her mother, she was too beautiful to be real.

But unlike Lynette, Lisa was vulnerable to human emotions. For her sake, and for Dane's, the hip-swinging, hula-dancing home wrecker had to go.

Chase only hoped that his little brother wouldn't screw things up hopelessly in the week before he could get to Hawaii.

CHAPTER
1

Y ou'll see," Dane said, giving his older brother an arch look. "I'm really going to enjoy saying 'I told you so.' There is nothing else like Nicole when she dances."

Chase bit back what he wanted to say about hormones and stupid men. It helped that he was ignoring his brother. If he looked at Dane, he would probably take a swing at that smug smile.

In the Kipuka Club's dim light, Dane watched Chase's face, hoping to see hidden enthusiasm or at least interest on the subject of Nicole. He saw nothing but hard angles, the pale flash of gray eyes, the inky black of his brother's short hair and mustache. If Chase felt anything more than fatigue and boredom, he wasn't giving it away to anyone, not even his younger brother.

Frowning slightly, Dane looked away, remembering another time, almost another man, a younger one who laughed at jokes and smiled at the sight of a puppy chasing a ball. But that had been BTB: Before the Bitch. After Lynette, Chase hadn't smiled much and had laughed even less. While

Dane sympathized—no one liked being taken to the cleaners by a pretty gold digger—he thought it was past time for his older brother to get over his mistake and get back to enjoying life. After all, Chase was hardly the first man to screw up in the marriage department.

Dane and Jan had spent a lot of time worrying about his older brother after he lost the custody battle. They were still worried. That was why they had decided that Hawaii was just the place for Chase to heal.

And Nicole Ballard was just the woman to teach him that Jan wasn't the only generous, gentle, loving woman ever born.

Chase drank from his beer glass and waited for the red-hot shimmy dancer to take the stage and have her body admired. The anger that seethed in his gut no more showed on the outside than a mainland volcano showed the molten stone that was its living core. He was a man who had learned the hard way that emotions were treacherous, particularly when beautiful women were involved.

Tonight there was most definitely a beautiful woman involved.

Though it had been seven days since Chase had seen Nicole Ballard in that snapshot, the image still burned in his mind. And his crotch. The woman in the picture was all sex and grace and energy, with long, golden-red hair streaming out as she spun around with a laughing child in her arms.

Once he finally had gotten past the sheer sexuality of the snapshot's impact, he had been caught by the combination of intelligence and vivid life in Nicole's face. Then with the next breath he would be punched all over again by the sensuous, fiery cloud of her hair and the delight of his own daughter at being whirled around in the heart of fire. Pele, woman of fire.

The picture haunted Chase.

It wasn't a pleasant haunting. Every time he looked at the photo, he thought of how easily Lynette had fooled him and of how vulnerable Dane was. Any man would be. Jan was no match for the red-haired temptress who was worming her way into the family's daily life.

No woman was a match for Nicole.

Every time he looked at the blurred snapshot, it was like a fist in the heart, sending a shock wave through his body. Each time it happened, his anger burned higher, hotter. Dane couldn't stand against such temptation for long.

No man could.

That was why Chase was sitting in a private Hilo nightclub, his body jet-lagged and his mind churning with what he had left behind professionally and what he had in front of him both professionally and personally. He had come to Hawaii sooner than he should have. He was still fielding faxes and e-mails and disbelieving phone calls from the vulcanologists he had been overseeing on two continents.

Worse, he hadn't even been allowed to unpack or

shower before Dane had dragged him to the Kipuka Club to see Pele dance.

At the moment Chase was tired, angry, and in general feeling savage enough to eat his meat raw. All things considered, it was the perfect mood for confronting an ambitious shimmy dancer. Unfortunately Jan, Lisa, and Sandi were running around backstage, so nothing useful could happen tonight.

He knew he should be grateful for the delay. He was in no shape to wage the kind of cold-blooded warfare it would take to defeat another Lynette.

But he wasn't grateful. He just wanted the whole nasty business behind him so he could concentrate on his daughter and Hawaii's famous volcanoes.

With a hidden, sideways look from ice-pale eyes, he studied his younger brother. It didn't take a mind reader to see that Dane was all but dancing with impatience for Pele to appear. Not for the first time, Chase wondered how deeply the red-haired predator had sunk her claws into his trusting brother. Not as deeply as she wanted them, obviously, or Dane would be asking for a divorce.

Well, Pele was shit out of luck, Chase told himself grimly. She didn't know, it, but her little shimmy show was over. She would just have to take her home-wrecking act on the road and find another rich, trusting fool.

Unconsciously Chase shifted his big body as though he was shouting numbers behind the line of scrimmage, waiting for the football to smack into his hands. He wanted to get on with the game, to get close enough to Pele to turn her greed against her. Then he would hammer in a wedge and break her wide open, ending the threat to his brother's marriage.

Until then, all he could do was wait, muscles clenched with the effort of holding back his disgust. He was careful to keep his feelings well hidden. He knew that Dane believed the woman to be virtuous, intelligent, warm, loving, kind, and all the other lies and lures females used to attract gullible males.

Chase wasn't gullible anymore. Lynette had well and truly cured him. Any lingering delusions he might have had about the true nature of the female character had vanished when Lynette called him six weeks ago and announced that she was tired of his sickly daughter, her new boyfriend hated whiny children, so Chase could just take her back. For good. She never wanted to see the little wretch again.

It was typical of Lynette that Lisa had been standing nearby listening while her mother dumped her.

Just the memory of Lynette's casual cruelty made Chase's whole body tense with rage. He had married because he wanted a child and thought Lynette did, too. It soon became clear that she hadn't wanted Lisa at all; she could barely be bothered to hold the baby. He had thought it just needed time, that not all women were natural mothers.

Wrong.

Nothing had changed, except to get worse. By the time Lisa was four, Lynette had been through a series of gigolos. When Chase had asked her to go to a marriage counselor or a psychiatrist, she laughed and said she didn't need anything but a bigger allowance from him; she was bored, so she picked up men.

Chase had refused to give Lynette more money. The next thing he knew, she hit him with divorce papers and demanded sole custody of Lisa, claiming that a daughter needed her mother and that Chase was always away. What she had really wanted was an open pipeline to the Wilcox family's wealth.

The judge had been taken in by Lynette's tiny, heart-shaped face and soft-voiced lies about the joys of motherhood. Chase had been left with no wife, no child except for minimal visitation rights, and no illusions about what women really wanted from men.

Motherhood, his **ass**. Lynette had held on to Lisa just long enough to find another wealthy fool to marry.

Chase was grateful to have his daughter back, in spite of the fact that it couldn't have come at a worse time for him professionally. When Lynette called, he had been in Mexico overseeing the work of three people on an emergency basis. The emergency had come about when the leader of the expedition got a lungful of El Chichón's poisonous fumes. A month in a sea-level hospital had been ordered. Chase had volunteered to supervise the work rather than lose the project halfway through the study.

If that wasn't enough, Mount Saint Helens had been swelling and rumbling with promises of new eruptions, and Chase had been within three months of finishing up the first phase of a long-term study of the return of life to the volcano's devastated slopes.

Neither El Chichón nor Mount Saint Helens was any place for a thin, shy seven-year-old who was recovering from pneumonia.

Chase had been sitting down to write a letter of resignation from the Saint Helens study when Jan called and asked if it would be all right for Lisa to stay in Hawaii with them for the summer. It had been typical of Jan that she acted as if he was doing **her** a favor when he agreed to let Lisa go.

Bloody idiot, thought Chase angrily, looking at his brother's dark, handsome profile. Didn't Dane know what an incredibly rare treasure he had in Jan? She was the shining exception to the bitter truth that women were whores selling out to the highest bidder.

So what in hell's name was Dane doing panting after a glorified stripper?

Hands fisted beneath the table, Chase wished that he was on Hawaii solely as a professional vulcanologist and not as an unwanted marriage counselor. To him, Hawaii wasn't the Big Island, it was

Volcano Island, the burning Eden that was the home of the world's biggest and most active volcanoes. He belonged up on the mountain's clean slopes, not in a dim club on a Thursday night waiting to meet the slut his younger brother was making a fool of himself over.

". . . is my brother, Dr. Chase Wilcox," Dane said, giving his brother an unsubtle nudge under the table.

Automatically Chase turned his attention away from the bitter thoughts churning in his mind. He curved his lips into a polite smile and shoved back from the table to be introduced to yet another volcano-observatory scientist, university ethnologist, or Hilo native. The Kipuka was a members-only supper club supported by a mixture of university types, volcano crawlers, national-park scientists and volunteers, and native Hawaiians such as Bobby Kamehameha, the club's owner and the drummer for the dancers.

When Chase got to his feet to shake hands with Bobby, he was surprised. At six feet five inches, with a naturally powerful build, Chase was usually the biggest man in any room.

Bobby was bigger. A lot bigger. He was easily four inches taller and at least sixty pounds heavier than Chase. Bobby had the deceptively smooth, almost soft-looking physique that full-blooded Polynesians often had.

Chase knew better than to believe the satin surface. He had played football with more than one islander. They tackled like a falling mountain and felt just as hard. Bobby's power showed in his calm eyes and in the strong hand gently gripping Chase's.

"I could have used you in college." As Chase spoke, his smile changed, becoming less professional and more personal. "The defense kept pounding me into the ground."

"You play pro?"

"Nope. Too small."

Bobby laughed, not believing it for a moment. "More like too smart. Dane told me about the Mount Saint Helens project, among others. Hawaii is honored to have you." The big man grinned suddenly. "Even if you are one more rich sonofabitch haole."

Chase gave a crack of approving laughter at the unexpected gibe. He let go of Bobby's hand, only to have the big Hawaiian grab on again. Broad, blunt fingertips traced the ridges of callus on Chase's palms and fingers.

"You no tell me he drum," Bobby complained to Dane, slipping into the easy rhythms of pidgin.

It wasn't the island's true pidgin, which would have been impossible for nonnatives to understand. Bobby spoke the languid, slangy version of English that was developing in the islands' yeasty cultural and linguistic stew.

"You no ask," Dane retorted, grinning.

Bobby said something in melodic Hawaiian that Chase suspected was distinctly unmusical.

Dane's smile got even bigger.

"Friends," Bobby added with great dignity and perfect enunciation, "should not have to ask about matters of such great, even grave, importance." He threw a thick arm around Chase's shoulders. "You me brudder. Long stay island, sure-sure."

Chase looked at the array of modern bongo drums set out on a corner of the stage and nodded. "Good thing you're not hung up on tradition here. Drumming on logs never appealed to me."

"My ancestors lived as well as they could, as often as they could, and took the best that was available to them at the time." Amusement and intelligence gleamed in the Hawaiian's black eyes. "That's the only Hawaiian tradition I care about upholding. I leave the poi and sixty-pound surfboards for the crazy haoles."

"I'm crazy, but not that crazy," Chase said, giving Bobby a friendly punch in the shoulder that would have staggered most men.

Bobby grinned and returned the punch.

Dane laughed with something close to relief. Jan had said that Chase and the sometimes prickly Hawaiian would like each other immediately, yet Dane had wondered. Some big men didn't like other big men around them. Chase wasn't that way. It was a relief that Bobby wasn't either. Since Nicole had introduced Dane and Jan into the supper club, they had made more friends in a month than they had in the previous two years of island living. Bobby Kamehameha was one of those friends.

The lights flickered wildly.

"The haoles," Bobby said wryly, "are restless tonight. I don't blame them. Pele's back. She's enough to make Mauna Loa's stone rivers melt and run again. Gotta go quick-quick."

With that, Bobby gave Chase another friendly whack and walked to the stage.

Dane looked sideways at his older brother. "Bobby has a Ph.D. in medieval iconography. His second one is in nonverbal communications."

"I believe it. After meeting him, I'd believe anything." Chase had a sudden, hopeful thought. "Is he Pele's lover?"

Surprise showed on Dane's darkly elegant face. Like his brother, Dane was taller than most men. Unlike Chase, Dane was built along the lines of a distance runner rather than a quarterback who had enough muscle and bone to take whatever punishment the other team's gorillas dished out.

"Bobby's married," Dane said.

"Since when has that bothered a woman on the make?" Chase's voice was as sardonic as the line of his mouth.

Dane simply shook his head. "Nicole's not like that."

Irritation and fatigue got the better of Chase. Before he could stop himself, he shot back, "She's a woman, isn't she?"

Dane winced at the bitterness in his brother's words. "Nicole doesn't sleep around. Period."

"Are we talking about Nicole, 'Pele,' or a white plaster saint?"

"Now you're catching on." Dane's smile was all teeth. "Pele is the nickname Bobby's mother gave Nicole when they first met—goddess of the volcano."

Beneath the table, Chase's hands balled into fists again. His brother was heading for disaster and didn't even see it coming. The laughter and affection in Dane's voice when he talked about Nicole made Chase want to hit something. His brother, for instance. But that wouldn't be smart, so Chase clenched his jaw against the need to hammer home the truth about the inevitable relationship between women and money into his naive younger brother's head.

"What does Jan think of this . . . dancer?" Chase asked tightly, substituting **dancer** at the last instant for the kind of word he never used outside the locker room.

"My wife is Nicole's biggest fan."

Chase's savage curse was lost beneath a flurry of drumbeats. The illumination in the club went from dim to zero. Spotlights bloomed and focused in shades of gold on the small, raised stage.

Pele had arrived.

CHAPTER
2

Nicole Ballard saw the sudden sword edge of light coming through the crack in the green velvet curtains. She smiled encouragingly to the seven teenagers lined up in front of her. At her signal they turned and faced the closed curtain. The girls shifted uneasily. It was their first performance ever.

For an instant Nicole rested her hand on the shining chestnut hair of Sandi Wilcox, silently reassuring the nervous girl. She and her friend Judy had been practicing in secret for months, wanting to surprise their fathers. The men knew that their daughters had been dabbling in dance, but they had no idea just how elegantly feminine their teenage daughters could be.

"Remember," Nicole murmured in a voice that went no farther than Sandi, "you're a goddess."

With a final gentle touch to the girl's hair, Nicole left the stage. Her bare feet made no noise on the floor.

Jan stood in the wings, holding the hand of a small, slender girl with clear gray eyes and hair as black and shiny as volcanic glass. When Nicole approached, the little girl held out her free hand.

Smiling, Nicole took the cool fingers and wrapped them in her warmth. Together they waited with breath held, nearly as nervous about the coming performance as the girls onstage.

The hula would tell an ancient story of feasting and sly gods and clever men. The chant had been passed through countless generations of Hawaiians until it had ended up in the files of the university's ethnology department. In the course of her volunteer duties, Nicole had discovered the chanted form of the amusing dance. With the help of Bobby's mother—a woman as graceful as she was gigantic—Nicole had reconstructed the most probable dance movements and taught them to the children.

The result was very much like the Kipuka Club itself, a mixture of tradition and possibility rather than the rigid preservation of rituals from a time long gone.

Tonight the girls wore neither modern cellophane skirts nor traditional ti leaves for their dance. In keeping with Bobby's pursuit of "the truth rather than the fact of tradition," the girls' costumes were more Samoan than Hawaiian—the best available, in Bobby's opinion, rather than the most "authentic."

In this case lavalavas got his nod of approval. The wraparound skirts were silk, short, splashed with vivid flowers against a dark background, and fit snugly around the hips. So-called grass skirts of cellophane were little more than a rustling, slithering striptease in Bobby's opinion. Lavalavas emphasized the grace of the body's movements, not the sex of the dancer. Each girl wore a matching halter top, a hibiscus flower over her ear, and a lei woven of fragrant plumeria.

There wasn't a purple orchid in sight.

Bobby had put his size-sixteen foot down, hard, on the subject of purple-orchid leis. They weren't a modern enhancement of the "best available" tradition of Hawaii. They stank. They weren't allowed past the front door. Or the back.

It was the same for Hawaii's famous steel guitar and ukulele music. No way. Never. Period. No matter how passionately the patrons pleaded or argued, the wailing, twanging music was forbidden within the Kipuka Club's carved wooden walls.

Nicole fully approved. Cellophane and steel guitars weren't on her top one hundred list of favorite things. They weren't even in the second hundred.

Orchids, however, didn't stink. They were delicate, gorgeous, sensual and . . . well, all right, a few orchids did smell like rotten food. But many had a delicate, heavenly fragrance.

Despite her personal delight in orchids, she had given up arguing with Bobby over the flowers. It was a small sacrifice in order to dance to the driving, exotic rhythms of bongo drums, Bobby's bass chants, and the husky, eerie notes of the Bolivian panpipes that he loved. Every time he could find someone else for the drums, Bobby settled in with his mystical, magical pipes.

Tonight Bobby was stuck with his bongos.

A subdued pulse of movement went through the novice dancers as Bobby shifted the beat from attention-demanding rhythms to a more fluid sound. He began chanting softly, telling the story of the hula in liquid Hawaiian while the curtain parted to reveal, not Pele, but seven young dancers.

There were muffled sounds of surprise from the audience as parents recognized their children beneath the colored lights.

Nicole smiled, knowing that hearing their names whispered through the audience was all the reward the nervous girls needed. The audience's surprise was complete, and it would only increase as the teenagers danced. They had worked hard. It showed in the easy grace of their hands describing legends in the dusky room. The hula was slow, fluid, each motion a separate phrase in an unspoken language.

When the music ended, the girls received enthusiastic applause from aunts, uncles, fathers, mothers, siblings, and neighbors. Smiling, trying not to giggle, Sandi hurried offstage with the other dancers and threw her arms around her mother.

"Did you see your dad?" Jan asked, grinning.

Sandi shook her head. "The lights were too bright. But I heard him. And I heard Uncle Chase laughing."

"Not at you, honey," Jan said quickly.

"Oh, I know that." Sandi's voice was easy, confident. "He was teasing Daddy about something. I could tell by his tone. Honestly, they're worse than me and Mark."

"Worse than you and your brother? Um, I'll have to get back to you on that," Jan said, hiding her smile by bending and picking up Lisa.

Lisa giggled and kept her fingers wrapped around two of Nicole's. With shining eyes, the little girl looked from one to the other of the two women who were helping to heal the hurt of her own mother's rejection.

From both wings of the stage, university students began filtering into position behind the closed curtains. Nicole gave Sandi a quick, one-armed hug and then nibbled teasingly on Lisa's fingers. Giggling again, the little girl let go of Nicole.

"Are you staying?" Nicole asked Jan.

"Can't. Dane will take you home. I've got to get Lisa to bed and finish my proposal."

"What is it this time?"

" 'Eden in Shades of Green.' "

Nicole tilted her head thoughtfully, then nodded. "That's a happy relief from the usual academic titles. I really like it."

"I hope the Pacific Rim Educational Foundation does, too. It will cost a bundle to do right. Did you know that no one has done a comprehensive, scientifically accurate botanical survey of these islands yet?" Jan demanded, her voice rising in disbelief and indignation. "When you think that—"

A flurry of drumbeats cut her off.

The rhythm tugged at Nicole, making her heart beat faster with the promise of the freedom of the dance.

"Let me know if you want to send a few drawings with the proposal," she said hurriedly to Jan. "I've got some of Waimea Canyon that are just that—shades of green." She kissed Lisa quickly. "See you tomorrow, honey." Nicole turned to Sandi and stroked her shining hair. "You were a goddess. I'm going to be out of a job."

Though Sandi giggled and ducked her head, her smile was brighter than the spotlights on the stage.

Just as the curtain parted, Nicole took her place at the back of the raised wooden floor. The advanced Polynesian dance students stood in front of her. Men and women alike wore colorful lavalavas wrapped low on their hips. Fragrant leis graced their necks.

The dancers earned pocket money and learned audience skills working in the Kipuka Club four nights a week. Some of the dancers were ethnography students who wanted to feel closer to their subject. Others were science majors looking for a change of pace or dive enthusiasts working on their aerobic stamina. Where they came from or where they were going didn't matter to Nicole, as long as they loved the dance enough to work at it.

Even though Nicole stood well out of the spotlights, the audience discovered her immediately. Murmurs of "Pele" rippled through the crowd.

Like everyone else, Chase leaned forward, straining to see the woman who dominated the stage even from the shadows. He saw nothing but a dark shape haloed by fire that twisted and shimmered with each liquid movement of her body. His breath caught when he realized that it wasn't fire he was seeing—it was hair the color of flames, a glorious fall of incandescent red-gold strands.

With heart-stopping grace, the woman's arms lifted, their smooth golden flesh framed by the silken violence of her unbound hair.

Pele, goddess of fire.

CHAPTER

3

For a moment Chase was afraid he had spoken the words aloud. In the next heartbeat he realized that he could have shouted them and no one would have noticed. A thunderous storm of applause had drowned out the drums.

When Nicole didn't move from the shadows, the audience sighed and settled back. Pele would dance, but she would dance to her own demands, not theirs.

Bobby's deep bass chant and gently throbbing drums wove in and out of the dancers' motions as he pursued his version of "traditional" entertainment. The effect was an elemental fusion of ancient and modern into an electrifying new way of approaching Polynesian dance. Sometimes he would switch his narration from English to pidgin, or to a rhythmic, humorous combination of the two that was unique to him.

The audience laughed while the dancers' movements and Bobby's chants told of men outwitting gods and one another. People clapped in time to the triumph of men over the sea and watched in taut attention as two lovers were tricked by a jealous spirit into throwing themselves into the lake of lava burning within Kilauea's black mouth.

Motionless, Chase watched as intently as anyone in the audience, but it was Nicole he watched, not the other dancers. They simply didn't exist for him. There was nothing onstage but the woman with burning hair and golden skin.

Unconsciously he leaned forward even more, trying to make out details of her appearance. He couldn't. She was too well concealed within her softly waving hip-length hair and the shadows at the back of the stage.

Gradually the rhythm of the drums changed from the stately dignity of the Hawaiian hula to the playful, sensual rhythms of Tahiti. One by one, all the dancers except Nicole stepped forward to display their skill at this new form of dance. Their movements were graceful, rapid, and demanding. Tahitian dance required as much strength and stamina as it did coordination and grace.

Soon bodies began to gleam like polished gold or mahogany. Away from the spotlights, darkness throbbed with the rolling thunder of drums. The rhythm increased in speed and intricacy, challenging the dancers to equal its driving presence. Those who couldn't keep up with the constantly increasing pace drifted to the side of the stage and sat like participants at a feast. From there they called out praise and subtle taunts to the remaining dancers, spurring them on.

The number of people standing on the stage shrank to five, then four, then two—Nicole and a young Polynesian scientist named Sam Chu Lin. He was barely as tall as Nicole's five feet ten inches. Like her, he wore a short lavalava. Unlike her, that was all he wore. As he faced her, his superb physical conditioning showed in every rippling muscle of his body. He swayed provocatively, tauntingly, daring her to equal him.

For the first time Nicole stepped fully into the spotlight.

Her hair blazed suddenly, vividly, drawing a low sound of awe and pleasure from the audience. Swaying rhythmically, she answered the male dancer's challenge with movements that exactly echoed his.

Bobby gave a short cry of encouragement and shifted the rhythm into an even more rapid pace.

Sam answered with sinuous, repeated, powerful movements of his hips. The motions were as difficult as they were frankly sensual. With each intricate movement, he inched closer to Nicole's teasing, gleaming body.

She didn't retreat. She moved her hips in a figure-eight motion that was so quick the print of her lavalava blurred into a halo of color around her hips. Her hair flew out as she spun and turned her back on Sam, giving him a clear view of her wildly gyrating and perfectly disciplined hips.

Then she smiled over her shoulder at him. It was a smile as old as Eve, a feminine challenge as fiery as the flame-colored hair that enhanced each fast, sensuous movement of her body.

Beneath Bobby's flying hands, driving rhythms pulsed out of the drums. It seemed impossible that anything could match them, but the dancers did.

As Nicole turned to face Sam again, he leaped into the air. When he landed lightly on the stage, his urgently moving body was closer to hers, so close that her hair licked over him like fire and clung to his hot, gleaming skin.

He smiled at her, an elemental male smile whose intent was as unmistakable as the potent motions of his body.

She answered with a swift, impossible quickening of her dance, her body burning brighter than her hair.

Chase felt like he had taken a fist in the gut. His breath went out with a thick sound that was almost pain. Blood raced through him until his own arousal pounded with the insistent beat of the drums. Each hot movement announced that in Tahiti, dance was an erotic ritual where both partners displayed their physical lures to a potential mate—strength, stamina, grace, and an elemental sensuality that was literally breathtaking to watch.

Chase would have given a great deal to be the man on the drums, driving the primitive rhythms to their inevitable climax. He would have given even more to be inside Pele, deep inside, driving that hot, beautiful body of hers higher and higher until she screamed with pleasure.

As the drumbeat thickened and increased yet again, Nicole and Sam danced toe to toe, their bodies moving so rapidly that individual motions were a blur. Taunting, provoking, challenging, dance and dancers were an eruption of sexuality that stunned Chase. There was no sound but the rapid, primitive thunder of the drums and the soft thud of bare feet meeting wood with each shift of the dance.

The beat increased as relentlessly as Chase's reckless hunger for the redheaded dancer. He didn't try to fight his need, because he didn't even know it was there to fight. He wasn't aware of himself any longer. He knew only the vivid, pulsing sexuality of Pele.

Sweat gave Nicole's skin an iridescent quality, as though she was burning from within. Her partner was working even harder. Drops of sweat gleamed, gathered in golden rivulets, and ran from Sam's body. His breath came in harsh gasps as he fought to keep pace with Nicole's incandescent dance.

But no mere man could match the goddess of fire.

With a hoarse cry, Sam dropped down among the dancers who were sitting on the stage.

Nicole's dance never even paused. With a provocative snap of her hips in Sam's direction, she turned and held out her hands to Bobby, inviting him to replace her exhausted partner.

Bobby answered with another quickening of the pounding beat of the drums.

The new rhythm swept through Nicole, exploding into passionate movements of her body that were both dance and something far older, as deeply rooted in the human soul as life itself. Fiery hair flying, body gleaming, smile flashing, Nicole gave herself wholly to the hot, sensual dance.

Bobby's hands became a dark blur over the drums, yet still he could not keep up with her. He held the violent rhythms at their peak for a long instant. Then, with a hoarse sound, he threw up his hands and surrendered to the woman who burned wildly in the center of the stage.

With a throaty, triumphant cry, she danced on alone, accompanied by only the wild beating of her heart and the audience calling **"Pele! Pele!"** as they celebrated her victory.

Without warning, the dance ended.

Nicole stood alone within the blazing spotlights, her breasts rising and falling rapidly, her arms held out as though to an unseen lover, her skin shimmering with heat, her hair the color of Pele's own burning lava fountains.

The room plunged into darkness.

The audience clapped and shouted for Pele, but no one answered. After a few minutes the lights came up. Men and women settled back around their tables and began talking again. Between the words and phrases, currents of excitement still echoed through the room where the fire goddess had danced.

Chase felt like he was on fire himself. He was grateful that the light level in the room stayed low, for his own savage arousal was all too apparent. Silently, uselessly, he cursed his body for its betrayal. The only thing that answered him was the hot drumming of blood through his veins.

He told himself that it would pass, he had been aroused before and life had gone on just fine. He could thank Lynette for that; she had taught him that sexual hunger was preferable to living in yoked misery with the wrong woman.

Slowly he let out a breath, then another, then another, until the vise of sexual need began to loosen. With narrowed gray eyes, he searched the faces of the other men in the room, wondering how many of them were grappling with their own stark arousal. He saw a variety of expressions— pleasure, excitement, humor, appreciation—but nowhere did he see a reflection of his own violent response to Nicole's sensual dance.

His only consolation was that Dane, while he had obviously enjoyed the performance, hadn't been aroused.

"Is it time to say I told you so?" Dane asked smugly.

"Just what did you tell me, little brother?" Chase's voice, like his thoughts, was raw and rough.

"That you've never seen anything like her."

Chase smiled thinly. "Outside of a red-light district, no, I can't say as I have."

"Chase Wilcox, closet Puritan!" Dane hooted in disbelief. "Say it again. I still don't believe it.

Tahitian dancing can be a little sexy, sure, but it's a long way from smutty."

"Couldn't prove it by watching the red-hot red-head. I'm surprised the cops haven't shut this place down."

Dane realized that his brother was serious. "What are you talking about? Look around you. The Kipuka Club is rated PG."

After a moment Chase forced a smile onto his lips. He knew that his brother was right. There were families gathered around tables all through the supper club, enjoying the food, drink, and professional conversations that were the Kipuka's hallmark.

Reluctantly he admitted that if he found Nicole's dance violently arousing, the problem was with him rather than with the dance itself. He had seen Tahitian dance performed before, had enjoyed the saucy rhythms, the curve of breasts and hips, and none of it had raised his heartbeat worth mentioning.

But that was before the fire-haired goddess.

All Chase could think was that the men in the club must be as blind as stones not to see the wildness in her, the hunger, the sexual heat.

My God, the sheer heat.

On the heels of that thought came another, one that made Chase's mouth curl slightly beneath the thick black sheen of his mustache. The women must be blind, too, or they would grab their men whenever Pele came onstage and take off like bats out of an erupting volcano.

"When does Nicole make her rounds of the tables?" Chase asked idly.

"Make her rounds?"

"Yeah. You know. Go to each table and smile and press the flesh and get tips stuffed into her lavalava."

Dane shook his head. "You've been keeping the wrong company, bro. You keep acting like this is a strip joint and Nicole's some kind of exceptionally well coordinated tart. If you try to stuff money in her lavalava, you'll lose your hand."

"I don't notice Jan dancing here," Chase pointed out.

"Try next Wednesday. That's amateur night. But if I catch your hands anywhere near **her** lavalava, I'll hire three men and break your arm."

Chase tilted his head back and laughed, really laughed, releasing some of the tension that had coiled so explosively inside him. The sound of his laughter was contagious. Nearby people looked around and smiled at him for no other reason than their pleasure in hearing him.

"I'm glad to see you have enough sense to be jealous of Jan," Chase said finally.

"Just cautious. Women fall into your hands like sun-ripe fruit. Jan makes life very comfortable for me. I don't want her too close to your lethal charm. After fifteen years of staid married life, she might get itchy and wonder if she missed anything by marrying real young."

Like you're itchy? Chase asked his brother silently. Aloud, he said, "Women trample me to get to you. You're so damned civilized and elegant you're almost pretty."

Dane grinned. "Yeah. Ain't it grand?"

As long as it isn't Nicole chasing you, yes.

Chase knew there was no way his brother could have a very discreet, very meaningless affair with Nicole and then go back to Jan a wiser man. But Dane didn't know that, and he wasn't listening to his older, wiser brother.

Chase felt like leaning over, grabbing his brother's shirt, and yelling, **Listen to me, damn you! You're going to screw up a wonderful marriage and never know it until way too late.**

Even as Chase wanted to pound on his brother's stubborn head, he knew that there wasn't much hope of words getting through. When their crotch was on alert, men were exceptionally vulnerable. Stupid, even. Shortsighted, certainly.

Except for Jan, Chase had never known Dane to react to a woman the way he did to Nicole. Open affection, pleasure, admiration. Full-on arousal couldn't be far behind.

If Chase had thought that shouting at his brother—or hammering sense into his thick head—would get through the testosterone blindness, he would already be shouting and hammering. But those direct approaches had never worked with Dane. Chase's charming brother did things his own way, in his own time, and to hell with the rest of the world.

Words wouldn't get through to Dane. Action would. A very special kind of action. The kind that would prove to Dane that he didn't know Nicole very well at all.

"Does Nicole do anything but dance?" Chase asked after a moment.

"Like what?"

"Work for a living."

"There speaks a man who's never tried Tahitian dancing," Dane said. "If that isn't work, what is? Didn't you see Sam Chu Lin? He was sweating like ice in a sauna, and it wasn't because he's out of shape. Hell, if I had his muscles, I'd burn mine."

Chase made a sound that could have meant anything or nothing. His wintry glance roved the room restlessly, searching for a flash of fire and grace and supple female strength.

Pele. Nicole. By either name, by any name, she was a woman to match the burning mountain.

"Nicole is an artist," Dane said.

Hardly able to believe what he had just heard, Chase gave his brother a sidelong look. "Oh, yeah, right. That's what all the exotic dancers say."

Dane fought a smile. "Could be, but I'll bet they don't strut their art in a bona fide gallery."

The arch of Chase's left eyebrow rose in a silent question.

"Didn't I tell you?" Dane grinned. "Nicole does line drawings and watercolors that are accurate enough to illustrate scientific texts and original enough to be sold as art throughout the islands."

Chase signaled a passing server, pointed at the two empty beer bottles on the table, and returned his attention to Dane.

"But don't take my word for it," Dane said dryly. "You'll see for yourself. She'll be working with you on your **Islands of Life** project."

"What are you talking about?"

"You asked me to find an illustrator. I did. Nicole."

"She's really capable of scientific illustration?" Chase asked in disbelief. Since the perfection of the thirty-five-millimeter camera, not to mention the newest digital models, few artists had the desire, the ability, or the control required for painstaking re-creations of nature such as Audubon had made famous.

"Did you see the Volcano Portfolio the national park put out a year ago?" Dane asked.

Chase nodded.

"The illustrations were all Nicole's."

"She's **that** N. Ballard?" Chase asked before he could stop himself. The last thing he wanted to be was impressed.

But he was.

The amount of talent, drive, and discipline that were required for someone to perfect both a gift for drawing and the more physically challenging gift of dance was impressive. He remembered the drawings for the Volcano Portfolio. He had been struck by the artist's ability to capture both the scientific facts of an erupting volcano and the more elusive emotional truth of a volcano's awesome reality.

A chill slowly condensed in Chase as he measured the clear pride and appreciation in his brother's blue eyes while he talked about Nicole's accomplishments. He sounded like a doting parent—or a man falling in love.

Christ, Chase thought wearily. **What chance does Jan stand against a woman like Nicole? Intelligence, artistry, and the kind of fire that burns a man to his soul.**

Pele incarnate.

Hoping that he was wrong, afraid that he wasn't, Chase began to question his brother in earnest about Nicole Ballard. Everything he heard made the chill inside him deepen.

"She's great with kids," Dane said warmly, glad to see that his brother was finally really listening. "Takes them on long hikes nearly every weekend, back up to the kipukas on Kilauea's slopes where nobody else goes."

"How did she find the kipukas? Or are you telling me that she's an explorer and volcano crawler along with all the rest?"

Dane laughed. "Nope. Bobby's kid showed her a batch of kipukas, and it was love at first sight. Same goes for the kids and Nicole. Love at first sight. Lisa follows her around like a gray-eyed shadow. Nicole is teaching her how to draw." The flow of words became a groan. "Oh, hell, that was supposed to be a surprise. Forget I said anything."

Great with kids, huh? Yeah, right. Lynette made a lot of noises about motherhood, too. You've picked a real winner, Dane. Just like your butt-stupid older brother.

The anger that had corded Chase's throat while he listened to Dane run on and on about the poor, sexy dancer who had just happened to catch the eye of one of the wealthiest men in Hawaii made it difficult for him to talk. He had to swallow some beer before he could trust himself to say, "So Nicole hula dances and paints nature."

"You make it sound so . . . ordinary."

Chase shrugged. He had to find a way to convince Dane that his redheaded saint had feet of wet, sticky clay. Otherwise Dane was about to make the worst mistake of his life.

Like Chase had when he believed Lynette's lies about love and family and marriage.

"Sounds like a hand-to-mouth way to make a living, dancing and drawing here and there," Chase said.

"She wasn't born lucky, like we were."

"Lucky? As in rich?"

Dane nodded. "I'd guess that Nicole pays her bills and not much more."

"Too bad. That's a hard life."

"She's not losing any sleep over it. She likes her life the way it is."

Chase bit back blistering words. **Don't you believe it, little brother. She's setting you up to clean your pockets right down to the lint in the seams.**

But, hell, that's just money. There's a lot where it came from.

Self-respect is harder to replace. I don't want you to have to look in the mirror and see just how many kinds of fool you were, to hate yourself every time you think about how an innocent child paid the price of your stupidity.

That was the part Chase couldn't forget, couldn't forgive: Lisa had paid for her father's bad taste in women.

"Well," he said with false calm, "I suppose Pele's lovers take up the financial slack from time to time."

The server approached with two frosty beers before Dane could reply. Chase pulled out a ten-dollar bill, threw it on the tray, and picked up one beer.

"Nope," Dane said, grabbing the other bottle for himself. "No lovers, no live-ins, no 'friends,' no nothing. Everybody's sister and nobody's woman."

"Bullshit," Chase said, forgetting caution.

"Same to you, buddy." Dane saluted his brother with the beer bottle. "I'm the one who knows her, remember? And I say she's alone."

Chase closed his eyes, concealing the rage he

knew would show. **Alone? Never.** Without a man to share her fire, Nicole would burn herself to ash.

But she really had Dane fooled.

"How long have you known her?" Chase asked, sipping beer.

"Long enough. She's as unattached as they come, and it isn't for lack of offers."

"I'll bet. I'll also bet that if she's turning men down, it's because they aren't rich enough. Scientists and university types aren't noted for the money rolling out of their pockets. A woman like her is expensive."

"You're way off base." There was an edge to Dane's voice that hadn't been there before.

"Bet I'm not. Bet I can get your perfect Ms. Ballard in bed before the end of the month."

"No way. Not even you, Chase. She hasn't dated since I've known her."

"How many rich men have tried her?"

There was a long, tight silence. Then Dane's hands relaxed from the fists they had formed. Almost curiously, he looked at his hard-faced older brother.

"None that I know of," Dane said. "Why?"

"Like I said, there aren't that many rich men around Hilo."

Dane took a slow breath—long enough to count to ten and remind himself of the special hell his brother had been put through by a woman who was as cunning as she was beautiful.

"Every woman isn't like Lynette," Dane said finally, "out for money and willing to do anything, hurt anyone, to get it."

Chase shrugged and sipped again. "The proof is in the pudding, little brother. You got lucky with Jan. A lifetime of luck. All you have to do is not screw it up." Then, before his surprised brother could say anything, Chase pinned him with a pale, crystalline glance. "What are you so pissed off about? If your Nicole is such a bloody perfect saint, then I'll be the first to apologize to you. And if not . . ." He smiled savagely. "Well, live and learn, right?"

Dane's lips stretched into a smile that was almost as hard as the one on his brother's mouth. "You're on."

Chase held out his right hand. Dane shook it.

Then Dane laughed triumphantly. **Gotcha!** "Jan is going to love this. She's been wanting to go on a vacation without the kids. I'll set it up for July first, because you'll be paying off your lost bet with two weeks of baby-sitting!"

So Jan wants a second honeymoon, does she? Chase thought. More likely she just wanted to get Dane away from that red-hot sex machine for a while.

"Win or lose, I'll take Sandi and Mark for two weeks this summer," Chase said. "Jan could use the break. She's looking tired."

Or like a woman worried about keeping her thick-headed husband from making a fatal mistake.

"Oh, you'll lose," Dane said, confident as a cat closing in on a mouse. "Nicole's not like Lynette. You'll see."

Chase simply leaned back and smiled. Nicole Ballard, alias Pele, was exactly like Lynette.

And he would prove it.

CHAPTER
4

Early the next afternoon Nicole rode the bus from Hilo to the national-park visitors center. She was accustomed to the bus trip, because she didn't have a reliable car—it was being worked on right now—and most of her part-time jobs were up on the volcano itself.

But it was no hardship to take a bus up a road where orchids grew in the ditches and giant fern trees arched protectively over the warm, damp ground. She enjoyed the changing vegetation as the bus climbed the gentle, lava-ravaged slope of the volcano. From Hilo's tropical rain forest at sea level, the bus climbed through croplands, then through native ohia and koa forests and lava flows, and finally to the top of the crater of the volcano itself, where there was little but bare black rock and steam vents.

While she watched all the changing shades of green, she ran through a mental list of what she had to do today. Not laundry, thank God. She had taken care of that first thing this morning, along with some gardening, housekeeping, and grocery shopping for Grandmother Kamehameha.

As for her own little cottage, it was as clean as it was going to get for a few more days. She needed to do some preliminary sketches for Grandmother's birthday more than she needed to dust. Bobby's mother had asked for a sketch of Benny, the youngest of her grandchildren. Nicole would make sure she got a good one.

She should also check with Jan again and set aside some time to go over sketches that might be useful to include with the written proposal for "Eden in Shades of Green." Then there was teaching; she had three classes of dance students, but not today. Usually on the days she didn't teach, she would put in four or five hours as a research assistant at the Volcano Observatory.

Actually, "research assistant" was too glorified a title for her work, but it kept the bureaucratic pigeonholers off the scientists' backs. What she did for them defied a single label. She handled logistics on projects for those scientists who couldn't organize their own wallets, much less something as complex as getting men and materials to the same place at the same time with the right equipment for some of the elaborate experiments being conducted on the volcanoes.

Sometimes she poured coffee and watered plants. Sometimes she filed papers. Sometimes she typed field notes into a computer. Often she put reports into English rather than the obscure technical language of experts, which sounded more like a chemistry textbook than human speech.

And sometimes she went with scientists to new lava flows and sketched them as they scooped scalding vapors into containers for later analysis. Once she had gotten so close that her sketch pad curled and her feet blistered despite her asbestos-lined boots.

No matter what she was doing, she absorbed the good-natured arguments around her, and she asked questions of the more patient scientists. She wanted to get some feel for the inner workings of the volcanic island that called to her as no other place ever had. Not only did the knowledge itself please her, she had discovered that the more she knew about the mysterious, majestic volcanoes seething beneath her feet, the more depth she brought to her drawings.

She loved that part of her work the best, the drawings, but the project she had been working on was finished. There was no point in starting another one until Dane's brother got up and running on his kipuka study. Then she would have some idea of how much time to budget, and when, for the kipuka project.

Until then she was on her own. While that was hard on the bank account, it was great for everything else. She had been wanting to finish her series of sketches on the Volcano House Hotel, which was perched on the rim of the volcano's huge mouth, overlooking what once had been a lake of heaving, molten stone.

The old frame building was newly painted a shade of dark brick red that contrasted with the black lava of the volcano rim and the thick growth of ohia and ferns that crowded right up to the edge of the cliff—and sometimes spilled over. She had already sketched the pathway along the rim beneath the Volcano House's big windows, the ragged cracks and deep holes where the old road had been abandoned to the restless volcano, and the tourists who ranged from nervous to bored to awed in the presence of the living volcano. Now she wanted a view of the hotel from the caldera floor, where cracks in the rock steamed with the volcano's hot breath.

The path down to the caldera floor was well marked. The many paths across the lava weren't. The floor of the caldera was made of molten stone that had cooled until it became a shiny black lid over the raging forces beneath. The type of lava she walked on now was called pahoehoe. It was slick, smooth, and hard, and once had been about the consistency of syrup.

Pahoehoe could be as thin as a fingernail where large bubbles had formed and cooled without breaking. There was no way to tell how solid the lava was except by walking on it. Since no one wanted to get sliced to the bone by breaking through a crust of sharp lava, the safe routes over the caldera were marked by occasional piles of stone. If there was any doubt as to what was a safe trail and what wasn't, all Nicole had to do was follow the dull ribbon left where many feet had worn off the original glossy finish of the lava.

Unfortunately, the view she wanted wasn't on the normal routes. She left the path and scrambled across a patch of much rougher aa lava. While this kind of lava was safer because it didn't form big blisters, it was like walking on knives. Every time she felt the sharp edges gnaw on her shoes, she remembered the first time the Hawaiian names for various kinds of lava had been explained to her. Pahoehoe had the same easy flowing, liquid sound to it as the lava itself had when fresh: pah-hoy-hoy. Aa lava, on the other hand, was rough and thick and sharp and thus had made its own name when the early Hawaiians walked barefoot over it, saying "Ah-ah!"

Nicole doubted that was how the lava had really been named, but she loved the story. And she was grateful for the tough hiking shoes she wore. They went well with her sturdy khaki shorts but looked odd with her flowered silk halter, which was part of an old dance costume and very comfortable. But all resemblance to Pele ended at the halter. Her hair was braided and pinned securely on top of her head. Loose hair was a nuisance when she was hiking or sketching.

After a few minutes she found the place where she had sat and sketched before. Here the aa gave way to a sinuous tongue of pahoehoe that was as black and shiny as the day it had cooled after its fiery birth. Once the stone had been thin and quick-flowing. Now it was a motionless mound curved into billows and swirls, as hard and nearly as bright as a mirror.

Bracing her sketch pad on her knees, she began a study of the old frame building that brooded over the frozen lava lake. She had been meaning to complete her series on the Volcano House Hotel for months, but something else always came up. Now that Dane's brother had arrived in Hawaii to lend his name and expertise to the **Islands of Life** project, she wouldn't have much time to work on sketches just for her own pleasure. But until Dr. Wilcox was ready to begin working on the project, she was free.

Not that she wasn't anxious to work on **Islands of Life.** She definitely was. The endurance and beauty of life in the face of overwhelming odds had always fascinated her. She felt a kind of sisterhood with the kipukas, survivors of past volcanic eruptions, past devastation.

She felt the same about the gradual return of life to barely cooled lava slopes. The grace and stubbornness of life made awe prickle through her, and with it a feeling of strength at being part of that resilient force. She was eager to work with and learn from Dr. Wilcox, a man who had made the study of volcanoes and returning life his specialty.

Her hand hesitated over the sketch pad for a moment. She wondered if Dr. Wilcox would be as funny and friendly and easygoing as his brother, Dane. She hoped so, because she would be spending a lot of time with Dr. Wilcox. But as long as he wasn't an octopus in drag, she wouldn't complain about his personality. She would rather spend her time in stony silence than deal with a man who thought he was God's gift to the inferior half of the human race.

It wasn't that she couldn't handle herself if Dr. Wilcox was as bad as Fred, the horny vulcanologist who acted like every female was dying to lie down for him. She handled Fred. She could handle anyone.

But she would have to spend a lot of time out in some very isolated kipukas with Dr. Wilcox. If he **was** an octopus in drag, the hours would be tiresome until he got the message and gave up. And he would give up. All the men did, sooner or later. She just kept smiling and wisecracking and saying no. Even good old Fred had given up.

Eventually. Sort of.

A shadow fell over her paper, blocking out not only the light but her view of what she had been sketching.

She looked up, blinked, and decided that thinking of the devil worked just as well as speaking of him. All six feet two inches of God's gift to Hawaiian skirts stood in front of her. About two inches away from her nose, to be precise.

"Hello, Fred," she said absently, returning to her sketch again.

And wondering for the hundredth time what women saw in "Dr. Fred." His broad shoulders, muscular legs, sun-streaked brown hair, and wide blue eyes didn't raise a quiver in her. She took that as just one more sign of her own frigidity, the kind of feminine coldness that even a volcano couldn't warm. Fred Warren had set more women's hearts pounding than anything on the island except a massive eruption.

"Hi, my little jalapeño. Saw you drawing. You looked lonely."

"Nope," she said cheerfully. Then she changed the subject in a way guaranteed to distract a scientist. She asked about his work. "She singing in harmony yet?"

Fred knew that she was asking about Kilauea's record of having harmonic tremors before most eruptions. "Getting there. Quakes are coming in swarms, but they're not really lined up in a row yet. She's working on it, though. Getting hotter and readier by the second."

"Must have heard you were back from vacation."

"So you missed me, huh?" He showed Nicole a double row of perfect white teeth.

"I died for you. Didn't you get the funeral invitation?" She leaned to one side so that she could see around him. Frowning, she measured the real Volcano House against the one she had sketched. A little more shadow along the edge of the building . . . yes, that would do it.

"You don't look dead." He glanced over the

curves filling out her hiking clothes and all but licked his lips.

"Miracle drugs. You survive, it's a miracle." She put her fist on his knee and pushed. Hard. "You're gorgeous, but you aren't a historic monument yet. Move it. You're in my way."

"This better?" He crowded right against her knees, giving her a close-up view of his brief hiking shorts and muscular thighs.

"Yuck. You ever think of shaving your legs?"

Fred laughed and backed up, shaking his head. "You dancing at the club tonight?"

She nodded.

"When are you going to do a solo in my bed?"

"Same as always—just as soon as you can dance or drum me right off the Kipuka Club's stage."

He grumbled and said, "No fair. Even Bobby can't do that, and he's as strong as a bull."

"Takes more than strength."

"Yeah? Like what?"

"Stamina. Finesse. Determination." She looked up at Fred suddenly. "And red hair."

"I'll dye it."

"A few pounds off wouldn't hurt," she agreed innocently.

Fred groaned at the pun and gave up. "See you tonight, beautiful."

"Yeah, but I won't see you."

"Why not?"

"Spotlights blind me."

"Ever heard of Braille?" he asked with a sideways leer.

"On your perfect body?" Dramatically she flung the back of her hand across her eyes as though she was about to faint. "Be still my beating heart." She lowered her hand and changed the subject again. "Marcie wants to know if the hotshot pool for this month is closed."

"Marcie?"

"The new haole from Washington State. Ph.D. Seismologist. She's sure she can predict eruptions from the quake patterns better than anyone else."

"Marcie." Frowning, Fred tried to place her. Every summer there was a flood of new people ranging from visiting VIPs to graduate-student gofers.

"Blond," Nicole said, shading in one edge of the building. "Cleavage from chin to navel. Green eyes that only women ever notice."

"Oh, **that** Marcie." He smiled slowly. "So she wants to play, does she?"

"I don't know about that, but she does want to get some money into the hotshot pool."

"Thanks. I'll check her out for tremors."

Shaking her head, Nicole watched Fred stalk off over the lava in search of more willing game. As soon as her glance fell on the side of the house again, she forgot about his relatively harmless lechery. It definitely needed more shading to catch the sense of age and weathering beneath the new paint. And over there, too, an echo of that shading on the rim itself . . .

She lifted her pencil and worked swiftly, losing herself once again. The insistent cheeping of her watch alarm finally broke through her intense focus. She muttered a few words, sighed, and shut off the alarm. Then she noticed the fading light.

"Damn! I set it for three-thirty, not five-thirty. Didn't I?"

The only answer was the position of the sun in the sky. Five-thirty. No doubt about it.

If she made the next bus, she would have just enough time to get home, shower, and race to the Kipuka Club before her advanced students finished their Friday-night act.

On second thought, forget the shower.

She leaped to her feet and started running across the volcano floor.

CHAPTER

5

Nicole finally managed to grab a shower in the washroom behind the Kipuka Club's stage. Still wet, she wrapped her costume into place and started pulling at hairpins and the scrunchies that kept her braids from unraveling. Impatiently she brushed her hair until it swirled around her like a warm cape.

Too warm.

If she hadn't liked the scent and feel of her hair sliding over her skin, she would have cut off the silky mass a long time ago. But there was something delicious about the texture and weight of her hair and the way it echoed every movement of her dance.

But why couldn't it have been black or brown or blond? she asked herself silently.

Because it's red came the swift reply—the words that her mother had used every time her tall, skinny daughter complained about her bright mop of hair.

Cocking her head, Nicole listened to the faint sounds coming from the stage despite the soundproofing. The students were chanting back and forth, ending their act with a dance of their own creation, a hip-twitching mixture of Tahitian and nightclub dance moves that evolved into a dreamy version of Hawaii's majestic hula.

She had just enough time to finish dressing. She hurried to a small changing room backstage and pulled traditional wrist and ankle decorations from a drawer. Just as she bent over to pull on her softly clashing shell anklets, the drums began a rhythmic pulsing.

She froze, knowing instantly that Bobby wasn't the drummer. This drummer was different. Cleaner. Quicker. More intense.

Bobby was very good.

This drummer was extraordinary.

Anticipation of her own coming dance bloomed in Nicole as she pulled a ginger-flower lei from the refrigerator. The cool petals made a wonderful contrast to the heat of her body. The flowers heightened the golden tone of her skin and deepened the fiery lights in her hair.

The thick tassels of dried grass she carried in each hand repeated the sunny color of the flowers splashed on her lavalava and halter. A cross between a long, soft brush and a small pom-pom with a handle, the grass tassels rustled and snapped with each motion of her wrists, emphasizing and enhancing the rhythms of the dance.

Soundlessly she stepped out, closed the door behind her, and went to stand behind the rear curtain of the stage. There she moved to the slow, stately rhythms of the hula, warming her body for the strenuous Tahitian dance to come.

Instead of accompanying the dancers with a chant, Bobby was playing Bolivian panpipes, an instrument made by natives of the high Andes Mountains of South America. The pure, husky sounds of the pipes tugged at something deep within Nicole.

Bobby played two pipes at once, each pipe containing half a scale. Harmony was possible. Barely. To get it, he had to move his mouth very quickly and blow in short, sharp spurts. The result was a ghostly staccato that evoked spirits chanting to one another across bottomless mountain chasms.

Shivers of pleasure coursed over Nicole's skin as the primal drums and husky pipes called urgently to the dancers. The possibilities of the dance raced through her, making her want to sweep aside the curtain and begin the sensuous movements.

Applause erupted as the stage vanished into darkness. While she stepped onto the stage through a slit in the curtains, the less experienced dancers streamed by her, leaving the advanced students on the stage. The dancers' quick comments told her that they had been as excited by the new drummer as she was.

Impatiently she looked toward the drums, but there wasn't enough light for her to make out more than the silhouette of a broad-shouldered, powerful man whose short hair was even darker than the nearly black stage. He could have been haole or Hawaiian, old or young or anything in between.

And his fingertips smoothed a sensual, pulsing rhythm from the drums that raced through her like wine. Each beat echoed in her blood and in her rippling impatience for the moment when she would turn and challenge the mysterious, powerful drummer on a stage empty of other dancers.

Suddenly the lights came up onstage, making Nicole's hair blaze from crown to hip as though each strand was truly made of fire. Murmurs of "Pele" raced through the audience, telling her that they hadn't expected her to appear this late in the night's entertainment.

The panpipes unleashed a husky, triumphant sound that was more electrifying than a shout.

The drummer hesitated for an instant, then settled in with the assurance of a river of molten stone pouring swiftly down to a waiting sea.

As had happened the night before, advanced dancers came forward to challenge one another, then fell away one by one until only Sam was left to face Pele. The drums slowed to a languid, almost taunting rhythm that exactly echoed the lithe motions of Nicole's hips as she danced barefoot into the spotlight. Grass whispered and rustled rhythmically in her hands, underlining each fluid movement of her torso. The ginger lei swayed against her breasts, caressing her skin with smooth, cool petals.

The rhythm of the drums changed subtly, picking up speed without losing either its clarity or its oddly taunting quality.

Hips gracefully swaying, she danced for a few moments with her back to the drummer before she turned the stage over to Sam with a flip of the thick grass tassels she held in her hands.

The panpipes picked up the challenge, urging Sam to greater and greater efforts. Smiling, he moved sinuously, quickly, with the muscular grace and potency possible only to a male dancer.

Nicole copied his motions, her hands speaking teasingly to him with every rustle of grass, her hips easily keeping pace with his.

The drumbeat reached a peak, paused, then started again with redoubled speed.

Sweat began to gleam on Sam's body, making him look like a beautiful polished idol. He leaped up and came down closer to Nicole. With every ripple and twist, his well-conditioned body spoke to her of the joys that would come when she stopped leading him on this sensual chase.

As an answer, she turned her back and danced, letting him see the grace and power of the hips that would never belong to him, for he was merely mortal, and Pele demanded something more of her lovers.

With a low cry, he jumped in front of her again, trying to entice her to give the contest and herself to him. At each beat, each thrusting rotation of his hips, he came closer to her, coaxing her senses with his display of strength and grace and sexuality.

Smoothly, heartlessly, the goddess Pele flicked her hips and picked up the pace in the same instant that the drummer did. For her, the sensation of neither leading nor following the rhythm was extraordinary, as though drummer and dancer were somehow joined. Eyes half closed, she tilted her head back and smiled like a woman opening herself for a lover.

She didn't see Sam's eyes narrow in male response, nor did she see the sudden tension in the drummer's body as her elemental smile ripped through him. She sensed only that the rhythm would change soon, becoming even faster, drumming Sam right off the stage, leaving only Pele and the drummer who courted her with every beat of their joined hearts.

Even as the change in rhythm came, she met it. Her body shimmered with life and sensual fire. Her hips described flashing, rhythmic arcs that were so quick no individual motion could be seen.

For a minute, then two, Sam stayed with her, but he couldn't keep up the pace. With a mingled cry of defeat and celebration, he sank to the stage with the other spurned dancers.

When Nicole turned to face the unknown drummer, there was an instant of hush, like a missed heartbeat. She held her arms out. Her body moved seductively beneath the silky fire of her hair.

Staccato rhythms poured out of the drums with renewed speed and potency, taunting her, daring her. Her hips moved in response, matching each beat, answering the male challenge with feminine grace and endurance.

And then she surpassed the wild drumbeats with passionate gyrations that brought cries of "Pele!" from the audience, cries that were echoed by the panpipes' hoarse, primitive harmonies.

Without hesitation the drummer matched the increased speed of the dance.

Matched her.

A sense of inevitability, of uncanny rightness, streaked through Nicole like lightning, bringing a new heat in its wake. **Here, at last, was a man who was Pele's equal**.

She forgot the audience, forgot the stage, forgot everything but the dance, giving herself entirely to the elemental rhythms called by the stranger's hard, skilled hands. She was no longer Nicole Ballard, haole. She was Pele, alive among the volcano's fires, calling for a lover to equal her dance.

And the drummer answered.

Thunder poured from the drums, a wild breaking wave of sound made up of distinctly individual beats. Each pulse of drumming was instantly met by a sinuous motion of Nicole's body, as though she and the drummer shared the same heartbeat, the same breath, the same network of nerves burning with messages of fire.

The panpipes gave out short notes, their panting cries telling of human endurance stretched to its breaking point.

The drumbeat increased yet again, a god calling to a taunting goddess. Her answer was an incandescent shimmer of motion and color, a woman on fire with the sensual demands of the drums.

She was Pele, inexhaustible, and the drummer was her more-than-human lover.

At a distance Nicole sensed the fatigue in her own body, the unintentional blurring of the clean motions of the dance. It was the same for the sound of the drums, a slurring of perfection.

And then she found out that she didn't want to dance the drummer off the stage. He deserved far better than that, for he had brought out the best in her in a way no man ever had. He had called out both the discipline and the wildness, letting her burn within his primal rhythms.

Now those rhythms were faltering.

With a soft cry she turned to face the drummer, holding out her hands in triumph and supplication.

Even as she turned, the drumming peaked. Simultaneously the stage lights vanished, leaving drummer and dancer equally triumphant, sharing the victorious midnight.

Into the silence and darkness came applause like storm waves breaking.

Nicole didn't hear anything but her own heart,

her own breath. She felt a man's powerful arms close around her, felt her own hands sliding over his hot skin, and then their mouths joined as though they were lovers separated since the beginning of time.

CHAPTER
6

Chase pulled Nicole against his body even as he opened her mouth beneath his. There was no hesitation in him, no awkwardness, simply a hot certainty that this woman belonged in his arms. He couldn't taste enough of her, feel enough of her, get close enough to her. His arms tightened around her until he arched her strong, lithe body hard against his. His tongue claimed her mouth fully, penetrated deeply, repeatedly.

With a husky moan she struggled in his arms, but not to get away. She wanted to be closer still, inside his very skin, as hot as the blood pounding through both of them. He tasted like heaven and hell, and she was stretched between, wanting to know it all.

Needing it.

To Chase, the sweet pain of her nails scoring his naked back was like a triple shot of whiskey. He forgot the stage, forgot the audience, forgot everything but the heat and taste of her exploding through him, destroying his normal control. His arms shifted, lifting her, pulling her legs around his waist. She clung to him like fire, surrounding him with the kind of heat and need he had never felt before.

Nor had she. She didn't know where she was or who she was. She knew only that this was the kind of fire the burning goddess within her had always sought and never found. Until now. Now she was the flame itself, twisting, burning, ravenous.

Dimly Chase heard Bobby's hissed warning. Only the knowledge that the stage lights would be coming back on at any moment gave Chase enough control to end the wild kiss.

Nicole must have heard the warning, because her long legs shifted and she slid down him in a motion that came within a breath of putting him over the edge and taking the fire she offered.

He managed not to lose control. But it was close. Too close. His heart beat like a drum beneath flying hands. His blood was a hammering rush through his hard, fully aroused body. He couldn't force himself to let go of her completely. With one arm he held her against his side, letting the sensuous perfume of crushed flowers and hot woman mingle with the heady taste of her on his tongue.

Never had he wanted anything the way he wanted Nicole right now. He could barely believe such need was possible. It was all he could do not to pull her down onto the dark stage and bury every hard, aching inch of his erection deep inside her untamed body.

Chase forced himself to move away from Nicole.

He wasn't an instant too soon. Though the curtains stayed closed, the lights came up.

Even under the slicing spotlights, he couldn't force himself to step completely back from her. Hidden from the lights underneath the flaming veil of her hair, his fingers held her wrist so hard he could feel the bones move beneath her flesh.

When he realized the strength of his grip, he told himself to let go of her. His fingers stayed locked around her wrist. The same primitive part of him that had almost taken her and to hell with the rest of the world simply refused to let go of her. He was afraid she would flick her hips tauntingly at him and disappear into the island's volcano like the legendary goddess of fire, leaving him to burn alone.

The curtains whipped apart. The audience was on its feet shouting, stamping, clapping, and whistling.

Sanity returned to Nicole like a bucket of ice water. For the space of one breath, then two, she couldn't believe what had just happened. She couldn't have wrapped herself around a stranger and done her best to crawl inside his skin while their mouths mated in a frenzy that was still racing through her in wave after wave of heat.

But she had done just that. She could still taste him.

She wanted to taste even more.

As they bowed together to the cheering audience,

she felt the stranger's vitality and power burning through her skin. She shivered in elemental awareness of a woman who has found her mate.

When Nicole understood what her body was trying to tell her, she froze. She wouldn't be vulnerable like that again. She simply would **not.**

If she could have bolted in that instant, she would have.

She couldn't. The man's determination to hold on to her was as plain as the callused fingers locked around her wrist. She was a tall woman, and her body was conditioned by the demands of dance and of hiking through Hawaii's wild countryside; yet she knew if she fought his grasp, she would lose. She couldn't free herself unless he let her go.

It should have frightened her. And it did.

But not as much as it intrigued her.

Reluctantly she understood that she was fighting against herself more than against him. She didn't really want to escape. Not yet. The core of her was still in thrall to the siren cry of the dance and to the dark stranger who had matched her as no man ever had. She remembered the silky caress of his mustache against her skin, remembered tasting him on her lips, on her tongue, remembered how it had felt to want and be wanted in return.

Waves of sensation surged through her, loosening her knees. She had loved being bent like a bow beneath the power of his sensual demands. She had loved feeling him shudder in return when her nails tested the strength of his naked back. Despite all common sense, despite all the sexual humiliations in the past, this stranger had responded to her with a male hunger that couldn't be hidden or denied.

And she had answered him.

The possibilities were as dazzling as they were terrifying. If she didn't get off the stage soon, her knees would finish turning to jelly and her confusion would be obvious to anyone with eyes.

As though Bobby sensed Nicole's need for time to gather herself, he walked out onstage, taking the attention from her. With a sweep of his thick arm, he gestured to the handsome, hard-faced man standing close to her.

"Welcome to Hawaii, brother. Pele waits long time, sure-sure." He turned toward the audience and said loudly, "Allow me to introduce Dr. Chase Wilcox—vulcanologist, biologist, and the hottest goddamn drummer I've ever heard!"

The volume of the audience's cheering shot up wildly.

For the first time since Chase had seen Nicole's flame-colored hair at the back of the stage, he was truly aware of the people beyond the footlights. Beneath his black mustache, his mouth curved up at one corner. He had come way too close to giving the folks a spectacle they never would have forgotten. As it was, he was lucky his lavalava was wrapped so that it concealed his arousal.

When he bowed in acknowledgment of the audience's enthusiasm, he felt Nicole tugging discreetly against his hard grip. He eased it, but not enough for her to slip away. Her skin felt too good against his palm for him to risk her escaping.

Nicole felt the measured grip and knew that she wasn't free. Not yet. Half dazed, she remembered wondering if Dane's brother had a sense of humor or was a womanizer.

Dumb questions.

Better if she had wondered what he would do if she fell into his arms and begged to be womanized.

A sideways glance at him didn't help to settle her mind. Tall, powerful, self-contained. He had the kind of dark masculinity most men would have killed for. His smile was piratical. He looked like he didn't have a care—or a brain—in the world.

She couldn't believe that this skilled, passionate drummer was the internationally renowned vulcanologist Dr. Chase Wilcox, the man who had been selected to author a big, glossy book about Hawaii's kipukas.

With a curiosity she couldn't conceal, she weighed the man standing so close beside her. He had dense black hair and fascinating ice-gray eyes. Once she got past their glittering beauty, she could see the intelligence beneath. And something more. Something . . . hard. His face was strong, angular, weathered, defined by twin black arches of eyebrow and a midnight gleam of mustache above a mouth whose heat and sensuality she could barely believe.

Hastily she dragged her mind away from his tempting lips to the rest of him. His shoulders were wide and well muscled. His naked chest was darkened by sun, thatched with curling, glossy black hair, and gleaming with sweat. A black lavalava rode low on his lean hips. The cloth's scattering of scarlet flowers only heightened his almost overwhelming maleness.

Everything about Chase Wilcox was hard, from the line of his jaw to the fingers that were clamped just short of pain around her wrist.

At Bobby's signal the curtains closed once more. He stretched his arms. With one hand he briskly rubbed lips that were nearly numb from the panpipes' demands. With the other hand he caught the back of Nicole's head and tugged. Automatically she braced her free hand on his heavily muscled shoulder and came up on tiptoe to receive his congratulatory kiss.

Chase's eyes narrowed when he saw Nicole's relaxed acceptance of Bobby's embrace. The kind of mutual physical ease they shared came only from being siblings, longtime friends—or lovers.

Logic said they were lovers, because they sure didn't come from a common gene pool. On the other hand, they could have been just friends.

Yeah. Sure. And he could have been the Faerie Queen.

The stab of anger Chase felt was as reckless as his refusal to release Nicole's wrist. He knew it, but it didn't change anything. He also knew if Bobby's big hand didn't let go of the silken fire of

Nicole's hair real soon, Chase would remove that hand himself.

Stupid thing to do, to feel. He knew that, too. But his normal self-control had gone down under the primal thunder of drums and the sexual heat of the dance.

"Hell of a dance, Pele. Good-good!" Bobby smiled at her from his much greater height. "Damn near set the place on fire."

"That's what you always say."

"Mean it tonight, sure-**sure**," he said, shaking his head. "Son of a bitch, but that was hot!"

"Then thank Dr. Wilcox, not me," Nicole said, kissing Bobby's cheek. "His drumming was as strong and wild as the volcano itself."

"Call me Chase." He smiled rather dangerously at her. "Anyone who dances like you do can't be long on formality."

Bobby let go of Nicole and gave the other man a fast, speculative look. The words should have been a compliment, but they didn't quite sound like one.

She heard the edge beneath the words, too. Her chin lifted in subtle challenge. "Really? Just how do I dance?"

"Like hell on fire."

She hesitated, searching his rain-clear eyes. "Sounds dangerous."

"Yeah," he said huskily. "And sexy. Untamed. Goddess of the unleashed volcano. But you know that already. That's why you dance."

She blinked. "Thank you—I think. But my name is Nicole, not Pele. Other than my hair," she added matter-of-factly, "there's nothing startling or unusual about me."

Chase gave Bobby a sidelong **Did you hear that?** glance. "Does she expect me to believe that?"

"You bet, haole. Why shouldn't you? It's what she believes."

Icy, measuring eyes went from the fiery crown of Nicole's head, then down her lush curves, to her bare, golden-brown feet. Chase had seen more conventionally beautiful women. A lot more. Hell, he had married the most beautiful one of all. In fact, he preferred women like Lynette—small, delicate, and coolly flawless rather than tall, flashy, and frankly female.

At least, he **had** preferred fragile and petite. But not tonight. Maybe not ever again. He had never felt anything as hot as Nicole's strong body arched against him, fitting him perfectly, flesh matched with flesh, female heat with male hunger.

And she had known just how he felt. It had been right there against her belly.

That isn't good, Chase admitted to himself. She was dangerous, sexy, and completely untamed. He had to keep himself on a real short leash. That was the only way he would win.

Pele had met her match. She would burn in his arms, not in Dane's. She wouldn't even know that she had lost her chance at the Wilcox wealth until it was too late. She was way too hungry to be cautious about having an affair with one brother while pursuing the other.

And this Wilcox brother had the bitter experience required to keep the upper hand in the sexual battle to come.

"Did you get your stuff moved in?" Bobby asked Chase.

Reluctantly he pulled his glance from Nicole's flushed, moist lips and looked at the man he had known for only a day and already liked, despite the irrational stab of jealousy. "Yes. Thanks. The cottage is perfect. But your mother isn't."

Bobby grinned. "Talked your arm off?"

"Nope. She was just damned stubborn."

"Insisted you call her Grandmother?"

"I don't mind that. It was when she refused to accept cash, credit cards, or traveler's checks that I got my back up."

The Hawaiian's laugh rumbled like a sleepy volcano. "We don't charge rent to family."

Beneath the dark mustache, Chase's lips softened into a whimsical smile. "Bobby, even if you checked all the way back to the Garden of Eden, I doubt you'd find much blood in common."

"So? You need a transfusion or something?"

Chase gave a bark of laughter before he shot back, "I need someone to take my damned rent money."

The smiling giant shook his head. "Ask Nicole

about blood and family and rent money. She's lived with us for years." He whacked Chase on the shoulder. "Talk you more later, brudder. Sure-sure."

With that, Bobby disappeared through the curtains into the noise and friendly professional wrangling.

Nicole waited for Chase to release her.

He didn't even look her way.

She tried one tug on her captive wrist. Nothing budged. She made a throat-clearing sound.

He turned and looked at her from head to toe. Glowing eyes. Lush breasts. Breathtaking skin. Hips that should have been against the law.

In a distant kind of way, Chase didn't blame her for wanting the richest man she could get. Women had been trading beauty for wealth for a long, long time. Why should she be different?

Because Bobby's family was rich both in land and in money, Chase didn't doubt that she and the big Hawaiian were lovers now or had been in the past. But whether old or new, the affair hadn't led to an offer of marriage yet. If it had, Nicole wouldn't be hunting Dane. Maybe Bobby hadn't been quite wealthy enough. Or maybe his wife had dug in and fought for her man until Pele let go and went on the hunt for easier prey.

For an instant Chase wished that his sister-in-law was a fighter, that he could pursue Nicole just for the pure, hot pleasure of the sex. But Jan wasn't a fighter. She was simply too gentle and too good for gutter brawling. If Dane asked for a divorce, she would give it to him even if it killed her.

Not that Jan's temperament made any real difference. No woman could measure up to Pele in a fight, in a bed, or anywhere else.

Every way Chase looked at it, Jan lost.

Unless he could get Nicole out of Dane's hair by getting her into bed. Soon. Very soon. Before she had a chance to do any more damage.

And after that kiss, **soon** shouldn't be a problem.

CHAPTER
7

Nicole's wrist tugged against Chase's hot, hard fingers. Nothing gave way.

"You have something of mine," she pointed out in a voice that was caught between exasperation and humor.

"You mean this?" Forcing himself to smile, Chase held up her wrist as if he had just discovered it attached to his fingers.

"Must be. See?" She put her left wrist alongside her right. "Perfect match with my other one."

"Can't argue that." He ran his fingertip from wrist to elbow, first along one of her arms and then the other. The visible shiver of her response short-ened his breath and quickened his heartbeat. "It's hard to find that kind of perfection," he said, look-ing into her eyes.

For a moment he forgot that he was going for a quick, cold seduction. In the slanting light from the stage wings, Nicole's eyes were a startling, luminous gold. The color was as vivid and as unex-pected as the pure fire of her body arched against his had been.

"And it's even harder to let go," he added thickly. "But I'm feeling generous tonight. I'll give your wrist back if you'll use it to have a drink with me."

Normally Nicole would have turned aside the invitation with a smile and a humorous excuse, but there was nothing normal about tonight. There hadn't been since the moment she had heard Chase's fingers seducing the drums, filling the night with sensual throbs that still quivered deep within her.

He was a stranger, yet during the dance she felt like she had always known him, always searched for him, always yearned toward the instant in time when he would come to her out of darkness and wrap his power and his hunger around her, teaching her something shattering about herself.

"I—" Her voice broke in a husky intake of breath.

She made herself look away from the clear, crystal depths of his eyes. She couldn't think when he looked at her like that. She could only feel, and what she felt was a sense of fire and rightness that would have frightened her if her mind had been working at all.

"All right," she said, her voice almost as thick as his.

His smile made her breath stop. Distantly she remembered that she was still hot and messy from the wild dance. "I'll shower and meet you back here in ten minutes."

He didn't release her wrist. "It takes longer than

ten minutes to get to the Kamehameha estate and back."

"There's a shower behind the changing room," she said, tilting her head toward the backstage area.

"Big enough for two?"

Chase felt Nicole stiffen instantly and withdraw. Silently he cursed himself for being a headlong fool. Just because she was in the business of selling herself to the highest bidder didn't mean that she was cheap, much less easy. Coming on to her like a boy who had just discovered a built-in Erector set wasn't the way to make her want him more than she wanted Dane. His brother had always been such a smooth, elegant, civilized bastard.

"Sorry," Chase said, stepping back. He released Nicole's wrist in such a way that his fingertips slid gently across her palm. "I'm hot and sweaty and must smell like old socks, but I'll wait my turn."

For an instant she closed her eyes, both savoring the sweet brush of his fingers and regretting her automatic retreat at his half-serious, wholly sexy invitation. But she didn't know him well enough to explain her own past, her own reasons for fearing sex.

She smiled hesitantly. "You don't smell like old socks."

Her low voice curled down his spine like a caress. "You sure?" he asked.

She nodded.

He gave her a slow smile that was made even hotter by his relief that she wasn't going to make him pay for trying to rush the seduction.

"Then how do I smell?" he asked teasingly.

"Like a man who enjoys the strength of his own body."

Surprise showed in his eyes. He had been expecting a sassy double entendre or outright flattery. He couldn't have said which surprised him more—her honesty or her insight.

She turned away and walked into the wings.

"Do you?" he asked.

She looked back. "Do I what?"

"Enjoy the strength of a man's body."

With what could have been a shiver, she looked away and walked toward the wings again. He watched her retreat for a long breath before he called out.

"Nicole? Do you?"

A husky murmur came back to him, a word that could have been **once** or **tonight** or both together.

But that didn't make sense. He must have been hearing things. He called out again, his voice low and resonant.

She didn't answer again. She simply tucked a towel around her hair, turned on the shower, and stepped within reach of the hot, pulsing spray. She enjoyed the rhythmic slide of water over her body and the feeling of renewal that came after a good dance.

Good?

She almost laughed out loud like a giddy school-girl. "Good" didn't even begin to describe what she had felt. If part of her hadn't been scared rigid, she would have pulled him into the shower with her and . . .

And what?

The shiver that came this time had nothing to do with pleasure. A hot kiss didn't make her less frigid when it came down to where it counted. In bed. She was a fool for forgetting what she had learned at such painful cost. When it came to the opposite sex—to sex, period—she just didn't get it.

That was something she had to remember. A man as sexy as Chase Wilcox would expect and deserve a hot partner. She wasn't it. Having her nose rubbed in her failure as a woman wouldn't teach her anything new. Her ex-husband had covered that ground quite thoroughly.

Deliberately she turned off the hot water. The shock of the cold made her gasp. When her skin felt as cool as her mind, she stepped out of the shower and dried herself. Thinking about nothing at all, she pulled on fresh thong underwear and went to the long cupboard where Bobby kept lavalavas of all sizes. She picked out an emerald green cloth with black orchids and a matching black halter.

After a long hesitation, she pulled out an indigo lavalava that looked like it would fit Chase. She left the cloth draped on the sink where he couldn't miss seeing it.

A few quick motions of her body had the lavalava and halter settled in the right places. She spared only a few moments more to weave her hair into an elegant mass that added defiant inches to her height. Years ago she had chosen the style simply because it discouraged men. There were few things the male of the species liked less than a woman who was taller than they were.

Her hands hesitated. The hairstyle wouldn't intimidate Chase. Even if she wore heels, he would still be taller than she was. With a shrug, she piled her hair up anyway. The style was cool, and Hilo was always warm. She needed no other reason than that to wear her hair as she pleased.

She opened her purse and took out a small vial of perfume whose fragrance had haunted her since she had first discovered it a year ago. The scent was like a breeze whispering in a rain-swept tropical garden: delicate, tantalizing, sensuous, deeply feminine—all the things that she knew she wasn't.

And I won't think about that either. Whimpering about it won't do one damn thing but make my throat sore.

Nicole picked up two slender ivory chopsticks. Each wore a cap of tassels made of strings of tiny golden bells. When the chopsticks were anchored securely in the coils of her hair, the bells gleamed and chimed sweetly with every movement of her head. She smiled at the pretty sounds. They reminded her of the past Christmas, when the

Kamehameha family had given her the beautiful hair ornaments.

Feeling more like her old self, she opened the door.

"Your turn," she said as she brushed past Chase in the semidarkness behind the stage. "I'll be at Dane's table."

The fleeting caress of soft skin, the elusive fragrance, the delicate chiming of bells exploded silently in Chase's senses. For an instant he was too stunned to move. Then he reeled in his jaw and opened the bathroom door with a jerk, angry at himself for being taken off guard all over again by Nicole's spellbinding sensuality.

My hat's off to you, little brother, Chase thought bleakly as he turned the shower on full. And cold. **How did you hold out this long, even for Jan and the kids?**

It was a fast shower. Chase wasn't going to leave Dane within reach of Nicole's fire for one second longer than he had to. Ignoring the lavalava draped over the sink, he wrapped a towel around his hips and got his clothes from Bobby's office, where he had traded them earlier for the lavalava he wore onstage. His slacks were black cotton, and his shirt was the same cold silvery gray as his eyes. He kicked into a pair of black beach walkers, settled his short, damp hair with a few impatient swipes of his palm, and stalked out to rescue Dane.

He arrived just in time to see Nicole leave a tableful of laughing, politely drooling men and go to

Dane. Rage flickered through Chase when his brother stood up and wrapped her in a big, close hug.

"They're going to pass a law against you." Laughing, grinning, Dane shook his head and released Nicole. "Whoa, babe! I still don't believe I saw that."

She winked. "Blame it on your brother."

"Yeah, he plays a mean set of drums. Only thing he's better at is volcanoes. Speaking of unpredictable, how's your car? Is it up to taking you home tonight, or do you—"

Coolly Chase stepped between his brother and Nicole, cutting off the questions. "If she needs a ride, I'll take care of it."

Dane knew his brother well enough to recognize the anger beneath the outwardly civilized words. He gave Chase an odd look, shrugged, and said, "Fine."

"Where's Jan?" Chase asked him bluntly.

"Working on the grant proposal, where else?"

"Maybe she could use some help."

"I'm staying out of her hair," Dane said, smiling. "What more could she ask?"

"Moral support?" Chase suggested, his voice both soft and cold.

Dane crossed his arms over his chest and said sardonically, "Who put the worm in your tequila? You know Jan. All she wants when she's working is peace and quiet. Hell, I'm the same way when I'm programming. The last thing she needs is me leaning over her shoulder every five minutes and asking if I can help. She's had enough trouble with this proposal as it is. Now that school is out, the kids are always underfoot. They're making us both crazy."

Silently Chase wondered if the proposal was taking so long because Jan was spending more time worrying about her husband and a certain redheaded hula dancer than she was about grant language and sponsors.

Rather bleakly, Chase congratulated himself on arriving in Hawaii just in time to keep his brother from fucking up big-time.

"Hey, my little jalapeño, that was one hot dance!"

The voice came from halfway across the room. The distance closed quickly as Fred towed a well-built blonde through the crowd toward Dane's table. Though small, the woman wasn't quite petite—certainly not from the waist up.

"Hello, Fred." Smiling wryly, Dane took in the blonde before he glanced back at the scientist. "Is this your latest entry into the haole summer sweepstakes?"

Fred grinned. "This is Dr. Marsha Sumner. Seismologist. You can see why—she walks through a room and everything quivers." He winked broadly at the blonde, who winked back. "Marcie, meet Dr. Dane Wilcox, computer wizard, Nicole Ballard, sex wizard, and Dr. Chase Wilcox, who claims to know volcanoes."

"Call me Chase," he said, holding out his hand. "It's a pleasure, Dr. Sumner. I saw the article you did for **Nature** comparing the summit tilt deformation of Kilauea preceding eruption to the movement before a Strombolian eruption. Very impressive."

She smiled. "From you that's praise indeed. Please, call me Marcie."

"Marcie," he agreed, releasing her hand slowly.

Nicole watched the two scientists and wondered how the brilliant blonde would look in a luau pit with an apple in her mouth. Then Nicole reined in her irritation and smiled at the other woman. As she did, she reminded herself that it wasn't Marcie's fault that she was blond, eight inches shorter than Nicole, and therefore much more feminine in the eyes of men.

Oh, let's be a teensy bit honest, she told herself bitingly. **You wouldn't care if Marcie sent every man in the room into a slavering frenzy—as long as Chase wasn't one of them.**

"Hi, Marcie," Nicole said, shaking hands and mentally cringing at the image of a redheaded giraffe looming over a Dresden china doll. "Did Fred initiate you into the hotshot pool?"

Marcie gave Fred a sideways glance out of very green eyes. "Did he ever," she murmured. Then she looked back to Nicole again. "You know, when I met you last week at the lab, I couldn't believe you were Pele. No offense," she added with a smile. "You just didn't come on like a professional hula dancer. But tonight—Jesus, Mary, and Joseph! Bet they registered that performance on every seismograph from here to Afghanistan."

"It was Chase," Nicole said, glancing at the tall man who stood beside her. Close beside. "He added something extra."

Marcie looked Chase over with frank female appreciation. "I'll just bet you did. You're enough to start harmonic tremors in granite. Speaking of which," she said, turning back to Fred, "have you seen the paper from four to six P.M.? Swarms of the sweetest little shakers you'd ever want to see. The mountain's warming up right on the schedule I predicted. No doubt about it."

Fred shrugged. "Maybe, darlin'. Maybe. Remind me to show you some of the paper from last September. She shimmied and she shook and she looked like she was going to come in six kinds of harmony. No juice, though. Not even any decent moans. Same thing happened later. The old fissure zone is still plugged solid. If she's going to come, Pele's going to have to find some new tricks."

A man at the next table overheard the discussion and offered his opinion as to the size and placement of the magma pool that was Kilauea's heart and which zones were the most likely avenues for future eruptions. Fred and Marcie turned toward him, both talking at once, their eyes alight with pleasure. The three-cornered argument spread with the speed of a burning fuse to other tables. Soon the discussion turned into the kind of scientific free-for-all that was the Kipuka Club's major attraction for its loyal members.

Chase listened to the voices raised in loud, decisive, sometimes in-your-face conversation. Smiling, he shook his head. "And to think you left home to get away from scientific shouting matches," he said to his brother.

"Yeah, and I promptly fell for a girl who became a botanist with a flair for writing grant proposals. Talk about being able to line up arguments in support of your position . . ." Dane smiled crookedly. "Jan in action is awesome."

Nicole looked from one man to the other, curious but not wanting to ask.

"Mom and Dad are both physicists," Dane explained to her. "Used to make me nuts with their arguments. I didn't understand how the hell an intelligent human being could get into shouting matches about particles of maybe-matter so small that they can be mathematically proven to exist only when they move backward in time." He looked down at the table and lifted his eyebrows. "On the other hand, maybe that's what happened to my beer."

Nicole snickered. "It moved backward in time?"

"Yeah. All the way to Prohibition." He sighed mournfully at the empty bottle.

A waiter materialized in response to Chase's signal—three fingers and an empty bottle of beer held over his head. He pulled out a chair for Nicole and one for himself at Dane's table.

Gratefully Nicole sat down. She was almost light-headed from the combination of hours of concentrated drawing followed by the all-out, wildly exhilarating dance.

Not to mention the kind of kiss that literally had made her knees weak.

The waiter returned with three beers, plus a large pitcher of water and a glass that he set in front of Nicole.

"Thanks, Pete." She smiled up at the young waiter. "You just saved my life."

He flashed her a pleased, appreciative smile that made Chase want to pull a shapeless muumuu over Nicole to hide her from all masculine eyes.

As though she didn't notice her effect on the male of the species, Nicole poured a glass of water and drank it down with swift, delicate greed. Chase watched each motion of her throat, the dark pink flick of her tongue licking up stray drops, and the smooth golden gleam of her breasts curving above the black halter as she sighed her pleasure at the refreshing, cool water.

Hunger swept through him, an almost violent need to touch her, hold her, know again the savage perfection of her body molded to his, her taste in his mouth, their tongues mating.

With growing smugness Dane watched his brother watching Nicole like a starving wolf . . . and Nicole totally unaware of it all. Dane had been worried by the hot currents of sensuality flowing between Chase and Nicole during the dance. It wasn't the idea of losing a bet that bothered Dane but the knowledge that Chase had used up more than his share of women since his divorce.

Dane had wanted Chase to get to know Nicole, to learn about her gentleness and spirit, her intelligence and humor, and above all her generosity. But Dane didn't want Nicole to fall for his brother. Not right away. Certainly not until Chase knew how special she was, how honest. Then his brother would be less bitter, more trusting, more like the man he had been before Lynette.

But until he softened, Chase was the wrong man for any woman to give her heart to, especially a woman whose heart had been as badly mauled as Nicole's must have been.

After seeing her dance to Chase's potent drums, Dane had wanted to take her aside and warn her that his brother was way out of her depth. Yet once off the stage, she treated Chase just as she treated most men—she was pleasant and yet aloof, like a family cat greeting a guest. No matter how the dance had appeared to the audience, it had been a performance rather than a real attraction.

A good start, Dane decided, settling back into his chair. Very good, in fact. Chase was hot and Nicole was cool. By the time he got anywhere with her—if he ever did—he would know that she was a good woman rather than a flashy piece of ass like Lynette.

After that . . . well, who could say? At the very least Chase would have to admit that Jan wasn't the only good woman on the face of the earth.

"I'm going to enjoy that vacation," Dane said softly, lifting his glass in a toast to himself for being so clever. He took a long swallow of beer. "I've earned it."

CHAPTER
8

"Did you say something, little brother?" Chase asked.

"I just wanted to be sure you could spare the two weeks," Dane retorted, his voice smooth and smug. He winked at Nicole.

"What two weeks?" Chase asked, looking at Nicole again rather than at his brother.

"The two weeks when you take Mark and Sandi."

Chase's head snapped around. He gave Dane his full attention. "Counting chickens?"

Dane just smiled.

"What chickens?" Nicole asked.

"Chase and I have a bet," Dane explained. "When he loses, he takes the kids while Jan and I go on vacation."

"Oh. That's . . . nice."

Nicole's hesitation came from the emotions she sensed seething just beneath Chase's calm exterior. She didn't know what was wrong, but she could guess. Impulsively she turned to him and rested her hand on his bare forearm.

"I know how busy you must be, and Dane's kids can be a handful. Not to mention Lisa," Nicole said. Then she smiled at the thought of the shy and quietly stubborn child who had Chase's radiant gray eyes. "Don't worry. If you lose, I'll help out. All the kids love picnics in the kipukas."

The affection she had for the children warmed her voice and the smile that came and went like the flicker of flame in a wind. Dane gathered up one of the red strands of her hair that she had missed braiding earlier and gave it a teasing tug.

"You're just a big kid yourself," he said. "That's why they put up with you."

"You bet. Of course, it helps that your kids are even smarter than you are."

Laughing, he freed her hair. "Yeah, they're something else, aren't they?"

Chase's expression settled into harsh lines. He knew from bitter personal experience that the second-fastest way to a father's heart was to seem interested in his children.

You don't miss a trick, do you, Pele? If Dane hasn't gotten the message your body is sending out, you can always make a fuss over his kids.

That was exactly what Chase's most recent lady friend had done. She had oohed and cooed over every snapshot of Lisa as though the girl was the most wonderful child since Christ. But the instant it became clear that the girl—rather than a handful of pictures—was going to live with Chase, the lady had wished him luck and gone hunting for another rich fool whose only responsibilities were to his stockbroker.

Lures and lies. But some of those lures are damned irresistible, Chase admitted, looking at the smooth, elegant fingers resting on the bare skin just above his wrist.

When Chase glanced up again, Nicole realized that she had left her hand too long on his warm forearm. With Dane or Bobby it wouldn't have mattered. They were married, and friends.

Chase was neither. He was something new, something entirely unknown. Touching him made her . . . restless. Being touched by him made heat race through her. The feeling was both exciting and scary.

She knew from past experience that she wasn't a sensual woman. At best, sex with Ted had been an uncomfortable event for her. At worst, it had been painful, and her fault.

All of it.

Her very experienced husband had explained it to her in humiliating detail the night he left her and moved in with a petite divorcée who had enough money to keep him in the style he had learned to take for granted with Nicole's money. As an added plus, the rich divorcée was a skilled, responsive lover. Nicole, on the other hand, was neither skilled nor responsive in bed, as Ted had discovered too many times.

Other than your hair, there's not one damned thing hot about you. You're a walking example of fraud in packaging.

The cruel and cruelly truthful words still echoed in her mind, especially late at night when being alone became loneliness, when her youthful dream of a loving partnership with a man became a nightmare of emptiness too painful to bear. She didn't doubt her husband's opinion of her sexuality. He had been a well-known connoisseur of women. She had been a wallflower.

Yet a part of her always hoped and dreamed that with the right man she would be able to respond in bed. With the right man she would know the heat of passion and the peace of companionship. With the right man she would be able to share herself, mind and body, and share his mind and body in return.

With the right man.

And it felt so very right with Chase.

It had felt right from the first instant she heard the drums speak beneath his hands. The single kiss on the darkened stage still sang in her blood, urging her to touch him again, to know again the fierce perfection of being in his arms.

Something deep within her insisted that the act of love with Chase wouldn't be painful or humiliating. She sensed it as surely as she had sensed the shifts in his drumming the instant before they happened. There was an elemental rapport between Chase and herself that defied logic or explanation.

He was right for her. She knew it.

She was right for him. Did he know it?

As though hearing Nicole's thoughts, Chase turned and caught her speculative amber gaze. The female knowledge in her eyes was as hot as his own hunger. He itched to draw her close and kiss her until they were both breathless and struggling to get inside each other's skin.

Wrong time.

Wrong place.

The kind of seduction he had in mind should be done in complete privacy rather than in the friendly, almost familial, and certainly loud surroundings of the Kipuka Club on a Friday night. Too many people were watching, and one of them was Dane.

He didn't need his younger brother overseeing every detail of male advance and female retreat with smug amusement in his eyes.

So Chase settled for reaching for Nicole's water glass instead of her lips. In some primitive way that was stronger than logic or experience, he needed to touch something that had touched her. The knowledge that she had held the cool, smooth glass, that her mouth had touched it, that the water had slid caressingly over her tongue, made this one glass irresistible to him.

"May I?" he asked, picking up her glass without taking his eyes from hers.

Wordlessly she nodded.

The delicate sounds of golden bells pierced the

blur of surrounding conversation. The sweet music sank into Chase like tiny, sensual claws, pricking him into full physical awareness. He poured a clear stream of water into the glass, set his lips on the rim where hers had so recently lingered, and drank.

He knew that she was watching him as intently as he had watched her. The certainty caused a sudden rush of blood in his veins, the heavy beat of sexuality swelling.

Dane took a swallow of beer, set down the bottle with a thump, and looked wryly at Chase. "I know you're going to accuse me of hedging my bets, but I need a ride home. No hurry, though. I've got some table-hopping to do."

Chase shot his younger brother a **Yeah, yeah, yeah** look. "Something wrong with your car?"

"Jan thought she'd be able to come here later, so I caught a ride in on the bus. But she called while you were onstage and told me it's slow going for her tonight. I was going to bum a ride with Nicole—"

"Sure," she interrupted with a sly smile. "There's always room for one more on the Hilo bus."

"Car's in the hospital again, huh?" Dane asked, sympathy and amusement in his voice.

"Until tomorrow. How did you guess?"

He grinned. "Psychic. That and the fact that your car is old enough to vote."

"But far too stupid," she retorted. "It doesn't know first from third."

"Told you the transmission was going." Dane gave his brother a sideways glance.

With a stifled curse, Chase accepted that there would be three for the road, not two. The only good news was that he and Nicole both lived on the Kamehameha estate, so the night wouldn't be an entire flop in the seduction department. It was logical to drop off his brother first, which would leave Nicole alone with him.

Finally.

What's the rush? Chase asked himself harshly. **You've got until the end of the month to win the bet**.

There was no answer but the heavy beat of his own blood. He wanted her. Now.

Right now.

Nothing cooled the hot rush of desire focused between his thighs, even the near certainty that he wouldn't get Nicole into bed tonight any more than he had lured her into the shower. She wanted to wait, to play. He wanted to spread those long legs and sink into her until she didn't know anything but the taste of him, the feel of him, and the screaming ecstasy they would share.

Dane, Chase asked silently, **how in hell did you hold out at all?**

Dane pulled himself out of the low-slung passenger seat of his brother's rented sports car. With a casual wave and a knowing smile that neither Nicole nor Chase saw, Dane headed up the winding walkway to his house. In the back, where Jan had her office, lights burned.

"Care to try for more comfortable quarters?" Chase asked when his brother disappeared into the darkness.

Silence.

He looked over his shoulder at his remaining passenger. Ignoring the protests of both Wilcox men, she had insisted on taking the cramped rear seat, which was more a luggage compartment than a true passenger space.

Next time, Nicole vowed silently, she would plan ahead better. The thought of struggling out of the backseat beneath Chase's very interested gaze made her mouth turn down at one corner. Bad enough to feel big and awkward. To prove it was humiliating.

He smiled at her. "Come on. Slip into something more comfortable."

Though she laughed at the old line, suddenly the back of the car seemed roomier than the front. Up there she would practically be on top of Chase. Even in normal surroundings he was a big man. In the small sports car he was huge.

Yet it was more than just size that bothered her. She had ridden in sports cars with Bobby, who was truly a giant, and had never felt a bit of the wariness, eagerness, and sense of sensual risk that was simmering in her blood now.

As Chase watched Nicole hesitate about moving up to the front seat, he wondered what was going on in her calculating little mind. He could see that she was suddenly wary of him in a very female way. Maybe she was afraid he would jump her.

After that kiss, he couldn't blame her.

After that kiss, he wanted to jump her.

Especially now, when she looked so very female, like a particularly fine amber carving nestled in black velvet folds. Fragrant amber.

In the soft, humid darkness her scent whispered to his senses, telling him that a living woman was only inches away from his touch. He wondered if, like amber, she would generate electricity when rubbed with silk.

Nicole brushed stray tendrils of hair from her mouth and flinched inwardly when she saw the slight smile beneath Chase's smooth mustache. She knew she must look like two pounds of hamburger stuffed into a one-pound bag. As she had so many times before, she wished that she had been born into a more delicate body. But she hadn't been. She was what she was—a tall, strong woman crammed into the backseat of a tiny car.

Sooner or later she would have to get out.

"Not much help for it, is there?" she muttered. "Might as well be comfortable for the rest of the ride."

Chase levered himself from the car and held out his hand to help her. After a moment she took it. Smiling, he watched her supple body uncoil from the cage of the backseat.

Most people would have looked awkward scrambling out of the Porsche's tiny compartment, but Nicole's dance-trained body had both strength and grace. Even when he tugged her forward unexpectedly, pulling her off balance and into his arms, she caught herself with catlike speed and flexibility.

She felt like Eden burning against him, a resilient warmth that went from throat to toe. As his arms closed around her, he wondered why he had always thought he preferred small women. What a waste. No matter how close a man his size held a tiny woman, part of him always went begging.

But not with Nicole. She filled his arms the same way she filled his senses. Completely.

"Chase, I—" Nicole began.

His head tilted toward hers and he bent over her, a potent shadow closing out the night sky.

"Shhhh," he interrupted softly, nuzzling her lips. "It's all right. I just realized that all my life I've wanted to kiss a tall woman wearing moonlight and fragile golden bells. One kiss, and I'll let you go."

For tonight, he added silently. **But not for long.**

CHAPTER
9

The memory of Chase's kiss was still tingling in Nicole the next morning. When he had kissed her, warmth and pleasure quivered through her, expanding with every heartbeat as they had the first moment she heard the drums speak beneath his hard and caressing hands. He hadn't been put off by her size or the subtle hesitations that came from her fear of not pleasing him. He had taken her mouth smoothly, hotly, completely, as though it had always been his.

The sense of rightness had swept her in a warm, silky wind. She had never felt anything like the delicate tremors of heat singing throughout her body. She had wondered if the feelings were proof that there was a chance for her as a woman, a possibility that this man could touch the passion she had always hoped lay inside her.

But she hadn't been certain last night that the kiss was proof of her own passion. She couldn't be certain this morning, no matter how much she yearned to have it be true.

Yet she was certain that she had felt sleek and soft and very feminine held against Chase's powerful body.

A passing car had reminded them that they were standing locked together beneath a streetlight in front of Dane's house. Chase's eyes had been narrowed, nearly silver, and he had released her very reluctantly.

Once out of his arms, she had hadn't known whether to kiss him again or run like hell. Part of her insisted that she barely knew him. Another part, the same instinctive part of her that kept insisting she could be a passionate woman with the right man, told her that she had always known him. It just had taken years to find him.

The tension between the two feelings had been unnerving, like walking across a newly congealed flow of lava and sensing the dangerous warmth welling up beneath the ground, waves of heat that betrayed the seething, barely contained molten rock just below the cool surface of reality.

Each step was a risk.

Each step was exhilarating.

When Chase had parked his car at the Kamehameha estate, she had smiled, whispered her thanks for the ride, and slipped away into the darkness of the overgrown trails before he could touch her again.

Risk. Exhilaration. Heart pounding like a drum.

She still felt the same way this morning. She

wanted to rush through Saturday so that she could go to the Kipuka Club tonight and dance to the dark, rhythmic thunder of Chase Wilcox's drums. She wanted to run away and hide. She wanted to see him.

She wanted, period.

Maybe she would see him this afternoon, when she took the present she had made for Dr. Vic to the volcano lab. If not then, surely tonight, when she danced . . .

But there were a lot of hours between now and dancing. She had discovered long ago that the best way to make time disappear was to concentrate on something else.

She grabbed her sketchbook and headed for the door of the small cottage that had become her home. Outside, the endlessly busy trade winds were piling mounds of clouds against the gentle swell of the volcano, hiding its dark, lifeless peak.

In the higher forests, ohia trees and the native koa that survived the mainland hunger for koa wood grew a startling green against the black tongues of recent lava flows. Scarlet-feathered i'iwi and apapane flicked like exclamation points through the mist-drenched silence, feeding on equally scarlet ohia flowers.

Farther down the slopes, nonnative species grew freely alongside native trees. The result was a thriving, mixed forest filled with life, including feral pigs and Kamehameha butterflies that were bigger than a man's hand.

Where ancient lava flows met salt water, the huge, flower-splashed grounds of the Kamehameha family estate tumbled down to a black-sand beach and the turquoise sea beyond. Like the Kipuka Club, the estate was a thriving combination of native and introduced species. Each plant had been cultivated for its flowers, its startling grace, its fragrance, or any combination of the three. Paths wound gently among ohia and jacaranda, coral and rainbow shower trees, with more ferns underfoot than Nicole could name.

No matter the time of year, regardless of mainland seasons, something in Hawaii bloomed next to one of its own kind whose spent blooms had already been transformed into food by the simple miracles of sun and rain.

Of all the beautiful trees on the Kamehamehas' sprawling estate, the jacaranda had always been Nicole's favorite. Unlike most tropical plants, all jacarandas shared a definite season for blooming, for fruiting, and for waiting. Today it was still the time of waiting. The first vivid rush of their blossoms would stay wrapped within the living silence of the trees, until just the right moment for coming undone in the sun. When that moment came, the buds would throw off their concealing shroud and burn like lavender flames against the intense green of the forest canopy.

Even now, while she watched, tender petals were swelling inside their dark wrappings. This was what she wanted to capture in a sketch—the tender, terrifying moment when the virgin bud came apart and offered itself to the sun.

And with every stroke of her pencil, she would pray that some of the jacaranda buds' innocent, terrifying courage would become her own.

Nicole . . .

Abruptly she stopped and looked over her shoulder, down the overgrown path, wondering if she really had heard someone call her name. She couldn't see much behind her. The path leading toward the big house was almost buried by lush foliage. So were the small cottages that circled the central house like wayward moons. Nothing to see but green on green and golden spears of sunlight.

In Hawaii's tropical rain forest, hearing was often more reliable than sight. Intently she listened as she peered toward the almost invisible openings in the greenery. These often were the only sign of the paths connecting the cottages. The cottages themselves were very private, reserved for family members and friends of the sprawling Kamehameha clan.

Nicole's cottage was the one closest to the sea. She had been given the run of the Kamehameha estate ever since she had discovered a very young, sweaty, scratched, and visibly defiant Benny Kamehameha up on Kilauea's rough slope. He was fighting tears while he stood at the edge of a frozen black-lava river overlooking a kipuka.

She had lived in Hilo and worked part-time at the national park long enough to hear of the

Kamehamehas and the Kipuka Club, so she knew where Benny belonged. She also could tell that he wasn't ready to go home yet. Instead of arguing about it, she opened her drawing pad and began talking quietly about the land and the bright native birds.

At first Benny hadn't responded. Then he had shared a few one-word comments about the birds and plants. After a while she discovered that he had run away from home after his first day of kindergarten and was never going back, because the other children had teased him about his limp.

Sketching as she talked, Nicole had worked quickly to capture the anger and hurt and intelligence she saw on his thin face as he stood and brooded over the green land falling away at his feet. When she finished drawing, she talked him into walking back down the mountain with her by telling him that she wasn't quite sure of the trail and needed someone to guide her.

Benny's ease with and understanding of the land had astonished her. The child was uncanny in his knowledge and agility. She told him so, pointing out that none of the kids who teased him could have matched his pace on that rough and broken ground.

By the time she returned Benny to his worried parents, he was thoughtful rather than defiant. When she gave him the sketch of himself standing like a prince on black-lava ramparts, he had been transfixed by the drawing.

So had his parents. They had also been dismayed to learn that Nicole was still living in a motel, waiting for an apartment she could afford to come up for rent in Hilo. Bobby's wife took Nicole's hand and led her to the three unoccupied cottages on the Kamehameha estate. She was told to take her pick of the cottages. Whichever one she wanted was hers for as long as she wanted it.

Rent? Please, don't insult your hosts. Can you put a price on a boy's smile?

That had been more than three years ago, and nothing had changed. Bobby and his wife refused to discuss rent. Benny smiled a lot. And Nicole fell in love with the spacious, sometimes overgrown grounds of the estate and the tiny cottage that was tucked just up the slope from the beach. Most of the year the cottage was private to the point of isolation, perfect for uninterrupted time to work on her dancing or her sketching.

Most of the year. But not when school was out. Then the place was alive with the shouts and arguments and laughter of children.

The sound came to Nicole again, a high cry like the wind rushing through a steep lava canyon.

"Niiii-colllle! Waaaiiit!"

Benny's thin, wiry body catapulted out of the undergrowth. He ran down the path toward her with an uneven gait that was blindingly quick. Sketch pad and pencils were clutched in his right hand.

"Slow down," she called out, laughing. "I'm not going anywhere."

Barefoot, nut brown, with a flashing smile that rarely failed to soothe Nicole's impatience at being interrupted, Benny was one of her favorites—though it was hard for her to choose among the island children who gathered around her like clouds around the mountain whenever they spotted her alone.

"Picnic?" he asked, excitement making his dark eyes shine with life.

"Not today, honey."

His eyes shifted to her sketch pad. "Watch?"

"Quiet?" she retorted.

He grinned and said not one word.

"Good-good," she said.

She enjoyed the coded exchanges and meaningful silences that were Benny's conversation. He acted like there wasn't enough time in life for him to waste it on anything as ordinary as speech.

He fell in line behind her on the path. He knew the rules when she was working. The first time he interrupted her was "free." Sometimes other interruptions might be tolerated, but only if they were very few and the questions he had were about painting or sketching or the plants themselves.

After that, any interruption had better mean something really urgent, like Kilauea splitting a new seam and pouring liquid fire over the face of the land. If it was anything less important, the chatty child was invited to go talk to the honey-creepers flitting brightly through the trees five thousand feet up the lava slopes.

The rules had never bothered Benny the way they did some of the other children. Silence came more easily to him than words.

Mouth shut, eyes wide open, he followed Nicole. She went to her favorite place, a little point of land where lava had licked out into the ocean at one end of a crescent-shaped beach. At the upper edge of the coarse black sand, coconut palms swayed and dipped in the breeze like stately dancers. The ocean was radiant with every tint, tone, shade, and combination of blue and green. Surf smiled, curled, and laughed whitely over the lava beach.

Though Nicole enjoyed the beach, it wasn't the isolation or beauty that kept bringing her back. It was the flowering trees that had been planted just up from the beach by Benny's great-grandmother when she was only nine. All of the trees except the scarlet-blossomed ohia came from other continents, yet each tree seemed to reach a peak in Hawaii's gentle Eden.

Coral trees blazed with color, their clusters of red flowers rising from each naked branch tip like a fistful of flame. Next to them, shower trees lived up to their name, producing fantastic cascades of blossoms that covered their branches. In other lands shower trees came in single colors—white or yellow or pink or pale orange. In Hawaii the trees had cross-pollinated until they transformed themselves into what the natives called a rainbow shower, a tree that produced flowers of all colors in soft-petaled rainbow drifts that had no equal anywhere else on earth.

Yet even the rainbow shower trees couldn't draw Nicole's eye away from the cluster of jacarandas that rose above all others. With their smooth, dark trunks, fernlike leaves, and delicate lavender flowers, the jacarandas pleased her in ways she couldn't describe, only feel. She loved to lie beneath the trees at the height of their bloom, to see sunlight glowing through thousands of pale purple blossoms, and to have sweet, spent petals swirl down around her in a fantastic amethyst snow.

But that particular glory was in the future. Today the jacaranda branches were naked of leaves and gleaming in the moist air. The trees were smooth-barked and had a dancer's grace. At the tip of every twig, buds were swelling almost secretly against the sun-washed sky.

Once, when she was much younger, Nicole had thought of herself like that: a bud swelling in silence, waiting only for the right conditions to bloom. Once, but not for a long time. She had learned that, for her, the sensual flowering was simply an aching dream.

For her, the years from thirteen to seventeen had

been a nightmare. Other girls had budded and bloomed all around her, while she had simply grown tall and then taller still, with no more curves than a slat fence. She hadn't been pretty in the way of other girls, petite, blond, and blue-eyed or dark-haired and curvy with mystery lurking in even darker eyes. The final insult had been delivered by the whims of fashion. Her light golden-brown eyes, pale skin, and fiery hair didn't blend at all with the pastels that were popular with the popular girls.

Other girls had boyfriends and admiring glances and bathing suits that revealed an intriguing feminine flowering. Nicole had simply kept on growing taller and taller, until she felt like a redheaded clown on stilts.

Then her body had begun to change in a wild rush, as though it realized that the blooming season was almost over. She was far too intelligent not to understand the connection between her increasing bra size and the increasing male attention.

Unfortunately, boys were no more interested in her as a person than they had been before her breasts grew. After the novelty of attracting whistles wore off, she decided that having a well-filled bra was as bad as being flat. Either way, she felt like an unwelcome passenger in her own body. The boys who noticed her breasts weren't interested in anything about her but how it would feel to get their hands under her clothes. When she refused to wrestle in the backseat of a car—or the front—they called her a tease. And that was the polite name.

Cynicism had come early to Nicole. It had stayed. She learned to fend off blunt male advances with the same breezy humor that she had previously used to hide her hurt at being ignored by the opposite sex.

Then she had met Ted. He didn't act like a starving octopus. He kept his hands to himself. He seemed interested in her thoughts and dreams. Later she realized it was her family's money that had attracted Ted, not herself. But that was later. In the beginning she had been thrilled that such a handsome, popular man would notice her, much less pursue her and beg her to marry him.

Dazzled, she had agreed. He wasn't a gentle lover. Her virginity had been an unhappy surprise. He had dumped a few state-of-the-art sex manuals in her lap and told her to study up on what men liked—there would be a test later.

She failed that test, and all the others he gave her.

Sixteen months into the marriage, her father went bankrupt. Ted cast an accountant's eye over the financial disaster, concluded that the money was gone and wouldn't ever come back, and walked out on his wife. To prevent the professional and personal contacts he had made since his marriage from seeing him as the cold fortune hunter he was, he announced that the marriage had failed because his so-called wife was a closet lesbian who refused even to have children.

That was the worst insult of all. She had wanted children. He had been the one who insisted there was plenty of time, they should grab what they could while they were young enough to enjoy it.

Nicole hadn't hung around California to see who believed her husband's lies and who didn't; everybody, even her own father, thought Ted was a warm, charming, loving man. So she had fled as far as she could, as fast as she could, leaving behind her girlish dreams and a broken marriage.

She knew flight was cowardly. She didn't care. There was nothing to stick around for but more of the bitter taste of humiliation and failure.

The instant she had stepped off the plane at Hilo, she felt a sense of homecoming that staggered her. It was as if the island itself had reached out to wrap her in a warm, welcoming hug. The island didn't care that she was too tall to be really feminine or that she was too cold to respond to a man sexually. Hawaii simply pulled her into its fragrance and warmth, asking nothing in return.

"Sad?"

The soft word slipped through Nicole's unhappy thoughts about the past. She blinked and realized that she was standing with her sketch pad tucked under her arm, staring at nothing. Automatically her free hand went out to stroke the smooth hair of the child who stood beside her.

"Mainland sad," she said huskily. "But I'm in Hawaii now."

Hawaii, where a stranger had kissed her and

made her believe that maybe, just maybe, there was hope for her as a woman.

"Always-always?" Benny asked quickly, repeating himself for emphasis in the Hawaiian style.

"I'll stay in Hawaii always-always," Nicole said, reassuring both of them.

CHAPTER
10

Nicole settled lotus-style onto an oversize chaise longue that waited beneath the jacaranda trees. That was her signal to Benny that it was time to be quiet.

A weathered wood table stood within arm's reach to one side of the big chair. The furniture had appeared beneath the jacarandas the day after Grandmother had discovered Nicole propped awkwardly against a tree trunk, spare pencils clamped between her teeth, frowning and sketching madly before the incoming afternoon rains veiled the trees in mist.

At first she had tried to sit on the ground to draw, but even the lush carpet of ferns couldn't blunt the edges of the lava beneath the green cloak of plants. In her typical generous fashion, Grandmother had quietly made sure that the new family member wouldn't have to stand in order to work her magic with pencil and paper.

Making no more fuss than a falling leaf, Benny settled just behind Nicole on the well-padded chaise. He positioned his own sketch pad and began to draw.

It was quiet but for the gentle, rhythmic surf and the sweet, erratic music of birds calling from the ohia's highest branches. Nicole heard the sounds only as a background to her concentration. Working quickly, cleanly, she sketched her favorite jacaranda. Though the tree was taller than all the others, it was beautifully proportioned, graceful in its strength, and somehow essentially feminine.

Every time she saw that tree, she thought of the ancient legends about women who were turned into trees to keep them safe from the sexual appetites of men.

Today her favorite jacaranda had been reduced by its natural cycle to pure, naked lines. No halo of amethyst flowers blurred the stately strength of the tree. No sighing, delicate, fernlike leaves distracted from the endurance of the trunk itself.

In this pause between rest and becoming, the tree called to Nicole's intelligence as well as to her senses, reminding her that the jacaranda's lush flowering was possible only because of the strength and resilience of the trunk itself. Without that silent, enduring power as a support, the buds pushing tightly from branch tips would never know the instant of blooming.

With an intent frown she went to work trying to capture all that she felt and thought about the jacaranda, femininity, life, and risk. At the edge of her concentration, she was aware of Benny coming and going as quietly as a breeze. He sketched with her for a time, then roamed a bit, then came back and sketched some more. At ten, he had learned the kind of patience some adults went a lifetime without finding.

When she thought to look away from her sketch pad again, she saw from the sun's position that she had been working for at least two hours. Her stomach was growling unhappily. The cup of coffee she had grabbed for breakfast just wasn't enough.

"Eat?"

The soft question came from the direction of a wildly overgrown path that eventually ended up at the big house.

"Eat," she agreed. "Hungry-hungry."

"Soon-soon."

There was a rustle of foliage, then the soft, uneven sounds of Benny running up one of the shortcuts only he knew about. Soon he would be back, lugging a basket of food that would feed five people.

The first few times he had appeared with food, Nicole had gone to the big house and protested that it wasn't necessary, she could certainly get her own lunch. Grandmother had simply smiled and continued sending huge piles of food down to the beach whenever her favorite grandson appeared with a hopeful grin and an empty basket.

In time Nicole finally understood that the Kamehameha family had adopted her. They treated her just like the daughters, nieces, aunts, and mothers who came and went from the estate in laughing waves. The Kamehamehas refused to take money for rent or for any of the other less obvious things they did for Nicole. She repaid the family in the only way they would accept.

She became one of them.

She taught their children ancient and modern dances, showed them basic drawing techniques, and gave her own drawings to any family member who looked at a sketch more than once. And she danced in the Kipuka Club, bringing to its small stage the incandescent sensual yearnings that Tahitian dances expressed so vividly.

"Picnic," Benny announced proudly.

Carrying a big basket, he popped out of what looked like a solid wall of ferns and bushes. He had an uncanny way of finding paths in even the most tangled, rugged places. His grandmother's big estate was like his very own playground.

Nicole laughed at the boy's smug grin. The clever Benny had managed to wangle that most prized of things—a solo picnic with the redheaded haole. The children's very own goddess.

Despite Nicole's denials, the island children half believed she actually was Pele reborn. She had given up trying to talk them out of it, just as she had given up trying to pay rent to Grandmother.

"Picnic," Nicole agreed.

Without any care for his own sketches scattered

on the end of the chaise, Benny started to unload the basket of food.

"Wait!" She snatched up the sheets of paper. "You'll ruin your sketches."

The boy's thin shoulders moved in a shrug. "Bad," he said, meaning his sketches.

"Good," she countered firmly.

He shrugged again and started laying out food.

On her half of the chaise Nicole spread out the sketches Benny had made of the jacaranda trees. With each new page she saw, she felt tiny, ghostly fingertips brush up her spine.

As always, there was something in each of Benny's sketches that made the landscapes surreal. Sometimes it was a subtly oversize blossom. Sometimes it was a tree whose leaves were upside down. Sometimes it was the suggestion of a face in the clouds. Often it was something that couldn't be defined, something as unique as the thin-faced boy who was now dividing fruit, bread, and smoked chicken between two plates.

Ignoring the sketches, Benny began to eat. Nicole joined him, consuming food quickly, but she couldn't stop looking at the boy's work. One sketch in particular was stunning. The drawing had an eerie, extraordinary sense of having caught the precise moment when a group of maidens quivered on the edge of taking root and becoming something they couldn't imagine.

Like Nicole, Benny had sensed that the jacarandas were fundamentally feminine. Unlike her, he was able to translate his intuition into a unique vision of a time and a place where myth, woman, and nature were one and the same.

"Good-good-**good,**" she said, catching the boy's chin in her hand. She held him that way until his big black eyes slowly met hers. "You have a wonderful gift, Benny. You see what no one else can, and then you capture what you see on paper."

"It's not like your trees."

The fact that he was taking the trouble to speak in a complete sentence told Nicole how important drawing was to the boy.

"Do you look like me?" she asked.

He laughed and gave her a glance that said he was very much Bobby's son. "No-no-**no.**"

"Then why should your art look like mine?"

He looked from his sketch to the tree, then from her sketch to the tree. "Different."

"Of course. That's how they should be. Different. I love your drawings, Benny. They make me see back into time. Paradise. Eden before the snake." She grinned suddenly. "Hawaii before haoles. No one else can make me see that. Only you."

The boy gave her a sudden, brilliant smile.

She kissed his shiny hair and ruffled it with her hand. Her watch face gleamed against his black mop. She was running late.

Again.

"Oops. Gotta go." Quickly she gathered up her

sketches of the jacaranda tree and the straining buds. "Lead me back to my cabin by the shortest way you know. I have to drop something off at the lab before Dr. Vic leaves for lunch."

"Ate," he said.

"Yes, we did. But they're on a different schedule at the lab. Haole time. They eat lunch at noon rather than ten."

"Sure?"

"Sure-sure."

He thought quickly, couldn't come up with a way to keep the beautiful Pele to himself any longer, sighed, and took her hand. "Sure-sure." As he ducked into the greenery, he muttered, "Haoles dumb."

Nicole snickered and bent double to follow him.

CHAPTER
11

By the time the Hilo bus finally arrived at the rim of the volcano, Nicole was sure she would miss Dr. Vic. Then she spotted him hurrying toward his car like a man with a mission.

"Dr. Vic! Wait!"

Carrying a big envelope, she ran across the parking lot toward the small, white-haired man who was one of her favorite people in Hawaii. He ran the lab with a quiet iron fist that kept the scientific prima donnas from turning the place upside down, yet he always made time to answer any questions she had. If he confused her more often than not with the depth and detail of his answers, she would just ask a different, related question until she understood.

"I have a drawing for you to look at," she said as she came up to him. "For your wife's birthday."

"Excellent." He smiled up at Nicole like a happy leprechaun. "I was afraid I'd missed you."

Unlike most men, Dr. Vic didn't care if Nicole was inches taller than he was. He just liked having someone to talk to besides scientists who were interested in only three things: volcanoes, sports, and sex, not necessarily in that order.

"So was I," she admitted. "I was drawing, and I forgot the time."

"Let's see," he said eagerly, standing on tiptoe as she eased the sheet from the stiff envelope.

Against a backdrop of misty blue, a jacaranda lifted its arms to the sun. The tree's bark was clean, smooth, as sensuous as the sunlight bathing its tightly budded branches.

"Oh, my." Dr. Vic touched the edge of the sheet with a hesitant fingertip. "Exquisite. Simply exquisite. Ettie will be thrilled."

Nicole smiled almost shyly as she slid the sketch back into its protective envelope. "I'm glad. A fortieth wedding anniversary should have a special gift. If you like, I'll frame it for you."

"No, no. I've imposed on you quite enough. How much do I owe you?"

"Don't be silly. It's just a sketch and you've spent hours explaining—"

"Nonsense," he interrupted, reaching into his shirt pocket for the check he had written earlier. "I thought this might happen, so I went to the gift shop at the national park and priced your drawings that are for sale there. Here you are."

"But—"

He gave her a smacking kiss on her chin, pressed the check into her hand, and took the envelope. "Thank you, my dear. Oh, before I forget it—Dr. Chase Wilcox was looking for you a minute ago.

Something about a kipuka project." He smiled slyly. "I understand you met him last night. Wish I'd seen it. Must have set the stage on fire."

"She sure did."

Nicole spun around at the sound of Chase's voice. For an instant his eyes were cold with something like contempt. Then he smiled at Dr. Vic.

"I'm asking for a rematch tonight," Chase said. "Come to the club and see for yourself."

"I'll bring Ettie. She loves the way Nicole dances." He gave Nicole a pat on her arm. "Thanks again, dear."

Chase watched the little man hurry to his car and wondered at the effect Nicole had on anything with a Y chromosome, no matter what age. He hadn't missed the swift, smacking kiss and the check changing hands. He even knew how much it was, because he had been at Dr. Vic's desk while he wrote it.

He had to take off his hat to the hula dancer—she wasn't afraid to ask a good price for her services.

With quick, sideways glances, Nicole measured Chase's tight stance. She half expected him to reach for her and finish what they had started last night. When he didn't do more than give her mouth the kind of look that raised her heartbeat, she was grateful.

At least the part of her that believed in logic, rationality, and such things was relieved. The rest of her simply yearned. But she kept her hands by her side. She needed some sign from him that he felt the same sense of rightness she did when they were together, a rightness that was based on far more than just physical attraction.

She needed to know more about Chase in a rational way as well as in the instinctive, almost overwhelming way that only he had ever made her experience.

"Anyone else waiting around in the lab to kiss and pat you?" Chase asked in a tone that wasn't quite humorous.

She blinked. "Er, no. It was just that Dr. Vic needed a present for his wife, and I—"

"Needed the money." Angrily Chase wondered what else she had done to earn the nine-hundred-dollar check that was dangling from her fingers. "Going to fix your car now?" **Or are you going to keep on flashing those golden eyes at Dane and offering rides?**

"I don't know. I'll have to take it up with my bank balance."

Chase changed the subject before he lost his temper and set back the seduction he had planned. "Do you have a few hours free now? I'd like to see some of the kipukas Dane said you knew how to find. Sounds like at least one of them might be perfect for the **Islands of Life** project."

Relief and eagerness gave Nicole's smile unusual brilliance. Exploring the kipukas would give them the time they needed to learn about each other.

Time alone with Chase would let them talk about anything and everything, to ask questions, to answer them.

She needed to reassure herself that his interest in her was real, that she hadn't dreamed him up from the depths of her own need, that he wanted to know her on as many levels as she wanted to know him.

"I have as many hours as you need," she said quickly, "as long as I get back to Hilo in time to get ready for work tonight."

"Work?"

"Dancing at the club. It's as close as the Kamehamehas come to allowing me to pay rent."

Remembering the casual intimacy of Bobby's kiss last night, Chase doubted that dancing was all she did for the handsome giant. But thinking about it wouldn't do anything for his already raw temper. "Great. Let's go kipuka crawling. Do we start here or do we need the car?"

She looked at what he was wearing—shorts, hiking boots that looked new despite some gouges here and there, and a short-sleeved shirt. "If you're sure that's what you want to do. The kipuka I'm thinking of is kind of a hike. Lots of aa."

"How do you think these boots got scarred?"

CHAPTER
12

About every five minutes Nicole glanced over her shoulder to reassure herself that Chase wasn't having any trouble keeping up with her. The trail she had chosen was little more than a series of twists and turns and small cairns set out across a piece of Kilauea's stony side. While the trail could be quite rough, the volcano itself rose very gently, almost secretly, from sea to summit.

As with all of Hawaii's volcanoes, Kilauea was shaped like a slightly curved battle shield. It was very different from the steep-sided, cone-shaped volcanoes of California, Italy, Mexico, or Japan. Hawaii's volcanoes were created by gentle, repeated lava flows, especially of the thicker aa lava, which lay like massive, carelessly thrown ropes across the Hawaiian landscape. Chunks of lava that once had floated on liquid rivers of stone like ice floes on the sea now were frozen in place. Jagged edges of aa stuck out like knives, ready to slash any careless hiker.

Not much grew on the part of the trail Nicole and Chase were walking over at the moment. The lava flow was largely pahoehoe. Its smooth, bright surface was easy on hiking shoes, but it broke down into soil very slowly. Seeds and roots just didn't have anywhere to take hold. Because of that, the trail was little more than a slightly scuffed thread twisting over the shiny surface of the land. The lava itself was black, smooth, and reflected the tropical sunlight almost like a mirror, redoubling the tropical heat.

Sweat gathered on Nicole's forehead, down her spine, and in the shadowed valley between her breasts. The hot slide of drops didn't bother her. Between Tahitian dancing and all the hours she spent climbing lava slopes, she was very much at home with the result of physical effort. As far as she was concerned, sweat wasn't a big deal. It was just the way bodies tried to cool themselves in the humid, wraparound heat on the wet side of the Big Island.

Chase wasn't bothered by sweat either, and for much the same reason—he was used to it. At the moment he was more interested in watching the deceptively slim legs ahead of him than in worrying about his increasingly wet shirt. Nicole's legs might be slender, but they were strong. She was hiking over the rough land at a pace that would have left a lot of men gasping and looking for a place to sit in the shade.

At first Chase had thought she was trying to walk him into the ground, and he had smiled to himself at the thought of disappointing her. But as the hike continued, she didn't give any of the subtle signals of a woman challenging a man. Then he had wondered if she was simply showing off her own well-conditioned body. Again, none of the signals were present. She glanced back to check on him from time to time, but she didn't linger or pose, inviting his approval.

Finally he decided that the brisk pace was her normal one. It showed in the regularity of her breathing and the grace of her stride. That got him to thinking about some other ways to test a woman's endurance and flexibility and balance. His breath quickened as he pictured the sensual possibilities.

How the hell can a woman look sexy in sawed-off hiking shoes, ragged khaki shorts, and a faded halter top with frayed ties? he asked himself half whimsically, half angrily.

The only answer was the elegant swaying of her hips as she walked up the trail.

With a mental kick to his own butt, Chase brought his attention back to the faint trail. As a vulcanologist he was accustomed to rough-country hiking, but Kilauea's slopes had some rather special traps for a careless walker. Sometimes ground that looked literally rock solid turned out to be a thin roof left by a fast-moving stream of molten lava long ago. Sometimes the ground underfoot was an even thinner bubble of cooled lava with nothing but air inside the fragile, now-cold shell. If a foot broke through the top of the bubble, the hiker stood a good chance of getting everything from a few cuts to a broken ankle.

Despite its built-in dangers, and perhaps even because of them, Chase enjoyed hiking Kilauea. The landscape was magnificent, a powerful statement of the living force of the earth itself.

Nicole stopped next to a particularly shiny formation of pahoehoe and bent down. "Have you ever seen Pele's hair?"

"A few nights ago." Chase looked at the braided red blaze that was almost concealed beneath the white scarf she wore Gypsy style on her head. "It was beautiful. Like fire."

She accepted the compliment with a quick, almost shy smile. Every time someone mentioned her hair, she remembered her ex-husband's repeated complaint.

The only thing hot about you is your hair.

"I meant the volcanic rock that's called Pele's hair." She pointed to a fist-size hole in the lava. Inside was something that looked like a flattened tangle of silver-gold hairs. "Look in the pukas— the holes in the lava."

Chase squatted on his heels next to Nicole and touched the shining hairs with a gentle fingertip, careful not to disturb their fragile beauty.

"I haven't seen this outside a specimen drawer or the pages of a textbook," he said reverently. "It's a miracle that something this delicate can come from, and then survive, such a violent event as the earth splitting open and bleeding rivers of molten stone."

For a moment he looked away from the shining hairs to the unusually clear sky. Against the horizon the massive, gently curved slope of Mauna Loa far overshadowed Kilauea's smaller mass. As he measured the bigger volcano, his eyes were unfocused yet clear, the look of a man appreciating something within the silence of his mind.

"What are you thinking about?" Nicole asked softly, hoping he would answer.

She needed to know more about Chase than his desire for her. Other men had wanted her—or at least wanted sex with her—but she had never wanted them in return, never wanted to explore them mind and body. Because of that, she kept wondering what it was about Chase that made him seem so different to her, what it was that made her want him body and mind.

She couldn't answer that question, yet she kept returning to it again and again, like a tongue pressing against a sore tooth. Maybe if she asked him enough questions, it would somehow let her answer the only important one.

Could she trust herself to him?

"What am I thinking about?" Half smiling, Chase gestured toward the smooth, brooding mass of Mauna Loa. When he spoke, his voice was husky, slow, the tone of a man thinking aloud. "Did you know that if you measure Mauna Loa from its base to its summit, it's the biggest mountain on earth?"

"But Mauna Loa isn't even fourteen thousand feet high, and Mount Everest is twice that," she objected.

He pinned her with his clear gray eyes. "Mauna Loa's true base is three miles below sea level. Its summit is more than thirteen thousand feet above sea level. That's nearly thirty thousand feet total. Taller than Everest."

She glanced out to the ocean as though she could see the submerged base of the volcano beneath the restless blue water.

"If you're talking about mass," he continued, "Mauna Loa is still the giant. Everest rises from the Himalayan Plateau, which is already about two miles high. Mauna Loa starts from the bottom of the ocean and takes up ten thousand cubic miles of the island. For all its fire and smoke and drama, Kilauea is little more than a boil on Mauna Loa's side, and the other small volcanoes on the Big Island are eroding away while we talk. But Mauna Loa is still alive, still growing, still the reigning queen of earth."

He looked away from Nicole's amber eyes to the indigo curve of the huge volcano. "The only mountain we know that's bigger than Mauna Loa is on Mars. Olympus Mons." He smiled briefly.

"Roughly translated from Latin, that means 'God's own mountain.' It's fifteen miles high. And it, too, is a volcano."

Her eyes widened with interest and surprise. "Is it alive?"

"So far as we know, it's extinct and has been for millions and millions of years. What we see now is what time and whatever passes for Martian weather have left of an incredible, once-living mountain whose base would have stretched from Los Angeles to San Francisco."

She sighed. "I wonder what an eruption would have been like."

He opened his mouth and then closed it without saying a word. He was trying to imagine what it would have been like to see Olympus Mons in action.

"How do you describe a mountain fifteen miles high blowing out immense rivers of fire while the surface of the planet itself trembled and shook?" he said slowly. "Maybe vapor condensed on the volcano's slopes, turning into rain that ran in wild torrents seven miles straight down to an empty ocean. Or maybe there was water on the surface of Mars back then, clouds and streams and rivers, even life swimming in a doomed sea."

Nicole closed her eyes and tried to imagine a mountain nearly eighty thousand feet high and four hundred miles across at the base. Dreamily she wondered what it would be like to stand on the lip of its awesome crater today and see Mars spread out below like a painting done in infinite tones of rust.

And then she heard Chase's deep voice say, "I'd sell my soul to have seen that mountain erupt. I'd sell my future for a chance to stand on its slopes even now." With a rough sound that could have been a laugh, he straightened and stood beside her. "But I was born far too late for the eruption and too soon for the exploration. I'll be dead long before man stands on any part of Mars."

The buried yearning in his voice made emotion thicken in her throat. Suddenly, fiercely, she wished that she could give Chase his impossible dream, could see his face as he stood on a mountain fifteen miles high and saw an alien planet spread at his feet.

"You have Hawaii," she said in a husky, intense voice. "It's not as high as the volcano you'll never see, but it's alive. You can hear its breath in the deep cracks of the lava, feel its warmth, sense its heartbeat beneath your feet. And sometimes you can see Hawaii's living blood pouring out, setting fire to everything, even stone."

Chase looked into her golden eyes and saw himself reflected, his own buried dreams and acceptance of what could not be.

I'll never stand on Mars. But I'll stand on a living mountain with the goddess of the volcano at my side.

I'm standing there now, and she is here, burning.

Making me burn.

"Yes," he said, his voice deep, "I have Hawaii, and Pele is my guide. What more could any man ask?"

Silently the answer came to him. He could ask to trust his guide.

Oh, but you can, he assured himself sardonically. **You can trust her to be like other women—selfish to the core.**

Hawaiians worshiped Pele, but they didn't love her. Those men weren't fools. They knew that a woman is as tricky and dangerous as a living volcano.

"How much farther is the kipuka?" he asked briskly, breaking the intimacy of the instant when he had believed that he saw his dreams reflected in a woman's eyes.

"Twenty minutes, maybe a bit more."

Chase looked dubiously over the rumpled, furrowed landscape. There was nothing in all directions but lava, lava, and more lava.

"It's there," she said, pointing across the black, stony land. "See? It looks like a tiny smudge of green on the far side of that aa flow."

"Green smudge," he muttered, shading his eyes and looking.

"Yes. The green is the tops of the tallest ohia trees."

"You're hallucinating."

Nicole laughed. Then she set out across the landscape that had been born in liquid fire. After a moment Chase followed, shaking his head. He was afraid he was being led on a long hike to nowhere.

Without so much as a look over her shoulder to see if he was coming, she walked at a clean, ground-eating pace until she came to a broad stream of aa rising like a black wall on top of an earlier flow of pahoehoe. The wall of aa was why she rarely came to this kipuka. It was a tough scramble up and across the lava, and tougher still to get down into the kipuka floor. She had never tried the descent, because she didn't want to risk injury when she was hiking alone or with Benny.

Unconsciously rubbing her hands on her shorts as though to assure a good grip, she headed for the six-foot-high wall of cold lava.

"You're kidding," Chase said, catching up to her.

"Nope."

"Hell."

She scrambled up onto the flow and began picking a path across. Along the way she scraped one palm, scratched both ankles, and picked up a few other small souvenirs of her trek over aa. But finally she stood on the other edge of the flow. At her feet lay an improbable green oval surrounded on all sides by a lava flow that was naked of plant life.

Less than ten acres in size, the kipuka was a miracle of survival surrounded by the desolation of the birth of new land.

On the uphill side of the kipuka, some irregularity in the old slope had divided the lava flow into two streams. Between the streams of molten stone, plants shriveled, steamed . . . and survived. When the lava flow combined again farther down the slope, it walled off the kipuka from the rest of the devastated land. Except for the kipuka's few green acres, life in all directions had been engulfed by burning stone.

Silently Nicole looked at the miracle of the kipuka's life in the midst of a barren, newly born land. Ohia trees grew in tall profusion. Flowers that looked like scarlet brushes grew at the tips of the graceful ohia branches. Ferns in more shapes and heights and kinds than she could name crowded over the hard rock floor of the kipuka, sending slender fronds toward the life-giving sun.

Every growing space from ground level to tree-top was filled by some kind of plant. The explosion of life was all the more startling for the sterile lava surrounding it.

Sensing Chase beside her, Nicole turned toward him. He was studying the lush greenery with a wondering expression that made her want to pull out her sketch pad and draw him. But she didn't know him well enough yet to ask his permission, and she wasn't bold enough to just go ahead while he was looking.

"Hard to believe, isn't it?" she asked.

"I've seen all kinds of freak survivals from volcanic eruptions," he said slowly. "Trees standing while others only inches away were blown to splinters. Flowers blooming where nothing had any right to survive at all. The tracks of mice that had burrowed out from under a blanket of hot ash. All unexpected. Freaks of fate."

She smiled almost sadly. "Freaks?"

"On the mainland, yes. But not here."

"What do you mean?"

"Kipukas are normal in Hawaii, not freaks. They're the inevitable result of lava rivers flowing slowly down sloping, uneven land." He made a rough sound. "And having said that, I've got to admit that it still looks like magic to me."

"Yes. Magic." She smiled. "It's as though Pele couldn't bear to burn all of life while she was adding on to her island home, so she saved a few places and plants that were special to her."

"That's a very Hawaiian explanation. Scientists prefer more ordinary reasons."

"Those are good, too." She glanced sideways at him. "For ordinary days."

A smiled flashed beneath his black mustache. Then he pulled a notebook from his backpack and began making cryptic entries about the height, width, and kind of lava flow that surrounded the kipuka.

The temptation was too much for Nicole. She got out her own sketchbook, flipped to the back, and began drawing him with swift, sure strokes. The lines she made with black ink were as intense and unflinching as the face of the man looking into a miraculous Eden surrounded by a destroyed land.

She worked quickly, almost secretly, not wanting to share the sketch with anyone yet, even him.

Especially him.

CHAPTER

13

Chase kept writing until he had filled several pages with notes. They would help him to recall the characteristics of this place even after he had looked at thirty others. This was all very preliminary, more of a lark than real work, but he had a feeling that the secret kipuka would be an ideal subject for the book.

"Is there a path down?" he asked without glancing away from his notebook.

Hastily Nicole closed her sketchbook, afraid that he would look up and catch her drawing him. "I don't know of any path. I went partway around the top once. It's pretty much the same on the other side as here. At least head-high aa, rough and as wickedly sharp as the day it first cooled."

"So here is as good as there when it comes to getting down?"

She nodded.

"Well, no help for it, then. I've been over worse. I think."

He stowed his notebook and scrambled down the sharp, rough wall into the kipuka. The last few feet were so steep and pocked with ankle-deep holes that he finally just jumped. When he had secure footing in the kipuka, he turned at the bottom and glanced back up. Nicole was at the top of the flow, looking doubtful.

"You don't have to come," he said.

"But I've always wanted to go down into this kipuka. I just didn't want to try getting home alone on a broken ankle."

"You're not alone anymore."

He held out his hand to help her climb down. The first few feet were fine. Then she hit the crumbling stuff. A chunk of lava broke off and turned unexpectedly beneath her foot. Instantly his hands closed around her waist. With an easy motion he lifted her and set her down on the kipuka's more even footing.

"Thanks." Her voice was too tight, almost breathless.

She hadn't expected to be picked up with so little effort. She thought of herself as substantial, not petite. The feeling of relative fragility next to Chase was both sensually intriguing and a bit unnerving. It was as though reality had shifted with the lava under her foot, changing her view of herself and the world.

"You okay?" he asked at her startled expression.

"Fine."

He looked down into her wide golden-brown eyes, wondering what she was thinking. He started to ask but got distracted by the feel of her supple flesh inside the circle of his hands. He flexed his fingers, testing the resilience of her waist.

He liked what he felt. A lot.

"You know," he said, shifting his glance from her eyes to her slightly parted lips, "I finally understand why men throughout history have paid a lot to have dancers as mistresses."

Nicole blinked, wondering if she had heard correctly. She knew she was distracted; the diamond intensity of his eyes made her want to put her hands in his hair and pull him down to her mouth.

"What?" she asked, more than a little dazed.

"Dancers feel good. **You** feel good." He closed her wide eyes with a lingering kiss on each lid. He flexed his fingers again, more deeply. "God, you feel better than good. You feel incredible, all tight and warm and flexible. You make a man wonder what it would be like to—"

At the last second he cut off his words, but he couldn't stop his thoughts. He wanted to have all of her wrapped around him, moving with him, wanting it as much as he did. He wouldn't have to worry about crushing her or frightening her or being too big for her.

She would fit him like a hot, satin fist.

Still savoring the unexpected caresses, Nicole slowly opened her eyes and licked her lips, wanting to taste him but not knowing how to ask.

Breath backed up in Chase's throat. His pulse slammed hard and heavy beneath the tan skin of his neck. Between one minute and the next he was ready for her, his erection pressing hotly against her belly when he pulled her into his arms.

"Chase?"

"Don't talk," he said in a thick voice. "Just kiss me. It's not enough, not nearly enough, but it will have to do for now."

He took her mouth, and his arms tightened around her as they had on the darkened stage. Her body flexed like a bow beneath his strength. He was arching her into his own body with a force that would have been painful if she hadn't come to him eagerly. Silently he told himself to slow down, take it easy, this was the first rather than the last stage of seduction.

Then her mouth opened, softened hungrily beneath his probing tongue. Shuddering, he thrust deeply into her, wanting all of her. Here. **Now.**

Part of him wondered at his own lack of control when it came to Nicole, but most of him cared only for the sweet fire of having her pressed against his body. She was pliant and warm and so soft that he groaned from the depth of his need for her. With barely restrained urgency his mouth moved over her face and neck and smooth, naked shoulders. Lips and tongue traced the small marks his teeth left, felt the trembling of her responsive flesh, the strength of her fingers kneading his back, urging him on.

Nicole didn't even know that she was moving

against Chase in a slow, sensuous dance. His mouth was both hard and soft, hot, consuming her with sensations she had never felt, never even dreamed.

Nor had she dreamed that a man would tremble at the delicate touch of her teeth on his jaw as she returned the wild, biting kisses he was giving to her. The salty taste and rough texture of his cheek swept through her, making her wonder how many other tastes and textures he had for her to discover.

The thought of all the possibilities made her breath catch. She had never felt like this before— hungry, wild, almost desperate to know all of a man's body in every way she could.

Chase felt the sudden passionate tension in her body as though it was his own. He **needed.**

And so did she.

With a low sound he took her mouth in a fierce kiss. His hands raked down her spine, cupped her tight buttocks, and shifted until he could rub every aching inch of himself over the sweet heat between her thighs. Her shudder of response was as exciting to him as the tiny sound she made at the back of her throat when she felt the blunt reality of his erection through layers of clothing.

Hungrily, slowly, he stroked over her again and then again, silently telling her that he would give her both deeper hunger and then shocking release. With each motion of his hips, his tongue moved deeply, claiming her mouth, mingling their taste until it was the same, hot and needy, like his hands stripping away her halter, leaving her breasts naked to the sun. To him.

With a startled sound, Nicole yanked back her hands and covered herself.

The defensive movement surprised Chase, for she had seemed as eager for the passionate love play as he was. And then he remembered that he was supposed to be doing just that: playing. This was supposed to be a teasing prelude, not hot sex in the cold lava beds.

Yet he barely had enough control to keep from taking her down onto the rough ground and to hell with cuts and bruises. The violence of his need shocked him, cooling his unexpected, fierce lust as nothing else could have.

"You're right." His voice was as harsh as the black stone beneath their feet. He couldn't stop looking at her, startled and half naked, like a goddess caught at her bath. "This isn't the time or the place. Turn around."

Numbly Nicole obeyed, hating herself for betraying the promise of passion with her own fear.

Struggling to breathe more slowly, Chase replaced her halter with deliberate motions, first waiting patiently for her to remove her hands from her breasts. She stood, trembling, while he fastened both halter ties with great care.

The casual brush of his fingers over her naked skin went through her like sweet electric shocks. She took a ragged breath, then another. She wanted to tell him that she hadn't meant to stop him, that she had covered herself without thinking because her husband had often hurt her breasts trying to force a response from her.

And that was only the beginning of the hurting.

She swallowed several times and tried to tell Chase why she had frozen. She couldn't. Her lips simply refused to shape the words. She was much too ashamed of her past failures as a woman to stand in the pouring sunlight and discuss her frigidity with the first man she had ever really wanted. The thought of saying something that intimate literally paralyzed her.

In frozen silence she stood with her back turned to Chase, her shoulders braced as she waited for the anger of a frustrated male to break over her head. It was her fault. Again. Her fault.

Always.

Chase couldn't miss the stiffness of her body. Though he put his hands gently on her shoulders, his thoughts weren't the least bit gentle. He was cursing himself for his loss of control with her. He had seduced enough women to know how it was done—and how it wasn't.

It wasn't done on a bed of prickly ferns and lava sharp enough to cut to the bone.

It also wasn't done by letting things get out of hand to the point that both people were frustrated and angry because the lovemaking stopped short of satisfaction.

Great going, hotshot, he told himself sardonically. **You've just nominated yourself for the Rutting Jackass of the Year award.**

And still he wanted her like hell on fire.

"Sorry," he said, brushing his lips across the soft skin at the nape of her neck. "Are you okay?"

For a moment she couldn't believe that the gentle caress and the quiet words were real. But they were.

He wasn't angry with her. He wasn't going to berate her for something she couldn't help, couldn't change, and couldn't bear living with. Her breath came out in a long, broken sigh of relief. Wordlessly she nodded in answer to his question.

"Let me see."

Gently Chase turned Nicole until she faced him. A single look reassured him. She wasn't angry with his lack of finesse and all-around bad timing. Relief went through him in a wave that made him feel light-headed.

The depth of his relief was as shocking to him as his nearly uncontrollable passion had been. Since his divorce he'd had only sophisticated, superficial, and physically satisfying relationships with women. Fun and games for both sides. Period.

He hadn't cared about anything more complex than returning the sexual release women gave to him. Nor had the women cared about getting anything more from him. Emotions weren't necessary for climax. In fact, they got in the way.

That kind of mutually cool coupling had worked well enough for his purposes.

Until now.

The magic of the redheaded dancer's body had brought him to the point of eruption with only a few kisses.

Remember what you're here for, Chase told himself savagely. **You're here for Dane, not for a quickie in the underbrush.**

And if you keep coming on to Nicole like you've never had a woman, she's going to decide that gentleman Dane looks like a better deal—wife and all.

Abruptly Chase turned away from Nicole. "Has anyone done a formal survey of this kipuka's biota?" he asked, his voice neutral.

Controlled.

For a moment there was no answer. He fought an impulse to turn back and look for emotions on Nicole's face. He shouldn't care whether she was happy or sad, relieved or vibrating with need. He already knew that she had wanted him, but not enough. She hadn't been anywhere close to losing her head.

He had. He didn't like admitting it, but Lynette had taught him that denial was a fool's way to live. He wasn't that kind of fool anymore.

It was up to him to keep his head in the future. Then he could raise the level of Nicole's need until she was like Kilauea on the edge of eruption, trembling on the brink of an explosive, mindless release that only he could give her. She wouldn't be thinking of money and marriage but of the kind of sex that made volcanoes look cold.

Afterward he would go to Dane, tell his brother that he had lost the bet. Then, finally, Chase would be free to . . .

What? What do I want after Dane's marriage is safe?

There was no answer for Chase but the thick pulse of his own need.

CHAPTER
14

Chase forced himself to stop, remembering how it had felt to press himself against Nicole's soft, hungry body. Thinking about it just eroded the very control he needed.

"Nicole?" he asked again. "Do you know about any studies?"

She swallowed hard and tried to be as casual as he was. He looked so calm, standing broad-shouldered and at ease, silhouetted against the kipuka's bright foliage. The passionate kiss might never have happened.

"No one has done a truly disciplined study," she managed. "Not here. Mauna Loa's kipukas are better known. Especially Puaulu."

When he pulled out his notebook again and began writing, she felt the last of her anxiety drain away. For a moment, while his back was turned, he had seemed angry with her. Now he was focused on the work at hand. Everything was . . . normal.

She sighed quietly in relief. She understood his concentration, so she didn't feel like he was shut-ting her out. She was the same way when she danced or painted; she used every bit of herself, ignoring the rest of the world. There was nothing personal about it. That kind of focus was simply necessary to get the job done.

"Spell Puaulu, would you?" Chase asked, frowning down at the name he had undoubtedly butchered. "I'm even less used to the Hawaiian language than I am to shield volcanoes."

Smiling, she spelled the word for him before she asked, "What kind of volcanoes are you used to?"

"Cone volcanoes, like Mount Saint Helens. Among other things, I've been part of the long-term study of the return of life to the slopes after the first big eruption."

He looked up from the notebook long enough to estimate the size of the trees in the kipuka that were growing along the margin of the most recent lava flow, springing up among the bleached bones of the trees that had been too close to the fire to survive. The age of the regrowth gave a rough estimate of the age of the kipuka itself.

Sensing Chase's concentration on the kipuka, Nicole watched him openly. His eyes fascinated her. They were crystalline, nearly transparent, with hints of blue and silver condensed around the pupil. They made a vivid contrast to his dark hair and skin.

"Did you study other volcanoes?" she asked when he looked down at his notebook again.

"I worked on the Heimaey Island volcano in Iceland, with time out for Surtsey Island and for the huge fissure fields on Iceland itself. Then South America, Mexico, wherever the earth burned."

"Did you like it?"

His pen paused over the page for a moment before he answered. She was the first person who had ever asked about his emotional response to the volcanoes that were his lifetime passion. "I loved working with volcanoes."

"What drew you the most?"

"At first it was the violence of the eruptions, pure and simple. There's nothing as exciting as feeling the earth shake beneath your feet and hearing the mountain roaring with a sound greater than any thunder, the kind of sound that makes your bones vibrate. Then comes the fire."

She watched his face, seeing shadows of remembered awe and excitement in his expression.

"It's unbelievable," he said slowly, "like being in on the birth of the world. In a way that's exactly what the fire and thunder are all about. Birth. Without volcanoes a lot of earth's land simply wouldn't exist."

"Or water?" she asked, remembering fragments of conversations she had overheard in the Kipuka Club.

"That, too."

"It seems incredible that the oceans could have come from cooled volcanic gases," she said. It was just one of the many things about the mysterious living mountains that intrigued her.

Chase looked up from his notebook, pleased that

she understood something about the volcanoes that had always fascinated him. And for good reason. If present theories were correct, volcanoes were literally the fountains of Eden, perhaps of life itself.

"It's true," he said. "Volcanoes are huge, immensely complex chemical factories. Even the air we breathe probably came from beneath the crust of the earth. And if that isn't enough to interest you, volcanoes make wonderful evolutionary laboratories. They destroy and they also create. They're God's own incubators."

"What do you mean?"

"If you think about it, in many ways the Hawaiian Islands are truly Eden. Their isolation from other landmasses allowed island life to take on shapes that are different from any other life anywhere else on earth."

Frowning, she tried to follow his line of thought, island life changing and growing in new directions, locked away from its source on the mainland.

"It's kind of like the Polynesian dances themselves," she said after a moment. "The first dance came from a mainland time and place long since lost in history. Each culture, each new island that people colonized, took that original dance and made something new of it, something unique. But still a recognizable dance related to other, older dances."

"Exactly." Chase looked at the lush vegetation growing up out of the dark lava. "One of the major differences between here and the mainland is that the plant seeds that came to the islands from other continents didn't have to fight animals in order to survive here, because in the beginning there weren't any land animals to speak of."

"What a strange place it must have been back then," she said, trying to imagine a land without animal life.

"Strange, but logical. A seed can fly on the wind or float in ocean currents or be carried in a bird's body. Animals—other than the smallest insects— can't."

"What about birds?"

"They're the exception to the animal rule, but at first there would have been only sea birds here, because there weren't any land plants to feed land birds." Chase glanced down at an entry in his notebook, crossed it out, and went on speaking as he wrote in something else. "Once a plant seed survived and took root here, the plant began changing."

"Why? Why wouldn't it just stay the same?"

"The plant had been adapted to an environment that was thick with competing life forms. Hawaii was different. There wasn't anything but bare rock waiting to be covered." He looked up again, watching the kipuka's varied greenery shift beneath the wind. "It's estimated that the seventeen hundred flowering plants that were native to the islands B.E.—Before Europeans—came from less than three hundred ancestral plant colonists."

"That's more than the number of dances that survived. We've lost so many to time."

"It's an old story." Chase's eyes searched the boundary between lava and life, black and green. "If we were above four thousand feet, this kipuka would be alive with the songs of honeycreepers. But their ancestral finch colonist wasn't immune to avian malaria or pox. When European man arrived with his barnyard animals and mosquitoes hatched from ships' water barrels, most of Hawaii's native birds died."

"Were the surviving birds somehow immune?"

He shook his head. "The introduced mosquito couldn't survive above four thousand feet. That's the only reason there are any endemic Hawaiian birds left at all."

Nicole thought of the rare flying jewels that brightened the island's upper reaches and felt her heart squeeze. "Thank God for altitude," she said starkly.

"Altitude slowed down the extinctions, but it won't stop them forever. There are other species of disease-carrying mosquitoes that can survive at high altitudes. So far those mosquitoes haven't found their way to the islands." Chase's shoulders moved sharply, as though in denial of what he knew was true. "But they'll get here sooner or later. There's world enough and time. And men are careless of their Edens."

His notebook snapped shut, speaking loudly about the emotion underlying his neutral tone.

"That's why you agreed to do **Islands of Life,** isn't it?" she asked. "You're afraid that Eden is living on borrowed time."

"I **know** it's living on borrowed time."

He looked at Nicole with gray eyes that had seen too many things lost before they had been found, much less understood. Too many possibilities gone forever. Too many cruel people who survived to perpetuate their cruelty.

"Yes," he said, looking away from her, "that's why I came to Hawaii. I knew that this would be my only chance to see landscapes and life forms that exist nowhere else on earth. These islands are proof that life bows to no odds. It survives. Somehow it survives."

"Reminds me of one of Fred's favorite sayings— something about 'nature, bloody in tooth and claw.' "

"Most of it is. But not here. This was a gentle Eden. Most native Hawaiian plants don't have thorns or poison to discourage browsers. Not even bad smells."

He reopened his notebook, then wrote quickly, turned a page, and gestured to the kipuka's lush life, so startling against the barren lava surrounding it. "In a way the Hawaiian Islands themselves are gigantic kipukas, safe havens for land creatures in the midst of the huge, hostile environment we call the sea. Once mainland life arrived here, there wasn't any need for it to be aggressive—to fight for water or sun or survival."

"Why? Surely even in Hawaii there was competition."

"Not in the beginning. Any kind of life was very rare. There was more habitat than there was life to fill it. After they arrived, plants and animals changed to meet the easier reality of this Eden. Green things lost thorns and poisons. Many of the birds and insects that came here on the wing often lost the ability to fly."

She started to ask why and saw that he was waiting for the question. "Do you mind?" she asked. "All my questions, I mean."

Smiling, he ran his fingertip down her arm. "Not a bit. People who don't have any curiosity are boring."

"Then why did birds and insects stop flying? To have a wonderful ability like that and then lose it . . ." She shook her head. "I can't see how it would benefit the birds."

"That's human-think. Flying uses up an enormous amount of energy. Taking to the air is good for survival only when the alternative is being eaten. Otherwise, especially for birds, flying is a waste of calories that could be better used making babies."

She smiled.

"In Hawaii, before European man arrived," he said, "there weren't any snakes or cats or even dogs. No land predators until the pigs the islanders brought with them. Birds didn't need to fly or even to nest in trees. The ground was safe. The birds that kept their ability to fly did it to bring ohia flowers within reach of their greedy little nectar-sucking tongues."

"Eden without snakes," Nicole said, trying to imagine it.

"Except for the two-legged variety."

She smiled wistfully. "Nothing is perfect. I'll take Eden however I can get it. Even with men."

Including a rich Adam?

Though Chase said nothing aloud, his mouth flattened at the reminder of what Nicole was really after. When she listened to him so attentively, asked questions, understood the answers, and all the time watched him with her brilliant, nearly gold eyes as though he was the only man on earth, it was hard to remember that he, not Pele, was supposed to be the predator in this particular Eden.

He looked away from Nicole's disarming, clear eyes, toward the wind-ruffled kipuka. Scents drifted up to him from exotic shrubs and flowers. He hadn't seen anything like this kipuka outside of botanical gardens.

Yet nothing smelled as good as the woman who stood so close to him that he could hear her quiet, even breathing and sense the warmth of her body.

Impatiently he forced himself to think of something else. The kipuka, for instance. Plants. Trees. Anything.

Near him, just within reach, grew a tangle of shrubbery that could have been a big bush or a thicket of small trees with heart-shaped leaves up to a foot across. A flourish of yellow flowers the size of his palm grew at the tips of some branches.

Using only his fingertips, he stroked one flower from edge to cup. The blossom shivered and swayed as though touched by a gentle wind. The petals were exquisitely soft, fragrant, flawless. Once he would have said there couldn't be any texture more pleasing to him.

Yet he had just kissed a woman whose mouth was more smooth, more perfect, more creamy. And the textures of her mouth would be nothing compared to the secret places of her body, hot and slick with need. The thought of exploring her satin depths rippled through him like a swarm of tiny, harmonic earthquakes, testing his resistance, warning of the explosion to come.

"Do you know of any endangered biota here, in this kipuka?" Chase asked.

His voice was too husky to be quite normal. His fingertip was slowly, lightly caressing the flower. She stared, unable to look away from the intensely feminine flower being so tenderly stroked.

"No, nothing endangered," she said. Then, silently, she added, **Just me. Do I count? I'm on the edge of losing my heart to a man I've known only a few days. That qualifies me as endangered, doesn't it?**

No? Then how about stupid?

But it didn't feel stupid to trust Chase. It felt inevitable, like plants losing their thorns and poisons when they found their gentle Eden. When she was with him, she discovered new things about herself. Each time he touched her, the discoveries multiplied.

Like now. She had just discovered that she was jealous of the flower that was shivering so softly against his fingertip.

"Then it would be all right for us to explore this?" he asked, his voice deep, his eyes watching her rather than the flower.

"Do we have a choice?" she asked huskily.

"There are other kipukas."

"Not here, not now."

Gently Chase picked the flower. "You're right."

He inhaled the delicate scent on a long breath. Then his tongue flicked out to try the deep, interior smoothness of the blossom, where its yellow shaded into a deep mahogany. Once, twice, three times, he tasted the flower before he caught the edge of a petal with exquisite care between his teeth. After a moment he released the creamy softness. There was no mark to show the sensual testing.

"Very nice," he said, turning toward her. "Do you know what this is?"

She said the first thing that came to her distracted mind. "A flower."

A smile curved underneath the midnight slash of his mustache. "You're sure?" His voice was deep, teasing.

Color crept beneath the golden tan on her cheeks. "It could be a morning glory that doesn't know it's nearly noon."

His smile widened. "Actually, I think it's a kind of hibiscus."

She touched one of the curving petals and reined in her muddled thoughts. "Actually, you're right. The natives call the plant **hau** and the flower **pua.** They were reserved for royalty."

Gently he tucked the blossom into the V of Nicole's halter before he bent and tasted the flower again. Shivers coursed over her when his black hair and mustache brushed against the rising curve of her breasts.

"I'm going to enjoy finding and tasting all the flowers," he said, letting his lips drift over her warm golden skin.

"Chase—" she began, her voice trembling.

"That's what we're here for, remember?"

"Tasting?" she asked, startled.

"And learning."

She closed her eyes and thought of all the things Chase Wilcox and this gentle Eden could teach her, wonderful things she had almost given up hope of ever knowing. But no longer. Now she sensed the possibilities trembling within her reach. All she needed was the courage to extend her hand. Herself.

She waited for fear to come at the thought of being as vulnerable as a jacaranda bud. Instead of fear, certainty bloomed as softly as a flower inside her.

If he asked for her, she would give herself to him.

She couldn't do anything less. If she held back,

she would spend the rest of her life wondering what might have been. And all of that time, every hour of it, she would hate herself for not having the courage of the simple living things that changed when they took root in a new, safer place.

There was no reason to hold on to fear any longer. She was his. She had always been his.

She just hadn't known it until now.

C H A P T E R
15

That night, as Chase settled into position behind the drums at the Kipuka Club, he told himself that he had his hunger for Nicole under control. He wanted her, sure. What man wouldn't? But he was riding the passion rather than having it ride him.

He kept on believing that right up to the moment Pele stepped out onto the small stage. Spotlights turned her skin to molten gold and her unbound hair to fire. Her hips moved with liquid ease, describing sensual arcs that made his blood pool thickly, hotly, focusing and hardening his desire with every heavy beat of his heart.

One look and he knew he had to have her. **Tonight.** He couldn't wait any longer.

On the drums his hands first whispered and then pounded out the elemental truth of his need. The other dancers simply didn't exist for him. Impatiently he drummed them off the stage. He wanted to be alone with the woman who danced like passion unleashed.

And then they were alone on the stage, thunder and lightning perfectly matched in dazzling display. Instinctively each knew when the other would peak, when the perfect match of sound and motion would begin to blur. Yet neither one of them wanted it to end. They drove each other higher, then higher still, until there was a soft cry and suddenly silent drums, midnight slamming down while wild applause broke over the stage.

Nicole found Chase even as he reached out to her. His mouth was hard, hungry, hot, like the powerful body flexed beneath her urgent hands.

"Come with me."

"Yes."

Hands joined, they fled into the darkness.

When the curtains opened again, the stage was empty.

Chase heard the startled silence and the spreading murmur of speculation as he quietly shut the club's back door behind them. Hand on the small of Nicole's back, he urged her toward his car. He didn't want to say anything. He didn't want anything to dim the feeling of triumph and relief that had come to him when she had simply whispered "Yes" and followed him into the darkness.

Deep inside, hidden even from himself, he had been afraid that she wouldn't want him as much as he wanted her.

Nicole gave Chase a quick glance and then looked away. She was grateful that he didn't want to talk.

She was having enough trouble hiding the nervousness that had hit her like cold water the instant she was no longer in his arms. She didn't think she could handle one end of any kind of conversation without giving away her fear.

She wondered if Hawaii's first thornless plant had trembled with fear when it unfolded its vulnerable leaves to the sun.

The door to the Porsche was open, waiting for her. She didn't know how long she had stood, staring at it. Quickly she pulled her hair forward over her shoulders and slid into place. When she fastened the seat belt, the long strands of her hair rippled and shimmered in her lap like flame.

The car started with a feral sound of power and leaped out into traffic. Nicole felt captured as surely as any woman ever thrown over a raider's saddle and carried away into the night toward an uncertain fate.

Helpless.

Eyes closed, she reminded herself of the moment when Chase's teeth had closed so delicately on the fragile flower. The image had haunted her, whispering to her that a man capable of such ravishing tenderness wouldn't hurt her.

Even if she failed to please him with her response in bed.

Chase drove quickly, silently to the Kamehameha estate. He sensed Nicole's unease. It didn't surprise him. They shared a mutual desire, but they didn't know each other very well at all. He was much bigger, far stronger. If he chose to hurt her, there wasn't much she could do to protect herself.

If the roles had been reversed, he would have been nervous as hell. But he didn't want her fearful and hesitant. He wanted her to be the way she had been onstage, coming to him eagerly. Burning for him.

When he ran a fingertip from her shoulder to the back of her hand, she jerked and made a startled sound.

"It's all right," he said quietly. "I won't be rough with you."

She gave him a look out of surprised golden eyes that told him he had guessed accurately what was on her mind. Then she smiled and touched his cheek with her palm.

"I know," she whispered. "I'm just . . . nervous."

Silently he caressed her again, thinking of how to handle the inevitable awkward moments getting from car to bed. He didn't want her to get cold feet. He wanted her the way he was—hot. As he pulled up to the estate, he decided she would feel more at ease in her own cottage than in his.

Neither one of them spoke while he handed her out of the Porsche and they walked toward her cottage. Beneath the moon's brilliant silver radiance, concealed landscape lights glittered among the foliage like captive stars. Wind smoothed through the trees. Leaves made soft sounds, as though pleased to be so gently stroked.

The scents of flowers and sea mingled in the warm night, making yet another kind of caress on Nicole's heightened senses. She felt her nerves uncurl and courage return with every step closer to her cottage. The estate was familiar. The cottage was her haven.

And Chase was a man like no other.

He opened the door to her small home and waited for her to make the next move. Moonlight poured through the wall of windows that faced the sea, giving a silver, unearthly radiance to the room's interior.

"The lights are on the right," she said.

His hand swept along the wall. Recessed lights glowed, gently illuminating the room. A single glance told him that Dane had been right—financially, Nicole lived very close to the bone. Her furniture was minimal, patterned after Japanese designs for living. A futon was stacked along the glass wall, waiting to be unfolded into a bed. Scattered cushions, a dining table big enough for two, and a desk completed the spare furnishings.

But the woman who lived here was anything but plain. Subdued flames twisted and shivered in her long hair as she stood in her own doorway, pausing as though uncertain of her welcome.

He caught a handful of the fire that was falling over her shoulder and between her breasts. Lifting the silky hair to his lips, he gently pulled her closer. He sensed the moment of hesitation before she put her hands on his shoulders and stood on tiptoe to be kissed. He reined in a flash of impatience that she wasn't fully eager; he was a grown man, not some teenager in rut. He knew how to seduce rather than demand.

"I don't blame you for not wanting to get close to me." His teeth were a flash of white beneath his dense black mustache. "After all that drumming, I need a shower."

"That's not wh—" she began.

Words and thoughts scattered when his lips fitted over hers. His tongue dipped into her mouth as delicately as though she was a flower reserved for royalty. The tip of his tongue tasted her once, then he withdrew as softly as he had entered.

"Shower," he said huskily.

As he spoke, her halter fell away from her breasts. She hadn't even been aware that he had undone the ties until she felt the air against her hot, naked skin. Reflexively she brought her hands up to cover herself, a protective gesture left over from the bitter time before Eden.

Her reaction didn't make sense to Chase. It could hardly be modesty or embarrassment about revealing her body to him. Her breasts were as firm and lush as her hips, and the narrowness of her waist was a temptation for any man's hands.

Just looking at her was enough to make his mouth water for the taste of her.

"Chase . . ." she said softly, and then her voice frayed. She wanted to explain her retreat, but she had no idea where to begin.

"How did you know," he asked, bending down until he could nibble on her right hand, "that hide-and-seek is one of my favorite games?"

His tongue traced the fingertips of her hand with hot, darting touches as his mustache nuzzled against the sensitive skin between her fingers. With the same ravishing care he had used on the flower petal, his teeth closed on her index finger. He nibbled delicately down the smooth skin, then inserted his tongue between two of her fingers, caressing them and the soft breast beneath.

Nicole made a small sound of mingled surprise and pleasure as he continued teasing her, teaching her how very sensitive her skin could be. Each time his tongue slid between her fingers to her breast, her breath caught. Each time his teeth tugged tenderly at a finger, her breath came out in an uneven rush.

She didn't realize that he was gently, carefully nuzzling aside the barrier she had raised until his tongue probed between her spread fingers and found the pink crown of her breast. With a thick sound of satisfaction, he tasted the nipple with swift darts of his tongue.

She froze, expecting to be hurt.

She felt only the firm, moist tip of Chase's

tongue exploring her textures, smooth to nubby, satin to velvet.

The seductive caresses continued until she shivered and felt herself changing, her nipple tightening into an erect bud. The feeling was so exquisite that she gasped.

Still he stroked her, drawing her nipple into a taut peak and then tugging on that peak with his lips. She forgot the painful lessons of the past and felt only the pleasures of the present streaming through her. Helplessly her fingers opened until she was offering herself to him rather than protecting herself from him.

A low thread of sound came from Chase as he took her gift. He drew her deeply into his mouth, suckling her with a rhythmic motion, drawing out breathless little cries with each shift of his mouth.

Nicole felt light-headed, almost dizzy. Her breast tightened even more, shaping itself to his insistent tongue, sending tiny quakes rippling through her body with each sweet tug of his mouth. It was like flying, like soaring, like nothing she had ever known. Closing her eyes, she gave herself up to the incredible sensations as she had already given herself to him.

"No," she whispered when she felt his mouth leave her breast. "Not yet."

The words were too soft for Chase to hear. It didn't matter. He wasn't ready to end the tantalizing intimacy any more than she was. With equal care he nibbled and nuzzled and probed the hand that still shielded Nicole's other breast.

If her fingers were slow to move aside this time, it was because she wanted to prolong the sweet anticipation of the moment when his tongue would curl caressingly around her, urging her to sensations that she had never felt before. Miraculous feelings, like being a bubble whirling in champagne, like breathing the softest kind of fire.

When at last his tongue slid between the barrier of her fingers, her nipple was already hard, waiting for his mouth. Wanting it. She couldn't control the throaty cry of pleasure that came when he captured the taut prize.

The husky sound she made sent heat ripping through Chase, threatening his control. **Slowly, slowly, you idiot. Don't devour her.**

But, sweet God, she tastes good.

He forced his mouth to release her, only to find that the sight of her wet nipple rising proudly between her fingers was even more arousing than her cry had been. He touched each nipple with a hungry fingertip, wanting only to taste her again, to feel the sensual trembling take her, to hear the hungry cries ripple out of her.

"Shower?" he asked, his voice deep. Then, almost harshly, "It's now or never, Pele. Your choice."

As his words registered, she opened eyes that

were dazed. She looked down at herself as though she couldn't believe that it really was Nicole Ballard standing half naked in the living room of her cottage, offering her breasts to a man.

No. Not half naked. Fully naked.

Chase's lean, nimble fingers had loosened her lavalava while his mouth caressed her. When he opened his hands, the cloth slid down her legs to the floor. Before she could draw breath to object or accept, her silky thong underwear whispered down her thighs and pooled at her ankles.

Kneeling in front of her, eyes narrowed, he made a sound as though he had just been struck.

"Fire goddess," he said hoarsely, looking at the pale perfection of her skin and the bright flame burning at the apex of her thighs.

Abruptly he stood up. He knew if he looked at her again, he wouldn't be able to wait another minute to sink into the lush fire. Already he had rushed her more than he wanted to, more than she was comfortable with.

Idiot. Rutting idiot.

Even as he raged silently at himself, he knew it was useless. His hunger for her was as unruly as magma on the edge of breaking free, a molten force seething and testing the boundaries that restrained its hot release.

He felt as though he had waited years for this moment. The pressure for relief was nearly unbearable.

She's not ready. Get it through your thick head.

She enjoyed the love play, but she wasn't ready for the rest. Not the way he was. Guts knotted. Feeling like he was made of twisted ropes of flesh.

Aching for it.

Needing it.

Burning alive.

"Shower?" Chase asked again.

Nicole simply stared at him.

He didn't know whether to smile or swear at her expression. She looked dazed, almost edgy, lost, surprised—everything but ready for him.

"Through there," she said, pointing toward the opposite side of the living room where a small door opened into the bathroom.

Before he could think better of it, he dropped to one knee and lifted first one of her feet, then the other. He took off the shell anklets and the mist-thin panties that had slid down her legs at his urging.

The scent of her made his mouth water all over again. He wanted to tease apart her legs as he had her fingers, to find the hidden textures, to suck on her tender flesh. But if he did that, they wouldn't make it to the shower.

They wouldn't even make it to the bed.

"Do you—" Nicole's voice broke when she looked down. His thick black hair lay like a shadow just below her navel. She sensed the warmth of his breath against the sensitive skin of her inner thighs. Suddenly she felt disoriented, almost weak. With the last of what passed for her wits, she blurted, "Do you want to go first?"

"First?" He looked up, startled. Then he smiled slightly. "No. And I don't want to go second either."

"Then what—oh," she said, understanding.

"Is 'oh' the Hawaiian word for two in a shower? If so, then most definitely **oh.**"

She felt heat climbing up from her breasts. Turning, she fled toward the shower before Chase could see her blush. She felt completely lost. Didn't know up from down. Floundering.

She knew what it was like to have sex with a man, but she had never shared a shower with one.

You've never been naked in your own living room with a man, either, she reminded herself, **and that didn't hurt, did it?**

Her nipples tingled and pouted all over again at the memory of his hot, gentle mouth. No, it hadn't hurt one bit. It had been like nothing she had ever known. The thought of feeling him that way again was dizzying, delicious.

She drew a steadying breath and turned on the water, letting it warm up while she divided her hair into two halves and pulled one over each shoulder. With trembling fingers she began to braid the right side.

Instead of barging in and running his hands all

over her the way he wanted to, he stood with his arms crossed on his chest and leaned against the bathroom doorway, memorizing the picture she made standing nude in front of the mirror.

Clean, long limbs. Elegant fingers. Lips flushed and moist. Her hair spilled over her creamy skin, concealing most of her body like a fiery cloak. Most, but not all. The sweet curves of her buttocks made his palms sweat. One tight pink nipple poked out through the silky strands she was impatiently braiding.

"Can I help?" Chase's voice was as light as he was determined to be; she had looked almost frightened before she fled to the shower.

"Can you braid hair?" Nicole asked in surprise, looking over her shoulder.

Straightening, he gave her a wounded look that made him appear ten years younger. "Of course I can. The first thing they taught us in summer camp was how to braid key chains for our fathers and necklaces for our mothers. I always thought it was the damnedest waste of time—until now."

She smiled.

He walked the two steps that brought him close to her. When she turned to face him, his hand stroked the long fall of hair that covered her left breast, tumbled in loose swirls to her waist, and finally blended with the fiery hair between her thighs.

At the first touch of his fingers, the tip of

Nicole's breast hardened so swiftly that it was almost painful. Almost, but not quite.

The difference was a stroke of sensual fire that was a revelation to her. Her eyes widened, and her breath came in sharply. He bent down until the tip of his tongue just touched the nipple that had responded so instantly to his touch.

"Hello," he said, nuzzling the taut flesh. "Do I know you?"

She was torn between laughter and a moan as his mouth tugged gently at the nipple. His sensual teasing was as new to her as the sensations radiating from her breast to the core of her body. Streamers of heat shimmered through her with each movement of his tongue.

He lifted his head and admired the tight, glistening peak his tongue had shaped. "Now I recognize you. We met just a few minutes ago. You have a friend nearby, don't you?"

Nicole made a throaty sound that was part laughter, part pleasure as Chase nuzzled between the red strands covering her other nipple. She let go of the braid she was working on and threaded her fingers into the much more satisfying thickness of his hair. Unconsciously she held his head to her breast, wanting to prolong the sweet caress.

His long fingers slid beneath her hair to curl around her breasts, taking their weight in his palms. For an instant fear shot through her, a defensive withdrawal from intimacy. Her husband's hands had been even more careless of her delicate flesh than his mouth had been, especially when he was aroused.

And she had little doubt that Chase was aroused. The evidence of it was plain and hard against his lavalava.

CHAPTER
16

Chase felt Nicole flinch away when his thumbs caressed her hardened nipples. Reluctantly he removed his hands from her breasts.

"Sorry," he said, going back to braiding her hair. "I'd better concentrate on something I'm good at."

After a few moments she said in a strained voice, "That's not it."

"You mean I'm not good at braiding?" he asked, then brushed his lips over the nipple peeking out from between strands of hair.

"That's not—" Nicole's breath broke. She swallowed and tried again. "It's just that—"

"Did I hurt you?" he interrupted, his voice quiet.

She shook her head, looked away, and wondered how she could tell him that it wasn't his fault. It was hers.

His index finger tilted her chin up until she had to look him in the eye.

"Tell me if I do," he said simply. "I know that a man my size can make a woman nervous."

She searched his gray eyes for a long moment, nodded, and felt her nerves relax again.

It was one of the hardest things he had ever done, but Chase confined himself to braiding her hair, ignoring the ruby-tipped temptation of her breasts so close to hand. Her hesitations and withdrawals puzzled him. Granted, he might have rushed her a little, but he was a long way from forcing the issue.

And she was a long way from being unwilling.

Suddenly he realized what was making her skittish. Mentally he kicked himself for forgetting, even for a moment, what was at stake. She must understand Dane as well as his older brother did. The instant she became Chase's lover, any possibility of seducing Dane away from Jan was gone.

No wonder she's nervous, he thought. But even as he understood, he couldn't help admiring the long, dark eyelashes that concealed Nicole's eyes as she looked down at his hands braiding her hair. **From what I've seen, Dane really likes you, but he hasn't climbed into bed with you, or you wouldn't be here with me.**

From Nicole's point of view, she was taking a real risk. Dane was better-looking than his older, bigger brother. Dane was also civilized, rich, more than half in love with Nicole despite his marriage. Pretty good cards to be holding in the seduction game. Yet she was gambling all that on a toss in the hay with a man who was rich, not very civilized,

and hadn't said one damn thing about liking or loving her.

But Chase wasn't married, and he was more than
willing to take her to bed.

He looked at her softly trembling mouth and
almost felt sorry for her. **You're hoping that I'll
still want you afterward, but you're too hungry
to wait and be sure. That's quite a risk you're
taking on me, Pele. More than you know. More
than you're going to know until you wake up
alone, with no rich Wilcox to comfort you and no
hope of one.**

**But there are other rich fools in the world.
You'll find one to take care of you. Women like
you always do.**

Chase finished the braid and backed away from
Nicole. As she lifted her arms to tuck her braids
into place on top of her head, he saw the elegant
sensuality of her body fully revealed for the first
time. It loosened his knees.

**God, I almost envy the man you finally sell
yourself to.**

Desire slammed through him in hot, rhythmic
surges as he looked at her, all of her. He wanted
even more than he saw, wanted what he couldn't
see, wanted the lush, hot, hidden flesh that would
wrap around him and milk him dry.

Turning toward the mirror, Nicole anchored the
braids on top of her head with the skill of long
practice. As she did, she felt Chase standing close
behind her, watching her in the full-length bath-

room mirror. The look on his face sent both fear and a strange heat through her. Her husband had looked at her like that when she was naked, and then he had taken her quickly, roughly, as though punishing her for something she had done.

She had learned to fear that expression on a man's face.

But Chase had been so very gentle with her. His caresses had given her more pleasure than she had ever believed was possible for her. The fact that he wanted her didn't necessarily mean that he would hurt her.

Besides, the picture he made standing behind her, naked but for the lavalava riding low on his hips, made her body tingle in hidden places. It was another of the new, delicious sensations she wanted to explore. When she met his eyes in the mirror, she hesitantly smiled.

With a single twisting motion, he stripped off his few clothes. He saw her eyes widen in surprise and something close to fear when she saw his readiness for sex reflected in the mirror. Smoothly he blocked the view of his erection by standing behind her. When his hands came up to rest on her shoulders, he felt her flinch again.

"Like I said," he murmured, brushing his lips across the nape of her neck, "sometimes I make a woman nervous. It's all right, Pele. I know my own strength. I won't hurt you."

As though his palms could taste her if he just went very slowly, very gently, he stroked her from her shoulders to her hips. He repeated the long caress, but this time down the front of her body, shaping her breasts and waist and the resilient curve of her thighs. The pressure of his hands eased her against him until there was nothing between them but the heat of their own bodies.

"Don't worry, little one." He kissed the curve of her neck while his hands caressed her thighs. "We'll fit together very well."

After a final, lingering stroke, Chase turned away, opened the shower door, and stepped in.

Nicole stared after him, too surprised to move.

Little one.

She shook her head as though to wake up from a dream. **Little one!** She had never thought of herself as small in her whole life. But then, compared to Chase, most people were just that. Small.

Bemused, she followed him into the shower, her nervousness overshadowed by the novelty of being considered petite. The fact that he obviously understood her fears about sex and wanted her anyway was a balm on her raw pride. She was right to trust her instincts.

She was right to trust him.

Realistically she knew that the first few times they made love would probably be difficult for her. Nothing, not even his gentleness, could magically erase reflexes learned in the past at such cost. But even as she accepted that, she knew that the tension in her body owed as much to anticipation as to anxiety. She wasn't afraid anymore that he would hurt her and keep on hurting her until he found his own satisfaction.

Chase stood to one side of the shower to make room for her and held his hand out to her. When she stepped forward, warm water spilled over her. Ginger-scented soap filled the steamy enclosure with fragrance. Lather slipped from his hands down his body as he soaped his shoulders. The glistening white streams heightened the darkness of his skin and the midnight mat of hair curling down his chest. The intriguing pelt narrowed to a finger's width at his ribs and ran like an arrow down his torso, pointing toward his sex.

She wanted to run her hands beneath the lather, to know each masculine swell of muscle and length of tendon, to feel the heat and strength of his body beneath her palms. But she didn't dare. In the early months of her marriage, when she had tried to please her husband, she quickly learned that touching him only shortened the time before he took her.

She wanted to stretch out every moment she had before Chase discovered her drawbacks as a lover. The sensations she was feeling now were too new, too fragile, too sweet to risk ending simply because she couldn't control her own foolish impulses to stroke him.

When Nicole reached for the soap, Chase shook his head and turned her so that she was facing away from him, shielded from the full force of the water by his broad back. Big, warm, soapy hands began rubbing over her skin. Strong thumbs traced the length of her spine with long, caressing motions. Broad, callused palms first stroked and then cupped the full curves of her buttocks, savoring her difference from him, making her feel sleek and very feminine.

When his fingers traced the shadow cleft at the base of her spine, she shivered with pleasure. He touched her hidden warmth once, tenderly, then withdrew with a slow care that sent stirrings of fire through her.

Very gently he closed his teeth on the nape of her neck. The helpless shiver of her response sent an answering echo through him. He slid his hands around her waist, seeking other pleasure points. Fingers spread wide, he pressed one palm just above her fiery nest of hair while his other found and caressed one breast. His hands moved slowly, skillfully, while his teeth lightly teased her sensitive nape.

Caught between the loving movements of his hands and his mouth, Nicole trembled. Then her body began to move in silky response, increasing the sweet pressure of his caresses.

She wished that she could stroke him without bringing a fast end to the delicious sensual play. For the first time in her life she wanted to touch a man as intimately as she herself was being touched. The hardness of his body had become an irresistible lure, and his strength excited rather than intimidated her now.

Even feeling his erection pressed against her hip

didn't frighten her. With his hands stroking her so sweetly, learning her, knowing her, teasing her, there simply wasn't any room for fear. All she could feel was heat climbing slowly inside her, radiating through her, making her tremble with tiny, secret ripples.

A lifetime of undiscovered sensuality was stirring and awakening beneath his gentle touch.

When Chase sensed the softening of Nicole's body, both triumph and desire raked through him. Her response told him that she wasn't worrying anymore about choosing the wrong rich brother. She was beginning to want him, truly want him.

She was beginning to come apart in his hands.

For an instant he was afraid that the feel of her slowly twisting hips was going to cost what self-control he had. Having her move against him like this was what he had wanted since the first time he had seen her dance to the slow beat of Bobby's drums, her hair swaying in blazing counterpoint to the stately elegance of the hula.

"Turn around," he said, his voice a husky command beneath the sound of the falling water. "I want your mouth, Pele. Do you want mine?"

Yet even as he spoke, he continued stroking her, making her choose between his caressing hands and the sensual promise of his kiss. The temptations were too new, too alluring. She couldn't make the choice. With a small, helpless sound, she tilted her head back against his shoulder, offering her mouth in the only way she could without interrupting the incredibly sweet seduction of his hands.

When Nicole half turned, her hip rubbed against aroused flesh. Heat exploded in him, making his pulse beat visibly in his erection. His tongue slid between her lips, tasting her, inviting her to taste him in return. She strained up to him, caught in a sensual vise that was tightening with each movement of his palm against the tangled, fiery hair nestled between her thighs.

He didn't ask her to choose again. He shifted his hands, turning her toward him. With shivering pleasure he eased his hot, aching flesh between her thighs, teaching her that there were many ways for a man to caress a woman.

Bracing his arms against the wall on either side of her, he let her feel some of the weight of his body in a long, slick caress. The coolness of the tiled shower wall against her back was heady, exciting, so different from the textured heat of the male body pressing against her, stroking her from her mouth to her toes and teasing the hot folds between her thighs.

Recklessly she put her arms around him, running her hungry palms down his back. In a wild, breathless silence broken only by the rushing of water, she learned the hard patterns of his muscle and tendon, the rippling strength that had fascinated her since the first moment she saw him calling elemental rhythms from the drums.

His back shifted slowly, powerfully beneath her

hands as he twisted into her touch, drawing every bit of pleasure from her hands while his tongue stroked hers, promising her even greater pleasures. The small, hungry sound she made when he caught her tongue between his teeth drew a groan of response from him. He thrust deeply into her mouth and moved slowly against her, caressing her with his whole body.

It wasn't nearly enough. He was just skimming the tender edges of desire. He had to be inside her, all the way in, until she clenched around him and cried out her climax.

The need to bury himself in her was an ache and a wild pressure. For an instant he considered taking her in the shower. Then he remembered her hesitations and knew that he had to keep his control for a little bit longer.

"I've had about all the shower I can take," he said, biting her neck not quite gently. "How about you?"

"I've never had so much fun in a shower in my life." Her voice caught as she looked at him, her eyes wide and catlike in the shower's filtered, steamy light.

Smiling, he rubbed against her again, drawing out the sensual moment. Her eyes half closed as pleasure shivered visibly through her. He jerked with a surge of heat that nearly undid him. For a shattered breath he almost let go and to hell with it, because he had never seen anything as sexy as her response to even the lightest of his touches.

But before he came, he would make her scream with ecstasy. Then he would know that her need was as great as his.

With an effort, he forced himself to turn away from her and shut off the water. He stepped out into the relative coolness of the bathroom and looked around.

"Towels?" he asked.

Then he saw her watching him in the mirror. Her expression was more curious than afraid and more appreciative than anything else.

"Forget the towels," he said thickly. "In this heat we wouldn't stay dry for more than a few seconds anyway."

His hand drew her out of the shower into a hot, slick embrace. She came to him without hesitation, molding herself to his powerful body, clinging to him with her mouth and hands. When he lifted his head, his breathing was quick, strained, and his hands moved restlessly, urgently over her body.

"I'm having a hell of a time keeping my hands off you long enough to get you to bed," he muttered.

"I don't mind." She smiled to herself while her hands rubbed across the fascinating textures of his chest. When she felt the sudden hardening of his nipple beneath her palm, she remembered her own wild pleasure when his lips had caressed her. "I enjoy this. Do you?"

He wondered at the note of surprise in her voice, but the soft, exciting pressure of her mouth against his nipple drove every thought from his mind except that of opening her legs and pushing into her until he could go no farther. His hands swept down her back, arching her against him. He wanted her hidden softness with a wild, nearly uncontrollable hunger that shocked him without reducing one bit of his need.

Nicole sensed the change in Chase. She didn't protest when he led her to the living room and flipped open the futon. When he urged her down beside him, she didn't hesitate. She would have loved to continue the exciting caresses they had shared in the shower, but she didn't resent the fact that he needed more. He had already given her greater pleasure than she had ever known; she could hardly deny him his own male release.

The scent of ginger and warm woman flowed over Chase when he pulled Nicole into his arms. Moonlight turned her into a quicksilver shadow, giving her a beauty that made his whole body clench. He slid his hand from her breast to the warmth between her thighs, wanting to know if she was as ready for him as he was for her. With barely controlled urgency he tested her softness.

What he found made him want to swear. She was ready enough that he wouldn't hurt her, but she was nowhere near the peak of feminine need. She didn't want him the way he wanted her, until he felt like he was tied in burning knots.

No surprise there, jackass. Courtesans and other head-hunting females are basically cold in bed, he reminded himself. **For them, real passion**

is an act. They don't want any more from a man than a meal ticket, and they pay for it in the coin the man wants most.

Sex.

When Nicole sensed Chase's hesitation, she kissed his shoulder and the pulse beating heavily at the base of his neck. "It's all right," she said, urging him closer.

The whispered words were all that he needed, more than he had expected. He took her without hesitation, savoring the hot instant of joining.

She was tight, much tighter than he had expected. He thought about withdrawing, wondering if he was hurting her. Then he felt her breath sigh out. The muscles clenched against him relaxed in a long, secret caress. She shifted and moved slightly, tugging at him.

The last possibility of control evaporated. He groaned and moved within her, letting the pulsing, bursting pressure of his hunger finally find release.

Nicole held him close, smoothing her hands over his hot skin, savoring the unique feeling of having pleased a lover and the equally rare sensation of enjoying the heat and weight of a man's body over her own. When he rolled onto his side, withdrawing from her, she made a small sound of protest. She had discovered a completely unexpected pleasure in being joined with him. Their separation made her feel empty and . . . restless.

Chase hesitated, then pulled her closer and

stroked her. The slow sweeps of his hand went from the moon-bright crown of her head to the alluring female curve of hip and thigh. Unconsciously she moved closer, wanting the feel of his skin against hers, hungry for the sweet intimacy he had showed her earlier.

The small movements of her body as she snuggled into his warmth, fitting herself to him with sensual precision, made his breath shorten all over again. He felt the thick, hot thrill of returning urgency, pressure growing with each beat of his heart. He bent over her breast, kissing her, and felt her tighten beneath his touch.

It took only an instant, like the tiny sound she made in her throat when his mouth tugged at her. An instant, and a blazing torrent of hunger leaped to life again.

Fire goddess. She would burn a man alive and never even feel the heat.

When Chase realized that he was on the verge of succumbing all over again to Nicole's sensual trap, he sat up quickly.

I've done what I had to. Dane's safe from her. Now I'd better get the hell out while I still have the strength to leave.

While I still want to leave.

He looked down at her, his eyes metallic silver in the moonlight.

"Chase?"

A long tendril of her hair had escaped the coils. It fell between her breasts in a soft ribbon that shimmered with subdued fire. He felt a moment of sharp regret that he hadn't taken down her hair and wrapped it around him, letting its silken strands bind him to her.

"Don't get up," he said. "I'll let myself out."

She blinked, trying to think of something to say. She had no experience with this sort of thing. "You—you don't have to leave."

"Lisa is with Jan and Dane. If something happens and they need me, they'll call my cottage, not yours."

The words were true as far as they went. And it kept him from saying the rest of the truth: if he stayed, he would take Nicole again and again, falling deeper and deeper beneath the spell of her cold fire.

She hadn't wanted him. Not really. Not completely. Not the way he had wanted her—all the fires of Eden raging inside him.

The way he still wanted her.

Swiftly Chase stood and retrieved his lavalava from the bathroom. He wrapped the cloth into place before he went back to the living room.

Nicole was standing by the front door, wearing nothing but moonlight.

Without meaning to, he found his fingertips tracing the length of the single tendril of hair that fell between her breasts and down over the smooth curves of her body. He lifted his hand, opened the cottage door, and stepped through.

As she moved aside to let him by, she held on to

the door with both hands. It was the only way she kept herself from clinging to him and begging him to stay and touch her gently for just a few more moments. But that would be stupid. Her marriage had taught her that once a man had what he wanted sexually, he had no further use for the woman.

"Thank you," she said shyly, looking down because she was suddenly embarrassed.

"For what?" Chase asked from the other side of the doorway. He knew that there had been no release for her. She must know it, too. She certainly hadn't bothered to hide it.

"For not hurting me."

The soft words were nearly lost beneath the sound of the latch taking hold as the she shut the door behind him.

For a long moment Chase stood in the silence and shadows, wondering at the sudden uneasiness sweeping through him. He felt like he was standing on the lip of a volcano that was supposed to be dormant, but wasn't. He could sense the sleeping volcano shuddering deep beneath his feet in ominous harmonic tremors, warning of an explosion to come.

Something was wrong.

Very wrong.

It's called postcoital depression, you jackass, he snarled silently to himself.

There was no answer but a feeling of unease spreading like cold water through his gut.

With an impatient curse he stalked toward his cottage. Every step of the way he told himself that nothing was wrong. In fact, everything that mattered was finally right.

Dane's marriage was safe from the fiery temptations of Pele.

CHAPTER
17

After a night of broken sleep and the kind of dreams that he hadn't had since he lost custody of Lisa, Chase's mood was savage. All he wanted was to get the next few hours over with. Then he would go out on the volcano and hike the desolate, steaming crater until he was too tired to get hard every time he thought about the image of Nicole naked in the moonlight, holding her arms out to him.

He shot out of bed, got up, and showered for the third time since he had left Nicole. No matter, he still could smell her, ginger and heat, and he could feel her soft, hungry hands on his body.

He didn't bother shaving. He just yanked on underwear, khaki shorts, and an old cotton shirt that once had been as dark as his hair but now was closer to the color of his eyes. With swift movements he rolled up the sleeves. He was impatient to see Dane so that he could get on with his real work in Hawaii—volcano crawling—rather than showing his younger brother how close an escape he had had from a sexy redheaded gold digger.

Sexy. God. What a pale word for Pele's physical impact.

No matter how Chase tried, the reality of his own nearly uncontrollable lust scraped at him. He kept reliving scattered moments—the silky fire of her hair, the odd hesitancy and heat of her mouth, her tiny cry when his tongue first touched her nipple, and the hot, tight, incredibly intense pleasure of sheathing himself deep inside her.

He had had sex with more beautiful women, and certainly more passionate or skillful ones, but Nicole was a fire in his memory and they were not.

She was also a fire in his body. He burned, and he didn't know why, but the evidence was hard and hot in front of him. He wanted her. **Needed her.**

Disgusted with his uncontrollable sexual response to even the memory of last night, Chase slammed out of the cottage. While he drove, the Porsche snarled for him, an oddly soothing noise. He pulled into Dane's long, curving driveway and parked at the rear of the house alongside Jan's zippy little car.

He hoped Jan was sleeping in and Dane was his usual bright-eyed, dawn-loving self.

Bougainvillea overgrew the detached garage and carport, shedding drifts of shocking pink flowers over everything. Chase picked his way through the greenery with respect for its weapons. As a recent arrival to Eden, bougainvillea still had plenty of wicked, inch-long thorns.

As usual, the back door of the house was unlocked. The front door was, too, but the back was closer. The smell of coffee greeted Chase when he entered. After a hellish night, coffee smelled like heaven. From the instant he woke up, he had been too impatient to make coffee or eat anything at his cottage. He just wanted to get the whole mess over with.

Dane sat alone at the kitchen table, reading the newspaper and sipping coffee. Chase let out a small sigh of relief. He didn't want Jan ever to know about Nicole and Dane. After all, nothing had really happened. And nothing ever would.

Now.

Chase wished he felt better about it, but he didn't. All he could do was put it behind him.

Dane gave him a shrewd look. "You're early. Lisa isn't up yet. Besides, I think this is the morning Nicole gives her drawing lessons." He grimaced and smacked himself on the forehead. "Damn, there I go again! Give me a bag and a cat and I'll let it out every time. You didn't hear anything about drawing from me. Again."

"Hear what?" Chase agreed automatically. He hesitated, wondering how to bring up the subject of the bet he had won and Dane had lost. "Where's Jan?"

"Sleeping. She was up until three polishing the proposal."

"Good." Chase felt a bit less savage. He had been

worried that Jan might come downstairs and over-hear a brotherly discussion about rich, gullible men and poor, shrewd women.

"Jan will be sorry you're sorry you missed her," Dane said ironically.

Chase shot his brother a hard look and decided that there was no civilized, gentlemanly way to open this conversation. After all, what had been done wasn't very civilized, and as for gentle-manly . . . His mouth turned down in a grimace of distaste.

On the other hand, women like Nicole could hardly expect to find a world full of **gentlemen** competing to pay the rent.

Rather warily Dane watched Chase pour himself a cup of coffee. His brother radiated anger or frus-tration. Given his knowledge of Nicole, Dane was betting on frustration. It would be good for his big brother to come up against a woman who didn't trip him and beat him to the floor after knowing him for five minutes. Abstinence built character, right?

With the smug amusement of a man who made love to a woman he loved as often as they both pleased, Dane was grateful that it was Chase who was suffering and building character thanks to sex-ual frustration. Dane was really out of practice at that sort of thing.

That didn't mean he wouldn't enjoy needling his older brother about it. In the kindest, most sup-portive way possible, of course.

"I thought after the performance at the club last night, you'd be tired enough to sleep for a week," Dane said blandly, turning to another page in the small newspaper.

Paper rustled loudly in the silence as he made a production of folding the sheets just so. He scanned the columns without interest, waiting for Chase to respond.

"Were you at the club?" Chase finally asked, sipping the scalding coffee. "I didn't see you."

"I came in later." Dane looked up at his brother with a mixture of curiosity and humor. "Must have had ten people tell me about your hot drumming, Nicole's hotter dancing, and the magic act."

Chase's black eyebrows lifted in surprise. "Magic act?"

"Yeah," Dane said dryly, bending over the newspaper again. "Now you see them, now you don't."

Chase took a deep breath. There would never be a better moment. "You lost the bet," he said bluntly, his voice rough.

Dane's head snapped up. There was shock in every handsome line of his face. "What?"

"We went back to Nicole's place. I stayed there long enough to make sure that she'd never go after you again—or if she did, that you wouldn't have her."

"What the hell are you talking about?"

"Fucking," Chase said brutally.

An image of Nicole's softness and beauty rose in his mind. Ruthlessly he shoved aside the memory.

He was old enough to know there was hell of a lot more to a book than its cover. The proof was definitely in the reading. Or in this case, in the sheets. Nicole had gone to bed with him for reasons other than passion, because she had shown him damned little of that.

Just enough of it to make him crazy, in fact. But that was his problem.

"You and **Nicole**?"

Dane's chair scraped across the floor as he came to his feet with a jerk that sent his empty coffee mug rolling to the floor. Crockery smashed on the tile with an unhappy sound. Both men ignored the broken mug. They were too focused on each other to have attention left over for anything else. They heard nothing except their own words.

Not even the sound of a soft knock followed by the front door opening.

"Of course it was her," Chase said impatiently. "Who else would I be fucking but Nicole? Or is some other gold digger after you, dazzling you with smiles and sweet lies while visions of bank accounts dance in her dear little head?"

For a stunned second, then two, Dane tried to understand what his brother was saying. It didn't make sense. None of it.

"You're crazy!" he said, shaking his head sharply.

Motionless in the middle of the living room, Nicole heard the male voices erupting from the kitchen. With each word she flinched. She felt like splashes of boiling lava were landing all around her.

On her.

But it wasn't hot. It was cold, freezing cold.

This can't be happening. I'm dreaming. I'll wake up soon, and it will be over. Just another bad dream.

The voices came again.

It wasn't a dream, and it kept on happening, words freezing her until she bit her lips against the cries clawing at her throat.

"She slept with you?" Dane demanded.

"Don't look so surprised. It happens all the time." Chase's voice was rough, impatient.

"Not with Nicole!"

"Oh, bullshit. She really had you going, didn't she, little brother? Well, if it makes you feel better, you didn't miss much. Like a lot of women with a good body, she thinks that it's enough for a man just to be in bed with her."

"What?"

The word wasn't a question. It was a measure of Dane's confusion.

Chase answered anyway. He had come to strip his brother of any male fantasies about Nicole, and that was exactly what he would do—even though he would rather shovel out campground pit toilets on the fifth of July.

"Women like Nicole can't believe that a man wants more in bed than a sexy body," Chase said in a clipped voice. "Most of them at least take the trouble to substitute skill for passion. Not her. Nicole is about as skillful in the sheets as a corpse."

"**Shut up, damn you!**" Dane's voice was hoarse, shocked. He was afraid that he understood too much. "I don't want to hear any more!"

"Tough shit." Chase's mouth thinned in violent disgust for the whole situation. But it was almost finished.

He couldn't wait for it to be over with so he could go to the clean slopes of the volcano. That was where he belonged. Not here, telling his brother what he should have been able to figure out for himself.

"You lost the bet," Chase said savagely, "but that's all you lost. You still have Jan, and she's a better woman than Nicole will ever be."

Nicole tried to turn away, to flee from the damning words, but her body didn't respond. She swayed slowly in place, fighting for balance, trying to understand what had happened, why it had happened.

It was devastating to know that Chase had seduced her as part of a cruel game. But knowing she had failed him so completely as a woman destroyed her in a way she couldn't comprehend. She simply felt it all the way to her soul in a single, tearing stroke that took the breath from her body.

The room dimmed to gray and started to spin around her. Instinctively she bent over and fought against fainting. Blindly clinging to an armchair, she willed her body not to betray her. She had to leave before anyone discovered her and knew that she had overheard. What had happened was bad enough. Seeing Chase, knowing that he knew, that Dane knew, having them look at her—**no, never. It must not happen.**

Only raw desperation kept her on her feet, and the silent screams in her mind demanding that she **get out! run! hide!**

Other words poured out of the kitchen, slicing into her in burning shards of ice, echoing in her mind as she fought for control of her body.

"What do you mean, I still have Jan?" Dane asked.

"Nicole was after you, little brother. Or, to be precise, after marriage and your bank account."

"You're wrong. Dead wrong."

"Don't give me that shit," Chase snarled. "I've seen how you look at her."

"Just like you look at Jan?" Dane asked, measuring his brother with cold eyes. "Just like Jan looks at you?"

CHAPTER
18

There was a moment of charged silence between the two brothers.

"You don't think—" Chase began, shocked.

"No," Dane cut in impatiently, "I don't. I know both of you too well. I know Nicole in the same way. Yes, I care for Nicole a great deal, just as you care for Jan. Nicole is a very appealing woman, and not just physically. I'd have to be blind and a liar to say otherwise. But if I'd been so butt-stupid as to make a pass at Nicole, she would have ducked. She's not like the females you've had since your divorce. And she most definitely isn't another home wrecker like Lynette, out for what she can get from men and to hell with anything else."

"Christ," Chase said, disgusted. "Nicole really has you going, doesn't she? If she's such a snow-white saint, why did she have sex with me after we'd known each other only a few days? Hardly the act of a virtuous paragon of womanhood, is it?"

"If she went to bed with you—"

"She did," Chase cut in impatiently. "Don't kid yourself about that."

"Then it happened because she wanted you enough to overcome—"

The rest of Dane's words were buried beneath Chase's sardonic laughter. Nicole's lack of real passion still grated on his pride. He had been so hot, nearly wild for her, and she had been controlled down to the last breath.

"She's cold to the core," Chase said. "She doesn't know the meaning of the word **passion**."

A wave of nausea hit Nicole. Icy sweat broke out and a salty taste filled her mouth. No longer caring if she made any noise, she shoved away from the chair's support and bolted for the downstairs bathroom.

She barely reached it in time. She was blindly, wrenchingly sick, as though the convulsions of her body could somehow wipe out the last terrible minutes when she had overheard herself being dissected as a woman and coldly dismissed by the very man she had trusted herself to, believing he was so right for her.

"What the hell?" Dane said, turning toward the sounds.

Chase turned and headed out of the kitchen at a run. "One of the kids must be sick."

He beat Dane to the bathroom. As he reached the closed door, he heard the toilet flush and the sound of water running in the sink. He yanked the door open, expecting to find one of the children.

What he saw shocked him.

Nicole was pale as salt, her eyes closed, and her

forearms were supporting her on the sink. Her hands were shaking so hard that the water she was trying to splash on her face was pouring down the front of her bright blue muumuu. Thin cloth stuck to her body in great dark welts of color.

Chase reached past her for a washcloth. He wet it and began to wipe her face as though she was a child.

When the cloth touched Nicole's skin, her eyes opened. Slowly she focused on Chase. With a broken cry she pushed away from him so violently that her back slammed against the shower door. The glass shivered but didn't break.

He caught her, steadying her. When she felt his hands close around her arms, she shuddered convulsively. With a low, ragged sound, she did the only thing she had the strength left to do. She turned her face away from the sight of him.

"Are you all right?" Chase felt her begin to sag in his arms. Her head rolled loosely. "Nicole!"

Weakly, futilely, she fought against being touched by him. She whispered "No," again and again as though it would make a difference.

If she could have died, she would have.

"Leave her alone," Dane said harshly.

"She needs help," Chase said. He supported her with one hand and controlled her weakly flailing hands with the other. "She's so sick with the flu that she can hardly stand."

Dane muttered a searing obscenity. "Something

made her sick, all right, but it wasn't the flu. Let go of her. Can't you see? She doesn't want you to touch her."

The bleakness of his brother's voice startled Chase. Then he realized what Dane was trying to say. The unease that had stalked him since he left Nicole last night congealed in his stomach, making it turn over. He took a harsh breath through his teeth and turned Nicole's chin so that she had to face him.

"How long were you in the living room?" he asked.

She closed her eyes before she could see him.

"Look at me," Chase said hoarsely. "How much did you hear?"

Her eyes opened, but she didn't see him. She looked through him, seeing nothing, wishing she could feel nothing as well. She would have sold her soul to be able to vanish.

"Let go of me." Her voice was thready, a stranger's voice. "I'm fine. Don't touch me. Don't. Please. Let go of me. Don't. I'm fine."

His breath came in with a rough sound. He looked from Nicole's pale face to the helpless pain on Dane's.

"What the hell is going on?" Chase asked.

"You won the bet," Dane said wearily, "but you lost, brother. You lost big. But not as much as Nicole did. **Shit.**" He closed his eyes for a moment, not able to bear looking at her agony. "Let go of her before you make her sick all over again. As a matter of fact, I'm feeling more than a little sick myself."

Chase didn't want to believe what was on Dane's face, in his voice, in the sag of his shoulders.

"Nicole?" he whispered, turning back to her.

She closed her eyes.

He looked at the pale, trembling woman he was supporting and felt bile rise in his throat in a burning wave. He didn't want to believe that he had let his distrust of women warp his judgment to the point that he had hurt someone whose only fault lay in trusting him. Wanting him.

There's a better explanation. There has to be. Flu and eavesdropping. That was it. It had to be.

When Nicole overheard the conversation, she realized that Dane was out of reach. A disappointment, to be sure, but hardly enough to literally sicken her. Women who made their living off men were tougher than that.

Or should be.

"Nicole." Chase's voice was gentle and very firm. "I'm sorry, but it had to be done. I couldn't stand by and let you break up my brother's marriage."

She had thought she couldn't be hurt any more. Big mistake. She could.

A ragged shudder went the full length of her body. The idea that people thought she was pursuing Dane was as terrible a blow as Chase's summation of her as a woman.

"If it's money you need, I'll—" Chase began.

"Shut up," Dane said coldly, cutting off his brother. "Christ Jesus, Chase, what's happened with you and women? Can't you see that Nicole didn't want me as anything but a friend? But she wanted you, and I'll bet she didn't put any conditions on an affair or ask for any guarantees or money up front, did she?"

Chase closed his eyes, praying that his brother was wrong.

And afraid, very afraid, that he was right.

She didn't ask me for one damn thing. And then she thanked me. Not for the pleasure I gave her, but for the simple lack of pain.

He swallowed against the acid coffee that kept trying to creep back up his throat. When he looked at Nicole again, her eyes were wide, fixed, and the skin around them looked bruised.

My God, what have I done to her?

"Nicole?" Chase asked gently, stroking her cheek with his fingertips.

With a small cry she flinched and swallowed convulsively, answering questions Chase hadn't even asked. She had overheard enough. Too much. It had hurt her in a way that he could barely comprehend.

There was one thing he knew without any doubt. She might have wanted him last night, but she couldn't bear his touch this morning. It literally sickened her.

Slowly, very slowly, Chase released Nicole and stepped aside.

"Nicole," Dane said, reaching out to give her a comforting hug, the way he would have his own children if they were hurt. "It will be all right, honey."

"No. Oh, no." Nicole backed away as far as she could from both men in the small bathroom.

"Nicole?" Dane asked, lowering his arms. "You know I won't hurt you."

"Yes. I know. Don't touch me. Please." Her voice was a raw whisper. "Don't anyone touch me. Not yet. Maybe tomorrow. Yes. I'll be fine tomorrow. But don't touch me now. Please."

For a long, long moment there was no sound but Nicole's ragged breathing as she fought to bring herself under control.

Watching her, cold waves of certainty broke over Chase. He had been wrong about her from the beginning. All the way wrong. Brutally wrong. Nicole hadn't been after Dane.

If she had been hesitant in the lovemaking last night, it came from something else. Fear. Simple fear.

She had been afraid.

What was she afraid of? Chase asked himself silently. **My size? That doesn't make sense. If she was afraid of big men, why was she attracted to me in the first place?**

"Nicole, I didn't mean to—" he began.

"That's all right," she said quickly, cutting across Chase's words, staring through him with a ghastly social smile. "I understand. Really I do. You wanted to protect. Your brother." Her eyes focused on Dane. Her laughter made both men flinch in sympathetic pain. "I'm sorry. Shouldn't laugh. It's not at you. It's just—the idea."

"The idea?" Dane asked softly. "Of what, honey?"

"Of marriage. Of marrying anyone. Even you, Dane. Being a man's **thing** again. Legally. Morally. All day. Every day. And the nights." Revulsion racked Nicole.

Chase had played football long enough to know how to control the nausea caused by pain. It was the only thing that kept him from being as sick as she had been. He finally understood the meaning of her whispered good-bye: **Thank you for not hurting me.**

She had been afraid to come to him because she was afraid of sex.

Yet she had come to him anyway.

"Nicole—" Chase's voice was raw with emotion, but she kept on talking, hearing only her own words, her unfocused eyes seeing things that made his stomach test the limits of his willpower.

He didn't know which was worse, hearing Nicole's shattered voice or hearing the voice in his own mind telling him that he had just made a hideous mistake—and someone else was paying for it, someone who couldn't afford the cost.

Thank you for not hurting me.

Chase began to swear softly, terribly, hating himself and the whole situation with an intensity that bordered on violence.

Nicole didn't even look at him. She didn't trust herself to. She focused on Dane and held her voice very carefully. She had to sound calm, normal, like nothing had happened.

"I'm going home. Tell Lisa . . ." Nicole's voice frayed into silence. When she could speak again, it was only a whisper. "Tell her I'll call."

"I'll drive you home," Chase said tightly. "You're in no shape to handle a car."

"I'm fine."

"Like fucking hell you are!"

"I'll drive her," Dane said. He put a warning hand on Chase when he would have stopped Nicole from edging past him on the way out of the bathroom. "You can follow and bring me home."

Chase started to object, then realized it was useless. **"Shit."** The savage word echoed as he stepped out of Nicole's way. Much more gently, he said, "We'll talk later, when you feel better."

"No." Her voice was very soft, very final.

"Yes." He held out his hand to her, only to have her flinch away again. He ran the hand through his hair in a gesture of barely restrained frustration. "I'm sorry, Nicole. God. I'm so sorry. I didn't understand. I really believed you were trying to break up Dane's marriage. Suddenly every conversation and letter was filled with Nicole this and Nicole that, and all Dane had to say about Jan was that she was busy on this or that project. I just assumed that you and he—"

"I understand," Nicole interrupted quickly, her mind working at frantic speed, focused on a single truth. **I can't hang on much longer. I have to get out of here before I fly apart.** Realizing that she had been holding herself frozen too long, she took a sawing breath. "You're right. Dane is funny, warm, intelligent. Gentle." Her voice caught on the edge of breaking. "So gentle. Any woman would want him."

"You left out rich," Dane said, giving his older brother a slicing sideways glance.

"Rich," she repeated obediently. "Excuse me. I really have to go now."

Chase saw that Nicole was clinging to her control by her fingernails. "Nicole—" His voice broke. "My God—I never meant—I didn't think I could hurt you that—that you—"

"It's all right," she said, talking quickly over his words, not listening. She couldn't bear to hear him, to look at him, to know what he really thought of her. She desperately wanted it to end—all the words, the fear, the tearing need to scream and keep on screaming and yet knowing she must not scream. Not yet. "I understand." She gave Dane another ghastly smile. "Sorry I was so obvious about liking you. I hope Jan didn't—"

The thought of Jan wondering if her friend was stalking Dane snapped the last of Nicole's control. With no warning she bolted past Dane and down the hall, catching both of the men flat-footed. She paused only long enough to scoop up the purse she had dropped on the living room floor.

When she heard the men calling her name, she knew they weren't going to let her go alone. She fumbled her keys out of her purse, jammed the correct one in the car's ignition, and heard the fickle engine roar to life.

Thank you, God.

Leaves and fallen blossoms flew wildly from beneath the spinning tires. She barely kept the car from fishtailing out of control. But she managed. Just.

Chase saw the little car accelerate. Cursing steadily, he spun around and headed for his own car.

Dane tackled him.

"Forget it!" Dane panted, struggling to hold on to his larger, stronger brother. "By the time you back out, she'll be long gone. No sense in having two emotional wrecks on the road at once. Not a damn thing you could do anyway, even if you did catch her."

With a controlled, violent motion, Chase broke Dane's hold. "I could see that she gets home safely."

Warily Dane circled Chase, knowing quite well that his brother would be happy to take out his anger the old-fashioned male way—a good brawl.

"What makes you think she's going home?" Dane asked.

"Where else would she go?"

"To the mountain." Dane gestured toward Kilauea. "Benny says she always goes there when she gets mainland sad."

The thought of some other man comforting Nicole nearly cut loose Chase's temper. "Benny? Who the hell is he? You said she didn't have any boyfriends!"

"Benny Kamehameha." Dane watched his brother with narrowed eyes, gauging his mood. He had never seen Chase like this. Raw. Wild. Dangerous. "Bobby's youngest son. He's ten. Surely Lisa mentioned him to you? Benny of the short sentences?"

Chase took a deep breath and slowly unclenched his fists. "Oh. That Benny. I see."

Dane saw that the danger had passed. "Do you? Nicole likes kids, and they like her. Of course," he added sarcastically, "she could just be buttering up the kids because they have rich daddies."

"Fuck you," Chase snarled, turning on his brother suddenly.

Dane's smile was razor thin. "Just wanted to be sure the hair shirt fit, brother. It's so hard to find clothes in your size."

Chase's mouth flattened into a line. "That's the second one."

Dane nodded, understanding the old phrase from their childhood. If he needled Chase again, he could expect a no-holds-barred fight.

"What is 'mainland sad'?" Chase asked carefully. His whole body was clenched with the effort of controlling himself. Like Nicole, he wanted to go away somewhere and try to understand how he could have been so brutally wrong. But he needed information about her more than he had to be alone. He needed that information with an intensity he didn't even question. "Is she homesick?"

Slowly Dane shook his head. "Nicole loves it here. She was born for the islands. It just took her a few years to find her way over here."

"Then what is it?"

"I don't know. I've never asked. She's never offered. I assume it's something to do with men, because she never dated. Until you. You were different."

Chase closed his eyes, realizing too late the simple truth. "So was she."

He turned away from his brother.

"Where are you going?" Dane asked.

"To the mountain."

"It's a big place. I don't think you'll find her."

"No, but maybe I'll find what she's looking for."

"What's that?"

"Peace."

CHAPTER
19

For the first few miles Nicole drove, she spent as much time looking in the mirrors as she did at the road ahead. Not until she reached the first of the sugarcane fields that had been transformed into cattle pastures did she begin to relax.

She was over the first, and worst, hurdle. Now all she had to do was hang on long enough to find the tiny kipuka she thought of as her personal sanctuary. Once she was there, she would be free to do whatever she wanted—cry or scream or curse—and most of all to ask **why** until either answers or the fragile peace of emotional exhaustion came to her.

She took an unmarked, rough spur road that went about two thousand feet up Kilauea's fertile, lava-scarred flank. The road ended in a thick lava flow. It was just one of the many black-stone rivers twisting down toward the sea and just one of many roads that ended beneath a cooled lava flow. The flows came from fissures that gushed liquid stone from the volcano's flanks whenever magma bubbled and seethed upward in response to shifts in the immense pressures beneath the earth.

Each frozen river marked a time of desolation and renewal, of plant life destroyed while more land was created. Death and rebirth, the paradox of the burning mountain.

Both the desolation and the creation called to Nicole. In a way that she couldn't describe, the ravaged land spoke to her, giving silent testimony to the stubborn endurance and ultimate beauty of life. For each savage moment of new land boiling up from the earth's molten interior, for each violent river of fire scorching through green vegetation, there was also a long time of tranquillity and renewal.

No matter how bad it looked after an eruption, the destruction was never total.

Within the lava flows themselves, kipukas survived. These tiny islands of life were landlocked arks that nourished plants and animals until it was safe to leave again. Then, once more, life grew and changed, meeting the new conditions of the newly born land, life creating something both soft and vital from the fertile ashes of destruction.

That was what Nicole needed as she stumbled over a track that only she and Benny ever walked. She needed to sit in the midst of life that had survived incredible devastation. She needed to look beyond the safety of the kipuka and see the tiny signs of life venturing out once more, colonizing land that was as hard and sharp as the moment it had cooled years and years ago.

What tiny, fragile flowers could do, she could do. Survive.

But first she had to find her own inner islands where emotions had survived the morning's devastation.

If nothing had survived, she had to know that, too.

Without kipukas it took longer for life to enrich the landscape of volcanic creation, but life **did** win out. Even islands that had been first covered with and then surrounded by half a planet's worth of water finally managed to rise above the waves and clothe themselves in ferns and flowers and sweetly singing birds. If Hawaii was possible, anything was possible.

Anything.

The kipuka was small, hardly more than an acre. It was a startling emerald garden bordered by the scrubby plants and grasses that struggled to conquer the brilliant black of a pahoehoe flow. Unlike most kipukas, this one was a small hill poking above the flow rather than a hole surrounded by walls left by more recent lava flows. The kipuka was thick with plants, because its lava floor was old enough to have crumbled into a thin, fertile soil. Ferns grew where other plants couldn't. Colorful kopiko and ohelo bushes were everywhere. So was the familiar ohia tree, raising its graceful crown, silently offering hundreds of bright red flowers to the sun.

Nicole eased through the thick growth, seeking her favorite spot beneath a many-trunked koa tree.

A remnant of once-vast forests, the tree with its thickly spreading roots had prevented other woody plants from moving in too close. The result was a sun-splashed opening where mixed grasses and small flowering plants like koali morning glories or white strawberries grew.

With a feeling of relief so great it was painful, she sank down onto the grass and leaned back against one of the koa's nearly smooth trunks. She didn't try to think, to question, to understand. She simply sat, letting the peace of the kipuka seep into her like a healing balm.

It was a healing she desperately needed.

After a while the tiny sounds of the kipuka resumed around her. It was a reassuring symphony of pollinating insects and immigrant songbirds moving like bright, musical shadows just behind curtains of green foliage.

Eyes closed, Nicole became part of the timeless kipuka. She asked nothing of herself except that she keep her thoughts from spiraling down in smaller and smaller circles. She didn't want her body to become as raw and tightly knotted as her mind.

Eventually, when she felt calmer, she allowed herself to think about what she would do when she left the kipuka. The impulse to flee the island was very deep. She had fled a disaster once before, and it had worked.

Had it?

Or had running simply set the stage for a bigger disaster? Chase Wilcox.

That unhappy thought kept her still for a long time.

Finally she decided that running wouldn't help. She had run halfway around the world once before. If she did it again, she would be back where she started.

No. She would be much worse off. Hawaii was her home. If she was driven from that, she would have nothing, nothing at all.

In any case, wherever she went, she would already be there, waiting for herself to arrive. Same woman.

Or rather, the same failure as a woman.

She doesn't know the meaning of the word passion . . . about as skillful in the sheets as a corpse.

With a cry, Nicole wrenched her mind away from Chase's harsh words. She would have given anything to doubt their truth.

No. That's stupid. That's how I got here.

She would accept his words.

Doubting the truth of her own frigidity was how she had fallen into the sensual trap with Chase. In the deepest level of her mind she had doubted her husband's judgment of her as a woman, so when something in her had seen Chase and said, **This is the man,** there had been no inner voice to warn her that she was being stupid.

Now there wasn't any doubt.

Her husband had been right.

She had been wrong.

In Chase Wilcox she had made the most agonizing mistake of her life. Now she had to accept the truth, live with it, and finally live beyond it, giving the islands of life inside her time to slowly spread out and heal the ruined landscape of her dreams.

If there was anything left to heal.

CHAPTER
20

P ele? She's not here," Bobby said.

    With an easy motion he popped the cap off an ice-sweating bottle of beer and handed it to Chase. Except for the two men, the Kipuka Club was empty, chairs tucked beneath freshly set tables, glasses shining along the bar, everything waiting for the Sunday night crowds to arrive when the doors opened at five.

"Do you know where she is?" Chase asked, taking the beer.

"Benny told me he saw her up on the mountain this afternoon."

Chase had looked for Nicole on the volcano, but he hadn't found her. As Dane had pointed out, the mountain was a big place. So Chase had come back to Hilo, even though he doubted that Nicole would show up at the Kipuka Club to dance tonight.

But she just might.

Thin as the possibility was, it was his best hope of seeing her.

"Was she all right?" Chase asked.

Bobby stopped in the midst of uncapping his own beer and gave the other man a sharp look. "First Dane, now you. What's going on?"

Chase watched creamy foam climbing the narrow neck of the beer bottle and sliding down the smooth brown glass. Bubbles caressed his knuckles with tiny, bursting kisses before he bent and licked up the savory froth.

"Thanks for the beer," he said, and saluted Bobby with the bottle. "Need a drummer tonight?"

The Hawaiian's black eyes narrowed. "I'm beginning to think I might need a dancer named Pele."

"Wouldn't surprise me."

"So you tell **me**. Is she all right?"

"If she can climb the mountain, she must be." Chase tipped the icy neck of the bottle to his lips.

Bobby said something in Hawaiian. He didn't offer to translate.

Chase didn't ask. He met the giant's black glare without flinching.

"Man trouble," Bobby said flatly. "Worse kine trouble. You be dat man?"

Until that moment Chase had thought Bobby's side trips into pidgin were both amusing and amazing, given the man's education. But this was like the harsh rumble just before a volcano explodes.

"Yes-no?" Bobby demanded.

"Yes or no," Chase said softly, "it's none of your business. Unless Nicole's your woman?"

"You slower dan aa," Bobby said in sardonic tones. "Dat wahine belong **no** man. No-no."

"Ever?"

Bobby lifted his beer bottle and didn't set it down until there was nothing left but a thin sheen of foam inside the bottle. In silence he opened another beer. Only then did he lean over the polished bar and look around the empty club in the mirror.

"You asking for a special reason?" Bobby said mildly.

"I'm asking."

"I get the feeling that's pretty special for you. Asking."

Chase's head moved slightly. It could have been a nod. It could simply have been that he shifted position. He gave away no clues, except perhaps in his very stillness while he waited for Bobby's answer.

"I don't know how she lived on the mainland." Bobby took a long drink of beer. "Don't give a damn either. When she came here, she looked like hell. Pale as death. Eyes like bruises. No life in her hair or her walk. Her idea of a smile made you want to cry."

Chase's eyelids flinched involuntarily. He had seen Nicole look just like that this morning. The image haunted him, making cool sweat break out on his skin as his stomach lurched.

"She didn't let anyone close," Bobby said. He had seen Chase's reaction, the flicker of eyelids and the drawn lines on the other man's face, and it made Bobby want to pound on something. But maybe he was wrong.

Maybe.

"She got work up on the mountain, did her job, and tried like hell to be invisible." Bobby smiled slightly. "Woman like Pele, that isn't easy. Some of the men gave her a try despite her stonewalling. At first she just ran from them."

Chase waited.

So did Bobby.

"And then?" Chase asked through clenched teeth.

"She started turning down the men with a quip and a smile. Her skin changed to gold and her smile was the prettiest flower on the island. And her walk . . ." Bobby's eyes half closed and his lips curved into a very male smile.

"Was it a man?" Chase asked, the words a bitter taste in his mouth.

"A boy. And a dance."

"I don't get it."

Bobby gave him a look that said he wasn't surprised. He had an unhappy suspicion that Nicole had come out on the losing end of whatever had happened between her and the only man who could keep up with her onstage.

"It's easy, haole," Bobby said coolly. "Benny ran away when he was six. She found him up in a kipuka only God and that kid knew about. She didn't know us, but she brought him home when we were going nuts trying to find him. My mother took one look at Nicole, said 'Pele,' and taught her how to dance."

"That's all?"

Bobby laughed hugely, a sound that wasn't as warm as it should have been. "Nicole doesn't ask for much. I couldn't believe the change in the next year."

"What change?"

"She smiled," Bobby said simply. "She laughed. She let herself be touched."

Chase didn't say anything. He didn't have to. What he was thinking was written in the rigid flex of jaw muscles.

For the space of one long swallow of beer, then another one, Bobby let him stew. Then he said, "I'm not talking about sex. I'm talking about family touching. Hugs and pats and kisses and kids on your lap smearing you with fruit juice and ice cream."

Chase didn't want to ask, but he did. It was better than watching Bobby drink beer. "No dates?"

The Hawaiian shook his head.

"No lover?" Chase persisted.

"Nope."

"You sound very sure."

"I am."

"Why?"

"I would have been the man," Bobby said simply.

Chase looked down at Bobby's big left hand where a worn wedding band gleamed.

This time Bobby didn't wait for the question.

"Hazel and I were sleeping separate then, and Nicole was like a little wounded bird to me. I knew I could heal her if she would let me. I wanted to. I used to lie awake nights thinking how it would feel to have her sleeping in my arms, that red hair of hers like a cool fire across my chest."

Absently Bobby spun the beer bottle on the bar top, watching the color leave Chase's face and then slowly return. "Why does thinking of her with me bother you? It never happened. Now it never will."

"Because you and Hazel are back together?" Chase asked roughly.

The other man shook his head. "We have an understanding about wounded birds of both sexes."

Chase couldn't completely conceal his surprise.

The big Hawaiian smiled slightly. "It works better for us than being separate did."

"Then what's the problem with you and Nicole?"

Chase heard his own his own words with a sense of shock. He hadn't meant to ask. But he had to know. The memory of Nicole's hesitations with him and her physical ease with Bobby and Dane were a real part of why Chase had misjudged her so completely.

The Hawaiian looked from his beer to the glittering length of glassware decorating the bar and told himself that it was a good thing his gut told him to trust Chase Wilcox. Otherwise there would be some serious ass kicking coming down.

There still might be.

"A while back some mainland scientist did an experiment," Bobby said slowly. "He raised kittens in a place that had only horizontal lines. No verticals. After four or six weeks he put the kittens in a cage with vertical bars."

Chase waited.

"The kittens kept walking into the bars," Bobby said. "They literally couldn't see them. Their little kitten eyes only knew how to interpret horizontal lines."

With an oddly graceful motion Bobby turned his back to the bar, propped both elbows on the polished surface, and watched the other man with eyes the color and sheen of volcanic glass.

"Keep talking," Chase said.

"I thought you were quicker than that."

"Yesterday I thought so, too."

Bobby's eyes narrowed into glittering dark lines. "It's simple, haole. Somebody conditioned Nicole to avoid sex. She literally couldn't see me as a lover, or any other man. The men who tried to make her see, lost her. I like Nicole too well to lose her just to tangle up some sheets. I want to heal her, not hurt her. She senses that, so she trusts me. But she can't **see** me."

"If I remember that experiment correctly," Chase said, "eventually the kittens adjusted to their new reality. They saw both horizontal and vertical lines."

Slowly Bobby nodded. "Interesting thing is that

no one tried to find out what would have happened if the kittens had been stuck back in the original cage, or in some variation, like a diagonal world. I'll bet it would have paralyzed them. They'd have been terrified to do anything for fear of slamming into more invisible obstacles."

Chase prayed that Bobby couldn't see what the words were doing to him: Nicole finally freed from one cage, only to slam into another one.

Christ Jesus, if only I'd known.

Bobby shifted onto one elbow. The thick muscles in his upper arm swelled with the sheer physical strength that was so much a part of him. The beer bottle looked like a toy in his hand.

"But we're talking about a woman, not kittens," Bobby said. "Nicole **saw** you. She took one look and decided that if any healing got done, you'd be the healer, not me." He smiled, but it went no farther than his brilliant white teeth. "You fuck it up, brother, and I'll be waiting for you."

Chase looked into the bottomless black eyes of Bobby Kamehameha. He didn't blame the Hawaiian for the blunt threat. If Chase had been in Bobby's shoes, he would have reacted in exactly the same way.

No, not quite. I would have trashed Bobby. I would trash any man who hurt Nicole.

The depth of his feeling startled Chase, telling him how guilty he felt for misjudging her.

"You don't have to wait any longer," he said flatly. "I'm here. So are you."

The beer bottle slammed down on the bar with enough force to dent wood. "Are you telling me that—"

Chase cut in ruthlessly. "I'm telling you that kittens aren't the only living things that can be conditioned not to see all of reality. Men can be, too."

A ripple of simple physical rage went through Bobby's huge body as he realized what Chase was saying.

"Are you seeing all of reality now?" Bobby asked, his voice low and hard.

"I'm working on it."

The Hawaiian's mouth shifted into a smile that was almost cruel. "Then you're figuring out what you lost." He flexed his dark, powerful hands. "I guess that's punishment enough."

"Wrong," Chase said softly. "I haven't lost. Stay away from her. If there's any healing to do, I'll do it. Hear me?"

A shadow of amusement crossed Bobby's broad face. It had been years since anyone had challenged him physically. And then it had been four men, not just one.

"Would it change your mind to know that I have a black belt in karate?" Bobby asked idly, looking down at Chase without even having to stand up straight.

"No."

"You think you can beat me?"

"In a fair fight? I doubt it. But I'd beat you, Bobby. One way or another. Count on it."

There was moment of tense silence before Bobby's smile flashed hugely. "It's a good thing I like you, haole son of a bitch. Otherwise we'd trash this club and each other while we sorted things out." He looked around at the tables and chairs and potted flowering plants. "Hell of a waste, too. Just redecorated last fall." Then he turned and pinned Chase with a fierce glance. "But if she comes to me—"

"She won't," Chase interrupted.

He headed for the front door with long strides and wished he was half as certain as he sounded. Even more, he wished he knew why it mattered so much to him that he be the one to heal Nicole's wounds.

But he didn't know why. He knew only that the feeling and the need went too deep to be denied or ignored.

CHAPTER
21

Leaving the Kipuka Club behind, Chase drove to the Kamehameha estate. He was hoping that Nicole had finally gone back to her home.

No such luck. Her car wasn't parked in front of the path that wound down to her cottage. He did a quick circuit of the driveway leading to the big house. Her car wasn't there either.

An anger that came from desperation spiked through him. He wanted to see Nicole, to talk to her, to explain to her that he had misjudged her, that he was sorry, that . . .

What? What else can I do?

Chase didn't know. All he knew was that his need to see Nicole was too deep for words.

When he got to his own cottage, the phone was ringing. Hoping against all logic that Nicole was calling him, he grabbed the receiver.

"Hello." His voice was tight, raw.

"Nicole called Lisa a few minutes ago," Dane said.

Chase let out a harsh breath. "And?"

"The drawing lesson is on for this evening."

"Where?"

"Here."

"I'm coming to dinner."

"No."

"Look—" Chase began roughly.

Dane kept talking. "If Nicole sees your car, she won't come in. If you arrive after her, she'll leave. You know it. I know it. Do you want the kids to know it, too?"

"Hell no, but—"

"Give her some time before you corner her again," Dane interrupted.

Chase swallowed a raw curse. He wouldn't have a chance to drum for Pele tonight because she wouldn't be at the club, she would be teaching his daughter how to draw. He wouldn't have a chance to talk with Nicole until . . .

Never, if she had her way. She didn't want to see him. Period. If he tried to force the issue, he would just make things worse.

If that was possible.

"All right," he said heavily, accepting what he couldn't change. "When should I pick Lisa up?"

"No rush. You can worry about moving her into the cottage when you're here for more than a few weeks at a time."

"That could be Christmas," Chase said, thinking of all the loose ends that needed tying up on the Mount Saint Helens project, plus the various Mexican projects. "I'm going to be commuting back and forth to the mainland for quite a while."

"And you're going to be spending most of the next few weeks hiking all over the island preparing for your book. Leave Lisa with us. We love having her around. She has the sweetest little smile."

"I know. I missed her like hell after the divorce."

Dane hesitated, then said bluntly, "Lynette damn near ruined Lisa. She needs a home, Chase. A real one. You can't give her that right now. Jan and I can."

"So can I."

"Can you?" Dane drew a deep breath. "I realized this morning that a lot has happened to you that I didn't know about. Lynette changed you."

Chase's hand tightened around the phone until his knuckles ached. He remembered all too vividly what he had done to Nicole because he couldn't believe that she wasn't another Lynette, out to wreck homes and lives for no better reason than pure selfishness.

"I won't argue that," he said finally. "But Lisa is my daughter. I love her, and she loves me. Don't fight me on this, Dane. You'll lose. I don't want it that way. There's been much too much hurting already, too much losing. It ends now. Here."

There was a long silence on the other end of the line, followed by a sigh.

"Sorry," Dane muttered. "My protective instincts are in overdrive. I'll call you after Nicole goes home. You can pick Lisa up tonight. I know you wouldn't do anything to hurt her. It's just—Damn it, Chase!"

"I know." His voice ached with the effort of

speaking calmly. "I'm sorry I hurt Nicole. I don't want to corner her. I just have to make her understand that it was my mistake, not hers."

"She'd rather be left alone."

"Scars aren't the same as healing. I learned that this morning when I realized how badly Lynette had scarred me. I thought I was whole again. I wasn't. I don't want Nicole to 'heal' the same way I did. I couldn't live with doing that kind of damage to another human being."

Dane let out another long breath. When he spoke again, his voice was warm, affectionate, full of memories. "That sounds more like the older brother I used to worship. You always were a rough son of a bitch, but you were also the one who taught me the meaning of the word 'decency.'"

Chase's laugh was short, almost sad. "Pull the other one, brother. You fought me tooth and nail over the damnedest things."

"Like I said, full-on hero worship. I had to keep testing myself against you to find out how much I'd grown."

"Now you know," Chase said, his voice layered with emotions.

"What?"

"You outgrew me."

Very gently Chase hung up. For a time he simply stood, seeing nothing. Then he went to the living room and sat by the wall of windows overlooking the garden.

The path to Nicole's cottage was an elusive,

flower-lined thread winding through the trees. He wanted to walk down it, sit on her doorstep, wait for her to return. He wanted her to understand. Somehow she had to understand.

His mistake, not hers.

He had to make it right again. Maybe then he would be able to look in the mirror without his stomach turning over.

And maybe not.

Once, when he had been studying an erupting volcano, the wind had shifted without warning. He had been wrapped in caustic gases and a rain of burning cinders. No matter which way he turned, he had been seared.

It was the same way now. Impressions of the morning kept erupting without warning, burning him.

Nicole's pale face and wounded eyes.

The clear knowledge that she would have walked through fire to avoid him.

A humiliation so deep it had literally sickened her.

Thank you for not hurting me.

His teeth clenched until the pain of it shot through him. He barely noticed as he stared into the night. He had not felt such helpless rage and fear since the day he stood in court and listened while his daughter was handed over to a woman who shouldn't have had custody of a stone.

There had been nothing he could do then. But there was something he could do now. He could talk to Nicole.

Corner her.

The thought made uneasiness spread through Chase, the kind of uneasiness he had felt and ignored last night. Tonight he wouldn't ignore what his instincts were telling him. Dane was right. Nicole wasn't ready to talk to the man who had cut her up so badly, so wrongly.

Yet he needed to talk to her. **Needed.**

He didn't know how long he could hold out against that kind of urgency, so he got back into his car and drove beneath the rising moon to the top of Mauna Loa, putting temptation beyond his reach. When he stood and looked out at the icy, lunar reality of the mountaintop, he knew he should have stayed home.

The mirror he had avoided was all around him.

CHAPTER
22

When Nicole's car pulled to a stop in front of the path to her house, the moon was well above the trees. Although she kept reassuring herself that she would be able to handle the unavoidable moment when she confronted Chase again, she wasn't eager for it. In truth, she was dreading it. When she saw that his car wasn't parked in its usual place, she was so relieved that her hands shook.

Coward.

All right. I'm a coward. So what? I'll be stronger tomorrow anyway.

As excuses went, it wasn't bad. It might just be true. Pleased with salvaging even a little bit of pride, she hurried down the path. Usually she stopped to touch to the cool, fragrant petals of the night-blooming flowers, but not tonight. Tonight she just wanted to hide from . . .

What? Chase Wilcox? Don't be stupid. He can't hurt you any more than he already has.

She stopped. Deliberately her fingers stroked a white flower the size of her hand. The memory of

Chase delicately tasting a hibiscus flashed into her mind, shaking her. She shoved the memory aside. She knew he was a sensual man. She didn't need to be reminded of it, for then her own failure as a woman simply loomed larger.

Like a corpse.

She fled down the path to her cottage, flung her purse onto a chair, and shut the door behind her. The room was stifling. She pushed open the windows, then the French doors leading into the garden. The filmy privacy curtains on either side of her began to lift and turn on the night breeze like streamers of fog.

Common sense told Nicole that she should shower and eat and go to work on her ideas for **Islands of Life.** Yet the instant the thought came, she rejected it.

Chase was head of that project. It was up to him to tell her what to draw, when to draw it, where to draw it. She had already settled that in her mind while she sat in her tiny, hidden kipuka.

She wasn't going to leave Hawaii.

That meant she wasn't going to leave any part of the life she had built for herself here either. After tonight she would continue dancing at the Kipuka Club. She would work at the observatory. She would illustrate **Islands of Life.** She would take Chase's daughter on picnics.

Nothing would change.

Nicole's glance skimmed over the futon. It was still open, the sheets still tangled. The memory of

those few instants when she had felt hot and wild at
Chase's touch raced through her, tightening her
body. The sensations were new, sharp, all but
unbearable. She had no defense against them.

With a choked sound she spun away from the
evidence of her stupidity. Dizziness made her
sway. She reminded herself she had missed two
meals and only played with the one Dane had put
in front of her a few hours ago. No wonder she was
light-headed.

Yet she knew that the truth was much more difficult than a simple lack of food. She wanted desperately to be capable of the kind of response that
would hold a sensual man like Chase Wilcox.

But she wasn't.

Nothing had changed. Nothing would change.
Nothing **could** change. She was the way she was.

Cold.

She had to remember that. She wouldn't survive
another mistake like the one she had made with
Chase. She wasn't even sure right now how she was
going to survive that one. The aftershocks of it
kept tearing through her unexpectedly, shaking
what little calm she had managed to find in the
kipuka.

Eat something, she told herself impatiently.

Her stomach flipped.

All right. Forget that. Maybe later.

First she would wash the sheets. Or at least
change them.

As though she was handling live snakes, she

peeled off the bedding and stuffed it into the corner of her closet along with the rest of her laundry. She told herself she couldn't smell the sweat and musk of sex on the sheets.

She lied.

She told herself she was disgusted.

Then why are you holding your hands against your face and breathing in like it's a fine perfume?

Hastily she scrubbed her hands against her muumuu. The cloth made a sound like smug laughter. The scent that tantalized her was in her mind, not on her hands. It was the scent of the few minutes in her life when she had felt like a woman.

I should have gone to the club and danced. Even if he was there, I should have gone. I'll drive myself crazy pacing this room.

She had to find something to do, or she would be in worse shape than she had been when she fled to the kipuka that morning. Without really thinking about it, she sorted quickly through a stack of CD cases. When she found the one she wanted, she put it in, hit the repeat button, and turned the volume up high enough to make the floor vibrate. Then she waited for the sensuous thunder of Tahitian drums to beat within the aching silence that was herself.

At first she simply listened, letting the primal rhythms sweep through her until they drove everything else from her mind. After a while it wasn't enough just to listen.

Like Chase, the drums called to her in a way she had never really understood. Unlike Chase, she simply accepted the lure of the drums without thought. She had accepted it from the first moment Grandmother Kamehameha had held out her hand, said "Pele," and taught Nicole's body the dances that had always lived in her soul.

When the CD cycled back to the beginning, Nicole threw aside her clothes, shook out her hair, and gave herself to the elemental, driving rhythms of Tahiti. She danced until the CD started over again, and then again.

And again.

She danced until sweat gleamed like molten gold and her hair was wild around her. She danced until she could remember nothing that had come before the endless moment of the drums' rolling thunder and could imagine nothing beyond this moment. She danced until she was a flame burning in the midst of darkness, and she and the drums were one, inseparable.

Whole.

CHAPTER

23

Chase sat by the open window of his own cottage and listened to the thunder of drums rolling through the darkness. He wished he could see Nicole dance but knew it was better this way. Less painful.

If he saw her, he would be forced to face how much he wanted her. With every drumbeat, every heartbeat, he measured his own emptiness.

"Daddy?"

Turning, Chase saw Lisa standing uncertainly in the doorway of her bedroom. He held out his arms and smiled.

"Having trouble sleeping, punkin?"

"Can't."

He smiled at the echo of Benny in her short answer.

As Lisa hurried to him across the wooden floor, the fanciful creatures on her nightgown looked like they were taking flight. Chase had seen the pale silk and golden fairies in a store window and had thought instantly of his elfin daughter. The delighted smile on her face when she opened her present tonight told him he was right.

"Drums keeping you awake?" he asked, lifting and settling Lisa's slight weight in his lap.

"Kinda."

"Just kinda? Kinda isn't enough to keep you awake. What else is kinda nibbling on you?"

Eyes as clear as rainwater looked up at him. Though she tried to sound brave, her lips trembled. "I woke up and thought you were gone. Really gone. Like Mother."

With aching throat and stinging eyes, Chase stroked Lisa's black hair, so like his own. And her need to be loved. That, too, was like him. Lynette hadn't understood love, hadn't needed it, hadn't given it, hadn't even known it existed.

"Never-never," he said huskily. "I love you, Lisa. When I go back to the mainland on business, I'll try to take you. If there are times when I can't, then Jan will kidnap you and hold you hostage until I get back."

Lisa giggled at the thought of her aunt kidnapping her. She snuggled against her father. "Love you, Daddy."

"Love you, too, Lisa." He kissed her hair, felt her cuddle closer, and thanked God that Lynette had decided she didn't want to play mommy after all.

"Stay up?" Lisa asked.

"Sure, punkin. Anything else keeping you awake?"

She shook her head. Fine, silky hair tickled his throat.

"If you think of anything, I'm here," he said. "That's what daddies are for. Listening."

"And hugs."

"Hugs," he agreed. And did.

Lisa's gentle presence eased some of the pain within Chase. For a time he and his daughter simply sat and listened to the urgent drums throbbing in the darkness. He believed now that Nicole didn't have anyone to kiss her hair and hug her and reassure her. She was alone in the same way he had been alone in the courtroom, stunned and disbelieving as he lost everything he loved at the stroke of a judge's gavel.

He wanted to go to Nicole, comfort her as gently as he was comforting Lisa.

He wanted to be comforted in the same way.

"Daddy?"

"Hmmm?"

"Nicole dancing?"

His eyelids closed against a sharp stab of pain. "Probably."

"But she told the club she didn't want to dance tonight." Like Bobby, Nicole had plenty of words for what was important. "Was it a white lie?"

"Maybe she changed her mind about dancing. Probably she just wanted to be alone."

Lisa was silent, thinking about the unpredictable world of adulthood. "Why?"

"Why not? Don't you ever start out to do one thing and end up doing something else?"

"Sure, but . . ."

"But?"

"I'm a kid."

"Adults have kids inside them."

"Like babies?" Lisa asked, startled.

He laughed softly. "No, punkin. I just meant that all adults were kids once, and part of them always stays a kid."

"Oh." She leaned back and looked at as much of him as she could see. "You must have been a really big kid."

"Guess so."

Lisa snuggled into her father. "I'm gonna be big like you."

"You'll be something better."

"What?"

"Big like Jan. A heart big enough to hold the world."

"And Nicole."

It was a moment before Chase could answer. "Yes, like Nicole."

Closing her eyes, Lisa relaxed into her father's strength. "I love Nicole. She always has time for me and never laughs at Benny."

Chase couldn't think of anything to say, so he made a noise that said he was listening.

The drumbeats stopped. He let out a long breath, hoping that Nicole had finally danced until she was tired enough to sleep. God knows he hadn't been able to sleep, even after a savage work-out at the local gym.

The drumbeats began again, rolling thunder through the night.

"Can't we watch her dance?" Lisa asked.

Just the thought of it made his heart leap. "Not tonight, punkin."

"Why?"

"She doesn't want an audience."

Lisa's full little lips pouted. "Sure-sure?"

"Sure-sure." He kissed her forehead. "If Nicole wanted people to watch, she would be dancing at the club. Right now she's dancing just for herself."

"Like Benny."

"Hmmm?"

"Benny draws and never shows. Except to me. He loves me."

"Everybody loves you, punkin."

"Mommy doesn't."

Anger flicked like a whip across Chase. There was no point in denying what the child knew for a fact.

"Remember that puzzle you tried to work at Aunt Jan's?" he asked.

"Dumb thing. Didn't work. Hate it."

"Don't hate it, punkin. It wasn't the puzzle's fault. It wasn't your fault. The blue pieces were missing, that's all. Your mother is like that. All the love pieces are missing. But you're not like that. You're whole. You'll work out just fine."

Lisa looked up at him with wide gray eyes. "You, too."

He smiled and said lightly, "Sure."

But as Chase sat and listened to the drums, he wondered how he had mislaid enough pieces to hurt a woman whose only sin had been to trust him before he trusted himself.

CHAPTER
24

Monday morning Nicole woke to the sound of someone knocking gently at her door. For a moment she froze, terrified that Chase had finally caught up with her.

"Nicole?" Lisa called softly. "Awake?"

Nicole's hammering heart settled into more even rhythms.

What on earth makes you think that Chase would come after you? she asked herself bitterly.

There was no answer but the same inner certainty that had once told her Chase was the man she had been looking for all her life without knowing it.

Well, you finally found him. Lucky you.

"Nicole?"

Hastily she reached out and pulled on the muumuu she had tossed aside last night in the heat of the dance. "Come in, honey."

The door opened hesitantly. "Sure-sure?"

"Sure-sure."

Sitting cross-legged on the futon, Nicole stretched and then held out her hand to the little girl. Smiling, Lisa ran to her second-favorite woman in the whole world.

"Where's Jan?" Nicole asked, yawning. "Or did Dane bring you here?"

"No, Daddy did. We're together now. Always-always."

The last bit of Nicole's sleepiness vanished. She came to her feet in a single lithe surge, as though she expected Chase to be right behind his daughter.

"Where is he?" Nicole asked.

"Asleep. When I woke him up, he said the drums kept him awake until nearly dawn."

"The drums?"

"Your drums."

The thought of Chase staying awake listening to the drums while she danced sent unfamiliar sensations sliding through Nicole. Hot, not cold. Unnerving.

"Sorry. Next time I'll turn down the sound."

"No-no. Fun-fun-**fun.**"

"Sure-sure-sure?" Nicole asked dryly.

"Yes-yes! I sat in Daddy's lap, and we watched the moon and listened." She smiled and looked through her long lashes at Nicole. "I wanted to come and watch, but he wouldn't let me. He said you were dancing for yourself."

Chase's insight was as unexpected as his attack on her yesterday morning had been. Nicole made a small, helpless gesture, then smiled at Lisa with more determination than cheerfulness.

"Are you staying with Ch—with your father all day?"

"I'm staying with him always-always."

"I see."

And what she saw was that it would be very hard for her to avoid Chase after working hours if Lisa was living with him. Yet she knew how much it meant to Lisa to be wanted by her father after being rejected by her mother.

"I'm glad for you, honey," Nicole said in a husky voice. "I know how much you wanted to be with him."

For a moment Nicole was tempted to send Lisa back home before Chase woke up, missed her, and started searching. The first place he would look for his daughter was the last place he had told her not to go: Nicole's cottage.

But when Nicole opened her mouth to tell Lisa she should go back to Chase's cottage before she was missed, she couldn't do it. Without saying a word, she closed her mouth.

I'm hiding again. But this time Lisa would be the one hurt.

The little girl was hypersensitive to adult rejection, especially a woman's.

"Have you eaten?" Nicole asked, taking Lisa's hand.

The girl shook her head

"Good-good." Nicole smiled. "We can have breakfast together. Just give me time to shower, okay?"

"I'll get Daddy up so he can—"

"No," Nicole interrupted sharply. Then, much more gently, "No, honey. Let him sleep. Why don't you try drawing the garden path while I shower? Remember what I told you last night about shadows all coming from the same angle and how things get smaller the farther they are away from you?"

Lisa nodded, her gray eyes serious.

With an encouraging smile and a wave in the direction of the drawing supplies, Nicole went to the shower.

And every step of the way she wished she could get her hands on the bitch who had made a seven-year-old child as serious as an adult. Lisa didn't smile often enough and rarely laughed. She simply vanished at the first sign of disapproval, as though she had no defenses against it, no sense of her own worth.

Nicole knew how painful and damaging it was to feel that kind of personal failure. It infuriated her that a child as gentle, bright, and loving as Lisa had been driven so far into a protective shell by a woman who wasn't worthy of the name.

The shower cooled Nicole off some, but she still got angry at the thought of Lisa's mother. When she went back to the living room, Lisa was drawing quietly. Every few seconds she would look unhappily at the lines she had drawn and the pencil in her hand.

Nicole knew that Lisa didn't have a tenth the natural talent Benny had, but it shouldn't prevent her from enjoying drawing. It was the pleasure, not the sketch itself, that was important.

"I like that," Nicole said, stroking Lisa's black hair. It was shiny and clean, silky and wild because it hadn't seen a comb for at least twelve hours. "I can feel the coolness of the shadows."

Lisa looked up at Nicole, smiled shyly, and returned to her drawing. She was less hesitant now, less critical of the result. After a few minutes she began humming quietly, totally unaware of the rest of the world.

Smiling, Nicole started slicing fresh fruit for breakfast. Before she was finished, Benny appeared at the cottage's garden door.

"Eat?" he asked.

Nicole smiled. "Sure-sure. But if you want eggs, you'll have to beg them from your mother. I'm out."

"Fruit." Benny managed to get a world of approval into the single word, telling Nicole that eggs weren't necessary.

He stepped into the room, graceful and sure-footed despite his limp. When he spotted Lisa, he broke into a beguiling smile.

"Li-sa," he said, accenting her name oddly, musically.

Her smile came and went so quickly that it was like a shadow of light chasing across her serious face. The two children had met on one of Nicole's picnics. Benny had been fascinated by the fragile little girl. It was a fascination Lisa returned in full.

"Hi, Benny," Lisa said. "How did you get here?"

"Home." He gestured with his hand toward the big house on top of the hill.

Lisa's smile came again and stayed. "Yours?"

Benny nodded.

"The garden, too?" she asked.

He nodded again.

"And the beach?"

"All."

Then he smiled and held out his hand to Lisa in a gesture that reminded Nicole of the time his grandmother had extended her hand and drawn Nicole into another world.

"Share all with you, Li-sa," Benny said. "Come."

Forgetting about her drawing, Lisa jumped to her feet.

Nicole was too startled at hearing six consecutive words out of Benny to protest when the two children ran through the French doors and into the beckoning Eden.

"No swimming until I get there!" she called after them.

Benny's answer was a wave that somehow managed to tell Nicole that she was being foolish—he would never do anything that might hurt the delicate, gray-eyed little girl.

Quickly Nicole packed fruit and honey muffins into a wicker basket, changed into her bathing suit, and gathered up her sketchbook. As an afterthought she grabbed a handful of towels. She stepped into the garden and hesitated, wondering if she should get a bathing suit for Lisa.

The thought of waking Chase stopped Nicole cold. She decided that Lisa could swim just fine in the cotton shorts and tank top she was wearing. As for Benny, he usually swam in whatever he happened to be wearing when the mood took him.

Although it was barely eight o'clock, the black-sand beach was already warm. So was the water. It was a warmth that varied only a few degrees throughout the year.

One of the hardest things for Nicole to get used to in Hawaii had been not only the lack of seasons but the lack of any real change in the weather at all from sunrise to midnight. On the wet side of the island, where most natives had always lived, the sun came up, the clouds came up, and the trade winds pushed them against the mountains for the afternoon rain.

The Hawaiian language didn't even have a word for weather. The closest it came was a word describing the rare days when the trade winds died and the southern winds blew, bringing a muggy, stifling heat to the islands. Then natives spoke of "volcano weather" and left Pele offerings of food and fiery drink on the dark, steaming floor of Kilauea's crater.

Nicole glanced up toward the direction where Kilauea rose. Automatically she looked for signs of an eruption with the same casual eye that mainlanders used to measure thunderheads as a potential birthplace of tornadoes.

Today there were no visible signals of the seething magma that always waited beneath the island's volcanic skin. The surface of the land was quiet instead of restless with the rhythmic quivering of molten stone. That faint shivering was the only outward sign of the magma relentlessly testing the hardened lid of former eruptions, seeking the fractures and fissures that would become channels for the birth of yet more land.

But despite its long period of quiet, Kilauea showed no signs of revving up for a big show. Neither did any of the smaller craters that ran in a chain down the mountain's flank.

Looks like the hotshot pool is going for a record, Nicole thought as she settled cross-legged onto a towel.

For several weeks rumors of a coming eruption had been racing like juicy gossip through the observatory. So far they were just rumors. Other than the patterns of tremors that the scientists argued about every night in the Kipuka Club, nothing had happened.

In any case she knew that the volcano wasn't on the edge of eruption, because all of the active rift zones were still open to tourists. When that changed, the road up to Kilauea would be lined with cars driven by expectant natives and tourists waiting for the big show. On Hawaii, volcanic eruptions were usually predictable and polite, and always awesomely beautiful. As a spectator sport they had no equal.

"Niiicolllle!"

She glanced up from her idle sketch pad in time to see Benny and Lisa burst from a clump of coconut palms and race over the sand toward her. Benny had a huge green nut in his hands. His uneven legs weren't a problem when it came to climbing. He shinnied up and down coconut palms quicker than a mainland cat.

The first few times Nicole had watched Benny climb a tall palm, she had held her breath with fear that he would hurt himself in a fall. Now she just licked her lips in anticipation of the fruit he would bring down. Raw coconut milk and meat was a taste she had quickly acquired on the Big Island, right along with macadamia nuts and pit-roasted pig. She had even tried poi. Once.

Benny pulled out a pocketknife and went to work on his prize. Nicole had never figured out how he got into the coconut with such a small tool. It took her a hammer and a hard stone to get the job done, or a cleaver as long as her arm.

The three of them ate in a companionable silence punctuated by tiny giggles from Lisa when various kinds of fruit juices trickled between her fingers and down her arms. Watching her, Nicole had the feeling that getting grubby was a relatively new delight to the girl.

"C'mon," Nicole said after they finished the

snack. Standing, she held out her hand. "Time to wash up."

Disappointment clouded Lisa's transparent eyes as she looked at the path leading back to the cottages.

"No. This way," Nicole said. She pointed toward the turquoise sea.

Lisa looked down at her juice-smeared shorts. "Can't."

"It won't hurt your clothes," Nicole said.

Lisa shook her head.

Benny touched her thin shoulder. "Swim with me."

"Can't. Daddy said." She took a breath so big her shoulders strained, then spit out the awful truth and waited for the worst. "Don't know how."

Benny was too surprised to say a word. The idea of someone not knowing how to swim was as astonishing to him as not knowing how to walk.

Nicole knelt next to the tightly waiting Lisa, whose little body was clenched against the disapproval she feared. "Swimming is like drawing, honey. Nobody is born knowing how to do it. But you can learn, if you want to. Do you?"

Lisa looked at the ocean and said slowly, doubtfully, "It looks awful big."

"That's okay. You're only in one part of it at a time."

The sound of male laughter froze Nicole in place for an instant. When she looked over her shoulder, she saw Chase standing in the shadow of the coconut palms. He was almost close enough to touch, wearing nothing but black swim trunks, his own potent masculinity, and a smile.

The sight of him was like a blow. She nearly went down beneath a sensual tide of memories. She had touched the rippling male power of this man, held him, felt him move inside her.

And failed to please him in any way at all.

Nicole flushed, then went pale. Silently she prayed that she was the only one to notice. She glanced around almost frantically. There was no subtle way to escape.

Chase ignored her panic. He had expected it. What he hadn't expected was her beauty in full sunlight, smeared with fruit juice and sand. His crystalline gray eyes admired the braided fire of her hair, her golden skin, and most of all the smooth, flexible strength of her body. Though her two-piece bathing suit was modest by tropical beach standards, it revealed a lush amount of curves. He wanted to run his hands and then his mouth over every bit of them.

He had seen the instant of sensual awareness and approval in her eyes when she'd looked at him.

He had also seen the color wash from her in the next instant as she searched for a way to avoid him.

"Daddy!" Lisa jumped up and threw herself into Chase's arms. Then her smile faded. "Oh, I forgot. I'm too dirty for hugging."

She pushed away from his chest and looked at

him with wide eyes, obviously expecting him to be unhappy with her.

"Are you? Where?" he asked, making a big deal out of looking her over and not seeing the food and the less identifiable stains that had come from racing through Eden down an overgrown path. "You look like perfect hugging material to me." Smiling, he cuddled her close and kissed her sticky cheek. "Mmmmm," he said, licking his lips. "Got any more of that coconut for me?"

Lisa's whole face brightened. Grinning, she turned her other cheek up to be kissed.

He gave it smacking approval.

With a secret smile she burrowed against her father's furry chest, confident again.

"Mother always got mad at me if I was dirty," Lisa confessed.

Chase spoke calmly in spite of the lash of fury that went through him. "Did she? Well, I'm not your mother. I think kids should play hard, get dirty, and take baths."

Over his daughter's head Chase watched Nicole kneel with a dancer's fluid grace and begin gathering up the remains of breakfast. Saying nothing, she tucked fruit and napkins into the wicker basket. After a few moments she stood with the heart-stopping grace he had to see each time to truly believe. When she shook out the towel, it became clear to the children that Nicole was leaving.

"Aren't you going to teach me how to swim?"

Lisa asked Nicole plaintively, unwrapping her arms from her daddy.

Nicole forced a smile. "That's what fathers are for."

"Me," Benny said. He stepped close to Lisa, silently saying that he would help Lisa learn to swim.

Smiling brightly, emptily, Nicole eased back toward the path up the hill. "You couldn't have a better teacher than Benny, Lisa. He taught every fish in the lagoon how to swim."

Lisa's eyes widened as she looked into Benny's clear dark gaze. "True-true?"

Wisely, he smiled and said nothing.

Chase set Lisa on the coarse black sand and said to Benny, "Take her down to the water and get her feet wet. Just her feet."

Solemnly Benny nodded. "Feet."

Chase ruffled Benny's hair and squeezed his lean shoulder approvingly. "I'll be right with you after Nicole and I work out some scheduling problems on the book."

The kids didn't wait to hear any more. Hand in hand, they raced toward the warm, softly foaming water.

"Just her feet!" Chase called again.

"Sure-sure!" both children said together without looking back.

Chase watched long enough to see Benny pull Lisa to a stop, then stand in front of her so that she would have to walk through him to get more than her feet wet.

"I like that boy's style," Chase said as he turned toward Nicole.

He was impatient to get the first, awkward words behind them. Somehow he had to make her understand that there had been nothing wrong with her. He had been the one at fault. Completely.

But when he turned around, there was nothing behind him except an empty garden path and palm trees swaying beneath the caressing wind.

CHAPTER
25

It was Thursday night before Chase managed to corner Nicole again.

"Are you going to run forever?" he asked quietly.

She turned toward him so fast that she almost lost her balance. For an instant she felt like there were iron bands around her lungs, squeezing out her breath. Air returned in a gasp, and with it came a surging blush that she was helpless to control.

Conversations around the Kipuka Club paused as people turned curiously toward Nicole and Chase. Though neither one of them had said anything to anyone except Dane, somehow people had concluded that something had happened between the untouchable Pele and the mainland lady-killer.

Rumors linking Nicole to a newcomer had been spread before, but she had put an end to them with a quip and a shrug. She hadn't been able to pull that off this time around. She knew she looked as pale and tense as she felt.

"Exercise is good for you," she said, shrugging, avoiding Chase's eyes, refusing to really look at him.

"Then let's exercise together."

Nicole went white.

"On the mountain," he said with false calm.

He hated the way she flinched from him. After nearly five days of stalking her, only to have her slide like fire through his fingers, his temper was more than a little raw. The fact that it was his own fault that she was running away didn't make him feel any better. It simply put an edge on his temper.

He hadn't known just how sharply memories could haunt, both the bad memories and the good.

Nicole haunted him.

And ran from him.

"Illustrations, remember?" he prodded. "Or have you decided to back out of the **Islands of Life** project?"

"No."

Her voice, like her face, was strained. Right now she was wishing she had resigned from the project no matter how much she needed the work. She hadn't realized how painful it would be to finally see Chase up close. It had been bad enough turning around time and again to find him watching her with his bleak gray eyes and then to know that sooner or later she wouldn't be able to escape.

Like tonight. She was trapped, forced to trade empty social words with Chase while humiliation twisted her heart and her stomach. And she had to endure it all under the very interested eyes of her co-workers.

They knew. All of them. She might as well have hung signs from every one of the Kipuka Club's ceiling beams.

"In that case, let's get going," Chase said neutrally. "I've made a provisional list of places, starting with the fire pit and going all the way to the sea. I figure it will take at least two weeks, more likely four, just to visit each area and select the various microenvironments that should be dealt with in detail."

Nicole nodded stiffly.

"With luck, we'll find everything we need on Kilauea," he continued. "Otherwise we'll have to shift to Mauna Loa. That would mean overnight camping." His eyes narrowed at the appalled look that came to Nicole's face.

"I thought you'd feel like that," he said, leaning toward her, his voice so soft that only she could hear. "Don't you know that the last thing I'd do is touch you again?"

Her eyelids flinched with helpless pain. She hadn't guessed that he would be so cruel as to bring up her sexual shortcomings again, and in such a public place.

When Chase saw her lips go pale, he heard the echo of his own words and realized that she had taken them wrong. Afraid that she would flee again, he put his hand on her arm and fought to keep his voice too low for anyone to overhear.

"I didn't mean— Damn it, there's nothing wrong with you as a woman," he said. "All I meant was—"

She turned away, cutting off his words.

"Nicole."

When she stopped and turned around slowly, Chase felt the curious stares of the people in the club like bugs crawling on his skin. It had been the same since Monday—people acting as though he and Nicole were living on center stage acting out their lives to a standing-room-only crowd.

What really bothered him was that Nicole was suffering the most from the scrutiny. Before their one-night affair she had joked with the people she met and turned aside any man who didn't get the hint with a quip and a smile. From her friends— men and women alike—she had received welcoming smiles, a friendly pat, even a quick hug if she hadn't seen the person for a while.

It was different now.

Every man who had been to the Kipuka Club last Sunday seemed to know that Nicole had joined the pool of sexually available women. To most men it made little difference beyond a certain speculative quality to their look, as if they were rearranging their mental landscape, putting her in a new category, and then forgetting about it.

Some men didn't forget. They acted like she had been stripped naked and thrown into an invisible sexual arena. Because they expected to be successful eventually, they pursued her more openly and relentlessly than they ever had before.

Chase understood exactly what had happened, and why. As long as the prowling males were sure that Nicole wasn't sleeping with any man, they took her rejection with reasonably good humor, especially when she made a witty joke of their attempts. But that had changed. Now the men sensed that she had been in bed with Chase Wilcox.

Chastity and humor had been Nicole's shield and weapon against the most persistent men. Though Chase hadn't meant to, Sunday night he had stripped those defenses from her. Now she was exposed. Vulnerable. What had once been humorous advances were now anything but a joke.

Knowing it made Chase furious, but there was nothing he could do about the men, no way he could protect Nicole. Not when she ran from him at every opportunity.

He couldn't decide which made him feel most like a piece of shit—her running, the men who pursued her like greyhounds going after a bleeding rabbit, or the male friends whose touch she now avoided.

For Nicole there were no more friendly pats on the arm, no small talk, no sense of being a friend among friends. Dane had mentioned her withdrawal to Chase more than once. Other people certainly must have noticed.

Chase didn't know whether she simply couldn't bear being touched anymore or if she was afraid of appearing to invite more than friendship from the men around her. The cause didn't really matter because the result was the same. She had cut herself off from the very people who might have reined in the more predatory men.

Nothing in the situation made Chase feel better about himself. The more he knew about Nicole, the more he understood how completely, and how cruelly, he had misjudged her.

This running away had to stop. It wasn't doing either of them any good.

"We need to decide on the drawings," he said.

"Make a list of plants you want illustrated and in which stages of development," she said tonelessly. "Tell me when and where you need me. I'll be there."

"Here. Now. We have to talk. This can't go on any longer."

For the first time Nicole met Chase's eyes. They were cold, metallic, like hammered silver. Her stomach twisted as she understood that there was no place left for her to run.

"Hey, my little jalapeño," Fred called cheerfully from a few tables away. He came up behind Nicole and slid an arm around her rib cage, just beneath her breasts. Just barely. "I've been looking for you."

She tried to step beyond Fred's reach.

His arm tightened, crowding her closer to him. He bumped his hip rapidly against her. "When are you going to teach me how to dance sexy?"

"On the thirtieth of February, just like I promised," she said, hoping that she was the only one who heard the strain in her voice.

Once Fred would have let go of her with a laugh and a shake of his head. Now he simply nudged intimately against her again.

She tried to pry his arm off without making a scene. He didn't budge, except to give her the hip shot again.

"Jalapeño, the moves I've got in me can't wait that long," he said. "Know what I mean?"

She sensed the savage tension in Chase's body as though her nerves were connected to his. She felt trapped, half wild. She couldn't bear being touched by the overconfident, overeager scientist one second longer.

"Joke's over," she said between her teeth. "Let go of me."

"Do I look crazy? The fun's just beginning." Fred trailed his hand from her ribs to her waist and back up again. "I'm going to teach you a few horizontal moves that will blow your hot little—"

Chase's hand shot out.

Fred's words stopped in a gasp of surprise and pain.

Chase yanked the man's hand off Nicole with a ruthless twisting motion that stopped just short of breaking bones.

Instantly she backed out of reach.

With a cold smile Chase closed his hand around Fred's and squeezed until the man's face was as pale as Nicole's had been.

"You know," Chase said casually, watching Fred with frankly lethal intent, "in the last few days

I've had a bellyful of your blue comedy routine. Clean up your act or I'll put it on the hospital charity circuit."

Fred's breath came out in a rush when Chase released his fingers. Warily Fred flexed his hand and looked from Chase to Nicole and back.

"I thought you were through with her," Fred muttered.

"You thought wrong," Chase said softly, his voice vibrating with anger. "Any man who wants to touch her better wait for an engraved invitation. **From her.** Pass the word, pal, or there's going to be a rash of broken hands on the mountain."

Fred hesitated, flexed his hand again, and shrugged. "February thirtieth it is," he said, glancing at Nicole.

"Sure," she said, her voice faint.

When Fred turned away, she shuddered, unable to control her emotions any longer.

"Are you all right?" Chase asked in a low voice.

"I'm fine," she said, the words too quick, too brittle. Then she whispered helplessly, "Oh, God, I hate being a **thing**!"

Chase remembered what she had said about marriage, about being a man's **thing**. It made him sick and angry at the same time. For two cents he would have cut loose and trashed the club, just for the bitter physical joy of it. But the club hadn't earned his anger any more than Nicole had.

"Let's get out of here," he said, his mouth grim. "You look like you could use some air."

Nicole stumbled as she turned toward the door. Her normal grace had deserted her.

"I'm going to take your arm," Chase warned, his voice low.

"I—" She stumbled again.

As he caught her to support her, he saw Dr. Vic close in from across the room.

"Nicole?" Dr. Vic asked earnestly. "Are you all right?"

She forced a smile onto her face. "Just a little tired."

The scientist gave Chase a hard look.

Chase gave it right back, too angry to be politic with the elderly professor. "Excuse us, sir. I thought some fresh air would help Nicole. The club is a little close tonight."

"Umm, yes. Fred is one of our best and brightest scientists, but he can be a little, er, cloying. I'll speak to him about it. I can put a stop to this sort of thing at work, but . . ."

"Bobby and I will take care of the club," Chase said flatly. "You just pass the word to the crotch hounds at the lab that sexual harassment is still a crime."

"Who else besides Fred?" Dr. Vic asked, looking unhappily at Nicole.

"Oh, you'll recognize them," Chase said with a narrow smile. "They'll be the ones in body casts."

Despite the danger that fairly radiated from Chase, his grip on Nicole's arm was gentle as he led her toward the club's side door. Gentle but unbreakable. He had waited as long as he was going to wait before they talked.

Running wasn't helping her, and it sure as hell wasn't doing him any good either.

In darkness and silence Nicole and Chase stood just beyond the partially open side door of the club. They were in a small fenced yard that ended at the alley. There was very little chance that anyone would bother them. The side door was the service entrance to the club, and everyone who worked inside was already there.

A curtain of mist lowered from the clouds and swept across the tiny yard. Nicole felt the rain as through glass, a coolness more sensed than experienced. Now that the running was over, she was oddly relieved, almost light-headed. She felt no need to go back inside out of the rain. She preferred wet privacy to a dry, crowded, avidly curious club.

Chase unzipped the windbreaker he was wearing and slipped it over her shoulders. She looked at him, surprise showing clearly in her pale brown eyes.

"That's not necessary," she said quietly. "I'm used to the rain. Hawaiian rains are like sunshine. Warm."

"Wear it."

He heard the anger seething just beneath the surface of his voice. With a quiet curse he ran a hand through his hair. Now that he had her alone, he didn't know where to begin.

How do you ask a woman politely, subtly, why the hell she slept with you?

No brilliant insight came to him.

Fuck subtle.

"Why did you sleep with me?" he asked.

Nicole turned her face up to the rain, accepting it just as she accepted that she had run as far as she could without leaving behind everything she loved. She wouldn't do that. No man was worth that. Not even Chase Wilcox.

"It seemed like a good idea at the time." Her mouth turned down in a bittersweet smile at her own expense.

"That's no answer."

"Why do you care? It's not going to happen again. Is that what's worrying you? That I might expect something from you? I don't. All I want is to be left alone."

"That's not—"

"No," she said, cutting across his words. "You thought I was after Dane. I wasn't. You apologized. I accepted. That's the end of it."

Slowly Chase shook his head. "But it hasn't ended," he said, his voice dark, strained. "I hurt you badly. You're still hurting. I want to . . . heal you."

Nicole closed her golden eyes and tried to think of nothing at all. "That isn't possible. You can't heal a corpse."

"What?" Chase asked, shaken.

"You're the one who pointed out that I was like a corpse in bed. You don't heal a corpse. You bury it and walk away." She fixed him with eyes that were like tarnished gold. "So walk away, Dr. Wilcox. The autopsy is over, the dirge has been sung, the grave is sealed, the—"

"Stop it," he interrupted harshly.

With an effort she bit back the scalding flow of words. After a moment she took a deep, ragged breath and wrapped her arms around herself as though she was cold.

Chase watched her with haunted, quicksilver eyes, hearing her words echo, trying to make them fit with the hesitant lover who had thanked him for not hurting her.

"What the hell happened to you before you came to Hawaii?" he whispered hoarsely.

Closing her eyes, she said nothing.

Very gently he put his hands on her shoulders. Beneath his palms her whole body radiated rejection and refusal.

"You haven't dated anyone, you weren't after Dane, and you were more frightened than passionate with me." Chase's hands tightened on her shoulders. "Why did you do it, Nicole? Why did you sleep with me?"

"Chalk it up to loose morals. I'm a slut."

"Bullshit!"

Her eyes opened. They were clear and hard. "But that's what you saw when you looked at me.

That's what I proved when I went to bed with a man I hadn't known more than three days. As you said to Dane, what 'paragon of virtue' would—"

"Don't do it," Chase interrupted, his voice low, warning.

"What?"

"Use my words like knives against yourself."

"But they work so well. Truth is like that. A knife."

He closed his eyes, disgusted and angry at everyone and everything, but most of all at himself. "Then use it on me. I made the mistake, not you. You're the furthest thing from a slut I've ever met."

"You thought I was as hot as my hair," she said. Her mouth turned down again as she remembered another man's words, another man's knives slicing her.

The only thing hot about you is your hair.

"I believed you were after Dane," Chase said, his voice both gritty and patient as he tried to make Nicole understand that it had been his fault, not hers. There was no need for her to look so drawn, so fearful, a woman waiting to be hurt again.

"I wasn't after Dane," she said dully. "I wasn't after anyone. Until you."

"I believe you, Nicole." He saw the surprise on her face as his words finally sank in.

"I— All right," she said. "Good. That's something."

"I've watched you since we—since that morning. I've seen how it really is for you."

Numbly Nicole turned her face up to the rain and waited to be told again about her failures as a woman.

"At the observatory you ignore the single men," Chase said, "or you top their sexy innuendos, and you don't give an inch otherwise. But you used to allow the married men to touch you. A hug here, a pat on the arm there, a slap on the shoulder and a smile. Why? Why them and not the other men?"

"You said it yourself. They're married. Safe."

Chase thought of Bobby Kamehameha and smiled thinly. "Not always, Nicole. Not always."

"They are to me! I would never—" Her voice broke beneath the tension that made her flesh like carved stone.

The need to flee was so great that it was like craving oxygen after spending too long holding her breath. She knew what Chase was heading toward. He was going to make her admit that she had wanted him. Then the depth of her failure as a woman would be even more humiliating.

She didn't know if she could endure hearing about it from his lips all over again.

And then she knew that she couldn't bear it.

Yet she couldn't get away. His hands had slid from her shoulders to her wrists, and he was gently unwrapping her arms from their defensive position around her waist. If she tried to move away from him, the strong fingers would close, holding her in place.

No way out.

Trapped.

CHAPTER
26

Carefully Chase took a breath and thought about what Nicole had said. He had to be certain he understood what she was telling him, what the words actually **meant.** He had learned how much pain it caused when he misunderstood her. He didn't want to hurt her again. He didn't think she could take that.

He knew he couldn't.

"And the single men?" he asked softly. "You avoid them because they aren't safe?"

Her shrug was jerky, harsh. Adrenaline flooded through her, yet she couldn't run, couldn't hide. Almost frantically she cast about in her mind for weapons, reasons, something, anything that would make him leave her alone.

Suddenly it came to her. Words were weapons. And the most lethal weapon of all was truth.

She should know. The truth of her own failure as a woman had destroyed her like a river of molten rock, burning alive everything in its path, covering the ashes with a thick layer of stone.

But she had survived.

She had even conquered her rocky shell enough to grow again, putting out tentative leaves and flowers of friendship, soaking up the affection that came in return like a plant soaking up warm rain and tropical sunshine.

"As far as I can tell," Chase continued gently, relentlessly, "you haven't slept with any other man in the whole state of Hawaii, **so why did you sleep with me?**"

Nicole shuddered and turned her face away from him to look at the tiny enclosed garden. "I've asked myself that at least a hundred times a day," she whispered, telling him as much of the truth as she knew.

"And?"

"It's pretty simple. I have a real talent for trusting bastards. You're my second, you see."

His breath came in sharply. Eyes the color of rain probed her drawn face. Pain accentuated her cheekbones and darkened her eyes. Her lips were moving again, but she was speaking so softly that he could barely hear. He leaned toward her intently.

"No, that's not quite true," she whispered, listening to her own thoughts, learning from them even as she spoke.

And it was anger she was learning. She had been wrong to trust Chase, but that didn't give him the right to destroy her.

"You're different from my former husband," she said. "Next to you, Ted was a legitimate son of gentle society. He was merely impatient with me and unkind about my shortcomings as a woman. You have a cruelty in you that cuts all the way to my soul."

She looked at Chase again, her face as calm as her words were bitter. "I hope that cruelty cuts both ways."

"Nicole," he whispered, understanding only her pain and the knowledge that being his lover had cost her much more than she could afford. Unconsciously he caressed the softness of her inner arm, wanting to reassure, to soothe, to pleasure her.

"No," she whispered, shivering.

Her body had come alive with the female certainty of Chase so close to her, reaching out to her. Burning her. His hand was strong and hard, gentle with her softer flesh in spite of the intensity that came off him in waves, like heat.

"Don't tease me with what I can't deliver," she said, her voice shaking. "Despite my past performances, I've just discovered I'm not a masochist."

"I know. You were made for pleasure, not pain."

As he spoke, he slowly stroked the length of her arm again. He saw her eyes widen in shock and felt the ripple of response racing through her so clearly it could have been his own body trembling, not hers.

She's turned away all men for years, yet she shivers at my touch.

The realization sent a shock wave of desire slamming through Chase. The force of it surprised him. He had felt nothing like it except the night he had been driven by his own need to take her too quickly, before he knew her.

Before he knew himself.

He wouldn't make that mistake again. She had been hurt too many times, yet against all odds, all cruel experience, she had turned to him for healing. He would never hurt her again. It was like hurting himself. The next time he held her in his arms, it would be a healing thing. For both of them.

Slowly Chase bent his head and at the same time lifted Nicole's wrist to his mouth. Her skin was silky, cool despite the frantic pulse beating just beneath her skin. As if she were a flower brought to his lips for a taste of honey, he touched his tongue to her pulse and delicately closed his teeth over her inner wrist.

Nicole's breath stopped. She wanted to run from his sensuality. She wanted to drench herself in his sensuality. Trembling, she swayed, caught between her own warring needs.

"This time I'll be good to you when we make love," he said huskily. "This time I'll give you the pleasure you deserve."

Desire and fear fought for control of her. Fear won. She tried to jerk her wrist from his grasp. He was too quick, too strong.

"Make **love**?" she asked in disbelief, her voice shaking. "Are you crazy?"

"Not anymore." Chase traced the shadow network of her wrist veins with the tip of his tongue, licking up raindrops and the indefinable taste of woman. "Give me another chance, sweet dancer. There's so much that we can share with each other."

"I don't have anything to give a man. Ask my ex-husband. Oh, God, why bother? Ask yourself!"

Nicole wrenched free and bolted back into the club.

Chase could have stopped her, but he was too shocked by what she had said. For long minutes he stood without moving, not noticing the rain pressing his shirt against his chest and making his lavalava cling wetly to his hips.

I don't have anything to give a man. Ask my ex-husband. Ask yourself!

Chase wished he could forget his cruel summary of Nicole as a woman. He couldn't. It ate at him like acid.

Even worse, it ate at her. She believed him.

A wave of pain went through him, making him grimace. **Christ Jesus, she believed it.**

If she had been a courtesan, his words would have been as true as they were brutal. But she wasn't a professional toy. She was a woman who had been taught to believe that she had nothing to offer a man.

Now that he knew that, everything about that night changed. Her responses to him had been generous and sweet and trembling with her potential for intense sensuality. A potential he had first ignored, then scorned.

284 ⁊ ELIZABETH LOWELL

A potential he would kill to have offered to him again.

"She dropped this," Bobby said laconically.

Slowly Chase focused on the rain-wet exterior of the club.

Bobby stood in the doorway, a dripping windbreaker in his huge hand, watching while pain pulled Chase's face into bleak lines.

Automatically Chase reached for his jacket.

Bobby jerked his hand, taking the jacket out of reach. "Stay away from her, haole son of a bitch."

"No." He took a sharp breath and said harshly, "I can't. Don't get in my way, Bobby. Two people hurting is enough."

After a moment the other man smiled oddly and lobbed the windbreaker at Chase, letting him push past the doorway into the club's dimly lit interior.

The room was full of refugees from the university and the observatory. Chase nodded to the people he knew but didn't stop to talk with anyone. Bobby hadn't delayed him for long, but it had been enough: Nicole had already slipped behind the stage curtain.

Savagely Chase threw his windbreaker into an empty chair. With angry motions he stripped off his dripping shirt, dumped it over the back of the chair, and went to the rear of the stage. Behind the curtain he took his position at the drums and waited motionlessly, his mind churning.

She's afraid of men, afraid of sex, yet she slept with me a few days after we met.

Why did she trust me?

Even as he began to drum, calling the dancers onstage, the question ate at him. It gave a hard edge to his playing, as though the drums themselves were asking questions of the night.

When the curtain rose and students stepped onto the stage, no glorious flame stood in the wings, waiting to burn. Nicole's absence drove into Chase, making him want to cry out at the pain he had given in place of the pleasure she deserved.

Why didn't I trust her?

The memory of a snapshot of Nicole came to him, a woman standing on a black-sand beach, her hair a glorious swirl of fire around her, and Lisa laughing among the flames. He had held that snapshot in his hand and stared at it until he was raw with hunger.

He wanted Nicole before he even knew her name.

He wanted her before he ever saw her lush body.

He wanted her before he saw her fiery dance.

A single look at a snapshot and he had turned his life upside down and flown to Hawaii. He had told himself that he was worried about Dane, that no man could stand against the temptation of Nicole.

Was that how it was for her? Did she look at me and want me enough to come to me despite her fear?

There was no answer but the primal beat of the drums speaking darkly beneath his hands.

I was so certain that Dane was in danger. Why?

That answer was simple. Chase didn't believe any

man could look at Nicole and not want her enough to throw over everything to have her. If he had sat down and thought about it rationally, he would have known that no woman could affect every man the same way.

But he hadn't thought. He had looked, wanted, and been certain in his gut that every man would feel the way he did.

One look.

Consuming desire.

The rhythms of the dance radiated from the drums, but beneath the complex beats the shadow of Chase's barely restrained emotions prowled through the darkened room. He had been in such a rush to taste the honey that he had crushed the blossom, and in the end had tasted only bitterness, given only injury.

Christ, if I'd only known . . . !

Sound poured out of the drums in a relentless thunder that pounded through the night, calling up a darkness that had nothing to do with a lack of light.

The students couldn't keep up with the furious rhythms. One by one, dancers sank to the stage floor, completely spent. They didn't even try to chant encouragement to the remaining dancers, for they didn't have words or legends to equal the drums' raging soliloquy of injury and regret.

Nicole came and watched from the wings, and her heart beat as wildly as the drums. Before Chase began to play, she had told Bobby that she wasn't going to dance, that she was going home.

Then the drums had spoken to her from the darkness, telling her things mere words couldn't describe.

She hadn't been able to refuse the seething rhythms of anger and isolation and regret. They spoke to her so exactly, so perfectly. She could no more turn away from their dark, syncopated violence than Kilauea could turn away from its own searing heart of molten stone.

With quick motions she took down her hair and stepped onto the stage. A murmuring swept through the room, a low wave of sound that was her other name.

"Pele."

From the first step, the first thud of bare heel on wooden floor, the dance was different. There were no flashing smiles, no teasing, flirting hips, no graceful fingers describing languid invitations. Tonight Pele's body described an anger that equaled the drums' wild discontent. She wasn't a laughing girl dancing her suitors into the ground. She was a goddess scorned, and every quick movement she made shouted her raging emotion.

Quick, graceful, dangerous, untamed as all fire is untamed, Pele claimed the stage, burning fiercely within the violent lament of the drums.

Neither drummer nor dancer noticed when the last student got up and slipped away from the stage. They didn't see Bobby lift his pipes to his lips once, then put his hands down before he blew a single note.

Though Nicole refused to look at Chase, had refused since the first instant of the dance, she knew nothing but him. She didn't have to look at him. He lived in the blazing center of her soul. He was the blood hammering wildly in her veins. He was the fire turning her body to shimmering gold.

Chase felt, understood, and accepted the transformation from wounded Nicole to furious Pele. He watched her intently, his glittering eyes reflecting both the savage regret of the drums and the searing accusations of the woman who called to him with every movement of her body.

He had wanted her.

He had taken her.

He had lost her.

He knew it, all of it. Knowledge was a torrent of lava pouring over his soul. Emotions he had no words to describe beat wildly within him, tearing at him, seeking a release that had no name . . . finally finding that release in the sweet violence of the drums and the dancer burning just beyond his reach.

The dance raged on, the rhythms quickening and then quickening again, separate pulses and movements compressed into impossibly small bits of time.

Distantly Chase realized that his hands had gone from aching to numbness to sudden, slicing pain.

He knew that he should stop beating the drums,
knew that with the next impact, or the next, his
skin would split beneath the relentless demands of
the dance.

He kept drumming. He needed to give something to the woman who had given him too much.
This was her dance, her moment, her time to
burn. Deliberately he stepped up the rhythm yet
again, building thunder into a savage, rolling
crescendo, knowing that she could meet the elemental challenge.

Yet even knowing it, he was stunned by the
unleashed fury of her dance. He held the violent
drumroll as long as he could, then threw up his
hands with a cry.

In the instant before the lights went out, Nicole
saw blood bright on his hands, on the drums, blood
welling in silent apology between her and the man
who had hurt her as no other man had, not even
her husband.

"Chase."

Her single involuntary cry was buried beneath an
explosion of applause from the audience.

In the darkness Nicole shuddered wrenchingly
and let go of the dance's savage, hypnotic fascination. She waited to feel Chase's arms coming
around her, his mouth claiming her, the hot, powerful length of him pressing against her until she
arched like a drawn bow.

She didn't know whether she feared or wanted
him—she knew only that she was trembling like

the mountain just before all the fires of Eden were unleashed, destroying and creating in the same instant.

The lights came on in a dazzling rush.

The stage was empty except for a woman with blazing hair and blind golden eyes.

CHAPTER
27

The next morning Nicole had a houseful of kids trying to get one another ready for a hike while at the same time not being ready themselves.

"Watch it!" Nicole said.

The warning was barely out of her mouth before Mark Wilcox grabbed the open, tottering jar of pickles and put it back on the counter, away from the edge. Not a drop spilled.

"Nice catch," she said, giving him a thumbs-up. "I don't know what I'd do without you."

He gave her a quick, pleased smile. At thirteen, he was already taller than Nicole, although he hadn't begun to fill out the raw promise of his bones. He had a long way to go to equal his father's build or the even more powerful one of his Uncle Chase.

"Hey, short stuff," Mark said to his sister. "You gonna play with that peanut butter or give it to someone who knows how to make a real sandwich?"

Sandi made a face at her brother and passed over the jar of brown goo. She knew what was coming next. As far as she was concerned, what her brother did with peanut butter shouldn't be allowed to happen in public.

With serene indifference to his sister's disgust, Mark built himself a sandwich of alternating layers of peanut butter, pickles, and mayonnaise. He piled the layers on until the bread sagged and flattened beneath the load.

Sandi made retching sounds. Her friend Judy went off in a storm of giggles. No sooner had she settled down than Benny came pelting through the garden. Normally he would have been followed by anywhere between two and ten of his cousins and siblings, but today the rest of the family was off to Oahu. Knowing that a kipuka picnic was on the schedule, Benny had stayed home.

Mark's best friend, Tim, was missing from the expedition due to a sore throat and a mother who couldn't be persuaded that her son's hoarse voice was the result of ragging on other players during a baseball game. Steve, the last third of the traumatic teenage trio, was running late as usual. They would meet him at the bus stop, if he made it at all.

"Ponchos?" Nicole asked.

A ragged chorus of words answered her query. The bottom line was that everyone who wanted a poncho had one.

"Canteens?" she asked. "Bus fare?"

Another ragged chorus.

"Okay, troops. Pack up your lunches."

"Li-sa?" Benny asked plaintively.

Nicole couldn't think of Lisa without thinking of Chase. As a result, her fingers clenched into the tough nylon of her knapsack. She forced herself to let go and hoped that no one noticed the small jerk of her hand that had marked the sudden hammering of her heart.

Last night, in the long hours before she fell asleep, the image of Chase's bleeding hands had haunted her. Knowing that he was in a cottage only a few hundred feet from her was a slow fire burning in the silences of her mind. She sensed that something had changed between them during her raging dance, but she didn't know what.

Whatever it was, it hadn't been enough to hold Chase onstage after the lights went out.

"Lisa is living with her father now," Nicole said carefully. "He may not want her to come with us today."

Though Benny said not one word, his disappointment tugged at her heart. She bent over and hugged him.

"Go ahead, honey," she said, smiling into Benny's black eyes. "Run up and ask if it's okay for Lisa to come with us."

"It's fine for her to come," Chase said from just beyond the open garden door. "As long as I'm invited, too."

"Uncle Chase!" Mark crowed, obviously delighted

by Chase's unexpected arrival. "Want a PBP and mayo to go?"

"Do I have a choice?" Chase retorted dryly. But it was Nicole he looked at. She was standing frozen in the center of her small kitchen. "May I come along?"

There was no way Nicole could refuse, even if she wanted to. And she wasn't sure she did.

"Of course," she said, turning away and stuffing her sandwich into the knapsack.

"Hold the mayo," Chase said to Mark. He looked down at his daughter. "You didn't tell me we should bring lunch."

"Don't have to. Benny's here."

The boy grinned and held out his knapsack. "Share."

"Are you sure there's enough for three of us?" Chase asked. "I get pretty hungry."

"See," Benny commanded.

Chase opened the bag and saw fried chicken and fresh fruit, scones and raw vegetables, enough food to feed four grown men. He gave the boy a grateful smile.

"Hold the PBP," he said to Mark. Then he turned to Nicole. "Ready when you are."

She didn't say anything. She couldn't. She was still frozen in the moment when he had reached toward Benny's knapsack and saw Chase's hands for the first time. His fingers were tightly bandaged and his palms had shadow bruises beneath layers of callus.

"Golly, Uncle Chase," Sandi said, staring at his hands, impressed and horrified at the same time. "What did you do to your hands?"

He smiled crookedly. "Played with fire."

"You get burned?"

"All the way to the bone."

Sandi's blue eyes widened. "That musta hurt a lot."

"Yes." Then he added softly, "But I hurt the fire more."

Only Nicole and Lisa heard the words.

Only Nicole understood them.

She looked away from the rain-clear depths of Chase's eyes to his taped fingers. Her hands trembled as she picked up her knapsack. She could still hear his reckless, relentless drumming driving her dance higher and higher, taking her to a level she had never danced before. He had seemed godlike, invincible.

But he wasn't. He hurt and bled just like everyone else.

"Okay, gang," she said. It was an effort, but she kept her voice neutral. "Which kipuka?"

"Kamehameha Iki!" everyone said instantly.

It was a unanimous vote for a lush, hidden kipuka more than halfway up Kilauea's slope. They had named the kipuka "Little Kamehameha" for Benny, who had led them to it.

"How about it, Lisa?" Nicole asked. "You feeling up to that kind of a scramble?"

"I'll help her," Mark said. "Right, squirt?"

"Me," Benny insisted.

"Me, too," Chase said. Then he asked Nicole, "Is the kipuka in one of Kilauea's active rift zones?"

"No. Why?"

"Bells went off on the rim this morning."

Instantly the children came to attention. They knew about the alarms wired to every seismograph at the volcano observatory. Whenever harmonic tremors lasted for more than ten minutes, bells went off, telling anyone with ears that seething, molten stone was pushing its way closer to the surface of the land.

Years ago the patterns of magma movement had been so predictable that the alarms were hardly necessary. But since 1975, when a big earthquake hit the mountain, everything had changed. The mountain had shifted, closing off old avenues for the release of magma without opening any noteworthy new ones.

Before the earthquake there had been four spectacular surface eruptions for every invisible intrusion of magma beneath the surface of the land. Now the ratio was reversed. Land was still being born on the Big Island, but it came silently, almost painfully, as though the mountain and the molten rock labored against invisible bonds.

In its self-made chains Kilauea was a much less predictable volcano. One day the mountain would shrug off the restraints, because nothing could stand for long against the immense forces at work beneath the gentle Eden of the land. When

Kilauea finally broke its chains, the fires of creation would leap free again. Then fountains of incandescent rock would shoot a thousand feet high in a dance as beautiful as it was powerful.

"When? Where?" the children demanded. Like everyone else on the island, they wanted to get front-row seats for the big eruption, if and when it finally came.

"It already was. Don't worry," Chase added as he saw the disappointment on their faces. "You didn't miss anything. It was an intrusion rather than an eruption." To Lisa he said, "That means the liquid rock never broke through to the surface. It just sort of squeezed between the cracks in the solid rocks down below."

Mark made a disgusted sound. "Another creeper. Man, I'm gonna be old and gray before I see a real eruption."

Chase laughed. "I doubt it. The hotshot pool will be claimed within a few weeks. Bet on it."

"I tried," Mark said indignantly. "Dad wouldn't let me."

Nicole managed not to laugh out loud as she looked at her watch. "C'mon, troops. Pele and the volcano wait for no man."

"How about women?" Chase asked blandly.

"Nope," Mark said. "Pele's a goddess. They don't wait for anything. Steve better hurry."

CHAPTER
28

By the time Nicole had herded everyone to the bus stop along the island highway, Steve came running up to join them. As the children paired off in the seats, Nicole found herself with Chase. She slid onto the bench seat, carefully leaving enough space for two men to sit down.

Chase filled it.

The children spent the bus ride betting pickles against peanut butter on just when and where the mountain would blow. They peered out the windows, hoping for some sign that soon they would be up to their lips in pickles or peanut butter and dancing fountains of lava.

As usual, the top of Kilauea was swathed in clouds and rainbows, telling the children from the wet side of the island what they already knew: it was going to rain. It rained almost every day, but only for a short time. They accepted it the way mainland kids accept sunshine or snow or smog.

Nicole spent the bus ride half listening to the kids and wholly wishing she wasn't so aware of Chase beside her, of his muscular thigh resting against hers whenever the bus rounded a right turn, and it seemed like the road was made up entirely of right turns. The first time she felt the heat of his skin against hers, she had flinched like she had touched burning stone. The second time his leg brushed hers, she flinched, but not as much.

By the fifth time she had tamed her reaction to a slight tremor when she felt his hair-roughened thigh touch hers.

Just over halfway up Kilauea's gently sloping flank, the bus made an unscheduled stop to let them off at the spot where an unmarked trail led to a popular island picnic spot. With Benny in the lead, they followed the trail until it unraveled into ferns, shrubs, and towering ohia trees.

As soon as the picnic spot was behind them, everyone shifted into hiking formation like a well-drilled team. Benny still led the way. Mark moved up to third place, behind Lisa. The other girls followed Mark, and Steve closed ranks after them, ready to help if needed. Nicole brought up the rear to keep an eye on everything.

Chase fell into line after her.

As she struggled through the overgrown stretches or scrambled down and up a steep ravine, she tried not to think of him just behind her. Some of the time she succeeded, but not often. Her skin tingled with a feminine awareness that was new and unsettling. She told herself it was simply nerves. She didn't believe it. Nervousness felt cold, not hot.

Even though there wasn't any real trail to follow, no one was worried about getting lost. Benny had an uncanny sense of place, a kind of three-dimensional memory that allowed him to see and remember forest landmarks that were invisible or unremarkable to other people. After the first few hikes everyone simply relaxed and trusted him to get them in and out of any place.

Having heard all about Benny's fey skill in the wild, Chase wasn't concerned about memorizing the trail—or lack of it. Other than noting changes in direction and obvious landmarks, he enjoyed the view directly in front of him.

Nicole's legs were long and graceful, strong and smooth. He remembered what it felt like to have that silky golden flesh next to his own darker skin. The memory was so vivid that he was almost grateful when his hungry train of thought was derailed by Mark's cheerful voice.

"Let's hear it for ocean jokes!" the boy called over his shoulder.

The kids all groaned in happy anticipation. Punning had begun.

"Do you know where fish come from?" Steve called out over the girls' heads.

"No, where?" they chorused.

"Finland!"

There were groans all around, then a pause.

"Why can't a shark sing 'do, re, mi'?" Sandi asked.

"Don't know," Lisa said bravely. "Why?"

"Cuz it doesn't have any scales!"

"Drown her!" Steve yelled, laughing in spite of himself.

"Was there a porpoise to that joke?" Mark asked slyly.

He smiled and bowed, acknowledging the round of boos that was his reward.

There was a long pause while they went over a rough part of the path.

"**Fin**ished?" Mark asked. "Maybe we should move on to bird jokes."

"You mean like the one about the owl that was so lazy it didn't give a hoot?" Chase asked. His innocent smile gleamed beneath the midnight slash of his mustache.

Nicole groaned.

"Is that a sketch?" Lisa asked eagerly. She turned to look at Nicole for an instant before giving her attention back to the uneven ground beneath her feet.

Before Nicole could answer, Mark jumped in. "If a hummingbird does in his brother, it's fratricide. If it's his father, it's patricide. What is it if a hummingbird does in a stranger?" He waited for a long moment of silence before he said triumphantly, "Humicide!"

Chase stopped walking, threw back his head, and laughed without restraint, enjoying his nephew's agile mind.

The sound of Chase's laughter rippled over Nicole like a warm, invisible net, wrapping around her, tugging her closer to him.

"Sketch!" demanded all the children except Mark, who waited modestly for Nicole's decision.

"Sketch," she agreed. "I've been **pun**ished enough for one day."

When everyone groaned, she smiled and pulled out her sketchbook and pencil. With a few swift strokes she captured Mark's face as it had been while he enjoyed the groaning applause of his friends.

She also captured something beyond the moment, the quality of his intensity and his unfolding strength, the man growing beneath the boy's handsome, smiling surface. The sketch didn't flatter Mark; it appreciated what he was and what he would become.

Chase saw Mark's pleased grin while he watched the sketch forming. He also saw the quick, shyly admiring looks his nephew gave Nicole when she wasn't paying attention to him. The glances told Chase that Mark had more than a little bit of a crush on her. Remembering what it had been like at that age, Chase doubted that Mark was even aware of why he enjoyed being with Nicole so much.

And then Chase wondered if Nicole knew.

She added a bloodthirsty hummingbird diving at Mark's ear with **hum**icide buzzing in its feathery little mind. The boy laughed with delight and took the sketch to show everyone else.

Watching the interplay, Chase realized that Nicole knew about Mark's fragile, unformed feelings toward her. The sketch told Mark that she approved of him, while the crazed bird shifted the boy's response to laughter. Deftly, very gently, she had made certain that Mark would have no reason to be embarrassed by his adolescent awareness of her as a woman.

Chase appreciated her tact, and at the same time wished she would show half as much gentleness to him. Surely she knew that he regretted what he had done.

Even as the wistful thought came, he dismissed it with an ironic smile at his own expense. He might want her consideration, but he himself had shown damn little consideration for her feelings. He was lucky that she didn't tell him to check out the kipukas in hell.

Benny led them from the thickly overgrown forest and across a smooth lava flow that had only a few lonely streaks of vegetation on its stony surface. It took the rain, sun, and wind a long time to break down pahoehoe's glassy surface, creating cracks and crevices to capture dust and shelter seeds.

Chase wondered how old this particular lava flow was. Relative dating was easy enough—the older lava was almost always underneath and the newer was on top. But whether an eruption was one thousand or seven thousand years old was a matter of opinion, not to mention outright shouting matches among the scientists. Even the kipukas were hard to date. In the tropics, trees didn't have well defined seasonal growth rings, for the simple reason that there were no well defined growing seasons. In Eden, all the days were pretty much the same.

The surface of the land wasn't that unchanging. Between one step and the next, pahoehoe gave way to aa lava. It had a much rougher surface, which allowed dirt to gather and ferns, shrubs, and grass to grow, and finally ohia trees. Born of fire, living on top of the living volcano, ohia had developed an ability to shut its pores when poisonous gases sighed out over the land. Other plants died, but not the ohia. It just held its breath until there was good air to breathe again. Unless the poisonous fumes continued for a long time, only direct fire could kill the hardy ohia.

Within a few hundred feet of the aa flow, the forest resumed as though the river of molten stone had never existed, had never burned away the old and created the new.

Overhead, clouds swooped low across the land, trailing streamers of warm rain. It came down hard, passed quickly, and left every little crease and crack of the land alive with water. Rills and narrow waterfalls danced through the green ravines, enjoying a brief white rush of life before sinking into the porous lava and disappearing. Some of the rainwater would reappear as springs and streams farther down the mountain. Most of it would simply vanish, returning to the ocean through seeps far below the breaking waves.

The landscape got rougher, as though barely cooled lava had been churned wildly with a huge stick and then left to harden. The children scrambled forward with the confidence of hikers who had been there before. They helped each other over the worst spots and went on without a fuss.

Chase noticed that Mark waited to see if Nicole needed help, only to be sent on with a wave of her hand. She went up the lava jumble gracefully, hesitating only once when her foot slipped on the rainslick leaves of a plant. Instantly Chase moved to her side, caught her arm, and supported her until she had her balance again.

The feel of his fingers on her bare upper arm made her heart lurch. Heat washed over her, followed by an instant of weakness. She was acutely aware of the texture of his skin and of the tape that protected his fingers.

She took a sharp breath and was surrounded by the hot male scent of him. Unable to stop herself, she looked up at him and saw his pupils widening in primitive response to her. For a moment she saw again his face above hers, his eyes dark with passion as he covered her body with his own.

Her heart stopped, then beat frantically.

"Nicole?" he asked quietly. "Are you all right?"

She closed her eyes, but that only increased her

awareness of the man standing so close to her. Her eyes snapped open. "Yes. You startled me. I'm not used to—"

When Nicole abruptly stopped speaking, Chase finished the sentence for her.

"Being touched by a man who isn't 'safe.' " His eyes searched hers. "It's all right. You know I won't hurt you."

Then he heard his own words, and his mouth turned down. He had hurt her very badly, and he hadn't even touched her while he was doing it.

"Not like this," he said. "Physically. You can trust me that far, can't you?"

Numbly she nodded, for it was the truth. Even when he had believed her to be a gold-digging little whore, he hadn't hurt her. His hands had been careful rather than harsh on her body. He had made her feel . . . good.

"Nicole," he said, his voice low, "let me make it up to you."

"There's no need." Then, quickly, before he could put into words the objections tightening his lips, she said, "You were better to me than my husband ever was, and he never felt guilty. Why should you?"

Chase remembered the instant when he had undressed her and she covered her breasts in defensive reflex. He hadn't understood then, but now it made the kind of sense that turned his stomach. "Did he hurt you in bed? Is that why—"

"Uncle Chase!" Mark called from the top of the lava flow. "Is everything all right?"

Relief washed through Nicole at the interruption. Now the uncomfortable conversation would have to end. Eagerly she turned toward the boy.

Before she could speak, Chase did. "Everything's fine. Nicole has a pebble caught in her shoe. Go on ahead. We'll catch up in a minute."

Mark hesitated until Chase turned around to face him fully. Even twenty feet away it was impossible to miss the command in Chase's gray eyes. The boy waved, turned away, and scrambled to catch up with the other hikers.

"Answer me," Chase said, but his voice and his touch were far more gentle than his words.

"He didn't beat me, if that's what you mean."

"That isn't what I asked."

Suddenly Nicole wanted to scream at Chase's insistent questions. **Can't he see that I don't want to think about it, to talk about it, to remember?** In her anger at his insensitivity she forgot to retreat, forgot to be humiliated by her own lack of response as a woman.

"You went to bed with me," Nicole shot back. "Can't you imagine why a man would get impatient and—and careless? A corpse doesn't have any feelings to—"

"Shit." Chase's mouth covered Nicole's and his tongue thrust between her teeth, stopping the scalding flow of words.

After the first overwhelming instant the kiss changed. His tongue touched hers slowly, tenderly. He sipped from her mouth as he had sipped from the heart of the flower.

Although the caress itself was very gentle, she couldn't have retreated from it if she had tried. His arms held her with a certainty that made her feel both fragile and completely safe. He was reassuring her with his touch that he wouldn't hurt her physically.

In that, at least, she had been right to trust herself to him.

The knowledge made warmth swirl in delicate currents throughout her body. The sensual heat softened her, changed her, made her breath into a sound wedged deep in her throat.

Her small, husky cry shuddered through Chase. He lifted his mouth and looked down into her face, wanting to tell her how very much he regretted the cruel things he had said in order to make certain that Dane never again thought about having an affair with Nicole.

The sight of her reddened lips made Chase forget everything but how good it had felt to join her mouth to his. With the same ravishing tenderness he had used on the flower, he caught her lower lip between his teeth.

She felt each serration of his teeth as a separate caress, felt the tip of his tongue tasting and stroking her captive flesh, felt the tiny, sensual shocks as he tugged softly on her lip. She wanted to stop breathing, thinking, to do nothing but feel.

"You're a woman, not a corpse." Chase groaned and dipped his tongue between her softened, parted lips. "All woman, from head to toes and most especially in between. And if I don't let go of you," he added huskily, "I'm going to embarrass the hell out of those kids."

But instead of releasing her right away, he kissed her again, slowly, deeply, saying with his kiss all that he didn't have words to describe. When he finally lifted his head, he saw hunger in her eyes, and fear.

"Don't be afraid of me," he said, his voice aching.

She shook her head. "It's not that."

The words were tight, as flat as the line of her lips. She tried to step back away from him but couldn't. He held her too closely, too powerfully. Too carefully. She felt naked, then wished she really was. She wanted to pull him over her, inside her.

Impossible.

All of it.

She would only hurt herself more. The way she was hurting herself now. Dreaming when she knew damn well what reality was.

"If you're not afraid of me, what—" he began.

"Let go of me," she cut in desperately. "Please, Chase. It—it hurts."

Puzzled, he released her. "Sorry. I didn't think I was holding you hard enough to hurt you."

"That's not what I meant."

Gently he stroked her cheek with the back of his hand. "Then what hurts, sweet dancer?"

She took a deep, broken breath. Running hadn't worked. Hiding hadn't worked. Maybe blunt words would. Anything was better than feeling like she was dangling between heaven and hell.

"Knowing that I'm only half a woman hurts," she said. "When I'm around you, it hurts even more. You make me want things that are just impossible."

"What things?" He touched the full curve of her lower lip with the pad of his thumb, but what he really wanted was to feel her softness shivering beneath his mouth again. "What do I make you want?"

"To be woman enough to please you in bed."

He couldn't conceal his shock. Of all the things he had expected her to say, that wasn't even close.

She almost smiled at the look on his face. Almost. But it hurt too much to be alive just now. Smiling was out of the question.

"Yeah," she said huskily. "Some joke, right? Go ahead and laugh. But don't wait for me to join in. I'll laugh tomorrow, or the day after. Or . . ." She shrugged and started up the trail, fresh out of easy words.

Stunned, Chase simply stared as Nicole turned away. Then his hand shot out and wrapped around her wrist, holding her close without hurting her.

"For the love of God . . . !" He shook his head

once, sharply, still barely able to believe what he had heard. "Did it ever occur to you that I didn't please **you** in bed? It sure as hell occurred to me."

"But you did," she said in a dull voice. "You pleased me more than my husband ever did. And I pleased you much less than a real woman would."

Just as Chase opened his mouth to tell her how wildly wrong she was, he saw a flicker of movement along the top of the lava flow. Someone was coming back to check on them.

With a sliding pressure of his fingers, he released her wrist and said quietly, "We'll talk later. In private."

"There's nothing left to talk about." Nicole's expression was as weary as her voice. "You felt guilty for hurting me. Well, it wasn't your fault, so you can stop worrying about making it right. It was the truth that hurt me, not you. I'm not much of a woman in bed and you're all man. Talking won't change that. Nothing will."

"Path?" Benny called from above their heads.

"No, thanks," she called back, understanding Benny's one-word question. "You don't need to find another way up for me. There's nothing wrong with this path that walking on it won't cure."

Chase watched Nicole disappear over the top of the lava flow. She moved cleanly, gracefully, and with an elemental femininity that made him want to grab her and not let go until she knew just how mistaken she was about herself.

But he couldn't do that here, with the kids waiting. There was nothing to do but follow her. He went up the lava wall in a coordinated rush, using strength where Nicole had used finesse, and wishing urgently that the two of them were alone. With each step he took, each rough scrape of stone against his bandages, her words echoed in his head.

I'm not much of a woman in bed and you're all man.

You're half wrong, Nicole, he retorted silently. **I can't wait until we're alone and I can show you which half.**

CHAPTER
29

Tantalizing thoughts of all the ways to demon-
strate just how mistaken Nicole was about her
sensuality kept burning in Chase's mind for the
rest of the hike. Thoughts were all he had. There
wasn't any way to talk to her privately or even to
touch her for the sheer pleasure of feeling her
tremble with the elemental female response she
had denied being capable of.

She didn't give him a single chance to get close to
her. Every time he looked, she was in the center of
a crowd of laughing kids. When they rested along
the trail, she either had her sketchbook out or Lisa
on her lap or both.

He was relieved that fear no longer darkened
Nicole's eyes when he walked up to her, but no
other emotion appeared either. In some uncanny,
maddening way she avoided him even while she
was looking straight into his eyes.

The third time it happened, he wanted to grab
her and lift her up to eye level until she looked—
really looked—at him.

Great, he told himself sardonically. **Grabbing her and shoving your face in hers is a really cool way to impress her with how sensitive and gentle and understanding you are. You might try remembering that kind of in-your-face assault on the defense is the least likely way to move a football, much less a woman.**

Ahead of Chase, hikers started dropping out of sight as they scrambled down into Kamehameha Iki. The kipuka was at least several hundred years old, for huge ohia and koa trees grew there. A deep, clear spring welled up at the north end of the kipuka, creating a mirrorlike pool. Scarlet blossoms were reflected in the water, along with the changing, rainbow-hung sky. Lush plant life cushioned the ground in shades of green broken by splashes of color from flowers.

The kids lost no time in peeling down to their swimsuits and washing off the heat and grime of the hike. Nicole posted herself on a fern-covered outcrop and watched the swimmers. Her actions were automatic—she always kept an eye on little Lisa, making sure she didn't get lost in the heedless, high-speed play of the older kids.

As soon as they both were cool, Benny signaled Lisa. The two of them stole off into a quiet corner of the kipuka. Nicole noted that Lisa wasn't playing in the water anymore, and returned to her sketching. She wasn't worried about Lisa being trampled playing with Benny.

Chase also saw the two young kids leave and relaxed. Lisa was safer with Benny than with anyone else; even the adults were counting on the boy to lead them out of the forest. Chase marked the place in the kipuka where Benny and Lisa had gone, and then turned back to watch Nicole.

He wanted to sit next to her, but the outcrop she had chosen was built for one, not two. After a quiet mental curse, he got out his own notebook and started doing what he should have been doing all along—taking notes on the varieties of plants growing on lava of different ages and types.

Every few minutes he glanced up from his work, making sure that the teenage water sprites weren't getting too wild playing their game of water tag. Satisfied that everyone was happy and accounted for, he returned his attention to his notes.

Without seeming to, Nicole watched Chase's increasing concentration on the kipuka around him. Part of her was relieved that he no longer searched her out with rain-colored eyes and stormy urgency. She told herself everything was fine now. She had finally made him understand that he shouldn't feel guilty for what had happened. It wasn't his fault that she couldn't respond to a man.

Maybe it wasn't even her fault. Maybe it was simply a fact, like the hardened lava twisting over the land.

Just a fact.

But it would have been so wonderful to stand inside his arms again, to know the shimmering sweetness of his tongue sliding over hers, to feel his heat and strength radiating through her. Even the thought of it was enough to send delicate currents of pleasure through her body. The memory of his mouth caressing her breasts made her nipples rise and tighten, adding more heat to the restlessness deep inside her.

It won't happen again, so quit torturing yourself. That kind of touching doesn't please a man, not really. A man wants more.

Chase knows he isn't going to get it. Not from me. I can't give it to him. So why would he waste his time petting me and frustrating himself?

The answer was simple. He wouldn't.

"Sad?" Benny whispered, appearing from nowhere to stand next to Nicole's lava outcrop.

She forced a smile onto her face and wished silently that Benny's emotional radar was less sensitive. A whole lot less. "Where's Lisa?"

"Hunting."

Startled, Nicole blinked. Then she remembered the special kind of hunting Benny had taught his small friend.

"Syrup?" she asked.

Benny nodded. "Sketch?"

"You mean she caught one?"

"Big-big." His smile lit up his dark, lean face.

Clutching the sketch pad, Nicole scrambled off her rocky perch. "Good-good! Where?"

"Close."

She gave a quick look around. No Lisa, but the older children had exhausted themselves for the moment and were sprawled on their towels making up awful puns. That should keep them occupied long enough for her to sneak off. Even if it didn't, Chase was keeping a close eye on everything no matter how many notes he wrote.

Nicole half smiled. It was a good feeling to share the responsibility for the kids with another adult.

With a last look over her shoulder, she tiptoed after Benny. As she twisted and wriggled through the tight greenery, she envied the boy's ease and silence. The instant he slowed down, she did. When he stopped, she crept up behind him and looked over his shoulder.

Still wearing her red bathing suit, Lisa sat cross-legged in the middle of a small, flower-dotted clearing. The back of her gently curled hands were supported on her knees.

Three huge butterflies rested with folded wings on the edge of her left hand, drinking from the tiny pool of sugar syrup cupped in her palm. Each butterfly was as big as her hand. Their velvety black wings were set off by splashes of orange and white.

Entranced, Lisa sat without moving, a look of breathless pleasure on her face.

Nicole memorized everything about the glade and the girl and the moment. She wanted to draw Lisa, but was afraid if she lifted her sketchbook she would startle the butterflies into flight.

Then Nicole sensed someone behind her. She didn't need to turn around to know that Chase was there, close enough for her to feel his heat and hear the intake of his breath when he saw his daughter sitting in the sunlight with a handful of black-velvet butterflies.

For long minutes no one moved, no one spoke.

The breeze shifted, sending a flurry of tree shadows over the seated girl. The butterflies opened their color-splashed wings, lifted with the new currents, and chased one another in wild spirals that took them out of sight among the trees.

Nicole let out a long breath and squeezed Benny's shoulder. "Thank you. That was beautiful."

The boy gestured toward the little girl, then toward himself, and said proudly, "Kamehameha." With that, he set off across the little clearing toward Lisa.

"The butterflies are named after the Kamehamehas, the last Hawaiian royal family," Nicole explained softly without turning around.

"So Benny is descended from kings," Chase said in a low voice. "And Bobby, too."

"Maybe." She laughed quietly. "I don't know of a native on the islands who doesn't boast direct descent from kings. But Bobby has one thing going for his claim."

"What?"

"Size. The Hawaiian kings and queens were huge. Seven feet wasn't unusual for male royalty.

And a woman under six feet tall was a shrimp," Nicole added in an unconsciously wistful tone.

Knowing she couldn't see it, Chase smiled and looked at her from head to toe, liking every inch of what he saw.

"They were big eaters, too," she said. "A few centuries ago Bobby would have weighed at least a hundred pounds more than he does today. That's why the butterflies are called Kamehameha."

"A four-hundred-pound butterfly?" Chase teased.

She snickered. "No. Just giants among their own kind. A four-inch wingspan."

"Daddy," Lisa called excitedly, looking beyond Benny to the underbrush where the two adults remained hidden. "Did you see me? Three butterflies! Benny says I must be related to the old kings to be such a good hunter."

"How did he say all that in one word?" Chase asked beneath his breath.

" 'Princess,' " Nicole retorted softly.

She sensed as much as heard the laughter rising in his chest.

Chase stepped out into the clearing. "I saw you. I didn't know you were such a good hunter. Do you think Benny can teach me to catch butterflies as well as you do?"

"We don't really catch them," she corrected quickly. "I mean, we sort of do, but we don't touch them or hurt them or anything. They touch **us**. It tickles like—like fairies laughing."

The voices of father and daughter floated back through the sun-dappled clearing to the place where Nicole stood concealed in the shadows.

"I know you don't hurt them, punkin." Chase scooped up his daughter and settled her in the crook of his arm. "Otherwise it wouldn't be any fun for the butterflies, would it? Or for us." With his free hand he reached down and ruffled Benny's thick hair affectionately. "What about it, Benny? Can the descendant of Hawaiian kings be bothered to teach a mere haole the secrets of butterfly hunting?"

The boy laughed. "Sure-sure."

Nicole watched while the three of them chose places and sat cross-legged in the tiny, warm clearing. Benny's voice had the clarity of a silver bell as he told Chase how to sit, how to rest his hands palm up on his knees, how to breathe quietly and slowly.

And all in four words.

Benny squeezed a clear, thick pool of sugar syrup into Chase's palm, stepped back, and added the most important instruction: "Wait."

"That's all there is to it?" Chase asked.

"Sure-sure," Lisa said. She pointed toward a velvet-winged butterfly settling onto a flower a few feet away. "She knows you're here. If she's hungry, she'll come to you."

"She?" Chase asked. "You sure?"

"Sure-sure. All pretty butterflies are girls. Like me."

"Makes sense, pretty girl," he said, hiding a smile. "What if it, er, **she** doesn't come to me? Do I chase her?"

"No-no-no," Lisa said instantly. "You're too big, Daddy. You might hurt her. You don't want to do that, do you?"

His smile faded. "No, I don't want to hurt anything that delicate and beautiful."

Lisa shifted a little, found a more comfortable way to sit, and waited while Benny put a few drops of the sugar solution on her hand. Silence and utter stillness claimed the clearing, as though even the wind was watching with breath held.

Nicole certainly was almost afraid to breathe as various butterflies skimmed and swirled over the flowers. No matter how many times they flew over or around or near the patient humans, none of the butterflies felt brave enough to land.

Finally a huge Kamehameha butterfly hovered around Chase's hand in a slowly closing, unpredictable spiral. Delicately the butterfly settled on the edge of his callused palm, then instantly fled, then settled once more, only to flit away again without drinking.

Chase didn't move at all, not even to present his lure more openly. He simply waited while the velvet wings fluttered closer and closer. At last the butterfly floated down to rest completely, safely, in the palm of his hand, drinking deeply of the sweetness he offered.

Nicole knew the exact instant when the butterfly trustingly drank. It was the moment when Chase looked up and found her concealed among the green shadows, wistfully watching a butterfly cherished within the hard curve of his hand.

CHAPTER
30

Tuesday, Chase and Nicole were hiking together again as they had every day since the picnic. It was the only time he saw her. His bruised hands wouldn't let him play the drums, and he hadn't trusted himself to watch her dance to Bobby's beat.

But during the long hours of daylight, he was with her. She led him to various kipukas, both well known and unknown. He surveyed the different islands of life, choosing the locations that would be best for his book. And over the many rough spots on the trails, he slowly, slowly, had accustomed her to his touch.

Now, as he helped her down a very rough portion of the path, he silently congratulated himself on his choice of kipuka for today's work.

The worse the trail, the more he got to touch her.

Until yesterday morning, when he introduced light hugs after really hard parts of the trail, he had made sure the touching seemed all very ordinary. Even the hugs he gave her were casual, not sexual.

He had no intention of doing anything that would make her rethink the promise he had given to her almost a week ago.

I'll never hurt you like that again.

It was the exact truth.

But not the whole truth.

He meant to make love to her, only this time there would be pleasure instead of pain.

Nicole had taken his words to mean that he would never try to seduce her again. What she hadn't figured out yet was that Chase simply couldn't walk away from her and what they could share as a man and a woman. He wanted her more with each day, each smile, each thought they shared, each silence, each touch, all of it adding up to a complex hunger that made him ache.

He had been very careful not to let her know the depth of his need for her. He didn't want to frighten her. He wanted her to come to him like the butterfly in the glen.

And like the butterfly, she kept coming closer, then retreating in a velvet flurry.

He sensed that she wanted him more with every touch, every easy silence, every conversation, every moment they spent together. He saw her yearning in the way her eyes followed him, in the softening of her mouth when she watched him, in the visible shivers that sometimes moved over her golden skin when he touched her casually.

It was driving him crazy.

The only thing that kept him from reaching out and grabbing her was an emotion that was even greater than his hunger for her. He **needed** to be certain that making love with her wouldn't hurt her. He couldn't bear hurting her again.

If that meant never making love to her, so be it. Somehow he would find a way to live without having her in his bed.

And each day he lived, he would curse himself for the unspeakable fool he had been eight days ago, when he had closed his hand and crushed the fragile wings of her trust in him.

It will work out, he told himself silently.

It had to. He couldn't live with himself otherwise.

Yesterday he and Nicole had hiked from Kilauea's caldera past the cone called Kilauea Iki, where in 1959 fountains of lava nearly two thousand feet high had showered ash, pumice, and globs of cooling stone over an ohia forest. The trees had lost their leaves, their bark, and their lives to the volcano, but their trunks hadn't burned completely. Their graceful skeletons lingered on, rising from the black, devastated land like ghosts of a greener yesterday frozen in time.

Chase felt the same way. Frozen in time.

He could control the physical ache of wanting Nicole. He couldn't control the agony of having had her and then destroying her, leaving behind a mental landscape more bleak than any volcanic devastation he had ever seen.

What made it worse was that she still didn't understand. She blamed herself.

He put the blame where it belonged. On him.

"Need a break?" Nicole asked, sensing that Chase had stopped on the rough trail behind her. When she looked over her shoulder, his clear, beautiful eyes were measuring the black rivers of lava twisting down to the turquoise sea.

"Just taking in the landmarks. You sure there's a kipuka between here and the ocean?"

For an instant she looked almost guilty. "It's not a true kipuka," she admitted. "But it's very special. It's the only place I've seen on this lava flow where anything more than Hawaiian snow grows."

He smiled crookedly. "Hawaiian snow," he said, shaking his head at her reference to the plant that was always the first to colonize cooled lava flows. "White lichen."

"Hey, when you're hungry for a white Christmas, you take what you can get," she pointed out. "Besides, from a distance the stuff really does look like snow."

"Um" was the most tactful thing he could think of to say. As far as he was concerned, the lichen looked like milk that had been tossed out and left to curdle in the sun.

Nicole paused on the margin between an old lava flow and a newer one. The aa ahead was intimidating, even to someone who was accustomed to walking on a jagged black jumble of stone.

Chase came up and stood beside Nicole. Close beside her.

She didn't flinch away. If anything, she might have leaned closer to him, but he couldn't be sure. He could only hope.

"Bad patch?" he asked.

She nodded and waited while he looked over the landscape for himself.

"You could go down that way," she said, pointing toward a thrusting ridge of rock only a few feet away. "It's shorter, but it's too big a drop for me."

"Okay. Wait here, and I'll try something."

He scrambled down a particularly nasty stretch of aa lava, muttering when pieces crumbled and broke off beneath his feet. Newly made or as old as the flow itself, the lava edges were sharp. They gnawed happily on his heavy leather hiking boots. While he would have preferred the lighter, cooler high-tech boots he had often used for hiking, the modern materials just couldn't take the punishment that aa ladled out the way leather could.

When Chase found secure footing, he turned around and held out his arms to Nicole. She came into them without hesitation, enjoying his strength and the tingling currents that spread through her when she was held against his body.

Gently he set her on her feet but didn't release her.

"Pay the toll," he said.

She smiled almost shyly.

He gathered her even closer, savoring the supple, feminine curves pressed against him. What had begun early yesterday as a joke had become the highlight of the hikes for him, and the reason that he chose the most rugged trails he could find. With each rough spot on the trail Nicole was becoming more accustomed to his hands, to the feel of his body close to hers, to being held and holding him in return.

She no longer flinched when he touched her.

It was a small thing, but it was balm for both their wounds.

Laughing softly, she hugged Chase, savoring how carefully he arranged her length along his body, matching curve to hollow, strength to softness. This was new to their hiking hugs, a closeness that had begun when he pulled her up a steep part of the trail.

She enjoyed the new way of hugging all the way to the soles of her feet.

After a few moments she knew that she should pull away and continue the hike as she had done just a few minutes back up the trail. But she didn't. When she had seen the rugged patch of aa coming up, shivers of anticipation had gone through her.

She had known that soon Chase would turn to her and hold her. Soon she would feel the hard muscles of his body shift and move beneath her hands as though he was savoring every bit of the casual embrace as much as she did. She felt the same about touching him. She memorized every instant of it.

And she wanted more.

Slowly she turned her head against his throat, unconsciously nuzzling aside the open collar of his shirt. She wanted to feel her cheek against his naked skin.

Chase felt the glide of skin against skin and was afraid the sudden hammering of his heart would scare her away. When she didn't withdraw, he let out a long breath. He spread his fingers until they all but spanned her back. Gently he shifted her from side to side, slowly rubbing her breasts across his chest. After an instant of stiffening, she sighed and softened in his hands, letting him lead her into an embrace that was more intimate than a friendly hug.

Closing her eyes, Nicole floated on the sensations Chase was creating with the slow, slow stroking of her body over his. Her breasts tingled and tightened, sending currents of heat streaking through her. Suddenly, vividly, she remembered the feel of his mouth on her swollen nipples and the sweet, rhythmic tugging that had made fire spiral through her.

"Chase?"

The catch in her voice was as exciting to him as the feel of her nipples hardening beneath her flowered halter.

"Yes?" he said, keeping his voice normal with an effort.

"I don't think this is a good idea."

"I thought we agreed that you liked being hugged."

"I do. It's just—" Her voice caught again as his hands shifted, somehow increasing the delicious friction on her breasts. "This is different."

"Is it? How?"

She tried to think of a way of explaining that avoided raising the subject of sex.

There was a long silence.

"You can touch me if you like," he said huskily, twisting slightly, subtly against her. "I'm not like your husband was. I won't fall on you like a starving dog on a lamb chop."

She made a choked sound that could have been a gasp of surprise or laughter or both together.

And she didn't withdraw. In the last few days she had gotten used to more than Chase's touch. She had also learned to enjoy his unexpected, sometimes outrageous, always reassuring, conversations about her past experience with her husband.

"Don't believe me?" Chase asked quietly. "Think about it. Even when I didn't know how badly you'd been hurt, I still didn't attack you when you touched me. Remember?"

What she remembered was how much she had wanted to run her hands over him that night in the shower. Even the harsh lessons of her marriage hadn't kept her from giving in to the point of stroking his chest with its fascinating patterns of hair and the muscles that shifted and slid so intriguingly beneath his skin.

His eyes had changed at her touch, becoming smoky rather than clear, dark rather than light. But he hadn't dragged her out of the shower and hammered her into the bathroom floor, which her husband had done once when he came home early and found her in the shower.

"Yes." She nuzzled again at the V of tan skin revealed by Chase's unbuttoned shirt. "I remember."

He waited, holding her so skillfully that every way she turned increased the sensuous pressure of two bodies discovering each other. He shifted his stance slightly, savoring the delicious hardness of her nipples rubbing against him.

"Are you afraid if you touch me the holding will stop and the sex will start?"

His voice was as gentle as the hands holding her close, shifting her, tantalizing her. She turned her face away from his skin long enough to look at the unforgiving black lava heaped around them. She smiled crookedly.

"Despite all the unlikely positions detailed in the sex manuals my husband gave me—no, I'm not afraid you have sex on your do-it-now list. With this aa for a bed, we'd bleed to death long before anything else happened."

Wisely Chase didn't tell her that if she was willing, he could lift her, wrap her legs around his waist, and have her right here, right now, with never a scratch on her beautiful golden skin. All it took was a man with unusual strength and a hunger to match.

He had both.

"Then you're safe," he said, smiling. "So go ahead, touch me however you want."

"But . . ."

He waited, watching the rise of color in her cheeks.

"Wouldn't that . . . that wouldn't be . . ." She made a sound that was halfway between frustration and embarrassment.

"Say it," he coaxed, moving against her again, tensing the muscles of his chest, increasing the sensuous pressure on her nipples.

"Won't that be hard on you?" she asked in a rush.

Then she heard her own words and blushed to the roots of her hair.

Amusement flickered in Chase's clear eyes as he smiled down at her. "No matter what your husband might have told you, having a woody and not having a woman isn't a fatal condition for a man."

Her flush deepened even as she returned his teasing smile. "Lucky for you, huh?"

"Damned lucky. Think about it, butterfly. I'm yours to touch any way you want."

Slowly he let go of her and turned away while he could still control his desire to stroke the tempting curves and hard peaks of her breasts with his hands. His mouth.

"C'mon," he said without looking back. "The beach can't be that far away. I'm ready for a swim."

Closing her eyes, Nicole tried to control the hammering of her heart.

She was on fire.

No man had ever held her like that, teased her sweetly until she ached, then smiled gently at her and turned away. With a small sound of confusion and frustration, she opened her eyes, watching helplessly while Chase covered the rough ground with a power and grace that made her want to run her hands all over him. And her mouth.

The idea should have shocked her. It didn't. Being caressed by him had become a temptation that was almost beyond her will to resist. The thought of touching him, of being able to find out how to caress him in return, how to please him . . .

That thought was definitely irresistible.

"Chase?" she called, her voice ragged.

He turned and looked back up at her. "Need help?"

She spoke in a rush, afraid she would lose her courage and with it the chance to touch him. "If I touch you, will you tell me if I please you?"

For a moment he thought she was joking—there was no way she could touch him and not please him. Then he saw the tension in her body as she came toward him, waiting for his answer.

She wasn't joking.

She really didn't understand how even her most casual touch gave him pleasure.

"Yes," he said simply as she came to stand next to him. "I'll tell you. Will you do the same for me?"

"What?"

"Tell me if I please you."

He saw the look of surprise on her face and wondered at it.

"I thought you knew," she said in a low voice. "Your touch has always pleased me."

His smile was bittersweet. He remembered how he had taken her too quickly, in ignorance and stupidity and anger, not even suspecting what a treasure he held.

"There's more to touching than not being hurt," he said.

Her breath caught on a cascade of sensual memories. "I know," she said in a throaty voice. She lifted one hand until her fingertips brushed across his mustache as lightly as a butterfly's wing. "You taught me that."

He tilted his head slightly, increasing the pressure of her touch. "And that pleases me more than I can say."

Her eyes widened in surprise until they looked like pools of liquid gold.

"Didn't you know?" he whispered huskily, turning her face up to his with a gentle touch of his hand. "Your pleasure multiplies mine." He smiled crookedly. "Of course, I'm not a saint. If you'd like to make me feel even better by kissing me, I wouldn't object."

"You're sure?" she asked, her eyes lighting with both laughter and anticipation.

"Real sure."

She braced her hands on his shoulders and stood on tiptoe. Even so, he had to bend down to bring his lips close to hers.

"It's the oddest feeling," she whispered.

"What?"

"You make me feel small, feminine, sleek. All the things I'm not."

"You're all of those things to me." He tested the resilience of her waist with his hands. "Or are you trying to say politely that I'm a little oversize?"

She smiled and pressed her lips against his jaw, his pulse. "Bobby's even bigger, and he doesn't make me feel this way. Small maybe, but not . . . mmm . . . delicious."

"Thank God," Chase said roughly. "The day he makes you feel edible, tell me. Then we'll see who eats what."

Her body moved with silent laughter.

Feeling it, he smiled. Then her lips touched his and all thought of laughter burned away in a single instant. Remembering the fragile, trusting butterfly, he held himself still. But he couldn't control the hungry tightening of his body when her tongue found his and her breath sighed into his mouth, filling him with her sweetness.

Slowly, hesitantly, she ended the kiss.

"I like that," he whispered against her lips.

"What?"

"Tasting you."

"Do you? Do you really?"

"Let's try again." He slid the tip of his tongue along her smile. "I might have been mistaken."

Her smile widened, parting her lips. With a feeling of pure luxury, she fitted her mouth to his and allowed herself the heady pleasure of kissing him without being afraid that the kiss would spiral out of control into sexual demands she wouldn't be able to meet.

As delicately as Chase had once tasted the flower, Nicole tasted him. The tip of her tongue found his, caressed gently, retreated, and returned. Tasting. Just that. So sweet a thing, tasting.

She sensed the quiver of response in the taut male muscles beneath her hands and hesitated, fearful of arousing him too much and having to end the intimacy far too soon.

"It's all right, butterfly," he said calmly. "Take as much or as little as you want. I won't hurt you or demand more than you want to give."

She looked up into his clear gray eyes and saw that he meant every word. She swallowed and spoke in a husky, hopeful voice. "Does that mean I can kiss you again?"

"Please. Yes. I love the taste of you."

With a sigh, she stretched up on tiptoe again and

threaded her fingers into his thick black hair. This time when she fitted her mouth to his, there was no hesitation. She was hungry to know again the heat and textures of his kiss, to feel the delicious velvet roughness of his tongue sliding over hers. To taste him.

This time when she felt the tremor of his response, it set off tiny shock waves of pleasure in her. **She was pleasing him.** She knew it as surely as she knew that he was pleasing her. Unconsciously she deepened the kiss, wanting more of him.

He felt the difference in her, a change that sent his blood gathering heavily between his thighs. He tried to tame the depth of his response. He couldn't.

So he simply accepted it, as he accepted that he wouldn't have the release his body was demanding with every hard, rapid beat of his heart. He had had release before. He wanted more this time. Much more.

He wanted Nicole.

For that, he would have to be patient.

Very slowly he shifted her supple, lush body with his hands, rubbing her breasts against his chest. The tiny intake of her breath as her nipples became more sensitive, more responsive, revealed that she was forgetting her fear and drinking more deeply of the sweetness he was offering.

He told himself it was sneaky and unfair to use

such masculine tricks on her, to turn her own awakening sensuality against her. To seduce her. She had never known pleasure with a man, so she had no defenses against it.

And in that lay his best hope of having her again.

CHAPTER
31

Nicole didn't know how long she stood on tiptoe kissing Chase. She knew only that at some point her bones turned to honey and his arms came hard around her, supporting her. When she finally surfaced from the slow mating of tongues, she could barely breathe.

She opened her eyes, wanting to see him, needing to know if he had enjoyed the kiss as much as she had.

"Yes," he said, answering the question in her eyes. "Oh, God, yes!"

She smiled, her teeth very white against her reddened mouth. With one finger she touched his full lower lip, loving the sensuous heat and resilience of his flesh.

His tongue flicked out and curled around her fingertip as it had once curled around her nipple. He pulled her finger into his mouth, sucking and stroking with his tongue.

Her breath caught, held, thickened.

"I like that," she said in a husky voice. "But it makes me kind of . . . I don't know. Restless."

Slowly she withdrew her finger, wondering at the very hot, very male smile on Chase's face.

"Then maybe we'd better get down to the beach," he suggested. "You can work off some of your restlessness in the water."

"I didn't bring a swimsuit."

"That's okay," he said as he set off down the lava again. "There's nobody around to see you."

She looked at his broad, retreating back. "Excuse me? Nobody? What are you, chopped liver?"

"I've already seen you." He turned around and looked at her with open male approval. "And I liked everything I saw, especially the color of your nipples fresh from my mouth." He smiled slightly. "I suppose that embarrasses you."

She opened her mouth to say yes, then realized it wasn't true. Not anymore. She let out a long breath and admitted, "It's hard for me to be naked with a man. I— It makes me nervous. Except for the time with you, the memories I have of being naked and—well, they aren't very good at all."

Chase closed his eyes and tried not to think of all the ways a man could make a woman feel bad in bed.

"Did I hurt you?" he asked, needing reassurance that in some way, at least, he hadn't been cruel. "That night. Did I?"

"No." She spoke quickly, because she saw a need in him that had nothing to do with desire. "I meant what I said. I never enjoyed sex before that night."

His breath came out with a ragged sound and he opened his eyes. "I don't deserve it, but I'm glad."

Not quite trusting himself any longer, he turned his back and picked his way down the jumbled dark river of lava.

After a moment she followed him. She felt unsettled in a new and intriguing way. She didn't know why. She just knew she felt like sunlight and champagne were fizzing in her blood.

The lava flow went all the way to the water. Together Nicole and Chase stood on a cliff and looked at the black tongue of stone licking out into the yielding sea.

"There must have been one hell of a blast when it all came together," he said quietly.

"I thought lava flows, especially pahoehoe, were slow, not explosive." She frowned, thinking about what she had seen. "I mean, sure, there's some steam when the lava creeps down to the sea, but it's more like backyard firecrackers than real explosions."

He smiled slightly. "You ever throw a few drops of water on a really hot griddle?"

"Every time I make pancakes."

"Well, that lava was once hell's own griddle with a whole ocean pouring over it. I'll bet tons of water and stone met and instantly vaporized with a sound like bombs going off."

She looked at the water and the lava and tried to imagine the wild clash of fire and water.

"That was what it was like at Surtsey," he said.

"We have film in the archives. A river of molten stone running down to an icy sea. The shock waves from the explosions made it sound like a battlefield. And in a way that's what it was. A natural war zone."

"What was it like to be there, to see and hear it?"

"Like watching God at work. Awesome."

Chase glanced to the left, away from the solid lava flow. There was a black-sand beach. After the lava cooled, a fringe of graceful coconut palms had taken root along the upper margin of the beach.

"Look," he said, pointing. "That's where the black sand came from. The explosive meeting of ocean and lava."

"I thought it came from old lava crumbling."

"A little probably does. But a whole lot of black sand comes from the moment when red-hot stone and seawater explode on contact."

Nicole looked at the peaceful sand curving out to embrace the sea. "I'm glad everything has cooled off."

Not quite everything, he thought ruefully, feeling the heaviness of his erection with every heartbeat. **But there's no danger of an explosion either.**

I hope.

Together they left behind the wild jumble of lava where the boiling blood of the volcano had once met the sea. As they walked toward a grove of palms, Chase took Nicole's hand. When they reached the grove, he kissed her palm, tasted it once with a lingering touch of his tongue, released her, and reached for the fastenings of his hiking boots. Bracing his butt against a tree trunk, he took off one boot and stuffed a sock into it.

She watched and thought about stripping naked in full sunlight with him. She doubted that she had the nerve.

"There are three ways we can do this," he said matter-of-factly, working on the other boot.

"Do what?"

"Go skinny-dipping. We can pretend we aren't—" he began.

She made a strangled sound and tried not to laugh out loud.

"Yeah, that's the way it strikes me, too." He looked at her with a wry smile. "The second way is we sneak sideways looks at each other and trip all over our own feet on the way to the water."

This time she gave up and laughed out loud. "What's the third choice?"

"We just take a good look and get over it."

With a single quick, twisting motion he stripped off his shirt. Then he pulled off his shorts and underwear and stood in front of her, naked.

"Of course, a man is at a real disadvantage in this situation," he said.

"He is?" she asked in an odd voice. Her glance traveled helplessly down his hard male body. Very male. **Very** hard. "Oh," she said, understanding what he meant about being at a disadvantage. "I see."

"Yeah, I'm sure you do," he agreed wryly. "I want you, and there's no damn way on earth I can disguise it when I'm naked. But I'm a man, not a baby. I don't expect to get everything I want the second I want it." He waited until her golden eyes came up to meet his. "Don't be frightened, butterfly. This is just my body's way of saying that, as a woman, you please me very much. Is that so bad?"

She let out the breath she hadn't been aware of holding. And she waited for fear to come.

She was still waiting several breaths later, looking at him, when she realized that the thought of pleasing Chase as a woman was not frightening in the least. She cleared her throat and tried to be as honest with him as he was being with her.

"No. It's good. I like the idea of . . . well, exciting you."

"Do you?" he asked with a slow smile.

She closed her eyes and spoke quickly, painfully, forcing out the words. "You won't be angry with me? Ted always was. He expected me to want him instantly, constantly. I'm not like that."

"Neither am I. I don't walk around ready to fuck anything female that will hold still for it."

Her eyes flew open at his bluntness.

"I know that might be hard for you to believe," he said, "considering the evidence in front of me. But it's true all the same. You have a potent effect on me. And it's **you** I want, not just sex. Hell, if it was just sex, I'd be in town right now, riding some faceless body. Sex isn't hard to find."

She watched as he turned and walked into the waves, leaving her to admire the fact that his tan was the same even shade of brown all over. Everywhere. When she realized she was staring, she flushed—and kept right on staring. Despite his size, his body wasn't bulky. He was simply powerful, coordinated, and **male**.

With fingers that trembled, she went to work on her boots. Then her clothes. Then she gathered her courage in both hands and walked into the water. Naked.

Chase stood waist-deep in the jeweled blue sea.

So did Nicole, but she was still half uncovered.

"Women," she said, her voice desperately normal, "are at a disadvantage in this case."

Accepting that as the invitation it was, he turned and looked at her. Slowly. Very thoroughly.

"Beautiful," he said simply.

And she was, with her wide amber eyes and the slanting line of her cheekbones stained with red. Long, elegant neck, as smooth as the shadow in the hollow of her throat. Her nipples were taut and deep pink and her breasts were the same smooth golden brown as her arms.

"I see you don't like bathing suits any better than I do," he said.

"I hate them. I like—" Her voice broke. She cleared her throat and admitted to him what she had never told anyone before. "I like to feel the sun on my breasts, and the breeze and the warm rain everywhere."

Her words undid whatever cooling effect the ocean had had on Chase's erection.

"Someday you'll feel me like that," he said, running his fingertips from her forehead to her thighs hidden beneath a bright surge of water. "I'll be all over you like a warm rain. I won't even take you. I'll just pleasure you." He lifted his hand. His wet fingertip touched first one nipple, then the other, leaving a diamond drop of water behind. "Think about it, butterfly. All you have to do is ask."

She couldn't help thinking about it. Ripples of sensual response coursed through her, making her nipples tighten even more.

He saw, and wished with savage urgency that he could simply pull her into his arms and seduce her.

But he couldn't. If she got afraid all over again and backed away, she would blame herself, not him. That would hurt her more than anything he had done to her.

He let a quiet breath out through his clenched teeth. He had to be the way he had been in the clearing—motionless, offering himself while she spiraled closer and closer to him on velvet wings. She had to come and drink the sweetness from him. Only then would she lose her fear of being crushed and thrown aside.

Even knowing that, he couldn't stop himself from bending down and licking the drop of seawater from one of her nipples.

"Salt is bad for the skin," he said almost roughly. "And you have such beautiful skin."

She watched with a shivering feeling of in-evitability while his head moved to her other breast and his tongue flicked out, touching her far too briefly.

"Chase." Her voice was tight, ragged.

He straightened, expecting her to retreat. "Yes?"

"I—I like that. I really like it. Would you do it again?"

Slowly he touched each of her nipples with a wet fingertip, leaving behind a drop of glittering water. This time he removed the drop with exquisite care before he took the taut peak into his mouth and tugged at it.

Heat shot out from the core of her body, fire snaking through every pore, molten need racing through her. Long before he turned to her other breast, her hands were clinging to him for support. His mustache stroked her like a silk brush before he drew her deeply into his mouth. She made a tiny sound in the back of her throat and arched her back, offering herself to him as she never had to any man.

By the time Chase finally released Nicole, she was trembling and breathing brokenly. Somehow he scraped up the determination to stop before it was too late.

And the next breath would be too late.

Closing his eyes, locking his jaw, he held her in his arms, just held her, letting the warm surge and retreat of the water bring her against him and then take her away.

After a few minutes of quiet holding, he trusted himself not to lift her up and fit her over his rigid, aching flesh, to feel again the satin heat and tightness of her surrounding him, tugging at him with every breath, every caress.

When he felt her stir in his arms, he reluctantly loosened his hold. Her cheek rubbed against his chest. Slowly she turned her head from side to side, openly enjoying his male textures.

"If I touched you the same way," she said softly, "would you enjoy it?"

"Yes, but you don't have to. I don't expect—"

The rest of his words shattered in a ripping intake of breath. Her tongue had found one nipple beneath the curling black hair on his chest. Even as he told himself he shouldn't react so much to an innocent little lick, he had to bite back a groan of sheer pleasure.

While she transformed his flat nipple into a tiny, hard nub, his whole body went taut, shivering.

She felt it, understood its source. The certainty that she was pleasing him was almost dizzying. So was his taste, his scent, the heat and power of his body radiating beneath her hands. Letting her explore him. Letting her taste.

Letting her.

In breathless silence she discovered how sensitive her tongue could be to textures as well as tastes, how good it felt to twist her body slowly against his, how much she liked pleasuring him as thoroughly as he had pleasured her. Finally she lifted her mouth, only to return to his nipple again and then again in sexy little forays, licking, biting lightly, wholly lost in the sensual instant.

Hard fingers slid beneath her chin, tilting her head back. When she started to ask what was wrong, his mouth claimed hers, leaving no room for anything except the hot, deep completion of his kiss.

A wave tumbled in, washing over them in a warm surge of water that went up to her collarbone and threatened to pull her from his arms. Even as her arms tightened to hold on to him, he lifted her beyond the reach of the wave.

"One of us," he said hoarsely against her mouth, "has to watch for the big ones. That would be you."

With that he turned her in his arms until she faced the open ocean. Slowly he pulled her back against his chest, fitting her hips into the cradle of his thighs. When he nudged against her, aroused and hard, he expected her to retreat.

She didn't.

"But now I can't touch you," she protested, looking at him over her shoulder.

The movement shifted her so that his erection ended up captured between her sleek thighs. He bit back a groan of outrageous pleasure. And need. The kind of need he had never known.

"You're touching me," he said almost roughly.

She flushed. "But not—not with my hands. Or my mouth."

Silently he admitted that it was just as well he was out of reach of her mouth and hands for the moment. The pleasure she took in his body was dangerously exciting. It made him forget all the reasons he had to be patient.

"Then I'll just have to touch you twice as much to make up for it, won't I?" he said.

"Are you sure?" she asked hesitantly.

"Yes."

"Sure-sure?" she pressed.

"Sure-sure," he said against her hair. "Let me show you, butterfly."

With one hand between her breasts and the other flattened over the blazing triangle just above her thighs, he pressed her even closer to his hungry body.

"Tell me what you like." He nuzzled her ear, then traced it with the tip of his tongue. "This?"

Slowly he thrust his tongue into her ear, withdrew, and thrust again.

Her breathing stopped.

He nibbled not quite softly around the rim of her ear until he felt her arch into the caress, demanding more. Smiling, nipping lightly, he continued along her hairline to her neck. There he stopped. With exquisite gentleness he used his teeth on the sensitive bundle of nerves at her nape.

The currents of heat that had been gathering in Nicole suddenly shot through her with a force that made her weak. She trembled and leaned against him.

"Yes?" he asked, repeating the caress, feeling her body soften even more in his arms.

"Y-yes," she said, her voice catching.

He bent over her nape again, and the trembling of her body rippled through him. His hands found the smooth weight of her breasts, caught the hard peaks between his fingers, and tugged the nipples exactly when his teeth closed on her nape.

She made a tearing sound of sheer pleasure.

Tenderly, relentlessly, he caressed her until she was crying with each breath and her hips were moving over him in slow, instinctive rhythms, seeking something more satisfying than his simple presence pressed between her thighs.

One of his hands slid down her body into the warm ocean, needing what she needed—to discover the even warmer woman waiting within her softness. He caressed the smooth skin of her thighs and the tangled silk of her red triangle as he gently bit her shoulder.

The combination of sensations made her gasp and press against him hungrily. His rubbed his erection between her thighs, holding her in a sensual vise that increased with each small, involuntary movement of her hips. Slowly, languidly, his fingertips found and stroked her soft folds.

"Yes?" he asked.

Her answer was a moan and a slow, rhythmic roll of her hips, as though the muted thunder of the breaking waves was the opening drumbeat of a sensuous dance.

The feel of her softness opening hotly over him made his whole body clench with a hunger that was more fierce than any he had ever known.

Pele—God, woman, you'll burn us both to ash.

With a throaty sound he closed his teeth on her nape again and pressed two fingers deeply into her softness. She cried out and shivered helplessly against his hand, utterly in thrall to sensations she never wanted to end. He stroked her repeatedly, felt every bit of the clench and tug of her satin body clinging to his probing touch.

Then he felt the shivering take her again, felt the liquid silk of her response flowing over him. Raw need ripped through him, tearing away his control, making him shake with the force of his hunger.

Another big wave came, pressing her against him in a warm surge of power, pushing him over a hidden edge. He turned her in his arms and lifted her.

"Wrap your legs around me," he said hoarsely.

His urgency and the sudden change of position caught her by surprise. She stiffened in his arms. "What . . . ?"

When he heard her uncertainty, he froze. Despite his promise, he was taking her, not waiting for her to come to him.

"I'm sorry, butterfly," he said painfully. "It won't happen again."

With the last shred of his control he let her slide back down his body into the warm sea. Gently he turned her and pushed her toward the black-sand crescent and the fringe of palms.

"Go back up on the beach," he said. "You won't have any problem with sudden waves there."

Automatically Nicole waded ashore. When she reached it, she discovered that Chase hadn't followed her. His absence made her feel empty, dazed. Lost.

She turned back to see where Chase was.

The sea was empty.

"Chase?" she called, looking around wildly.

No one answered.

Moments later a dark body broke the surface of the ocean out where the waves were coming apart. Chase swam smoothly, powerfully, spearing beneath the breaking waves and reappearing on their far side.

Nicole watched him with an aching in her throat that she didn't understand. It seemed like forever before he turned and began swimming back to her, riding the wild whiteness of breaking waves.

It won't happen again.

She trembled, and tears flowed hotly down her cheeks, and she didn't know why she cried.

CHAPTER
32

Ten days later Nicole sat cross-legged on the oversize garden lounge and wondered if Chase would call tonight as he had for the last nine nights. From the mainland.

Three time zones and thousands of miles away.

Sorry, butterfly. Something came unstuck. I have to go for a while. Lisa is coming with me.

Nicole envied Chase's daughter. Talking on the phone with him was wonderful, hearing the husky burr in his voice, making him laugh, laughing in turn; but talking wasn't enough. It wasn't the same as feeling his strength when he hugged her, smelling the unique scent of him on her hands, seeing his eyes go smoky when she tasted him.

Every night he told her about the quivers and burps of Mount Saint Helens that continued decades after the major eruption, and the pile of paperwork that threatened to bury him alive. She told him about the sketches she was doing and that dancing at the Kipuka Club just wasn't the same without him. He put Lisa on the line, and she asked about Benny and kipuka picnics.

They weren't the same either.

Lisa sent kisses and hugs and put her daddy back on the line. He and Nicole talked a while longer, a lot longer, more every time. They talked about anything and everything and nothing at all. Even though it made her ache to hear his voice and not be able to see him, to touch him, she didn't want the connection to end. Neither did he. They talked until long past midnight in his time zone.

And every night when she finally hung up the phone, she cried. She wanted to see Chase so much that she felt like she was being scraped with a dull knife.

He said he would get back as soon as he could, she told herself for the tenth time in as many minutes. **Now, get to work so you'll have time to play when he does come back.**

There was a lot of work to do, but the drawing wasn't going very well. No matter where she looked or what she looked at, all she could see was his face, his smile, his hands on the drums. On her.

Stop it, she snarled silently at herself.

Sitting cross-legged on her big garden chaise, she lectured the dreamy-eyed woman who had taken over her mind. After a while she was able to concentrate on the jacaranda trees arching overhead. They had burst into bloom, lifting masses of lavender flowers in silent, generous offering to the sun.

Thousands upon thousands of blossoms shivered when the breeze slid caressingly over their soft surfaces. Some of the blooms came undone with the gentle pressure and were swept away on transparent currents of air. In time those flowers floated to the ground to lie heaped in sweet windrows that swirled with each new touch of the breeze.

Normally she loved these days when the jacaranda bloom was at its peak and blossoms showered the land with a fragile lavender rain. But for the last ten days she had done little more than sketch unhappily during the daylight hours and pace her cottage after dark, waiting for Chase's nightly call.

When she slept, it was badly.

When she awoke in the night, it was to a body quickened by sensations that made her breath catch in her throat and stay there until the dawn came. Just the thought of the time she had spent in his arms was more than enough to send heat lancing through her, tightening her until she wanted to scream.

It had been like that since the day he had led her into the sea and taught her how much more he knew about her body than she did. Now she waited for him to come back with an intensity that made her tremble like a wire strung too tight. She didn't know why she trembled. She knew only that she did.

Maybe today. Or tomorrow, she thought, doodling on the edges of a failed sketch.

She wanted to return with Chase to the warm, creamy sea. She wanted him to miss her the way she missed him, to lie awake nights and spend his days distracted, to not take three breaths without thinking of her.

So you pleased him a little, she told herself. **So what? The world is full of women who can please him a lot more than a little.**

That was something she tried not to think about. She didn't succeed.

With a silent curse she threw down her pencil and stopped pretending to be sketching the jacaranda trees.

"Bad day?"

Nicole spun around so quickly at the sound of Chase's voice that her sketchbook went flying. There was no hesitation, no shyness in her greeting. She simply came off the chaise and into his arms and held on to him as though that was the only thing keeping both of them alive.

He held her the same way. "Miss me?"

Her answer was a shudder and a ragged sound that was all emotion.

"That's the way I missed you." He buried his face in the fragrance of her braided hair and inhaled deeply. "I thought if I couldn't see you or touch you, I wouldn't want you so much it felt like I was breathing broken glass." His laugh was short, harsh. "I was wrong. I keep being wrong about you, butterfly."

He picked her up, held her against the length of his body, and let her presence in his arms flood through him. She pressed her face against his neck and clung to him with every bit of her dancer's strength.

All that Chase had been thinking and feeling since the moment he realized just how badly he had misjudged Nicole came pouring out in a torrent of words. He knew it was too soon to say such things, but his own exhaustion and her abandoned greeting swept away common sense.

"I kept thinking about how Lisa smiles when she sees you coming up the path," he said. "Then I'd remember your laughter at one of Mark's awful puns and the way you listen, really **listen,** when I talk about the islands." He found her mouth and kissed her deeply, fiercely, shuddering at her open, wild response. "I remembered that, too. The taste and the heat of you. I don't want to be without you anymore. Marry me, Nicole. Let me—"

"**Marriage?**" she interrupted, pulling back in shock.

Even before Nicole spoke, Chase felt her rejection in the sudden stiffness of her body. Too late he remembered how she felt about marriage.

Being a man's thing. **All day. Every day. And the nights.**

Closing his eyes, he cursed his foolish dream savagely, silently. Just because she jumped up and threw herself into his arms didn't mean that she wanted to risk belonging to him in any important way. He had shown her only a little of the fire buried within her body, let her taste just a bit of the wild honey.

Naturally she had missed him. She didn't know that any man could kindle the flames and drink the sweetness of mutual sensuality with her.

"Sorry, butterfly." He set her on the ground again. "I never should have asked. Blame it on jet lag and the heat of the moment. Like I said, you keep taking me by surprise. You make me respond at every level. I make you respond somewhat at one." With a bittersweet smile he touched the tip of her nose with his lips in a casual kiss. "But then, nobody ever said life was fair."

Nicole tried to hold on to her spinning thoughts long enough to make a sensible statement. She couldn't. "I didn't mean— It's just that I hadn't thought about— After Ted, I promised myself that I would never, ever, **ever**—"

Chase kissed her gently, stopping the tumble of words. "It's all right. I understand. You have no reason to trust me with your happiness and a lot of reasons not to."

He let go of her and backed up several steps, putting her out of reach. With every breath he berated himself for jamming three weeks of work into ten days so that he could rush back to her.

And ruin everything.

"Please don't," she said in a raw voice. "Don't feel guilty about what happened that morning at

Dane's house. I know you'd never hurt me. Don't you believe me?"

"I believe you," Chase said wearily. "But the absence of pain isn't enough. Not for sex. Not for love. Certainly not for an enduring marriage. Mind. Body. Soul. That's what marriage has to be to work. I didn't know that the first time around. Lisa paid the price for my stupidity. But I know now. All or nothing at all."

"Does that mean you won't—that we can't—" Nicole closed her eyes and clenched her hands together so fiercely they ached. "Please don't go away from me," she whispered. "I couldn't bear it. You make me feel so many things that I didn't even think were possible for me."

"Any man could do the same."

Her eyes flew open. "That's not true!"

"Oh, it's true," he countered calmly. Then his mouth turned down in a sad smile at her disbelief.

"But it's only with you—" she began.

"I just happened to be the man you saw when you were starting to split the past's cocoon," he said, interrupting her before he could hear any more of the words that cut so deep and hurt so much because he wanted so desperately for them to be true, really true, all-the-way-to-the-soul true. The way it was for him, but not for her. "For you, I'm a stage that will pass."

"No," she said, tears brimming in her eyes. "That's not true!"

With a choked sound she threw herself back into

his arms and held him fiercely, shaking with emotions and thoughts that were too new and much too powerful for her to sort out, much less understand.

For several minutes Chase held her and spoke in a matter-of-fact voice about matter-of-fact things. His voice and his words belied the darkness in his eyes and the grim brackets etched deeply on either side of his mouth. Slowly the harsh tension began to leave her body.

"What's this I hear about a big luau?" he asked.

She drew in a broken breath and accepted the neutral topic. After another breath she was able to answer him. "It's the annual Kamehameha bash. Pig in a pit. Fires on the beach. Dancing all night. Everything tourists think of when they think of Hawaii."

"Where will it be?"

She pulled away from him just enough to point toward the tangle of greenery that led from the high ground where they stood to the beach below. "Down there."

He stroked her hair lightly and stepped back from her arms. "When?"

"Tomorrow night."

"That soon? Good."

Something in his voice made her go still. "You're going back to the mainland again, aren't you?"

He nodded.

"When?"

"Soon." Silently he added, **A lot sooner than I'd hoped. But it's the only way, butterfly.**

I can't trust myself around you. I almost took you that day in the ocean, and I want you far more right now than I did then.

She watched him undo his tie with a few quick jerks. For the first time it registered on her that he must have come straight from the plane, not even taking time to change out of his mainland business clothes.

"Where's Lisa?" Nicole asked.

"With Benny. Somehow he knew we were back. He was waiting at the cottage door."

Her throat tightened as she saw the lines of strain beneath his exterior calm. "You must be exhausted."

"I've been up most of the last three nights. I got most of my paperwork done when Lisa was asleep." He yanked, and the tie hissed out from beneath his collar. He unbuttoned more buttons, took a long breath, and let it out in a sigh. "Have any sketches for me to look at?"

"None that I like."

The corner of his mouth lifted very slightly. "Do you ever like them?"

"Not very often," she admitted.

"Then it's a good thing I have the final say. I'd hate for my words to have to carry the whole **Islands of Life** project."

The thought that he might need her profession-ally startled her. Silently she watched while he unbuttoned his shirtsleeves, rolled up the cuffs, and then started back up the trail.

"Can you meet me at my cottage in about an

hour?" he asked without looking back. "That will give me time to clean up and eat before we look at the sketches."

"Eat?"

"Dinner. My stomach is still on mainland time."

"I'll make you something," she called after his retreating form.

"That's all right, butterfly. I've been cooking for myself for years. I'm getting pretty good at it."

Nicole watched Chase merge into the greenery along the tangled garden trail and wondered why she was crying. He was back. She could see him, touch him . . .

And he seemed farther away than ever.

C H A P T E R
33

When Chase came to Nicole's cabin that night, Lisa was with him. Nicole was glad to see the little girl and disappointed at the same time.

You can be alone with him later, Nicole told herself briskly. **Now let Lisa know she's welcome.**

"Hug?" she asked the girl.

"Hug-hug!" Lisa said, and leaped up into Nicole's arms.

Holding her, Nicole spun around and around, making her little armload laugh with delight.

Despite the pain of seeing Nicole and knowing how badly he had screwed up something beautiful, Chase smiled to see his daughter's pleasure. She was getting over Lynette's casual cruelty, and part of the reason Lisa was coming out of her shell was the redheaded dancer who was spinning her.

"If I had known you were coming," Nicole said, stopping and kissing Lisa's cheek, "I would have bought some peppermint ice cream."

"Benny did," Chase said. "Like I said, that boy is uncanny."

"He's perfect," Lisa said quickly, defending her friend.

"Perfectly uncanny," Chase agreed.

"Is uncanny good?" she asked doubtfully.

"Sure is." He took his daughter's hand. "Means he's a wizard."

"Oh." Lisa shrugged. "Well, of course he is. He's Benny."

Chase smiled. "That he is. Remember our deal?"

She nodded and turned to Nicole. "I'm going to draw while you and Daddy work. Is that all right?"

"Sure-sure. You know where everything is."

"Fourth drawer?" Lisa asked, wanting to be certain.

"That's the one."

When Lisa skipped off into the kitchen, Nicole tried not to stare at Chase. The shadow of a half day's growth of beard lay across his jaw. Fatigue or something less easily defined had drawn his face into dark planes and angles that shifted when he smiled or spoke, but never really softened.

"Sketches?" he asked, yawning.

"Over here."

The futon was in its couch mode, folded to more or less comfortably support a seated adult. A folder of sketches lay on the floor in front it.

No matter what its present shape, Chase didn't trust himself to sit down on the same futon where he had once taken Nicole. He was too tired, too unhappy, too close to the edge of his control. If she sat next to him, he wouldn't be able to keep his hands to himself, even with the bright-eyed little chaperone in the kitchen.

Bending over, Chase raked up the folder in one hand and flipped it open with the other.

"Some of the sketches aren't of native fauna," Nicole said quickly, "but they should give you an idea of how I treat subjects in close-up as well as part of a whole landscape."

He nodded and began sorting through the sketches. He had meant to work quickly, almost impersonally, but the drawings simply took him by the throat and wouldn't let go. Each line was distinct, crisp, yet each flowed into another line, capturing the seamless grace of nature itself.

A solitary bird dodging waves at sunset.

A palm tree dancing with the wind.

A green coconut that could have been a fertility goddess.

An asbestos-shrouded scientist edging up to take a sample of molten lava.

The absolute desolation of newly created land.

The graceful, almost living sweep of pahoehoe curving back on itself like a snail.

He looked up and saw her watching anxiously. "These are wonderful," he said simply. "You draw both the fact and the art of nature."

Before she could do more than smile, he was looking at sketches again. He went through them once, twice, three times, and each time he murmured fragments of praise. The words didn't mean as much to her as the fact that he was obviously impressed by her work.

One sketch in particular compelled him. The drawing was almost stark in its simplicity: a single jacaranda bud at the tip of a supple twig. The bud was swollen to bursting, but neither the color nor the softness of the coming bloom showed in the tightly furled bud.

Chase studied it for a long, long time. Then he looked up, pinning her with his bleak eyes. "This is a brilliant drawing, Nicole. On the verge of sweet becoming, but the bud will never bloom for us, will it? Caught forever between all and nothing at all." He looked back at the bud frozen in time. "I don't know when I've ever seen anything quite so beautiful or even half so sad."

He put the sketches back into the folder and handed it to her, careful not to touch her in any way.

"Keep going in this vein," he said neutrally, "but concentrate on native fauna when you can."

"What about a new kipuka? I mean, going there. Hiking."

And all the rest. The hugging and the holding, the heat and the pleasure.

"Not tomorrow," he said, yawning again. "Too much work at the lab. Maybe when I get back from my next trip to the mainland. But you don't need to wait with your sketches. The native fauna is the same no matter which kipuka it's growing in." He turned toward the kitchen. "C'mon, punkin. Time to go. Your old dad is worn out."

Lisa came running out of the kitchen and launched herself at her father. He caught her, lifted her high, and tucked her squealing under one arm.

"Thanks for sharing the drawings," he said as he walked to the door. "Are you dancing at the luau?"

"Only if you drum for me."

He hesitated. "Sure, Pele. It's a deal. We'll see you at the luau."

Nicole didn't know how long she stared at the door Chase had closed behind him. It must have been a long time, because night had gathered thickly in the garden outside.

Too much work at the lab.

You don't need to wait.

We'll see you at the luau.

She didn't know she was pacing and crying until she felt the cold glide of tears off her cheeks. She kept pacing, kept crying, kept hearing him, kept seeing him.

Missing him.

He's back, so why am I still pacing? Why am I still missing him?

Why am I crying!

No answer came but the unvarying rhythm of her feet over the wooden floor. She glanced toward the CD player, then looked away. Even dancing didn't appeal to her right now. Nothing did.

Except Chase.

Marry me, butterfly. Be with me all the time.

With a throttled cry she paced the living room

over and over. Remembered words followed her like shades of darkness.

Don't look so sad, butterfly. You can respond to other men. But I won't leave you until you know that's true. The honey will be here until you open those velvet wings and fly away.

Her hands clenched and she paced more quickly. She didn't want it to happen like this. Too fast. She needed time. She needed to think. She needed—

Chase.

Are you dancing at the luau?

Only if you drum for me.

Sure, Pele. It's a deal.

The time between now and tomorrow's luau yawned in a chasm as deep and wide as the night.

Damn it! Why is he doing this to me!

There was no answer except the seething, unpredictable currents coiling deep inside her. She was like Kilauea itself, racked by hidden, secret forerunners of an explosion to come.

He hadn't kissed her. Not even once. Not even casually.

She had waited and waited, her heart a wild thing caught in her ribs.

Why didn't he kiss me?

Then she understood, and she wanted to scream.

If she wanted him, she would have to come to him like the butterfly in the forest. The sweetness was there, waiting for her. All she had to do was light within his hand and drink.

She closed her eyes and saw the jacaranda bud quivering with potential.

On the verge of sweet becoming, but the bud will never bloom for us, will it? Caught forever between all and nothing at all.

"Chase," she said hoarsely, putting her face in her hands. "You want too much from me! You're too much man. I'm too little woman. I'll disappoint you and destroy myself."

All or nothing at all.

And like the bud, she was imprisoned between.

CHAPTER
34

By the time morning came, Nicole was as restless as the melted rock seething beneath Kilauea's black shield. She had almost gone to Chase's cottage many times during the long hours of darkness. She wanted to see him, to talk to him, to . . .

What? she asked herself impatiently. **What do you want?**

There wasn't any answer in the moon-silvered night, just a mixture of fear and restlessness, loneliness and longing.

There wasn't any answer in the rising sun and the dazzling rainbows arching down from the clouds.

There wasn't any answer in the blazing glory of sunset and the excited speculations of the scientists at the luau about Kilauea's latest harmonic stirrings.

There wasn't any answer in the familiar faces gathered around the luau fires on the beach. There wasn't any answer in the conversations of friends.

Worst of all, there was no man with rain-colored eyes and midnight hair and a bittersweet smile to break her heart. There was nothing for Nicole at the luau but the feeling of being frozen between past and future, pain and pleasure, nothing and everything.

And then the drums began to beat.

Nicole turned away from Bobby in mid-word, leaving him to watch her retreating back with rueful understanding. She didn't even notice. She had room for nothing in herself but the elemental summons of the drums.

Come to me.

Barefoot, her hair tumbling freely to her hips, she came to stand in front of Chase. She wasn't aware of the applause or the sudden end to conversations around her. Nothing existed for her but the drums and the man who made them speak to her soul.

His hands moved quickly and the drums called out to her in complex, driving rhythms.

Dance for me. Dance. For me. Dance!

Nicole shook back her hair and let the rhythms take her body, giving herself to the drums. To Chase. Her hips moved sinuously beneath the blazing curtain of her hair. Firelight gleamed on her skin, giving it a lush golden color. The lavalava she wore low on her hips was the same golden-red as her hair.

Wrapped in fire, she moved elegantly, sensually, letting her body speak for her, dancing for the only person in the world besides herself.

Chase.

Minute by minute he watched her through narrowed silver eyes while his hands moved skillfully, relentlessly, driving toward a climax that would demand everything from himself and the drums and the dancer.

Burn for me, Pele. Burn. For me!

And she did.

Time stood still while she danced out at the edge of her control, giving herself to the wild, sweet violence of the drums. Finally her body couldn't sustain the blazing demands of the dance any longer. With a cry she threw up her arms, surrendering the night and the victory to the intricate thunder of the drums.

The drums stopped in the same instant Nicole did, leaving only the bonfires to burn among the stately rhythm of the breaking waves.

Chase stood and smiled, acknowledging the applause. Then he stepped back into the shadows of the palms and disappeared.

Nicole stared in disbelief at the place where he had been. It was empty. She called out to him, but the sound of clapping hands overwhelmed her words. When she started after him, she was slowed down by the enthusiasm of her friends. She put them off with a smile and raced to catch up with Chase.

There was no one waiting for her on the moonlit path.

No one waiting for her in her cottage.

No one waiting in his.

Wearily she returned to her own cottage and waited for him to come to her.

Nothing came to the cottage except the sounds of laughter floating up from the beach. When she could take no more of the numb waiting, she stripped off her clothes and stood for a long time in the shower, wishing she could wash away memories as easily as tears.

At last the steamy confinement of the shower lost its appeal. She put on a black silk blouse and an ankle-length lavalava. As she anchored her hair in place with ivory chopsticks topped by tassels of chiming bells, she admitted to herself that she really didn't want to go back to the luau.

She didn't want to stay in the cottage either.

She wanted Chase.

Obviously he didn't want her.

Slowly she walked back out into the garden and down the twisting, overgrown path to her jacaranda grove. Brushed by moonlight and warm winds, the blossoms were shimmering silver clouds crowning midnight branches. Petals lay in drifts and shifted in pale streamers over the ground. At each sigh of wind, more blossoms floated down, falling soundlessly to the warm earth.

With a weariness that had nothing to do with her recent dance, Nicole stretched out on the oversize chaise. The petals pressed between her body and the cloth cover of the chaise felt cool. Every breath of wind sent more petals drifting down to settle over her body as softly as a kiss.

For a long time she lay without moving, letting the silent, fragrant cascade of blossoms swirl around her, trying very hard to think of nothing at all.

Finally she slept.

Only then did Chase step out of the shadows and come to stand by Nicole, watching her sleep in the moonlight, all her fires banked. As he looked down at her, he told himself how many kinds of fool he was to be here. He should have kept walking along the beach, kept counting the thundering waves or the stars or the number of steps he took away from the woman he wanted more than he wanted to breathe.

He wanted her in too many ways.

She wanted him in only one way.

Sex wasn't enough to ease the need inside him. Sex alone would only make the need worse. Much worse. It would be unbearable to make love to her and lose her all over again because she didn't love him. Couldn't love him.

He knew that, just as he knew he should have kept walking alone in the night. Yet here he was, counting the silent flowers drifting down to rest on skin that was softer and more fragrant than any blossom.

She wanted him, but not enough.

He wanted her.

Too much.

The way he had hurt her weeks ago. Too much.

Nothing he did could take back that morning, those cruel words, the bitter destruction of the first budding of love. In those few scalding minutes he had lost her.

All that remained of what might have been was her own buried sensuality. He could release that, giving it to her and to himself, a burning gift and epitaph to what might have been.

Making love would free her from the cruel past.

And enslave him to a cruel future.

He knew that as surely as he knew there was nothing else he could give to her but the velvet wings of her own sensuality and the freedom to fly.

There had been no one for him like the woman sleeping in a gentle storm of falling blossoms. She had shown him how wrong he was about women and love. She had healed the black scars that life had left on him and scarred herself in turn on the uncooled fires of his rage at women. The least he could do was heal some of Nicole's scars.

And when it scarred him in return . . . he would survive. He had Lisa and Dane and Jan, people who loved him, people he loved. It would be enough.

Who are you kidding? Chase thought bleakly. **You can't even imagine not having Nicole to talk to, to laugh with, to dance for you. No matter what you tell yourself tonight, tomorrow you'll be on your knees praying that she'll find life without you to be as lonely as hell.**

And then she'll come to you, needing you and only you.

Won't she?

With a sad smile at his own dream of love, Chase sat next to Nicole on the broad chaise. Still asleep, she turned toward him. At every stirring of her body, golden bells sang. Their tiny notes were unexpected, sweet. They pierced his soul.

Very gently he slid the ivory chopsticks from the piled coils of her hair, letting it spill like cool fire over his hands. This time he would know the full glory of her hair wrapped around him. And if the memory of it was more salt in the wounds of his loss, so be it. He had given her too much pain to hold back simply because he knew that pain would come to him in turn.

As Chase set the ornaments aside, ivory and gold gleamed and sang softly in the moonlight. Slowly he bent down to her. At first he simply breathed in her warmth, her scent, her presence. The moon shadow of her eyelashes lay like black lace on her skin. He kissed the fragile shadows, then the delicate warmth of her eyelids, the smooth hollow of her cheek, the sensitive inward spiral of her ear, the sensual curve of her lips.

And he felt her come alive at his touch, felt her lips opening to him, her breath washing sweetly over him.

"Chase?" Her voice was husky, dreamy, neither fully awake nor asleep. "I looked for you. I wanted to drink the sweetness from your hand." Her breath came out in a broken sigh. "I couldn't find you."

His hands tightened in her hair. "I know," he murmured, sipping gently at her lips. He had been running from the hurt of loving and not being loved in return. If he had any sense at all, he would still be running. "I'm here now, butterfly."

"Don't leave me." She threaded her fingers deeply into the rough silk of his hair.

"Not until you know that you can fly." Then he took her mouth before she could ask what he meant.

All her questions vanished as his tongue caressed her, showing her again how complex a simple kiss could be. Feeling the first currents of fire stir deep within her body, she made a soft, broken sound and kissed him in return.

Her hands trembled as they slid from Chase's hair to the flexed power of his shoulders and back. Her fingers dipped into the open collar of his shirt, tracing lines of tendon and muscle, tangling in the curling midnight hair of his chest. She tried to search lower, wanting to know the delicious power of teasing his nipples into hardness.

His shirt was in the way. She made a frustrated sound and tugged at the cloth.

"Tell me what you want," he said. "It's yours."

With exquisite care he bit her lower lip, silently showing her how gentle he would be.

"You," she whispered.

She opened her eyes and saw him looming over her. He was huge, blocking out the stars. Shivering, smiling, she savored the certainty that his strength wouldn't be turned against her. The twisting, trembling feeling deep in her body wasn't fear.

It was anticipation.

"I want to touch you like I did before," she said. "And then I want you to teach me other ways to touch you."

His breath came in swiftly, hotly. With slow movements he eased his hands from the silky bonds of her hair. Watching her eyes, kissing her between heartbeats, he unbuttoned his shirt and let it slide to the ground.

"Better?" he asked.

"You're so beautiful. . . ." She smiled when she saw his expression and pulled him down on the chaise beside her. "I know, men aren't beautiful. But if something as powerful and wild as a volcanic eruption can be called beautiful, why can't you?"

He laughed, not knowing that the sound sent more currents of fire through her. Then he felt the heat of her mouth tracing a path across his chest, and laughter wedged in his throat. She gently scraped her teeth over one of his nipples.

When she felt the sensual tightening take him, she smiled against his skin and tugged lightly at the tiny, hard nub she had called from his flesh.

"I love doing that to you," she said, nuzzling against him. "I love feeling your response."

Torn between laughter and the nearly painful clench of desire, he could barely get the breath to speak. "That makes two of us. Definitely. Two."

"Is that a hint?"

She raked lightly across his chest, found his other nipple. She felt his heartbeat quicken as she tasted, stroked, and savored him. Then she began nibbling across and down his chest, following the dark path of hair as it narrowed to his waistline.

Chase's breath came in and stayed. Women had touched him before, and a lot more intimately. But never had he felt so savored, so enjoyed, so deeply aware of the power of his own body as seen through a woman's eyes.

With loving deliberation Nicole's hands and mouth traced every line and ridge of muscle, every hollow, every shift in the pattern of dense hair. When she found his belly button, she stabbed it lightly, repeatedly with her tongue. His response pleased her. She returned again and then again, until finally the lure of more exploration called her away. Her tongue slid along the line of skin just above his low-riding lavalava.

After a few minutes of that unexpected, shimmering torture, Chase buried his hands in her long hair and slid down to capture her mouth with his own.

"Come here, Pele," he said huskily. "Give me that sweet, teasing tongue."

His words licked through her like fire, telling her that she had pleased him. She opened her lips eagerly, anticipating the hot instant when his tongue would thrust inside.

Aware that she was waiting for him, he held back, wanting her to wait, knowing it would be all the sweeter for the tiny disappointment.

"Chase, why—"

The question became a moan of satisfaction as she felt his tongue stab deeply, claiming her softness. It was a kiss unlike any she had ever known, taking everything, giving everything, calling to the untamed currents of fire swirling deep inside her.

She shivered as her whole body tightened in a wave of sensual response. Her hands clenched in his hair, holding him to her mouth. She kissed him as wildly as he was kissing her, arching up against him, trying to get closer to him and then closer still. She wanted him covering every bit of her.

His palms rubbed over the silk of her blouse, soothing and inciting her with the same long strokes. He circled but never touched her breasts while her breathing quickened, her eyelids fluttered down, and she twisted slowly beneath his touch. He saw her nipples hard against the silk and knew that they ached to be caressed.

His smile was a slash of white as he ran his hands over her face and shoulders and hips, her arms and her thighs and her belly, teasing her relentlessly, watching her body shimmer and twist as she sought the caress that always eluded her.

"Don't you want to touch me?" she finally asked, her voice as ragged as her breathing.

The answer was a soft, broken laugh and his hands held in a pool of moonlight so that she could see their trembling.

"Then why?" she asked.

She gasped when his fingertips brushed over her silk-sheathed nipples and fire burst through her.

"That's why," he said. "And this."

He captured a pouting nipple between his thumb and forefinger and squeezed not quite gently.

She gave a wild little cry and arched helplessly while pleasure stabbed through her in sharp, hot pulses.

He released her, only to brush his fingers teasingly over the hungry peaks again and again. He was rewarded by the fierce rise of her nipples beneath the black silk.

She made a breathless sound that could have been his name. "You don't know what you're doing to me."

His smile flashed in white contradiction before he caught the hard peak of one breast between his teeth.

The thin silk wasn't a barrier. It heightened the sudden heat of his mouth on her aching breast and the wet velvet caress of his tongue. She gave up trying to breathe and simply held him to her breast. She needed the sweet, tugging warmth of his mouth more than she had ever needed anything.

When he turned his head away, she cried out in disappointment.

He pulled her mouth to his, drinking deeply,

stilling her cry. She held him, twisted against him, and his fingers moved over her ankle-length skirt. Swift tugs, a slither of black silk, and the lavalava unwrapped to reveal the golden warmth of the woman beneath. Without freeing her mouth he undid each of the blouse's tiny buttons. When he spread his hands apart, silk fell away, leaving her naked in the moonlight.

Her hands came up, shielding her breasts.

CHAPTER
35

In an aching voice Chase said, "I won't hurt you. Don't you know that yet?"

"Oh, yes." Nicole smiled. "I know. Remember?"

When he saw her almost shy, completely sexy smile, relief and a blinding desire swept though him.

"I remember," he said huskily.

Slowly, gently, he traced the length of her body as he had while she was clothed, teasing her despite the fact that his hands were shaking. She didn't know what that smile had done to him.

But she would.

"So you like to play," he said, bending down until he could tease the fingers shielding her breasts.

She felt the warmth of his breath and the damp, resilient tip of his tongue. He outlined each finger as though he was memorizing its shape. He nibbled on her fingertips.

He made no attempt at all to slide his tongue between her fingers and touch the sensitive breast beneath.

When he began the same tender tracing of her other hand, she shivered and gave a soft sigh. His teeth tugged at her little finger in response. He pulled it into his mouth, sucked slowly, then released the sweet flesh with a reluctance that was another kind of caress.

Her hand loosened, offering the taut peak of her breast to his mouth. He made a deep sound of pleasure and accepted the gift. Her response was a shudder and a tiny cry that ripped through him. His mouth changed, less gentle now, more urgent.

"Yes," she whispered as she twisted slowly against him, wanting more, not even knowing that she was describing aloud the need growing in her. "Harder. Yes, like that. **Yes.**"

Her husky words and her nails flexing into the muscles of his back were like fire burning through him. He swept his palms beneath her shoulder blades and arched her body to meet his hungry mouth. With barely controlled force he suckled her, tugging and tasting and tugging again.

She clung to him, knowing nothing but the currents of fire pulsing through her, fire created by the man who held her imprisoned between his hands and his mouth, freeing her from years of sensual doubts.

After a long time his hands slid from her back to her hips. He kneaded her hungrily, deeply. She moved in unconscious response, seeking him. With languid, teasing strokes, he smoothed her full hips and curving thighs. His mouth followed his hands, biting gently down the length of her body until she shivered and called his name.

"Do you like that?" he asked, kissing the silky flesh of her inner thigh.

Her answer was a broken laugh followed by a gasp as his mouth moved higher, finding and caressing her with shocking intimacy. Instinctively her hands moved between their bodies, shielding her softness.

"Mmm, hide-and-seek," he said, kissing her fingers. "I'm glad you like to play the same games I do, Pele."

Nicole tried to speak, to explain that it wasn't a game. The words backed up in her throat at the first caressing touch of his tongue between her fingers. He nuzzled and bit delicately on her fingers, silently proving how very gentle he could be. He kissed and tenderly touched, whispered her own beauty against her skin until shivers of need coursed through her, a helpless trembling that shouted the fires burning inside her, demanding release.

"Come to me, Pele." Lips and teeth tugged at her fingers, teasing and reassuring. Hungry. "Dance for me."

Long before her hands gave up the sensual contest, her hips were moving in slow, liquid rhythms. His hands caressed her in the same deep rhythms, urging her to release the hot currents seething inside her. He called to the passion he knew waited within her, seeking the bursting, incandescent moment of release.

Gently he nudged aside the last barrier, leaving her open to him. He heard his name as a trembling sound on her lips and breathed her own name back to her. He touched her with exquisite care, taking her to the edge and holding her there until she was shaking and crying his name with every breath she took. He lifted slowly, memorizing the picture of her totally yielded to him in the moonlight.

Then he bent down to her again, all teasing gone. Now, finally, he would know her. And she would know herself.

The feel of his caressing, searching mouth took the world away from Nicole. She tried to say his name, to ask what was happening to the body she thought she knew so well.

She couldn't speak.

She couldn't even breathe.

All the hot, fierce currents that had gathered in her burst free, tearing her body from her control. She burned wildly, deeply, and she burned for him, his name a broken cry on her lips as wave after wave of pleasure shattered her.

Chase gathered her against his body and held her until the sweet burning began to ebb, leaving her dazed and breathless within the strength of his arms. Finally she managed a full breath as her body slowly began to become her own once more. She held his face between her hands and blindly, softly, kissed him again and again, trying to tell him how beautiful it had been.

"I didn't know—" she began, only to have her voice break on an unexpected aftershock of pleasure.

He smiled and kissed her gently, ignoring his own hunger surging violently against the lavalava he still wore. His skin was as hot as hers, as slick with sweat, and his breathing was as broken, but he didn't seek his own release. He had promised himself that he would simply pleasure her and then let her go, taking no more from her than the knowledge that he had given her something to balance the agony of that morning at his brother's house.

He knew that was a way of running, of protecting himself from making the kind of memories that would haunt him to the grave—sliding into her, joining them, completing them.

He didn't know how he could walk away after that. He didn't even know how to try.

"I'm glad it was good for you," Chase said, his voice dark, deep. "Very, very glad."

He smoothed back the thick, silky mass of her hair and kissed her forehead. Silently, slowly, he stroked her back, gentling her, bringing her wholly back to herself after her wild flight. When he felt the long sigh of her breath against his neck, he brushed his lips across her cheek and simply held her.

She made a rippling sound of contentment and nestled closer, savoring the peace of lying with him as much as she had savored the sweet violence of ecstasy sweeping through her. Both the fire and the peace were wholly unexpected, miraculous. She couldn't absorb them fully enough.

For a long time they lay quietly in each other's arms and watched the silver spirals of blossoms drifting down from the moonlit sky. The petals touched her hair, her cheek, the womanly curve of waist and hip. Fragile flowers settled on the tousled midnight of his hair, on the muscular swell of his shoulder, and brushed sweetly over the mat of hair on his chest.

Nicole fell asleep, giving herself to Chase in another, deeper way, trusting him with her sleeping body. He savored that gift to the last bittersweet drop.

It was time to release the velvet woman who had trusted him enough to drink both sweetness and fire from him.

"Wake up, butterfly," he whispered. "It's time for you to fly away."

She slept on, wholly relaxed, utterly at peace.

He picked up her long lavalava and dressed her, wrapping her in black silk, trying to control the fine trembling of his hands as they inevitably brushed her warm flesh. Slowly he smoothed her unbuttoned blouse over her arms. So slowly. Too slowly.

But it was so tempting to hold on to the excuse to stay near her.

He told himself that he could dress her without caressing her. He was still telling himself that when his hand accidentally brushed across one breast. The nipple pouted up at him in instant response. Pulled against his will, he bent over and brushed the nipple just once with the tip of his tongue. Just once.

And then twice. Three times. Then his mouth opened over her, cherishing and tasting and loving her responsive flesh. Smiling, she half opened her eyes and yielded her body to him without hesitation.

Forcing himself to sit up and stop caressing her was the hardest thing Chase had ever done. He had to close his eyes, shutting out the vision of her proud nipple glistening from his mouth. With hands that trembled he began to button her blouse.

Her hands moved behind his, unbuttoning.

"Nicole," he said, his voice gritty, "this is hard enough as it is."

One of her hands smoothed up the length of his muscular thigh, sliding beneath the lavalava, finding and testing his hunger.

"Yes, it is hard, isn't it?" she said. Her smile was as sultry and sweet and intimate as her hand cradling his rigid flesh.

Chase shuddered and made a sound deep in his

throat. "Oh, God, butterfly," he said hoarsely, capturing her hand. "Don't."

"I didn't know that you liked to play keep-away, too."

Deliberately she moved her fingers beneath his, pressing and rubbing over the hot male flesh.

He knew he should pull away, stand up, run, do anything but what he was doing—sweetly, hotly teaching her how to please him, guiding her hand beneath his until he was shaking and there was nothing left for her to learn.

"You once said we would fit together very well," she whispered, pulling aside the folds of black silk that wrapped her hips. "You were right. Fit yourself to me, Chase. Slow and hard and deep. Deep most of all."

The thought of it sent fire raking through him all over again. "You don't have to, butterfly. It won't be any better for you that way than it was with my mouth."

She gave up trying to make him understand with words alone. Threading her fingers deeply into his hair, she tugged his head down toward hers.

In one last instant of self-preservation he pulled back.

Her surprised, hurt look defeated him. With a groan of surrender, he let her take his mouth while he slid his hand between her thighs to take the softness between her legs. His fingers moved slowly, finding and stroking the sultry heart of her desire until she came undone, melting over him.

Only then did he come completely to her, fitting his aching flesh slow and hard and deep inside her. The cry of pleasure she gave when he filled her was more exciting to him than her curious, caressing hand had been.

Suspended in an agony of pleasure, savoring every instant of her trembling beneath him, he held himself utterly still. When he could stand the sweet pain no longer, he began to move fully, deeply. He let her measure him again and again, felt her eager acceptance in her soft cries and in the satin flesh closing slickly around him.

She began to dance in slow counterpart to the man inside her, stroking him with every sinuous motion of her hips. He groaned as the sweet pressure of her around him shifted and changed, tugging at him, caressing every bit of him. He held on to the languid, deeply sensual dance for long, long moments, until the coil and shift of her body stripped away his control.

Then he came to her without reservation, moving powerfully, feeling his own violent tension echoed in her body. When he felt his own strength slamming into her, he tried to hold back, afraid of hurting her—and then it was too late to do anything but thrust into her while ecstasy exploded savagely through him, blinding him, shaking him to his soul.

Feeling his climax sent her over the edge, a long, spinning fall into pure fire. Her nails dug into the clenched muscles of his buttocks as she burned out of control, crying her wild pleasure against the rigid muscles of his neck, as blind and shaken as he was.

"You were wrong," she managed finally, her voice ragged. "It was better this time. You were inside me."

He groaned and held her even more tightly, more deeply, letting her heat and sweet, sultry flesh caress him. The feeling was so silky, so exquisite that for a moment he couldn't even breathe. Never had a woman taken the world away from him. He couldn't fight it. He couldn't even think why he should fight it. He could only yield as she had yielded.

Completely.

She felt him change inside her, stretching her, filling her. Her breath caught and fire welled up again, consuming both of them.

The moon was setting before they could bring themselves to undo the sweet tangle of arms and legs and gently caressing hands. It was even longer before they slowly walked up the trail to her cottage. They shared a languid, slippery shower that ended abruptly when she discovered ways not only to please him but to drive him over the edge of his control.

This time when he lifted her urgently and told her to wrap her legs around him, she didn't hesitate. She wanted it as much as he did, aching to have him inside her while the shower poured hotly over their joined, straining bodies.

As dawn came, he was locked deep inside her again, drinking the wild cries from her lips, coming apart even as she did, sharing the ecstatic burning. When he could breathe again, he bent and licked drops of moisture from between her breasts. She smiled dreamily and caressed his thick, tousled hair. He nuzzled the full breasts he had come to know so well during the long, consuming night.

"Do you have any last doubts about your ability to please and be pleased?" he asked, kissing first one nipple and then the other.

Her hands paused in his hair. She laughed softly and moved her hips against his body, glorying in his growl of response.

"Not a single doubt," she said, sighing and drifting downward into sleep even as she spoke. "If either of us pleased any more, we'd die of it."

He smiled sadly, thinking what a sweet death it would be. But she didn't see his smile, didn't feel him withdraw, didn't understand that the pain of knowing he had to leave turned in him like knives.

"Spread your wings, butterfly," he whispered very softly as she slept. "I'll keep my word and set you free. And I'll pray every second I'm alone that someday you'll understand, forgive, and fly back to me."

CHAPTER
36

L i-sa soon?" Benny asked.

Despite the emotions twisting through her, Nicole smiled down at the wistful boy.

She couldn't think of Lisa without thinking of Chase. Thinking of him brought confusion and anger and regret and a kind of pain she had no defenses against. Every time she closed her eyes, she saw again the note that Chase had left three weeks ago on her kitchen table, dark words surrounded by sketches of swollen buds and volcanic deserts.

If I stay, I'll ask more from you than a butterfly should have to give. Your body, your mind, your future, your love. I would give you the same in return.

I know you don't want that. Not from me.

You've found your wings, and what beautiful wings they are. I don't blame you for wanting to fly to a man you can trust all the way to your soul.

I regret hurting you more than I can say.

It cost me more than I thought I had to give—a chance to love.

Then why didn't you stay? Nicole asked silently. Uselessly.

She knew the answer. She just didn't like it.

All or nothing at all.

And that was what she had now. Nothing at all.

She had tried to imagine herself with another man, touching and tasting and sharing the wildfire and peace she had shared with Chase. Her stomach had turned over at the thought of such intimacy with anyone else. She didn't want another man. She wanted Chase.

And she was terrified of that wanting.

She had barely survived Ted's massive insensitivity to her mental and physical needs. If Chase ever tired of her or misused her as Ted had, she wouldn't recover.

Ted hadn't been able to destroy her because she hadn't given enough of herself to him. If she gave any more of herself to Chase, she would be lost. Already he was part of her, as deeply embedded in her as her own heartbeat.

It had happened so quickly, so completely. She had trusted Chase instantly, instinctively.

And she had been wrong.

No. Not wrong. Just too quick. If I'd waited, he would have known I wasn't hunting Dane. Then there would have been no morning after, no need to fear trusting Chase.

If wishes were horses, beggars would ride. There was a morning after. I am afraid.

And I miss Chase. God, how I miss him!

Nicole realized that Benny was watching her, waiting patiently for her answer to his question. With an effort she pulled her mind away from the warring emotions that had all but paralyzed her since she had awakened and found Chase's note.

"Lisa's coming in on the afternoon flight," Nicole said. "Didn't your father tell you yesterday morning?"

Benny nodded.

She forced herself to smile again. "Nothing has changed since then. Dane will pick Lisa up at the airport, and she'll go hiking with us tomorrow."

"Kamehameha Iki?"

"I don't know. That depends on the reports from the observatory. Kilauea has been pretty lively the last two weeks."

He shrugged. To him active volcanoes were like weather, a part of life. "Kamehameha Iki," he said firmly. "Li-sa like much-much. You Pele. We safe."

She smiled and ruffled Benny's hair affectionately. "What a lot of words. You must miss Lisa."

"Li-sa mine," he said matter-of-factly, and turned toward the garden doors.

She stared after him. Even Bobby had remarked on the attachment between the two children. They enjoyed a mutual-admiration society that had begun instantly and deepened every day. It had given both Lisa and Benny a confidence in themselves as people who delighted the adults as much as it bemused them.

The cottage seemed very empty without Benny.

Why isn't Chase coming back to Hawaii with Lisa?

Doesn't he miss me at all?

How can he ask me to marry him, make love to me as if I was truly Pele, and then just walk away?

There were no answers but the ones implicit in the note he had left behind. He cared enough for her to want her to be happy. He believed she couldn't be happy with him because she couldn't trust him, really trust him, all the way to her soul. So he had showed her that she could trust herself. And then he had left her to find a man she could trust.

Could love.

It was all there in the note, along with Chase's regret and pain and loss. She had all the answers. She just didn't like any of them.

Especially the certainty that in the end she had hurt Chase as badly as he had hurt her in the beginning.

The thought of it went through Nicole like a torrent of molten lava, searing her until she wanted to scream or cry. But she couldn't do either. All she could do was ache to be with Chase, to hold him, to comfort him and herself.

Chase, I didn't mean to hurt you!

But she had. Badly.

With a feeling close to desperation she looked around the cottage and tried to think of all the ways there were to kill time until the picnic tomorrow. Everywhere she looked, sketch paper lay crumpled, thrown in frustration at the corners of the room. She was afraid that the day and night to come wouldn't be any better.

Grimly she grabbed a sketch pad and began to draw. Even as she lifted her pen, she knew that tomorrow morning there would be an even bigger mess of rejected sketches littering the cottage.

CHAPTER
37

By the time Benny and three other Kamehamehas appeared at Nicole's door the next day,
wadded-up sketching paper studded the cottage
from the highest shelves to the farthest corners.
Failed watercolors torn to confetti added color and
variety to the litter.

Benny took one look at Pele's smoldering amber
eyes and decided that even one word on the subject
of her housekeeping would be one too many.

His sister, Mira, wasn't that wise. "What happened?"

"Nothing," Nicole said tersely.

"Oh." Big black eyes measured the storm of
paper littering every surface. "I used to tell Mama
the same thing. She didn't believe it either." Mira
hesitated. At fifteen, she was old enough to know
that adults sometimes needed to be left alone. "We
don't have to go hiking today."

"I've been looking forward to it," Nicole said
flatly. "I need to get out."

Benny smiled with relief and hustled his sister

and cousins out the garden door before Nicole could change her mind and cancel the hike.

Hands on hips, she looked at the drifts of paper. They reminded her of the luau, when jacaranda blossoms had lain in fragrant drifts around the chaise and Chase had made her feel as beautiful as the night.

More beautiful. In his arms she had truly been Pele, goddess of fire.

The sound of Lisa's excited laughter broke through Nicole's seething thoughts. She reached the front door just in time to open it and catch a small, energetic body in her arms.

"I missed you," Lisa said, hugging her hard. "Is Benny here?"

Nicole smiled despite the pain lancing through her. Lisa's eyes were the same rain-clear gray as Chase's. "He's in the garden. Where's Dane?"

"He and Daddy let me off at the gate. They'll pick me up there later."

Numbly Nicole released Lisa.

The girl raced off to the garden, calling Benny's name in a high, clear voice. Nicole barely heard. All she knew was that Chase was back. He had been only a few yards away.

And he hadn't even said hello.

Doesn't he want to see me?

The answer came swiftly to her, like a black knife twisting. **Did you want to see him again after you ran out of Dane's house?**

Trying to get past the anguish of their mutual pain, she closed her eyes and wrapped her arms around herself.

He was here.

So close.

She wanted to go to him, to hold him, to know if he had truly meant what he said in his note.

A chance to love.

"Nicole?"

Slowly she opened her eyes and focused on Mark. "Oh. Hi. Is everyone here?"

"All six of us. Sandi, Judy, Lisa, Tim, and Steve. We all crammed into the car with Dad and Uncle Chase. But don't worry. We made lunch at home. Uncle Chase told us not to mess up your kitchen."

"Oh," she said again. She couldn't think of anything else to say. All she could think was that she had to see Chase again.

A chance to love.

Mark looked at her oddly. "You feeling okay?"

"Sure. Fine. Just a little . . . slow." She gestured at the litter of paper. "I worked late last night."

Mark's eyebrows climbed as he took in the extent of the mess. "Who won?"

"Not me." Nicole's mouth turned down. **And not Chase. We both lost. We're still losing.**

The agony of it was literally breathtaking.

"Uh, you sure you're up to a hike?"

"First Mira, now you. I must look like death warmed over."

"Well, uh . . ." Mark changed the subject,

because he didn't want to tell one of his favorite people on earth that she looked like hell. "Uncle Chase told me to tell you to be sure to stay clear of the southwest rift zone. It's not official yet, but they're going to close that part of the mountain anytime now."

"So it's finally singing in harmony," she said, rubbing her arms as though she was cold.

"Huh?"

"Harmonic tremors. Swarms of them. That's how they know the magma is moving up inside the mountain," she said absently, still caught in the agonizing net of her thoughts. Then she shook her head and forced herself to concentrate on something besides her painful, consuming need to see Chase.

"So where are we hiking?" Mark asked.

"Kamehameha Iki. It's nowhere near the Great Crack," she said, referring to the fourteen-mile-long fissure that lay like an open wound down Kilauea's southwest side. "Is anything happening on top yet?"

Mark shook his head. "That's where Dad and Uncle Chase are going later. Uncle Chase told me to bring a cell phone on the picnic, and Dad told him it was a waste of time."

"He's right. The cell coverage where we're going is a joke. A bad one. I'll take a radio. One of the stations is sure to come through."

Nicole turned to rummage in her kitchen drawer for the tiny portable radio she rarely used. She found it, turned it on, and was rewarded by a blast of fusion retro-rap music. Quickly she turned it off.

"What good will the radio do us?" Mark asked. "You can't talk into it."

"If the mountain goes, it will be on the news. We'll hurry back and drive up for ringside seats."

A swarm of kids came rushing in from the garden just in time to hear her words. Like the mountain, they were more than ready to go. They hustled Nicole out and didn't give her a moment's peace until the bus door closed behind them. All during the ride they talked in rising voices about the chance to finally see the fabled mountain blow.

"Nah, it won't blow," Mark said. "Not like Mount Saint Helens did. Uncle Chase told me the lava that comes out of Kilauea is usually thin and fast, so it doesn't get stuck inside the mountain's throat and build up pressure like that mainland volcano did. Poor old Saint Helens literally blew its top. Kilauea just sort of lets it all bubble out quietly."

That started an argument about just what constituted "quietly." Were fountains of fire eighteen hundred feet high quiet? As several of the kids had parents who worked at the observatory, there were plenty of opinions to go around.

Nicole listened with half her attention while she herded everyone off the bus, counted noses, and came up with the right number. Just ten, though it sounded like twenty. While the children chattered

and hiked along the very faint trail that their summer picnic jaunts had made through the forest,
Nicole kept counting kids and coming up with the
right number. It was something she did so automatically that she barely had to think about it.

That meant she could spend too much time
thinking about Chase and what she would do when
the hike was over. The thought of not seeing him
was too painful to consider. She had missed him
unbearably in the past few weeks. Each day had
been worse, not better.

Yet the thought of going to him and giving herself wholly to him terrified her.

**What if he doesn't want me after all? What if
that's why he didn't come to see me?**

Nicole stumbled and barely caught herself on the
rough ground. The thought of being rejected by
Chase was numbing.

**Trust him. Trust yourself. Take this chance for
love.**

The arguments raged in her head without letup.
She made the rest of the hike on automatic pilot,
her mind locked between trust and fear. As usual,
it was warm on the mountainside. As usual, it
rained for a time. As usual, the small pool in the
center of the kipuka felt like Eden reborn.

What wasn't usual was the sudden, sharp leap of
the earth beneath their feet.

Lisa screamed and tried to run toward Nicole,
only to trip and fall.

"Everyone sit down!" Nicole ordered as she

gathered Lisa into her arms. "There may be after-shocks or even more quakes." She sat down herself and bent over the little girl who was huddled in her lap. "Are you okay, honey?"

Tears trembled in Lisa's eyes. "My ankle hurts."

Nicole looked at the ankle. It was scraped, bleeding, and beginning to swell a little. "Can you move it?"

The girl grimaced, but she wiggled her foot and ankle.

"That's enough," Nicole said quickly. "It's not broken."

The ground beneath them shivered and trembled as if the island itself was cold, but Nicole knew it wasn't cold that caused the shaking. It was magma pushing up Kilauea's throat, pushing and pulsing in response to shifts deep in the earth that no one truly understood.

"Looks like someone will be claiming the hotshot pool anytime now," Nicole said. "Want to go back and get good seats for the show?"

"It's probably just another intrusion," Mark said. "I'll see if anything's on the radio."

Nicole turned on the radio and held the speaker to her ear. After a few minutes of moving the dial through the few stations she could receive, she lowered the radio and looked at the children.

"Nothing about the volcano," she told them. "I'll try again in a few minutes."

Beneath them the ground shivered and trembled very faintly, a kind of deep humming that never really stopped. Despite her reassuring smile at the kids, Nicole wished desperately that there was someone along who knew more about Hawaii and volcanoes than she did. This might be perfectly normal behavior preceding a perfectly normal intrusion or even an eruption in the southwest rift zone.

Or it might be a disaster taking shape around her and the children. The earth seemed to vibrate beneath her feet, but the motion was so subtle now that it was more sensed than felt.

Nicole's instincts stabbed her with sudden, sharp warnings. **Get out. Get out.**

She didn't question or fight her instinct to flee. She couldn't. It was simply too powerful.

"I think," she said as casually as she could, "that if we don't get going, the best seats at the top will be overrun by tourists."

"What about lunch?" Steve asked.

"We'll eat while we walk. Less to carry that way."

There were a few grumbles, but not too many. The faintly shivering ground whispered to instincts that were much older than logic. The children didn't know why; they just knew it was time to go.

Nicole took the scarf off her hair and used it as a makeshift bandage on Lisa's ankle. "How's that, honey?"

The girl nodded and pushed to her feet. With breath held, Nicole watched while Lisa put weight on the ankle. She limped but was able to walk.

"Okay?" Nicole asked.

"Sure-sure." The little girl managed a smile. "Like Benny."

The ground quivered, a beast testing its chains.

"Fall in," Nicole called.

The children picked up their lunches and began walking. Lisa's limp got worse with each step along the rough mountainside. Anxiously Nicole watched her. The little girl was still keeping up, but she wouldn't be able to much longer.

Radio held to her ear, Nicole worried about Lisa and the rest of the children. She impatiently flipped from station to station until she found one where an excited announcer was talking about earthquakes and Kilauea. What she heard made her heart stop, then beat with redoubled speed.

Kilauea was waking up. The first sharp jerk of the earth had closed old fissures and opened new ones. No one knew how many. But they did know one thing: the eruptions were happening on a whole new section of the mountain.

Suddenly the wind shifted, blowing down rather than up the mountain.

"Something's burning," Mark called from his position at the middle of the column. "I can't see it, but I can smell it."

The children agreed loudly. Nicole held up her hand for silence and listened intently to the radio. The description of the new rift zone made her mouth go dry even as her palms slicked with cold sweat.

No, it can't be. They must be wrong.

Mentally she calculated the distance to the road as she listened to the announcer's excited description of Kilauea coming apart and pouring fountains and rivers of incandescent stone over its flanks. Already the road to the caldera had been cut in several places by lava.

Closing her eyes, Nicole prayed that Chase wasn't on one of the sections of road that was barricaded by new lava flows. Then she forced herself to put her fears for Chase out of her mind. She couldn't help him, but she could help the children.

"Benny," Nicole called.

Her voice carried to the front of the hiking line, where the youngest Kamehameha was confidently leading them through the trackless forest of fern and tall ohia. He raised a hand to show that he had heard her.

"Can you get high enough in a tree to see where the smoke is coming from?" Nicole asked.

Benny didn't bother to answer. He simply sized up the trees around him, accepted a boost from Mark, and scrambled up until the branches were too thin to support his weight. He looked around once, twice, three times, as though memorizing the land.

"Mountain burning!" he said, his voice high.

Nicole's eyelids flinched. It was what she had expected, but she had hoped fiercely that the radio announcer was wrong.

"Can you see any lava?" she called.

"Smoke."

"Is it from burning trees or is it in great big plumes going all the way to the clouds?" Nicole asked, keeping her voice calm with an effort.

"Trees."

"Can you see a way down to the road?"

Benny hesitated a long time. "Sorry-sorry, Pele. Big line smoke between."

A chill went over Nicole.

They were cut off from rescue, and all around them the land was on fire.

CHAPTER
38

Nicole forced herself to breathe past the freezing instant of panic. Ten young lives depended on her. She had to think and think fast. Chase and Dane knew where their children had gone hiking. The men would know the kids were cut off from the road.

The radio poured static and excitement in her ear. She made out just enough words to know that they weren't the only ones to be caught by the mountain's sudden shift. Search-and-rescue operations were being mounted by air, land, and even sea.

In her mind she retraced the trail between where they were now and the road that they couldn't reach. Somehow she had to get everyone to a place where they could be seen from above.

And, if necessary, airlifted out.

"Can we get to the slick pahoehoe flow that's halfway back to the road?" she asked.

"Yes-yes," Benny said instantly.

"Is there smoke in that direction?"

He moved his hand in a circular motion that took in the land all around them. "Smoke everywhere."

"Do you see any helicopters or small planes?"

He gave the sky the same careful survey he had given the land. "No. Just smoke. All-all, Pele. All-all."

"Come down, Benny. And thanks. You've helped us."

She turned and faced the children who were waiting anxiously in front of her. Sandi moved to stand next to her older brother. Mark bent over and said something as he put a reassuring arm around her. The gesture was so like Dane that Nicole wanted to smile and cry at the same time. She took several measured breaths. She had to stay calm. And she damn well had to **appear** calm.

"The radio announcer said that Kilauea is splitting some new seams," she told the children. "We're supposed to go to a road or a clear area where we can be spotted from the air. Then a helicopter will come and get us. Benny, you take the lead again. Mark, help Lisa up onto my back."

"I'll carry her," he offered quickly.

Nicole shook her head. "Thanks, but it's not that far." **And I'm a lot stronger than you. I won't be a year from today, but it's not a year from today. It's now, and we're trapped on a burning mountain.**

"But—"

"If I need help over the rough spots, I'll yell for you," she said, cutting off his objections.

Unhappily Mark lifted Lisa onto Nicole's back.

She smiled over her shoulder at the girl. "Hang on tight, honey, but around my shoulders or my chest, not my neck. Ready?"

Lisa nodded.

"Benny, I want you to keep going until you're in the center of that slick pahoehoe," Nicole said in a tone that told everyone this wasn't a suggestion. "When you're there, sit down and wait for the helicopter."

"Sure-sure."

She smiled at him and turned to the rest of the children. "It's very important that you stay together. If it gets too smoky, take off your shirts and breathe through them."

The kids all nodded.

Mark whipped off his shirt and handed it to Nicole. "If I need something to breathe through, I'll take some of Steve's shirt."

She hesitated, then took the shirt. "Thanks. This will be easier to tear than my silk halter. And Mark, if I fall a bit behind," she added casually, "don't double back for me. Lisa and I will be fine. You bring up the rear of the kids." She saw the quick concern for her and the protest forming on his lips. "You're the strongest of the boys," she said in a low voice. "If someone needs help, I'm counting on you to be there."

He wanted to object, to stay with her no matter

what, but a single look at her eyes told him all he needed to know. There was no give in her.

As Benny took the lead, Mark fell into place at the end of the line of hikers. Nicole walked behind him, carrying Lisa. They hiked at a good pace and without the usual jokes or sibling byplay.

For the first time in her life Nicole was grateful for her unusual size, as well as for the years of dancing and hiking that had conditioned her body. Lisa might have been small, but she wasn't a handful of feathers, and the miles they had to cover were on a path that was little more than crushed ferns pointing the way between trees, shrubs, and bigger ferns.

The wind shifted again. Now it blew from behind Nicole. The air was rough with smoke, a reminder that somewhere above them, burning lava was spreading down the mountain.

Nicole coughed and kept walking, hoping for another shift of wind. With every step she was falling a little more behind. She couldn't see the children ahead of her anymore. She couldn't even hear their occasional complaints about the pace Benny set. All she could do was follow the faint trail left by nine pairs of feet tramping in front of her.

Gradually the forest changed, thinning out and then getting lush again according to the rhythms of old lava flows. The air stayed the same, thick enough to taste. Every shift of wind brought more smoke swirling down the mountain in billows. Despite the makeshift scarves Nicole had ripped from Mark's shirt, she and Lisa coughed constantly

And always, always, Nicole listened for the crackling sound of fire overtaking her. So far all she had heard was the roaring of her blood in her own ears. The forest was too wet and lush to catch fire from a few random blobs of hot stone raining down. But a river of lava was different. The intense heat of the molten stone dried out everything close to it. Plants heated to flash point and went up in small explosions along the edges of the lava flows. Both the lava and the burning forest pumped out a lot of smoke. It made a misery of breathing.

Just when Nicole had begun to think she was lost, the plants around her thinned to almost nothing. The glassy pahoehoe ahead of her once had flowed like burning syrup down the mountainside, filling crevices and hollows. Though the lava had been fully cooled for more than a hundred years, it was still too harsh an environment for plants to take hold.

Mark stood at the edge of the shiny flow, looking anxiously toward the thick forest beyond. When he spotted Nicole, he ran over and lifted Lisa from her back.

"Hang on, squirt," he said to Lisa.

The girl wrapped her arms around his thin shoulders and hung on.

Nicole smiled wearily and stretched the kinks out of her back. "Everyone here?"

"Yes. They're waiting in the center of the flow just like you said to do. A small plane flew overhead about twenty minutes ago."

"Did it see you?" she asked sharply.

"It wagged its wings."

She closed her eyes, feeling dizzy with relief. Until that moment she hadn't admitted to herself how frightened she was. "Thank God."

On the pahoehoe there weren't any trees or tall ferns to block everyone's view of the mountain. Even through the haze of smoke they could see long lines of more dense smoke writhing skyward, marking outbreaks of lava. The molten stone itself was still hidden, revealed only by the fires it set among the wet green forest.

Nicole watched the smoke creep lower and lower down the mountainside. The wind was unpredictable. It pushed smoke here and there and back again, revealing and concealing the land at whim. The only certainty was that the air was getting thick enough again to make them cough.

"Listen!" Mark said.

The faint, distinctive **whap-whap** of a helicopter rotor came down through the murky sky. Soon a small chopper landed gingerly on the uneven ground. Nicole herded the kids toward the open passenger door.

The pilot glanced from the ten children to the tall woman standing braced against the backwash of the rotors. She looked at the helicopter's small interior and then at the pilot.

Neither of them said a word.

She stood at the door and boosted children inside until they were packed in the helicopter like fish in a tin. Mark was the last one in. He turned to help Nicole, only to find that she was hurrying away.

"Where's Nicole going?"

The pilot didn't answer.

The helicopter shuddered up to full power, and Mark understood. "Nicole!" he yelled through the open door. "Come back! There's room! You can have my place! **Nicole!**"

With one hand the pilot held Mark in the seat. With the other he slammed and locked the door. Then he poured on more power and put the bird into the sky.

Mark beat his fists against the transparent door and watched Nicole until he couldn't see her any longer. But he could see a lot more of the mountain.

And all of it was on fire.

By night the lava would look like a wild network of liquid red and gold. By day it looked like a black, many-fingered hand wreathed in smoke. That hand was reaching down toward the island of pahoehoe where Nicole waited alone.

"I'll come back for her," the pilot shouted over the noise of the engine.

Mark turned away from the frightening view and looked into the pilot's sympathetic eyes. With a jerky nod the boy went back to watching out the window.

The pilot spent most of the short flight to Hilo Airport talking on the radio. He told the search-and-rescue coordinator that he had found the kids the airplane had reported. There were ten kids, not nine. He was bringing them in to Hilo, and would someone be damned sure there was a fuel truck standing by.

As soon as the helicopter touched down, Mark spotted the tall figures of his father, his uncle, and Bobby running across the apron toward the chopper. The kids poured out of the helicopter and ran toward their parents. Mark carried Lisa to her father's eager arms.

Chase took his daughter's small weight with a feeling of gratitude that made his throat ache. He surrounded her with a hug. She returned it with all the strength in her small arms.

"She's okay," Mark assured his uncle. "Just a sore ankle."

Chase nodded and looked over Lisa's black head for the fiery hair that had haunted his dreams.

The helicopter was empty.

There was no one else nearby but the pilot, who was hauling a fuel line toward the machine at a run. With growing unease Chase looked all around the apron. When he turned back to Mark, tears were streaming down his nephew's face.

"There wasn't—enough room," Mark said, his

voice breaking. "She wouldn't let me—trade places. It was burning—behind her. Everywhere. Burning."

Chase made a sound like he had been kicked. With a terrible effort, he kept his voice gentle while he unwrapped Lisa's arms from around his neck.

"Go to Uncle Dane, punkin," he said, kissing his daughter, handing her into Dane's arms. "He'll take you home."

"I want Nicole," Lisa said suddenly, and burst into tears.

"So do I."

The pilot saw Chase running toward the helicopter. "That your wife back up on the mountain?"

"I'm working on it," Chase said roughly.

"Hell of a woman," the pilot said, pumping fuel with grim haste. "She saw right off there wasn't enough room. Didn't say a word. Just stuffed the kids in the cockpit and jumped back out of the way. The boy damn near bailed out after her. Barely got the door locked in time."

"Was she hurt?"

"No."

"Did you get GPS coordinates?"

"Yeah, for all the good it will do me. Global positioning satellites in the sky don't mean shit if you can't see the ground."

"Smoke?"

"Thick enough to chew." The pilot jerked back on the fuel nozzle. "That should do it. It's not far for a bird. Pure hell on foot, though. I'll radio in as soon as I find her."

"I'm coming with you."

"Too damned dangerous," the pilot said bluntly. "That old mountain is coming apart all over."

"We're wasting time," Chase said as he jumped into the passenger seat.

The pilot climbed into his own seat. "Good enough. I can use another pair of eyes. Even with the GPS . . ." He shrugged. "You ever used one of these helmets?"

"Yes," Chase said curtly.

"Put it on. Can't hear much otherwise."

With that the pilot concentrated on bringing his chopper back to life. The instant the machine was ready, the tower gave them clearance. The helicopter leaped into the sky.

The panorama of the burning mountain unfolded below Chase. His trained eye quickly picked out the pattern beneath the chaos of billowing smoke. From a point just over halfway up the mountain, long fingers of molten lava were spilling out, setting fire to the forest wherever they touched. Several major fissures shot fountains of boiling lava into the air. Other fissures simply pumped rivers of lava quietly down the slope. Slivers of green forest lay untouched between the new flows.

Potential islands of life were forming as he watched. Some of the kipukas were too small to protect their plants. Everything alive burned up in streamers of smoke. Other kipukas were big enough for some of the plants to survive between the molten pincers of lava.

There was so much smoke it looked like everything was on fire, even the air itself.

"How the hell did you find the kids in this mess?" Chase asked.

"Observatory plane spotted them first. The woman had them parked in the middle of a big patch of pahoehoe. No trees to burn or to hide them. Good thing, too. Never would have found them otherwise."

The pilot checked the GPS reading, veered to the right, and skated down on a long descent, coming closer to the rivers of burning stone with each passing second. Heat rising from the lava buffeted the helicopter, but the pilot held his course.

Chase throttled the impatience hammering at him, the raw fear that he was too late.

He should have been down there with her.

I was going to have it all my own way. I was going to heal her and set her free and then wait for her to fly back to me.

But she can't fly. She's trapped down there, and I'm trapped up here in this goddamned tin can.

"How much farther?" he asked, his voice harsh.

"Under that smoke somewhere. We're right on the coordinates."

Chase stared down into the rolling billows of smoke. "I can't see shit from here."

"Going lower will be dangerous."

"Like being down there alone on the ground isn't dangerous?" Chase asked savagely.

"Just so you know."

"I know."

"Good enough. Keep your eyes peeled. I'm gonna have my hands full."

The engine noise changed as the helicopter dropped down through the smoke. The pilot kept one eye on the GPS readout and the other on the altimeter.

Chase stared out into the murk. A blur of smoke-mantled green forest unreeled dizzyingly beneath the helicopter. The chopper's skids were barely above the tallest trees.

After a few minutes the pilot switched directions and flew another leg of an imaginary grid. The forest raced by, green on green. Smoke swirled up wildly. Eden burning.

The thought of Nicole alone down there made sweat gather along Chase's ribs and slide coldly down his spine. The helicopter was dangerously close to the treetops, and still it was all he could do to make out shapes on the ground. The air was thick with ash and sometimes reeked of sulfur.

His hands clenched into hard fists. The sulfur smell told him that there was a fissure nearby pouring gases into the air. Some of them would be poisonous.

Hurry, he yelled silently to the pilot. **Hurry!**

The forest vanished.

At first Chase thought it had been blacked out by the smoke. Then he realized that they were skimming over a cooled lava flow.

Pahoehoe, where nothing could grow.

Long minutes went by while he stared at the ground through shifting veils of smoke and saw nothing but shades of black, slate, gray, everything but the colors of life. Suddenly he caught a shimmer of red-gold in the midst of black and gray, old lava and new smoke. At first he thought it was fire. Then he knew.

"There!" he said, pointing. "Two o'clock!"

The pilot switched directions and swooped down like a hawk. The closer they got, the greater Chase's fear, until it was a hand wrapped around his neck, choking him.

Nicole lay facedown on the lava, motionless but for her hair rippling like a banner over the dark rock.

Chase leaped from the helicopter before it fully settled to the ground. Calling her name, he ran to her. Finally, painfully, she turned toward his voice. He lifted her into his arms and buried his face in her hair. She coughed terribly, unable to speak, clinging to him as he carried her into the helicopter.

They were barely strapped in before the helicopter shot upward, tunneling through smoke toward the clearer air of Hilo.

CHAPTER
39

Fountains of lava danced against the night sky, sending dazzling rivers of stone burning down Kilauea's seamed flank. When the outside of the lava flows congealed into dark rock, it formed a shifting, temporary lid on the seething rivers. As the volcano continued to pump out more molten stone, the dark lid of each flow broke many times. The burning rock inside made patterns that were like captive lightning. The sight was both savage and beautiful, a view back through time to the birth of the land.

In awed silence Nicole watched from a safe vantage point. It wasn't merely the distance from the incredible upwelling of molten stone that made her feel safe, it was Chase's arms around her and his voice murmuring in her ear, telling her what was happening to the mountain beneath them.

"There's a new Great Crack pouring out lava for half the length of the mountain. Already one of the lava tongues has gone all the way to the sea." He brushed his lips over Nicole's hair and smelled her ginger shampoo. He still went cold at the memory of seeing her laid out like a sacrifice on the black lava. "The island will be a little bigger come morning."

The fountains gushed higher for an instant, pulsing with rhythms alien to man, incandescent with the violence of creation.

Nicole trembled.

He nestled her closer against his chest. "Don't be frightened. Every last person who was trapped on Kilauea has been rescued. No one was even hurt. You saw Lisa tonight. She's running around like a little gazelle." He laughed softly. "So is everyone else on the island, trying to find the best place to watch the mountain dance."

"It's so powerful. So beautiful. Unearthly."

"It's the beginning of everything." Softly he kissed her hair and let the scent of her reassure him at the most primitive level. She was alive. Unhurt. In his arms. "Without the volcano there would be no land, no trees, no ferns, no flowers, nothing but the sea. Eden was born in fire, and only fire keeps it alive."

She shivered again and leaned back against him. She enjoyed sitting cradled between his long legs, her back against his chest, his arms around her, his breath stirring warmly on her neck.

It was as though the last three weeks had never happened, as though he had never gone to the mainland, as though she had never huddled in the middle of black stone and prayed that she would live to see him again.

So much had happened.

And nothing had changed.

In the hours since he had lifted her into the helicopter, he hadn't said anything about his trip to the mainland. She had been afraid to ask him when he was going again, if he was glad to see her, if he wanted her to stay with him tonight.

He hadn't asked her anything at all. He had simply held her, watched her reunion with the worried children, and then asked everyone to come up the mountain with him again after dinner. He wanted them to see how beautiful the volcano could be. When the children had finally tired of the spectacle, Dane and Jan had taken them back down the mountain, leaving Nicole and Chase alone on a mound of picnic cushions.

"Chase?" Nicole asked, her voice suddenly uncertain.

His arms tightened around her. He didn't want to hear her next words, her hesitant thanks for rescuing her and then a plea to be set free again.

He couldn't let her go. Not now. Not ever. He would take whatever she could give and try not to ask for more.

"It's all right," he said. "You're safe."

As he spoke, he lifted the silky mass of Nicole's unbound hair and let it fall over his shoulder and down his back like a fiery cape. The red-gold lights of Kilauea gleamed within her hair, reflections of the dancing fountains of creation.

His mouth found the soft skin at the nape of her

neck. He tasted her delicately, testing the smooth flesh with his teeth and tongue. He heard her breath catch, felt the tiny tremors of her response. When his palms found the full curves of her breasts, she sighed and let her head fall back on his shoulder.

"Yes, butterfly," he breathed into her ear, "come to me. Drink the sweetness."

Beneath the long black muumuu she wore, her skin tingled as though brushed by fire. His hands moved lovingly from her shoulders to her thighs, pressing against her, urging her even closer to his heat, caging her gently between his legs.

Restlessly, hungrily, her palms moved over the masculine textures surrounding her, enjoying the hair-roughened, flexed power of his legs. She tilted her head up and turned toward him, wanting to taste his lips.

His eyes were closed against the moonlight and the dancing fires. His expression was harsh, intensely male. He was absorbing every instant of touching, every tiny movement of her hands, everything about the woman half reclining against him.

Heat washed through her, a need that was as complex and unknowable as the mountain itself. As she lifted toward his mouth, his hands slid beneath her muumuu, gliding up her legs until he captured the softness waiting between. Her breath came out in a startled moan as fire burst through her, consuming her. Her hips moved slowly, slowly, telling him how much she enjoyed the intimate caress.

A thick sound wedged in Chase's throat when he felt Nicole's silky movements beneath his hands. He stroked her for a moment longer before sliding his hands higher, seeking the tempting peaks of her breasts, finding them, tugging sweetly at them until she cried out and arched into his hands.

A shudder of pure need racked him. He wanted her with a force that was both pain and pleasure. His hands swept up her body, peeling away the soft black folds of cloth, leaving her wearing nothing but a dark lace triangle that couldn't conceal the fiery hair beneath.

An instant later Nicole was completely naked and Chase's hands were teasing her breasts again. She wanted to turn and capture the hot, hungry mouth that was buried in the curve of her neck, but the sensation of his hands caressing her nipples was too exquisite. He held her in sweet captivity.

His fingers looked dark against her pale flesh, hard, exciting. When his hands drifted down her body and nestled between her legs, she gave up any thought of trying to turn over in his arms. Her breath came out in a broken cry of pleasure that was his name.

Hearing it, he smiled against her neck. He bit her nape even as his fingers found and caressed the slick, taut focus of her desire.

Nicole's whole body burned with the response

only Chase had ever called from her. Her nails
swept up the length of his bare legs, but his hiking
shorts kept her at bay. She wanted to touch him, to
know the hard leap of his flesh when she satisfied
him. She could feel him pressing against her back.
She twisted against him just as the first, shivering
waves of pleasure took her, melting her.

He felt the fire washing through her softness, fire
overflowing at his touch, and he made a husky, triumphant sound. "I've spent three weeks trying to
figure out how to get you to fly back to me."

"All you had to do was—" Her words ended on a
gasp of shocked pleasure.

He raked his teeth not quite lightly over her nape
and stroked deeply into her, glorying in her
untamed response. She strained into his imprison-
ing, caressing embrace in a sultry dance that made
him want to eat every inch of her and then sink
into her until sweet annihilation consumed them.

"I thought of using Lisa," he said, "of telling
you how much she loves you, needs you. But Lisa
will be grown up in the blink of an eye, and I'll
just be beginning to know how much I want you,
need you."

"Chase, I—" Her voice broke as his hands
moved skillfully, taking her to the edge of fiery
release.

Holding her there.

"I'll take whatever you want to give me," he said,
pressing her tightly against his hungry body,

stroking her, feeling the sultry rush of her response. "Just don't fly away from me. Stay and drink from me. Let me drink from you. Don't ask me to let you go. I can't."

She cried out and fought to hold back the waves of pleasure melting her. Trembling, her hands closed over his, stilling his caressing fingers.

"Nicole," he whispered hoarsely, "don't you want this?"

Slowly she turned in his arms, stroking his rigid erection with every languid movement of her body. Her hair spilled over both of them, veiling them in fire.

"Nicole?"

She unbuttoned his shirt, pushed it aside, and sighed as she tasted his hot, salty skin.

He couldn't stop a shudder of pleasure and relief. Her teeth scraped lightly over his nipples, her tongue stabbed, and her hands finished undressing him. When he was naked, she stroked him hungrily, holding him between her palms, enjoying every bit of his arousal as he smiled darkly and moved with her touch.

"I love your taste," she said, bending down to him, "your textures, the heat of your body. I love your words when you talk about the land and your smile when Lisa falls asleep in your arms. I love **you**." Her voice trembled with the emotions that were sweeping through her, melting her body into his. "Be part of me. Now. Always."

As he took the gift of her body, he gave her the words that burned within him even more fiercely than his passion for her.

"I love you, Nicole. I'll die loving you." He caught her mouth in a consuming kiss and sank deeply into her, becoming part of her.

Completing both.

Around them fountains of molten stone danced and pulsed. The fires of Eden burned, washing everything with the incandescent light of creation.

AUTHOR'S NOTE

Although I have written many types of fiction, I will always have a place in my heart for stories that revolve around a growing relationship between a woman and a man. While I no longer write that form of brief, pure romance, it was wonderful to revisit two lovers and to rebuild a story that has been out of print for more than fifteen years.

In those intervening years, the story that began life as a short romance called *Fires of Eden* grew into a longer, fuller book called *Eden Burning.* With the freedom to add pages came the ability to put in new scenes, to flesh out old ones, and to look at the relationship between Nicole Ballard and Chase Wilcox in a different way.

Some friendships ripen through the years. For me, *Eden Burning* is one of them.